ABOUT THE AUTHOR

One of the fathers of the Nordic Noir genre, Kjell Ola Dahl was born in 1958 in Gjøvik. He made his debut in 1993, and has since published twenty novels, the most prominent of which form a series of police procedurals-cum-psychological thrillers featuring investigators Gunnarstranda and Frølich. In 2000 he won the Riverton Prize for *The Last Fix*, and he won the prestigious Brage and Riverton Prizes for *The Courier* in 2015 (published in English by Orenda books in 2019). His work has been published in fourteen countries. He lives in Oslo. Follow him on Twitter @ko_dahl.

ABOUT THE TRANSLATOR

Don Bartlett completed an MA in Literary Translation at the University of East Anglia in 2000 and has since worked with a wide variety of Danish and Norwegian authors, including Jo Nesbø, Roy Jacobsen and Karl Ove Knausgård. For Orenda he has translated several titles in Gunnar Staalesen's Varg Veum series, including *We Shall Inherit the Wind, Wolves in the Dark,* the Petrona award-winning *Where Roses Never Die, Fallen Angels* and *Bitter Flowers*. He has also translated four books in Kjell Ola Dahl's Oslo Detectives Series for Orenda – *Faithless, The Ice Swimmer, Sister* and *Little Drummer* – as well as *The Courier* and *The Assistant*.

THE LAZARUS SOLUTION

KJELL OLA DAHL
Translated by Don Bartlett

**ORENDA
BOOKS**

Orenda Books
16 Carson Road
West Dulwich
London SE21 8HU
www.orendabooks.co.uk

First published in the United Kingdom by Orenda Books, 2023
First published in Norwegian as *Lazarus* by Aschehoug Forlag, 2022
Copyright © Kjell Ola Dahl, 2022
English translation copyright © Don Bartlett, 2023

A catalogue record for this book is available from the British Library.
This book has been translated with financial support from NORLA

ISBN 978-1-914585-68-5
eISBN 978-1-914585-69-2

Typeset in Garamond by www.typesetter.org.uk

Printed and bound by CPI Group (UK) Ltd, Croydon CR0 4YY

FSC
www.fsc.org
MIX
Paper | Supporting
responsible forestry
FSC® C171272

For sales and distribution, please contact *info@orendabooks.co.uk*
or visit *www.orendabooks.co.uk.*

1

Jomar Kraby was late. Gunvor had been waiting for him, but now she wanted him to stay away for a bit longer, because she had spotted Orina, who was early. Slim, dark-haired and wearing light-coloured trousers, Orina stood out from the crowd. Gunvor cast around for the Russian Embassy car, but couldn't see it. Orina stopped in front of her, and they greeted each other in Soviet fashion, air-kisses on both cheeks, then crossed the street side by side.

Gunvor was seized with a sudden shyness and wondered what to say, as she looked around again for Kraby. He was nowhere to be seen.

Orina talked about the heat wave that had been hanging over Stockholm for several weeks and expressed a hope that it wouldn't end just yet. She asked Gunvor if she had been swimming much this summer.

They entered Humlegården Park and made a beeline for an empty bench. Gunvor said that she sometimes went to the Vanadis pool on Sundays, which was true; only to sunbathe though, she said. But she hadn't been swimming for a while – not since they last met anyway. She got panicky in water, she told Orina. This was only partly true. In fact, Gunvor wasn't at ease in a swimming costume. She could lie on a rug in one, but swan around...? No. Gunvor felt her bottom was too big and her thighs too fat for that – something Orina would never have to worry about.

'You can swim, though, can't you?' Orina asked.

Gunvor nodded.

After sitting down, Gunvor caught sight of the embassy car – a black GAZ – as it pulled over and stopped in Sturegatan.

Orina told her that she loved the sea and had been for a long swim on Sunday. 'Not many women can do that. I'm proud that I can. I'll take you along so we can swim together.'

Gunvor felt a warm flush spread through her abdomen at the thought.

Orina said that Madame Kollontai lived on the island of Storholmen, and now Orina's department was moving there too. She would be stationed there for the next few weeks. 'So it'll be harder for me to see you at short notice.'

Gunvor gazed down at Orina's hands, struck by how elegant all this woman's movements were. What she wanted to say was knotted inside her.

Then she burst out with it, heedless of the outcome: 'Let's arrange to meet, shall we, just the two of us?' she said in a rush, fearful of how Orina might react. 'Then we'll have more time than we do meeting like this.'

Orina stared straight at her. 'You and me? Alone?'

Gunvor nodded.

Orina sat on the bench, thinking. Gunvor was suddenly afraid she had gone too far – had let her feelings run away with her. She was about to retract the suggestion, when Orina raised her chin and looked her in the eye.

'If there's somewhere we can swim, perhaps you could come to Storholmen?' Orina took Gunvor's hand in hers. 'One Sunday when I'm free. I'll have a look for somewhere. Don't forget your swimming togs though, even if there's no mention of them on the invitation.'

Orina stood up. Gunvor stayed on the bench and followed her with her eyes. What grace she had; those long legs of hers and the lissome way she walked.

Reaching the GAZ, she turned and waved, then got in. The car drove off – but had to brake for Jomar Kraby, who crossed the street and continued down the pavement.

Gunvor waited until the car had gone. Then she grabbed her bag, stood up and followed him.

Kraby was dressed in black, as always, apart from a red neckerchief. On his head he wore a Panama hat. It wasn't hard to keep him in her sights. His lean body was arched like a wind-filled sail, his head bent over his feet, as though he was struggling not to be blown backward. With every step he raised one leg high in the air like some spindly insect groping its way forward over unfamiliar terrain. Where the street ended in Stureplan square, he turned left into a restaurant known as the Anglais. Gunvor waited for a few seconds before following him in.

Standing just inside the door, she watched Kraby greet with a bow the Norwegian artists and actors dotted around, then he proceeded to his regular table. Immediately the waiter was at his side, placing a tankard of beer and a small glass of port in front of him. The waiter waited. It was like a ritual. Kraby emptied the port into the beer then raised the glass tankard, drank and put it back down.

Gunvor walked towards his table.

Kraby gave his order: the usual. His voice was hoarse; his face a pale yellow, dominated by a broad mouth, a long nose and very bushy eyebrows. He had been a good-looking man once, Gunvor thought. In his younger days Jomar Kraby must have been quite a Casanova. Now the skin around his skull was beginning to tighten. His eyes were deep set amid a myriad of wrinkles, rippling like water towards the base of his imposing nose. The fingers that held the tankard were long and bony. Two joints on the middle finger of his left hand were missing, the result of carelessness when using a straw cutter on the farm in Lunner where he grew up before moving to the capital and becoming a writer and social commentator. Gunvor had heard him tell the story many times. Malicious tongues, however, maintained that the finger had been chopped in half by a jealous husband, and that it was the relationship with this man's wife that was the real reason Jomar crossed the border from Norway into Sweden.

He raised his tankard and, with his free hand, pulled out a chair. 'Take a pew, Gunvor.'

Gunvor sat down. Shortly afterwards the waiter appeared with the food. Kraby was served beef tartare: meat, capers and an egg yolk.

'This is a luxury I can permit myself for as long as the restaurant has meat and I have money,' he said, unfolding the serviette wrapped around a knife and fork.

Gunvor shook her head when the waiter turned to her. 'I'm not staying.'

Kraby broke the yolk with his fork and spread the egg across the meat. 'Normally I eat tinned sardines on bread.'

Gunvor coughed. 'Torgersen sends his regards.'

Kraby started eating.

'He instructed me to tell you to drop by the office.'

Kraby chewed.

'Today. As soon as you can.'

Kraby swallowed, took a swig of beer and put down the tankard. 'How is she, our friend Orina Vasilikova?'

Gunvor didn't answer.

'I saw the two of you,' he said. 'While I finish this, why don't you go to the toilet and check that you took the right bag when you parted company?'

Gunvor eyed him without speaking.

Nonchalantly, Kraby continued to eat.

'Well, can I tell Torgersen that you're coming?' she asked, getting up.

He didn't answer.

Gunvor left. His comment about the bags had unsettled her, but she wasn't sure whether Kraby actually knew what had happened or just said such things to keep her on her toes.

2

After finishing his meal, Jomar Kraby lit a cigarette. It was still early in the Anglais. The worst imposters hadn't turned up yet.

Pandora hadn't, either. It didn't matter; he had a meeting to go to. So he paid, went out and made his way to Mäster Samuelsgatan.

Occupied Norway's Legation in Stockholm was spread across several addresses. The main office was in Banérgatan. The Press Office was there, too, while the Legal Office, the Liaison Office, the Refugee Office and the two Military Offices were housed elsewhere. Ragnar Torgersen was in charge of the Refugee Office's secretariat. He had a responsible job – there were tens of thousands of Norwegian refugees in Sweden.

The Legation took care of its own security. As Jomar trudged the last few metres up the hill, he saw Borgar Stridsberg on duty in front of the door. His jacket was tight and the bulge by his armpit revealed that he was armed. Jomar came to a halt, said hello and asked him if he had heard from his brother, a shrimp fisherman.

'No news is good news these days,' he replied. 'When they shot my father, I was informed at once. Do you want to see Torgersen?'

Jomar nodded, waited for Stridsberg to open the door, then went in and up the stairs.

In the ante-chamber Gunvor was sitting at her desk behind a typewriter, and she told him to go straight in. Jomar knocked on the glass door and opened it without waiting for a response.

Ragnar Torgersen was sitting behind a huge desk with a pen in his hand, busy taking notes. He was wearing a grey suit, and his tie was knotted so tight the mere sight of it made Jomar gasp. His complexion was ruddy; his head was covered with grizzled hair, cropped, like the spikes on a hedgehog. He was the kind of man who still possessed a touch of the nobility that the Eidsvoll Assembly had tried to eliminate in 1814 when drawing up Norway's new constitution – a nobility the pince-nez over his nose enhanced. But a dead cast to Torgersen's eyes also lent him an appearance of inaccessibility, a veil that Jomar was able to see through, because he knew the cause. Torgersen's only son,

Hjalmar, had died the previous autumn while being tortured by a Norwegian collaborator.

There was a deep armchair placed in front of the desk. Torgersen performed his well-rehearsed party piece: he arched both eyebrows in such a way that the spectacles pinched to his nose loosened and fell. He caught them with his left hand and extended his right to indicate the vacant chair to Jomar.

Jomar knew that if he sat in the armchair he would sink right down, as helpless as a duckling in a well. So he took one of the wooden chairs from the conference table by the window, carried it to the desk and seated himself.

Torgersen folded his hands and leaned across. 'Are you writing anything at the moment, Jomar?'

'What do you mean?'

'Are you bringing your creative mind to bear on a novel or an essay, or indeed on anything at all?'

'Not at the moment, no. Why?'

'Daniel's dead,' Torgersen said. 'Daniel Berkåk. He was shot. In Norway. Just across the border.'

Jomar replied that he had heard the rumours, but not the name of the victim, which was true.

'It was a few days before his body was found,' Torgersen said, leaning back in his chair. 'You know who Berkåk was, don't you?'

'We probably met, said hello.'

'Berkåk worked closely with the Press Office and the Mi-2 Military Office. When he wasn't working as a courier in Norway, he was gathering intelligence. Anonymous appearance, not very tall, slim, combed-back blond hair, steely eyes.' Torgersen raised his hand and placed his index finger against his chin. 'A lump here, on his chin.'

Jomar nodded pensively. He remembered the man.

'Berkåk was carrying documents and newspapers,' Torgersen said. 'A rucksack full. The latest edition of *Håndslag*. The idea had been to distribute it across Østland. The documents were for the Resistance leaders, but before he could deliver anything, he was shot. When his body was found, there was no sign of any documents or newspapers.'

'Were the documents in code?'

'Of course.'

'No problem then?'

'Can't you see the gravity of this? One of our couriers is murdered and vital documents have gone missing!'

'You don't think it was the Germans then?'

Torgersen shook his head. 'If German soldiers had been behind this, or the border police, they would've taken the body with them, but Berkåk was found by a forester, almost by accident. Had he not been, he would've been lying there for months.' He took a deep breath. 'This is not the first incident. Papers have gone missing from files too. We can't go on like this. Disloyal is one thing, but now a courier carrying confidential papers is killed. One of our most trusted men, slaughtered like an animal. What's going to happen next? These are not normal information leaks, Jomar. This is a breach in a dyke. If we can't plug the leak, we'll drown. We can't let this happen.'

'Trying to fight disloyalty at the Legation would be tilting at windmills,' Kraby said. 'There are disloyal staff in all the legations in Stockholm, working for the British, the Germans, the Americans and the Russians. That's why they're all here, fishing for info from each other.'

'This is quite different. Daniel Berkåk was murdered!'

'Strange,' Kraby said.

'What's strange?'

'With such leaks, you'd expect the third-party beneficiary to be someone in the German Abwehr in Oslo, such as the man leading the Intelligence Office, Fritz Preiss, but you said the Germans weren't involved.'

'Did I?'

Jomar leaned forward and opened the cigarette box on the desk. On seeing the contents, he inclined his head in respect.

'Of course, it's possible the information has been passed on to the German authorities in Norway,' Torgersen said, and then corrected himself: 'No, actually, I'd say it's highly likely that it's been passed on to them. But it wasn't German soldiers who killed him. Which, of course, makes everything far worse.'

Jomar took a cigarette and examined the side seam. It was probably Virginia tobacco. He ran the cigarette under his nose, sniffed and savoured the aroma, then grabbed the lighter on the desk. It was shaped like a dragon. A flame shot out of the dragon's mouth when he pressed the tail.

'Have you considered the arsonist angle?' he asked, blowing smoke into the air with the satisfaction of a passionate smoker. 'Whoever shouts "Fire!" is probably the person who started it.'

Torgersen shook his head firmly. 'The woodsman who found Berkåk is a thoroughly decent fellow, and our couriers vouched for him. I know it's easy to suspect him, but in fact I don't.'

'What's his name?'

'Arnfinn Bråtan.'

'Arnfinn? He was the man who guided me across the border.' Jomar nodded, persuaded that Torgersen was right. He doubted Arnfinn Bråtan was behind the courier's death.

Torgersen began to clean his spectacles with the cloth beside the desk pad. 'The government – ours, in London – wants the case investigated.'

'It's interesting to hear all this,' Jomar said, his eyes half closed, 'and of course I'm humbled that you've let me into your confidence, but I still don't understand why.'

'London asked me what I thought, and in my opinion you're the right man for the job.'

Jomar's eyebrows shot into the air in disbelief. 'Have you taken leave of your senses?'

Torgersen shook his head. 'I've thought this through carefully.'

'How could I – of all people – find out anything about this business?'

'By using your grey matter.'

'The Norwegian Legation is full of competent staff who know how to work with this kind of material,' Jomar said. 'Politicians, military officers, saboteurs, police from back home, and the quick-witted Norwegians who trained in Scotland.'

'We can't broadcast to all and sundry that we're investigating this. That would sow division. It would set people against each other, and we Norwegian exiles fighting for a free homeland have to stand together. This has to be a covert operation.'

'So you've come to me, an impecunious bohemian and alcoholic?'

Torgersen ignored him. 'I'm convinced the explanation for this murder is to be found here, in Stockholm. If the situation is as I believe it to be, we have a mole in our midst, someone with sources in the Legation, in which case we need someone who can investigate from the outside. Someone who's independent and impartial.'

Jomar shook his head, but Torgersen raised a pre-emptive hand. 'First, no one will suspect that you have a hidden agenda. And, least of all, that you're running errands for the authorities. In addition, you're independent, mature and experienced enough not to allow yourself to be duped by the bigwigs. You're an artist; hence you have the imagination to think outside the box. To my knowledge, you have no personal or careerist agenda within our pathetic political set-up outside Norway. I don't believe you have any loyalties you should be ashamed of. And, from my experience, you don't have any hobby horses. At any rate, none I know of. If you're the person I think you are, you hunt for angles and contexts, which so-called specialists, and particularly bureaucrats, are unable to do. Best of all, however, is your appearance. What you say is true. You look like a bohemian and an alcoholic. It's the best disguise there is. Even Sherlock Holmes understood that.'

Jomar didn't allow himself to be taken in by this flattery. He took a deep breath, ready to speak, but Torgersen raised his hand again.

'As I said, I have the backing of our exiled government in London.'

'London,' Jomar said, letting silence reign for a few seconds. 'What about the heads of the Norwegian Legation here?'

Torgersen folded his hands and breathed in. 'London turned to me. Directly to me,' he said, searching for the right words.

Jomar let him search. The fact that others in the top echelons of the Legation hadn't been informed made the case all the more delicate. He couldn't be part of all this. The mere thought of having to manoeuvre between machinating parties in the administration – it would be like sitting on top of an ant heap, naked.

'Hundreds of people work in the Legation offices,' Jomar said. 'How do you imagine I can find out who the leak is?'

'What we want to know, Jomar, is why Daniel Berkåk was murdered as he made his way to Norway. We want to know what the motive was. Daniel Berkåk's dead. There's nothing we can do about that. What's so awful is that nothing's happening about it. The crime has fallen between every conceivable stool. The murder took place in Norway. So no authority in Sweden is interested in investigating the case, even if Berkåk lived in this country. And I can't phone the Norwegian Statspolitiet, the Stapo, and ask them how the investigation's going. They'd just snort with derision. They're not interested in investigating the murder at all. For the Stapo and the German authorities in Oslo, Daniel's death is a stroke of luck. They'd like to see our couriers dead, and everyone else working against them.' Torgersen tapped his forefinger on the desk as he continued: 'Whoever's behind this has to be punished.'

'You said yourself the Stapo want the couriers dead. But what if our Nazi friends are behind this?'

'Then it'll come out during your investigation,' Torgersen said, in a slightly irritated tone now. 'Your employer is the Norwegian government in London – but this is highly unofficial. The government-in-exile has no authority to initiate an investigation in Sweden. You'll have to work undercover, with the greatest possible discretion, and you will report to me. We have to bring these people to justice, if not here in Sweden, then at home in Norway when we can once again hoist the Norwegian flag over the Palace Square in Oslo.'

Jomar smoked, staring glumly at Torgersen. 'You've missed out a couple of tiny details,' he said. 'Such as the fact that Daniel was killed in Norway, and that I had to leave Norway to avoid arrest by the Germans.'

'As I just said, I'm sure the solution to this case lies in Stockholm.'

'There are two cases. The leaks are happening in Sweden, but the murder took place in Norway. This might be two sides of the same coin, but it doesn't have to be. To presuppose that the two cases are connected before starting a thorough investigation would be amateur.'

'As I said, you're the right man for the job.'

Jomar didn't answer.

'There's no risk involved for you, Jomar, but I need your help.' Torgersen sat up straight: 'Say yes, but not just for me. For Norway, Jomar. Our homeland needs you.'

Jomar met Torgersen's doleful eyes and asked himself if he wanted this. Working on a practical project was quite different from writing. If he had been at a different stage in his life, he would have remained true to his original position, despite appeals to serve king and country. He would have said 'no' out of a fear that committing to worldly activities would destroy his creativity and the urge to write. But it was a long time since Jomar had written anything at all. His brain was desperately searching for something to write about, but it had been doing so for a long time, to no avail. Now, with Torgersen's questions, he glimpsed a straw to cling to. The assignment was immense, opaque and so impossible that Jomar thought there had to be a loose thread somewhere, a thread he could unravel, and sooner or later this process might provide sustenance for his pen.

Eventually he said: 'Who were the documents and news-papers for?'

Torgersen lowered his voice another notch. 'Only Berkåk knew that.'

Jomar leaned forward, using the opportunity to snaffle another cigarette from the box and put it behind his ear while contemplating the first that was now so short it was almost burning his fingertips. With a heavy heart, he crushed it in the ashtray.

Torgersen opened the desk drawer and took out a wad of banknotes, which he smacked down in front of him. 'Your re-muneration, Jomar. Cash in hand every week.'

Jomar sighed. 'Look at me.'

Torgersen clipped on his pince-nez.

'What do you see?'

Torgersen smirked. 'I see you haven't shaved today.'

'I'm an artist,' Kraby said, 'a romantic, a dreamer. I'll drink this money.'

Torgersen shrugged. 'Drink it then. I don't care. The fee takes into account that the Swedes censored your last play. You won't get it published as a book either. You just said you weren't writing anything new, but you need an income, and you need to activate your imagination and creativity. You still have an ana-lytical mind. You're the only person I know here in Stockholm who can mix effortlessly with the exiles in the Theatercafé and the social circles around the Norwegian Legation.'

Kraby leaned forward again. 'What if I can't solve the crime; what if I can't shed any light on what happened?'

Again Torgersen shrugged his shoulders. 'Well, then we'll have tried.'

Jomar thought aloud: 'For me to have any chance of cracking this, I'll need to be able to move between circles, mingle with the élite, when they don their best bib and tucker and go to public receptions. The Norwegian Legation's spread across the whole city. More departments are appearing all the time, and every single sector has its own tin-pot tyrant. Presumably I'll have to confront them, every single little bag of wind that London hasn't involved in this investigation. How will my voice carry any weight at all in the conversations I'll need to have with them?'

Torgersen opened the desk drawer. 'Finally, a relevant question,' he said, passing Jomar a document. 'Here.'

Jomar took the document and held it up to the light. As always, he was impressed by the bureaucrats' appreciation of finer materials. The paper was top quality, robust, nice to hold in your hand, resembling a parchment from bygone times – a watermark, a monogram at the top, the official stamp and the signatures. It was a letter of authorisation with the king's seal, signed by two ministers from the government-in-exile: Justice Minister Terje Wold and Foreign Affairs Minister Trygve Lie.

'You know how rumours spread in Stockholm,' Kraby said. 'Two minutes after I've spoken to someone, a whole crowd of Norwegians will be speculating about what's going on.'

'I'm aware of that. We've managed to live happily alongside rumours ever since the Germans invaded our country. However, this investigation must not become public knowledge. If you hit a brick wall with the bureaucrats, you can show them this document, provided that they take an oath of silence. Afterwards you can explain that the investigation will be followed by a report you send to London – via me. The summary of your actual work won't be included in the report, but your assignment gives you the right to question people in our Legation. However, this only applies to Norwegians. Our government-in-exile has no authority in Sweden. You should use this document only when it's absolutely necessary and only with high-ranking Legation officials. Be discreet. You'll still be Jomar Kraby – the lush and the poet the teetotallers and the hotheads laugh at, as far as their limited abilities allow.'

Jomar Kraby lowered the document. 'Who knew where and when Daniel Berkåk was going to cross the border?'

'A coterie only. As he was carrying newspapers, I'd imagine the journey was organised internally at the Press Office.'

'What about Gunvor?'

'Gunvor's salt of the earth. She was with us on the raid against the officers' brothel in Oslo, known as Löwenbräu.'

'I know,' Kraby said. 'But even women with their hearts in the right place can make a poor choice of comrade. Besides, she's a Catholic, so she can sin multiple times and always be sure of God's forgiveness.'

Torgersen rose to his feet, walked to the door and opened it a fraction. 'Gunvor.'

She came in and stood by the door.

'Gunvor's been fully briefed about the assignment,' Torgersen said.

Jomar said that must therefore mean Daniel Berkåk had been to see her before he set off.

She nodded. 'I gave him the documents.'

'What about the newspapers he had to take with him?'

'He already had them. The Press Office gave him them.'

'Did you know when Berkåk would leave?'

'No one knew. He never spoke about where he was going or when he was leaving. He went back and forth across the border and knew the area like the back of his hand. He had several identities, and no one knew which one he would use on his next trip.'

'So Berkåk came here, and you gave him the documents. Accordingly, only you and Torgersen knew about them?'

Gunvor shook her head doubtfully. 'Peder Svinningen in the Legal Office knew about them. Svinningen came to the office while Daniel was here.'

'What did he want?'

'He was banging on about refugee routes again. In the Legal Office they think we aren't capable of administering the flow properly. Whenever anyone comes from the Legal Office, they nag us for maps of the routes and names of the border guides and couriers.'

Jomar glanced across at Torgersen, who was wearing a vexed expression.

'Nothing's ever enough for them. Svinningen's desperate for power and influence. The tune they're playing at the moment is that the Legal Office should be responsible for our activities. There's always antagonism. Daniel Berkåk's murder has raised the stakes. Svinningen and his crew have come up with the notion that Daniel would still be alive if they'd been administering Norwegian refugees in Sweden.'

Jomar Kraby nodded pensively. Rivalry had already reared its ugly head; this suggested Torgersen had a hidden agenda. Svinningen wasn't only in charge of the Legal Office. He also had a reputation as the strong man in the Norwegian Legation in Stockholm. So what might it mean that the government-in-exile had chosen to ignore a strong man when launching an investigation into Daniel Berkåk's death?

Jomar thought about the banknotes he had just stuffed into his pocket, observed Torgersen and wondered whether it would be possible to keep this assignment away from the intrigues of various top Legation officials.

Torgersen appeared to have read his mind. 'This has nothing to do with internal bickering, Jomar. Don't forget, the initiative comes from London.'

Kraby glanced at Gunvor again. 'What did you think when Svinningen bumped into Berkåk here?'

'Not much. Daniel Berkåk knew a lot of people. He knew Svinningen too.'

'Where did he live?'

'Hammarby.'

'Alone?'

Gunvor nodded.

'A Legation flat?'

She nodded again.

'So there's a spare key?'

'Come with me,' she said, leading the way to the ante-

chamber and a wall cupboard behind her desk. 'Here,' she said,
took a key, jotted down the address on a pad, tore the sheet off
and passed it to him.

Jomar stuffed both items in his pocket with a smile.

'What's the matter?'

Jomar lowered his voice: 'Just for form's sake, Gunvor, why
do you swap bags with a Soviet Embassy employee?'

'I don't,' she said in an equally muted voice.

Jomar stared at her.

She sighed, looked down, then away and finally straight at
him. 'It was a letter,' she whispered.

'A letter from someone in Norway?'

'It's harmless.'

He had to smile at her choice of words. Gunvor knew as well
as he did that one of the Legal Office's tasks in Stockholm was
to keep an eye on the so-called 'opposition' – the collective term
Svinningen applied to Norwegian Communists.

'Of course, Gunvor. Madame Kollontai and the Soviet
Embassy are harmless. Is that why we're whispering to each other?'

'I'm telling the truth. It was a letter from Norway to one of our
allies. The handover has to be discreet because the Legal Office will
go mad if it reaches their ears that letters are passing between the
Soviet Embassy and our Resistance movement. They don't accept
that diplomacy is about looking both left and right. I deliver one
letter and get another back. My job is to pass it on to the intended
recipient, and don't ask me who that is because I can't say.'

Jomar changed the subject. 'Are you seeing anyone at the
moment?'

'Seeing?'

'Are you going out with anyone?'

'Jomar, I haven't said a word about Daniel Berkåk, money or
anything else related to this office to anyone.'

He grinned. 'So you're not seeing anyone? Maybe you'd like
to go out with me?'

After a deep intake of breath, she slapped him.

3

The oncoming gravel road rushed towards him, bordered on either side by grassy banks and cotoneaster bushes, guelder rose shrubs and lilac trees, their blooms withering now. Gable apexes towering up to the sky revealed the presence of the detached houses concealed by this shrubbery screen. As soon as the building at the top of the hill hove into view, Kai pulled the cord, only to discover that another passenger had already rung; the bulb at the front of the bus was lit.

His seaman's kit bag slung over his shoulder, Kai made for a flower shop next to a hairdresser's. Inside, he inhaled the fresh scent of greenery. The female assistant picked out individual carnations from the bucket as he pointed to them. Then she wrapped the bouquet in newspaper.

Kai tucked the flowers under his arm and walked down to the railway station. On the platform two German officers were talking. They didn't notice him as he stood waiting for the train. Kai thought about his elder brother, Atle, who would certainly have engaged them in conversation. Or, at any rate, nodded to them. Atle had always been more courteous than he was. More confident. Bolder. When Kai started school, stories were still circulating about his brother's derring-do. At the age of ten Atle had climbed up a school drainpipe, three floors, swung himself onto the roof tiles with a clatter and run along the ridge, while down in the playground the pupils cheered and the teachers yelled at him. When Kai left school, Atle's long-jump, high-jump, 800-metres and 3,000-metres hurdles records still stood. Atle was the coach's obvious first choice for the Slemdal-Besserud stage of the Holmenkollen relay race. He bounded up the steep hills like a mountain goat and, one by one, left his competitors for dust. At home, Atle was his big brother. A helping hand he could always reach out for. A lodestar – one phase of his life.

There were still only three people on the platform when there was some air movement around the bend. The train pulled in almost without a sound. The headlamps resembled two eyes. The driver in the small cab turned the crank to slow down and the train gently kissed the buffers and drew to a halt. The doors opened with a dry click. A solitary passenger stepped out. Inside the train the conductor noisily straightened the seats. He finally emerged – the signal that the three passengers could board. Kai was the last to get on and found a seat two rows behind the officers. They were speaking German.

The sound of laughter drifted in from the platform. The conductor, who had been standing with the driver, smoking, shouted to someone further away and boarded the train. Kai bought a ticket from him, and sat staring out of the window as they started up.

Soon they passed a military camp – red flags with a black swastika inside a white circle waving in the wind. At the next stop lots of soldiers got on. They moved down the train, all with a rifle strapped to their shoulders. When they saw the two officers, they stopped, raised their arms and shouted 'Heil Hitler.' The officers returned the salute.

Kai exchanged glances with a woman sitting opposite him. She rolled her eyes and searched for confirmation that he had no sympathy for their guttural shouts either.

Kai looked away and out of the window again. Thinking about Atle, who had started work on the railways after he had finished full-time education. Atle had been a star at school. But Kai and studying had not been such a natural match. In fact, his schooling had gone so badly that when he'd turned fourteen, his father had taken him to an office where they signed him up for the merchant navy. His mother had cried and refused to allow him to go to sea. Kai and his father had stood firm. They won. That summer Kai signed on as an ordinary seaman on a collier plying between Liverpool and Cuxhaven. This life had created a distance between him and his family, and he'd returned only when his father died. And he hadn't seen much of Atle before he had to leave again.

The next time Kai signed off, the boat was docked in Marseille, where he met the woman who was to take him with her to Paris. It had all been so natural for them to get together. They were a man and a woman from the same social background, with the same political schooling, the same convictions and the same desire for each other. She had been the one who wanted to go to Spain and defend the Republic. He was the one who went. He still struggled to understand himself – to understand why and how it had happened. One day he was holding hands with a woman in a Paris café; the next he was at war. He couldn't blame her. She was the way she was – in her infidelity too. The man she fell for was like Kai: a seaman and a Communist. The only difference being that he refused to risk his life. So he stayed around, ready for her to cling on to, so she could avoid the consequences of her politics. That was where she and Kai differed, he thought now. He chose to follow his convictions; she chose passion. He gazed down at his hands: he was still alive and still surrounded by enemies. It is one thing to understand yourself; it is quite another to understand what has happened to your brother.

When Kai and Atle met again, it was at their mother's funeral. Atle wore a railway uniform when he was at work, but a different one for political meetings: dark blue with a red-and-gold sun cross sewn on the arm. He was wearing it at the funeral. It had struck Kai that Atle would never have had the nerve if his father had still been alive.

Or maybe he would have defied his father? No, he wouldn't have dared. Wearing the symbol at the funeral wasn't defiance though, Kai thought. It was outright rejection. Atle might as well have spat on his father's grave. But that was his business, Kai had reflected, from where he was sitting, grieving the loss of his mother, returning from a civil war and finding himself forced to accept that Atle had become a stranger to him.

Atle had still been charging around like a crazed horse, but his course had by then been set – away from Kai and everything they had in common. It had been no time for Kai to express his bafflement or ask probing questions the evening they got drunk and divvied up whatever there was to inherit from their parents. They were just two brothers who hadn't seen each other for two years. At that moment, that night, mollified by their reunion and drunk on aquavit, Kai felt their situation was perfectly viable: they were brothers – they might disagree on politics, but they were still brothers.

The following day, though, the wonderment he felt at his brother's transformation was almost worse to deal with than his hangover. Kai had to accept that Atle's previous role as his hero was reduced to that of a pest. The kind that wanted to hear stories about the war in Spain. Who wanted to hear about military action and would not take no for an answer. In the end, Kai gave in and told him about a boy chained to the village pump on the day he entered a town square in a lorry. It transpired that the boy, in his teens, was going to be shot. Kai asked the troop leader what the boy had done. Apparently, he had been deployed in the trenches and had decided to desert. He had charged out of the trench towards the enemy, waving a white kerchief and shouting: Don't shoot, don't shoot. What the boy hadn't realised was that the trench where he was posted curved round, and the trench he stumbled into was a continuation of the one he had left. That was why he was chained like a calf to a stake, waiting to be shot by the comrades he had wanted to betray. Kai laughed out loud at the irony of the story, but Atle's mouth was pinched shut; he didn't consider the story amusing. Kai could have told him that. War is anything but amusing.

The train stopped in Smestad station. The two German officers got up and made for the doors. When they opened, the officers stepped out, followed by several soldiers. Kai watched them and saw the fortified entrance to yet another military camp with menacing swastika flags flapping in the breeze. The train carried on and Kai pulled the cord.

◈

There was no one around as he strolled into Vestre Cemetery and passed the heavy architecture of the chapel and the crematorium. A sweet fragrance Kai was unable to identify wafted through the air. Did it come from the flowers in the beds or the pile of earth beside the open grave? The clay mass was partly covered by a tarpaulin. The black hole awaiting the coffin yawned open to the sky. Kai went looking for another grave, but couldn't remember exactly where it was, so he started examining the names on the stones.

At last he found it. The sparse grass in front of the headstone told him it hadn't been dug long. Beneath the names of his mother and father, and after the date of decease, a third name had been engraved: *Atle Fredly*.

Kai had no close family anymore, no one to go home to. For several months he had lived with the realisation that he was on his own, but as he read the three names, the definitive finality instilled in him a gravity he had not felt before. He remained like this, standing, thinking, stirred by a memory, a smell. The smell of Atle. The smell of sun.

He knelt down, unwrapped the carnations and placed the bouquet in front of the gravestone. Straightening up, he spotted a woman on the shingle some distance away. She was pushing an elderly man in a wheelchair. He was sitting slightly hunched up and crooked, with a rigid grimace on his face, while the woman stared at Kai. She was wearing a plain cardigan over a dress. Her bag hung from a strap over her shoulder, and from under her smart hat blonde curls protruded. Kai looked away and again focused on the grave. He read the date of decease once more. Atle had made it to thirty-two before departing this life. Kai was five years younger. Atle had died in the war – in a Norway that was still at war. It was by no means a foregone conclusion that Kai would live any longer than his brother.

When he raised his head again, the woman and the man in the wheelchair were making for a bench. Kai reflected for a few more minutes. He was completely alone in the world now. No one would always have him in their thoughts.

Finally, he tore himself away. The sun beat down on his forehead as he followed the path to Frogner Park and the Vigeland sculptures. The last time he had been here, a few years ago, this park had been under construction. They had made some progress now. Statues of men and women towered up on both sides of the bridge and along flag-stone paths laid in symmetrical patterns. In the distance, children could be heard playing.

The din the stonemasons were making drowned out the children's shouts as he approached Tørtberg. Kai contemplated the huge wooden structure that had risen around the sculptures. The contours of a massive column could be discerned through small peepholes in the plank-work surrounding and hiding it and the workers inside. As he continued down towards the construction site – which was to be a water fountain – he heard someone behind him. It was the woman pushing the wheelchair. She nodded to Kai, who politely returned the gesture.

Kai found a bench in the area above the pond, sat down and watched the odd couple. The man was bent over in the wheelchair, and his hat was perched perilously on his head. The woman placed the chair in such a way that he could see across the pond. Then she turned and approached Kai with a determined step. When she stopped in front of him, he stood up and shook her proffered hand. She introduced herself as Sara Krefting. Her voice was deep and soft, and suited her. Now her head was bare. Her hair was golden yellow and thick, and held in place with slides. Her eyes were light blue, and a smile revealed a line of perfect teeth.

'I saw you in the cemetery,' she said. 'You're Atle's brother, aren't you? I knew him. You're different, but there are some similarities.'

Kai nodded. Feeling that he had to explain himself – why he had laid the flowers. However, he felt no inclination to tell her the truth, so he used a story that chimed with the seaman's kit bag. He said he had been at sea and had signed off just today. That was why he hadn't been able to attend the funeral.

In response to what he told her, she straightened up and scrutinised him more closely. 'You signed off? Today? From a boat?'

He nodded.

'A German boat, you mean?'

'Yes. Why?'

'Do you know how your brother died?'

Kai said he knew what the priest had written to him after they found Atle's body. It must have been a brutal death. Had there been any developments, did she know?

She didn't answer; her expression became more pensive.

'How do you know my brother?'

She nodded towards the kit bag on the bench. 'If you've just come ashore, have you got somewhere to stay?'

Kai picked it up. 'I haven't got round to thinking that far ahead. The plan is to find a cheap boarding house.'

'Out of the question,' she said with a solicitous furrow between her eyes. 'You can stay with us.'

This was a turn-up for the books. Stay with them?

She read his astonishment. 'It's the least we can do for you and your brother. My husband and I.'

They both turned to the old man, who was still sitting at an angle in the wheelchair, a rictus grin on his face.

Kai apologised and explained that he didn't want to be a burden to anyone.

The words bounced off her. 'We've got more than enough room.' Her hand gripped his. 'Promise me you'll come.' Once again her expression had taken on the sympathetic, solicitous look. 'Come and stay with us for a few days. I have some things to tell you about your brother. We have a lot to discuss.' With that she let go of his hand and rummaged through her handbag. Then passed him a card. 'Here's the address. Do you think you can find your way there?'

'Sure,' he said. 'Give me a couple of hours.'

Kai watched them as she pushed the wheelchair down the flagstone path. He was amazed that she hadn't introduced him to her husband. Especially as she had invited him to stay in their house. How old could she be? Forty? Forty-five? The husband had to be close on eighty – at least. Unless the illness he was suffering from had aged him. Kai looked down at the card. It said she was a dentist. That made sense, with a smile like hers.

◈

He jumped on the tram outside Frogner Park and stood on the platform all the way down to Studenterlunden. Afterwards he strolled around aimlessly. Passed shop windows and ran a critical eye over himself. Noting that his appearance could be more presentable. So he ended up buying a suit and a couple of shirts in Adelsten Jensen. Choosing them was easy. He didn't have much money so bought what he could afford – but the suit was a good fit. The sleeves finished where they should, and the assistant, a somewhat haughty individual with a tape measure around his neck and two watery eyes peering over spectacles, knelt down, plucked at the material and concluded there was no need to let out the waist or the legs.

After the clothes had been paid for, how much did he have left? Maybe it was enough for a decent meal. His purchases tucked under his arm, he wandered around, looking for somewhere to eat. He walked straight into two German guards. Kai avoided eye contact, feeling like a slave as he passed them, head down, striding out as briskly as he could.

◈

As afternoon became evening, he was sitting alone at a table by the wall in Cecil's. His selections from the menu were made with judicious care. He ate and drank only what he could afford. Around him sat German officers with Norwegian women. Power attracts, he thought to himself, and as soon as the thought was articulated, one of the women burst into laughter, revealing a lot of teeth and gums. He looked down and lit a cigarette. The last of his money would go on this meal. He needed a job, and once again he was reminded of the vicious, brutal way in which his brother had lost his life. There was nothing he could do about that though. Being utterly alone was a new situation for him, but it also contained a sense of expectation. Again his thoughts turned to his family, to his father, who had worked at the sausage factory in Fredensborgveien and had been alone at work the day everything went awry. The workers on the new shift found him in the giant meat grinder. He had been trying to free a blockage and had left the motor on while he stood over the machine, poking at the minced meat with a stick. Apparently, the grinder had caught the sleeve of his overall and dragged him up into it. It must have all happened in seconds, the factory foreman said. His mother had cursed his eternal haste, his sloppiness and all his short cuts as much she mourned his passing. For Kai the bereavement was harder. He felt the unpleasantness of the bizarre way his father had died as intensely as his grief. It always hurt Kai to think about his father. His emotions were never pure; his sense of loss was mixed with anger, his sorrow mixed with shame.

Nor could he talk about the accident with anyone, not even with his mother or Atle. His brother had felt little shame about his father's death, but his anguish had been boundless and found release in tears. Atle and his father had argued about everything while he had been alive. When he died, though, Atle turned to mush.

Kai took out the business card the woman in the cemetery had given him and flicked it between his fingers. There was no one waiting for him. 'Come and stay with us for a few days.' Should he take her at her word? Or was her invitation just a pleasantry, a polite way of rounding off the conversation because she had known Atle? Should he find accommodation elsewhere? Or should he visit this couple? The answer stared him in the face. He had no money. In a way, this was par for the course. It was as though his brother had sent him this woman. As though Atle had been looking down through a hole in the sky and had sent an angel to help his destitute brother.

4

The house was detached and white, with a hip roof and black tiles, two round pillars at the entrance and blackout curtains in the windows, which lent the building a sombre quality. The wrought-iron gates gave a low whine as he opened and closed them. On the flagstones in front of the door he pulled the cord above the nameplate. Soon he heard footsteps and the door opened. There she stood, like an elf in the light coming from all the rooms. She was wearing a grey skirt and a loose blouse. Her blonde hair hung down to her shoulders.

'Ah, how nice. Come in.'

Her smile was as gleaming white and friendly as before. A wave of perfume hit him as he crossed the threshold: scents of vanilla, incense and flowers. As he went to remove his shoes, she raised a hand. 'Don't bother.'

She was wearing sandals with heels. Kai followed her into a room lit brightly by two chandeliers. The blackout curtains had kept this well hidden from outside. Her husband was sitting in a chair with a glass in his hand.

'Reidar,' she said. 'This is our guest. Atle's brother.'

Kai bowed, and her husband looked back at him, clearly un-interested.

'Come with me,' she said, leading the way up the stairs. Her heels click-clacked on the steps as she climbed, almost sideways, and at quite a pace.

On the first floor there was a corridor. She stopped here and opened a door with a gilt handle.

'This is the bathroom. It's yours. Ours is further along.'

There were tiles on the floor, the bath had lion feet and the taps were made of brass. She turned and they almost crashed into each other.

'Whoops,' she said with a smile before opening the door opposite the bathroom. 'Here.' The ceiling lamp came on when she turned a switch.

The room was large and light. The bed was broad and covered with a crochet quilt. A white wardrobe dominated one wall; an equally white dresser the other. On top was a clock inside a glass dome cloche. The hands appeared to be made of gold and pointed to Roman numerals, indicating that it was just after nine in the evening. There was a mirror hanging above the dressing table. The blackout curtains were drawn in this room too.

'Hungry?'

'I've just eaten.'

'Make yourself at home,' she said. 'And come downstairs for a drink. We have a lot to talk about.'

For a few seconds he stood listening to her footsteps on the stairs. When all was quiet, he sat down on the edge of the bed. The second hand of the clock glided smoothly past the Roman numerals. He might as well go down, Kai thought. He

unpacked his kit bag. Laid his possessions on the dressing table
and changed into his new suit and shirt.

◈

Downstairs, the husband was sitting in the same place. Studying
an illustrated book through a magnifying glass. Kai caught a
glimpse of a hunting lodge, a tiger, and men dressed in khaki
and pith helmets.

Kai coughed.

The man didn't react.

Kai looked around the room. It was like a library, with books
lining shelves behind vitrine doors. There was some art on two
of the walls. One painting aroused his curiosity: sea, horizon,
the sun hanging over an islet at the mouth of a fjord, and an
open boat on the water. The other was a jumble of lines and
bright colours.

The kitchen door opened. Sara Krefting angled her head
when she saw him. Complimented him on his suit, and added
that he was young and good-looking. More attractive than his
brother. 'How old are you, Kai?'

'Twenty-seven.'

She held a bottle in her hand and raised it with a questioning
look. It was whisky. It could not have been easy to get hold of.
He gave a nod.

'Just a tiny bit of ice in the glass please, if you have any,' he
said.

She disappeared into the kitchen and he could hear her
breaking ice.

Soon she was back; she poured the whisky and passed him
the glass. As he took it, she stroked a finger across his hand.

Kai glanced across at her husband, who was still studying the
big book, taking no notice of them. When Kai looked back, she
met his gaze and stared into his eyes.

He was first to turn away. 'Nice house you've got.'

'We're doing the best we can,' she said. 'But it isn't easy. As you can imagine.' She began to talk in indignant tones about the government that had escaped to London when the Germans invaded.

'The king just fled,' she said, her voice tinged with steel. 'With the whole of the government. They ran off with their tails between their legs. The rest of us can't do that, run away from problems. We're forced to sit still and watch while the British lay mines around our coast and sink our Hurtigruten boats, and innocent people drown. Isn't that right, Reidar?'

'What?' The man hadn't heard.

With a little smile playing on her lips, she shook her head at her husband. 'Don't bother about Reidar, Kai. He's hard of hearing. Tinnitus. An injury sustained working with explosives. It's terrible in our country. This clown, Quisling, who's elevated himself to some kind of Führer. The truth is he's at Terboven's beck and call. He dances to his tune, he really does. Things are not good.' She went to the drinks cabinet and poured herself another. With her back to Kai, she began to talk about his brother and the injustice of his death.

'An execution, a cowardly execution,' she said, turning with a glass of red wine in her hand. She took a sip, then placed the glass on the table. 'Killed for no reason and then thrown in the river,' she added, sitting down on the sofa, her knees together, before straightening her skirt and covering them.

Kai cast around for a free chair. There wasn't one, so he sat down beside her.

'Thank God he was found,' she said. 'So at least he had a grave.'

Kai cleared his throat. 'Do they know who did it?'

'Who did it? It will've been some coward under cover of darkness. The police haven't managed to catch him yet. They're useless too.'

Kai leaned back. He was aware Atle had been murdered, but that was all he knew. From the day he read the priest's letter, he

had wanted to know more. Not only to have some clarity about
who had committed the murder, but also why and, not least,
how. Perhaps he would never find out, he thought. Norway was
at war, and the person, or persons, who killed his brother
probably acted as if they had every right to do so.

'Penny for your thoughts, Kai.'

'I was thinking life is short. We never know what's around
the corner.'

'There's something you can do though,' she said. 'You can
still do something for your brother.'

'What do you mean?'

She jumped to her feet. 'Reidar?' She wriggled past Kai and
across to her husband, who was shuffling towards the stairs, his
back bent, a stick in his hand. 'Are you going to bed, Reidar?'

The man continued towards the stairs without uttering a word
or turning round. He took one step at a time, tightly holding on
to the handrail. She hurried over and supported him.

Kai listened to the sound of their footsteps getting fainter on
the floor above.

In his mind's eye he saw a shadow, then a body fall and break
the surface of a wild river. He saw a corpse, swollen and partly
decomposed. He saw it, even though he didn't want to think
about it. He jumped to his feet as if to dispel the images.

It was late, it struck him, and realised he may have just been
given a hint. His hosts were withdrawing for the night. He
should probably turn in too. He grabbed his glass and drank
up, but hung on to say goodnight to her. She was taking her
time. He liked the whisky and cheekily allowed himself a refill.
He had managed to finish that glass as well by the time she came
back down.

'I'm tired too,' he said. 'It's been a long day. Thank you for
the drink, fru Krefting.'

'Sara,' she said. 'To you, I'm Sara, Kai.'

'Sara,' he said, heading for the stairs. 'Goodnight.'

'Kai,' she said before he had got very far. 'Come here.'

She held the bottle in her hand, leaned forward and filled his glass.

Kai went back, sat down and sipped the whisky. He could feel himself getting tipsy. When he put the glass back down, she was holding something in her hand, which she passed to him.

'Open this.'

It was a little leather package. He placed it on the table, loosened the ribbon tied around it and unfolded the soft leather. There was an envelope and a photograph inside. Something heavy slipped out from between them and fell onto the table with a clunk.

He picked up the medal and examined it. A matt-black metal cross with a decorative silver edge, *1942* embossed on the lower arm and a swastika in the middle.

'*Ein eisernes Kreuz, erste Klasse*. Iron Cross, First Class,' Sara said in a solemn voice.

As he weighed the bravery award in his hand, he had images of his brother in his mind.

'You're smiling,' Sara Krefting said softly, nodding to the Iron Cross. 'Atle deserved it.'

She picked up the photograph. It showed a group of soldiers chatting cheerfully in a field. A rippling meadow behind them, a line of black treetops – spruces – towering up between the land and the sky in the background. The soldiers were standing beside a handcart. One of them was sitting on a motorbike. Atle was in the middle.

'He was pinning the medal to his chest,' she said, pointing to the photograph.

Kai knew Atle had volunteered, but had never seen him in a German uniform. Now he noticed that Atle had stripes on his arm; he was an *Unteroffizier*, a sergeant.

Sara took the envelope and passed it to him. It bulged and wasn't stuck down. 'Open it.'

Kai let go of the medal and opened the envelope. It was stuffed full of banknotes.

'It's all yours, Kai – the money too.'

He looked down at the notes. Five-krone notes, ten, a hundred, a big one, folded over. The zeros on it told him it was a thousand-krone note. This was a lot of money. He had to clear his throat to make his voice carry.

'How come you have all these things?'

'I claimed the medal and the photograph when I found out your brother was dead.'

'What about the money?'

'It's a present for you.'

He looked up at her, but no explanation was forthcoming.

'Why did he get it?'

'What do you mean?'

'The medal. Why was he awarded it?'

'For showing valour and fortitude. It was a battle, the twenty-fifth of September last year, outside a town called Grozny. Atle was wounded. He had killed many of the enemy and held a machine-gun post for several hours. Until he was hit in the shoulder by a dum-dum bullet. It caused terrible damage. They wanted to amputate the whole of his arm, but he wouldn't let them. Afterwards, he was awarded this honour. There aren't many Norwegians who have this decoration, Kai. Your brother was a real man. He would've gone far if he'd been allowed to live.'

Kai took a sip of whisky. He could feel a fuzziness behind his eyes. It was a wonderful feeling. It had been a long time since he had felt the effect of alcohol and, in these circumstances, it was good to get drunk, even if he was unsure what was having most influence on him, the whisky or the place – this brightly lit palace ruled by the sylph sitting so chastely with her legs together. Yellow light and brown nectar, he mused – and a sweetly scented Siren. He had to smile and picked up the envelope containing the money. 'What about the gift? Where has that come from?'

'From someone who wants you to carry out a mission.'

'Someone?'

She nodded.

'A mission?'

She nodded again.

'Who wants me to carry out a mission?' He looked at her with a curious expression on his face while she eyed him wordlessly.

Someone, he wondered. It must be someone with a lot of money, and who else could that be but her?

'There's one thing I'm unsure about,' he said. 'Do you know why he was killed?'

She didn't answer.

'What had he done?'

She clenched her teeth, and her face hardened. 'Nothing. The question is whether you're man enough to avenge his death.'

'Avenge?' That was a word he hadn't expected. 'What do you mean?'

She looked him in the eye. 'I'm asking you if you'll do it. If you're half the man your brother was, you will know the answer.'

This direct, implacable tone wrongfooted him, and he struggled to find the right words. 'We don't know who did it, do we?' he said, but realised she wasn't listening. She was still staring into his eyes, and it was clear she was telling him something.

'I know you didn't sign off from any boat today.' She leaned forward and spoke in a whisper. 'You were interned for six months, in Grini concentration camp. They released you today.'

She got up, went to the closest cabinet and opened the glass door.

Kai's brain was racing. How could she know about the camp and his release? Well, there was only one answer to that question. Yet he couldn't bring himself to believe it, not that instant at any rate. But he didn't understand the connection. He would have to ask straight out when she turned round.

But Kai quickly decided not to say anything. Because now she was holding a gun. It was black and much too big for her small hand. Her eyes locked on to his, she came back and sat down. Then she soundlessly placed the gun on the table.

She has done this before, Kai concluded. He raised his head and met her eyes again. They sat like this for a long time, neither of them backing down.

'This is what you need to avenge your brother,' she whispered. 'But we're getting ahead of ourselves, Kai. I've heard you've had quite a life. You went to sea when you were fourteen. You were in France when you were nineteen, and then you went to Spain. You volunteered to fight with the Reds in the Spanish Civil war. You stayed there until you returned to France.'

'You're well informed, fru Krefting.'

She grabbed his hand. 'I told you. Call me Sara. Let me guess, Kai. Why did you go back to France from Spain?'

He looked down at her hand. The veins on it stood out like a river delta, signalling maturity and experience.

'I think it was because you deserted,' she whispered. 'That's no disgrace. After all, you did risk being shot at by your own side. I think that's why you signed on to join the Foreign Legion after the Reds had been beaten. You wanted to disappear, become invisible, because you'd deserted. Am I right?'

She wasn't, but now he could read her. Sara Krefting was the kind who, when aware of some elements of a situation, filled in the rest with her fertile imagination. Being able to see through her in this way gave him the upper hand, but he nodded anyway, to retain this hold over her. He was under no obligation to tell the truth to anyone. This woman had her sources, but Atle could not have been one of them. Because Kai had never told his brother about the Foreign Legion. Sara Krefting must have another source, and it was becoming increasingly obvious who it was. It could only be one person. The German officer at Grini. The man with the smooth voice who had released him earlier in the day. If she was on such intimate terms with this officer, that suggested she had much more power than he had hitherto supposed.

'Betraying the Reds is no disgrace.' Her voice was a whisper again. Her head was only centimetres from his. 'The Reds lost in Spain, which was always going to be the case. Then you signed up for the Foreign Legion, but you didn't stay long. Let me guess. You deserted again? Was it too hard being a soldier twenty-four hours a day? I can understand that. You were so young. You'd already lived in trenches for a long time. Perhaps you dreamt about a woman, perhaps you even met one?'

Kai looked down at her hands. They were fondling his arms. Small, experienced hands, with red fingernails, running down his arms, going back up and stroking him again.

'You're a handsome man,' she whispered. 'I'm sure you found a woman and pleased her, but you were escaping from the Foreign Legion. You wanted to come home, to Norway. Instead you were arrested. Where did they catch you?' Her face was so close that the sweetness of her breath mingled with her perfume. Again Kai felt the fuzziness of intoxication, unsure whether it was the whisky or the perfume that was more responsible for his state. Her blue eyes searched for his, but he didn't want to meet them, and looked away. She was welcome to this part of his past.

'In Berne,' he said. 'I was arrested by the Swiss military police.'

'Were you released?'

He shook his head.

'You escaped,' she said. 'You fled once again and came to Norway, and this is where you signed on to the German boat we were talking about earlier today. The one carrying weapons to Narvik, but you didn't stay there long either. You wanted to sign off, but they refused, so you ran off again. Then you lived from hand to mouth here in Norway until you were arrested by the Gestapo.'

Kai gave her a serious smile.

'What is it?'

'I know when I'm beaten.'

'What do you mean?'

'You know these things because the German officer is an ac-
quaintance of yours,' Kai said. 'The bastard who let me go this
morning. You were waiting for me in the cemetery because you
knew I would visit my brother's grave. Quite a plan. The
German said I would be contacted. I thought it would be by a
German in uniform, but then you appear. The Queen of Sheba.'
He drained his glass and moved to stand up.

'Look at me,' she said firmly.

When they were eyeball to eyeball, she gripped his hands
again and held them tight.

'You were sent to Grini. It was a rough time, but you were
set free. Listen to what I have to say. You'll soon be completely
free, if you help me.'

'If I help you? Supposing I agree, what will I have to do?'

'You'll have to report back to me.'

'About what?'

'About the people you know. The Reds, Kai. Your parents
were party members, weren't they?'

He nodded.

'Your brother was an exception, but you followed your father
and joined the party. You went to sea, and the beliefs your father
imposed on you as a child meant you ended up in Spain, with
the Reds you thought were your family. But they destroyed your
life. You had to watch your comrades being killed, and when it
became too much for you, they went after you, intending to
shoot you. That was the thanks you got for risking your life to
fight for them. You don't have much love left for the Reds, Kai.
Together we'll beat them. We'll eliminate them, and then we'll
avenge your brother.'

The cat was out of the bag, partly. Again he felt the mental
hold you have over people who believe they know everything,
but don't.

'How will we do that?' he whispered back. 'Have you got any
specific plans of action?'

It was her turn to look down now.

He picked up the photograph. 'I'll take this. You can keep the medal.'

'Wait,' she said as he made to leave. 'I'll keep the medal. It's a wonderful memory of your brother. Atle was a good friend. We worked together quite a lot.' Her hand held out the envelope with the money in. 'This is for you.'

'Why?'

'So that I can see you're the person I think you are.'

He had to give it to her: she was good. She knew how to play her cards right. He stuffed the envelope and the photograph into his inside pocket and took the gun. He studied it. German manufacture. A luger. It felt good in his hand. He took out the magazine and confirmed it was fully loaded. When he went through the loading motions and squeezed the trigger it replied with a dry click. Then he shoved the magazine back in and activated the safety catch. Looked up. Saw that she liked to see him handling the gun.

'Are you telling me you know who killed my brother?'

'A man who lives in Stockholm,' she said, sipping from her glass. 'His name's Daniel Berkåk. He comes over here – into Norway, that is. Crosses the border regularly. You'll be told when he's coming. You have to be there, at the border. Your cover will be that you're escaping to Sweden. As soon as you've shot Berkåk, you'll have to dispose of the gun. Throw it in a river or bury it under a rock. Then you complete the cover operation and cross into Sweden as if you're an escapee. On the other side you'll be arrested by Swedish police. It's important you don't have the gun on you when you're captured. The police will transport you to a refugee camp. There you'll be interrogated by Norwegians. Many times. They'll ask you why you fled from Norway. Don't lie to them. Anyone who lies trips up at some point. Tell the truth. Tell them about your work on boats, how you escaped, tell them you were arrested, tell them about your incarceration in Grini. The only thing you should keep quiet about is avenging your brother's death. When they ask you why you fled to Sweden, say you want to fight for your country, you're ready to do anything for Norway.'

Kai placed the gun back on the table, stood up and went upstairs without another word, without even a rearward glance. Went into the bathroom. Went to the toilet. Afterwards he washed, scrutinising himself in the mirror.

What an idiot he had been today. The plan had been to lie low. To avoid German soldiers and officers. The slippery German in Grini must have known. The officer hadn't trusted Kai. Working for them, giving them the information they wanted, in return for freedom, was one thing, but the officer must have realised that Kai had no intention of keeping the deal. That was why he had decided to outmanoeuvre him. The German had set the bait. A woman. *Come and stay with us. I knew your brother*.

Kai walked naked from the bathroom to his room. Lay down on the duvet. Heard her moving around on the floor below. Then he got up, switched off the light and lay back down on the bed, but under the duvet now. Staring into the darkness. How crazy life could be. From a prison camp to this perfumed room in one day. His mind went back to his brother. Atle, who joined the SS, became an *Unteroffizier*, was awarded the Iron Cross and died.

As he was descending into sleep, he heard a noise by the door; he opened his eyes wide. The hinges creaked. The door opened gently; a strip of light fell across the floor from the corridor. A glimpse of her shadow appeared in the doorway; the duvet rustled. Then her lips were there. She tasted of toothpaste.

5

Jomar Kraby took the bus up to Södra Hammarby, where Daniel Berkåk lived, in a three-storey house, one of many in a row.

As he approached the entrance, he could see two heads peering out from behind their respective kitchen curtains, but when he raised his hat and bowed, both heads quickly disappeared.

On the first floor a piece of paper protruded from under one of the doorbells. *Daniel Berkåk*, it said. Jomar tried the key he had been given by Gunvor and entered a hallway with a recess for coats and a door that led to a toilet. Inside, there was a smell of soap and after-shave.

Jomar continued into the sitting room. There was a desk and a wooden chair under the window, and two armchairs had been placed against the opposite wall either side of a sideboard with a radio on top. Three rifles were propped in the corner. A door led into a kitchenette with a gas ring, a table and a sink.

Jomar took one of the guns. Norwegian manufacture. A Krag Jørgensen with a dioptre rifle sight and a chamber for five bullets. Empty. After replacing the gun, he opened the last door – to a bedroom. There was a bed under the window and, in the corner, a wardrobe. In it hung a suit on a solitary clothes hanger. There were a few shirts neatly folded on one shelf, and below, underwear. Jomar felt the suit pockets. Empty. On the bedside table was a glass of water. In the drawers, nothing.

Returning to the sitting room and the desk under the window,

he sat down on the chair. In the top drawer there were some
folded newspapers, a pen, three pencils, a rubber and some ration
cards. In the second drawer a half-bottle rolled around. Swedish
vodka. This was so tempting that he went to the kitchen and
found a glass in the cupboard above the gas ring. He poured
himself a snifter, drank it and licked his lips, then sat down at
the desk again. There was something under the desk blotter. Two
notebooks. Jomar flicked through them. There were a lot of
notes. Some lists. A number of disconnected sentences Daniel
Berkåk had considered worth jotting down. Some of them
credited with the author's name: Sandemose, Øverland, Nordal
Grieg. A whole poem. Inger Hagerup's 'Aust-Vågøy' – about the
German reprisals after the raid on the Lofoten Islands. Jomar
smiled as he read it. He liked her a lot, and this poem was a gem.

In the second notebook there was a newspaper cutting. It was
from the Press Office's bulletin: *Håndslag*. It was about three
patriots from Odalen who had been executed by the Germans.
Jomar had also heard about the incident. The names of the three
victims were listed, and one was Sverre Berkåk. That was of
interest at any rate. Who was he? A brother? The father? Or an
uncle?

There was less writing in this book and it was of a different
kind. Lists of addresses. Beyond that, times of the day. He recognised one of the addresses. It was the German Legation's
Intelligence Office. None of the others though. He put the
notebooks in his coat pocket. Then he poured himself another
drink and stood weighing the bottle in his hand. He concluded
that neither Daniel nor anyone else would miss it, so slipped it
into his other coat pocket and left.

6

When Jomar again boarded the bus, it was to go to the
Norwegian Press Office, where he occasionally took odd jobs.

Several of the journalists were dubious about Jomar's radical past. The famous non-aggression pact that Foreign Ministers Molotov and Ribbentrop had signed in 1939 meant that all patriots with their hearts located on the right were sceptical of patriots on the left. Neither the fact that Hitler had invaded the Soviet Union two years later, nor the fact that the Soviets had today blunted Hitler's war aims, forcing the Germans into a retreat in the east, thus gaining the upper hand over the Third Reich, appeared to affect the entrenched scepticism.

Jomar Karby's outspoken criticism of the Nygaardvold government's disarmament policy in the thirties, together with his contempt for Norwegian politicians' vacuous indifference to Germany's rearmament and war-mongering during the same years, had given him a reputation as an agitator, which stuck to him however much he disliked it. On the other hand, Kraby's censored stage play had reinforced his status as a persecuted patriot. Jomar wasn't always welcome at the Press Office, but he did receive the editor's blessing whenever he felt like sharpening his quill.

In the editorial department he walked over to Sigurd Friis, who was in the process of mounting a cartoon. Sigurd was a little younger than himself, closer to forty than fifty, but still blessed with wavy black hair and had a huge beard shaped like a horseshoe around his mouth.

Jomar said he had heard about Daniel Berkåk's tragic death.

'Absolutely dreadful,' Sigurd said. 'Too dreadful for words. Shot and abandoned in the densest forest. As if there wasn't enough devil's work in our country already.'

'I barely knew him,' Jomar said. 'Where was he from in Norway?'

'South Hedmark. Actually, he was a smithy by trade. He'd been working as a mechanic when he fled across the border last summer.'

'A mechanic? Working here in the Press Office?'

'He probably felt more at home in the Intelligence Unit, but he was a kind of newsman. So he was often here. Quite a guy, in fact. At home he ran an illegal newspaper all on his own, but had to flee after a raid on the house where he kept his mimeograph machine. He crossed the border and was arrested on the Swedish side, and given an emergency visa and a one-way ticket to Kjesäter refugee camp. He was recruited pretty much as soon as he got there, and driven to Öreryd in Småland for commando training. You know, swimming in the Nissan River, cross-country running and all the things Swedes shouldn't know that we do. After a few weeks' training he was sent on his first mission to Norway with documents and underground newspapers and so on.'

'All the way from Småland?'

'Exactly. Not the easiest job in the world. First of all, he had to get closer to the border. That was why he took a job as a forester – on a false passport. Then he was sent on a so-called *huggarkurs*, a logging course, in Ragunda, in Jämtland. As soon as he arrived, he made his escape and crossed the border to Norway via Östersund and Meråker. Three weeks later he was back in Stockholm and ready for the next fight. That was impressive. From then on he was working here, and going back and forth across the border. He probably did it fifteen to twenty times. Knew his way around, especially in the border areas by Eidskog, Magnor and Austmarka.'

'A tough nut?'

'One of the best.'

'Politically?'

'A patriot.'

'Did he wear his heart on the left or the right?'

'Don't know. He was more of a moral than a political man, I think. He volunteered for the Soviet-Finnish Winter War. He fought against the Soviet invasion there, and at home he committed himself to fighting the Germans. Why do you ask?'

'A patriot has been killed. That affects me.'

Sigurd Friis leaned back, his brow furrowed with suspicion.

'The killing has upset a lot of people,' Jomar said. 'Patriots, people with influence. One of them has asked me to do a bit of digging.'

'Who?'

'I'd prefer not to say.'

Friis smiled. It was a wry, knowing smile that was unable to compensate for the tristesse of his droopy walrus moustache.

Jomar produced the notebooks he had found in Daniel Berkåk's flat. Took out the newspaper cutting about the three patriots who had been executed in Trandum Forest.

Friis nodded. 'Sverre Berkåk was his father. He was in the Skarnes Resistance group.'

'Did it happen a long time ago?'

'Last autumn, not so long before Christmas. Daniel was devastated. He talked about it non-stop.'

Jomar nodded too. He could understand that.

'The three who were shot were arrested after the Germans received a tip-off.'

'Did Daniel know who the informer was?'

Friis smiled. 'The informer was killed a short time after. I think the police even had Daniel on their list of suspects.'

Jomar needed some clarity here. 'So Daniel's father was shot by the Germans after an informer gave him away? Then the informer was killed, and the Norwegian police suspected Daniel of having killed him?'

Friis nodded again.

'Yet he went back to Norway?'

'Berkåk was a wanted man long before the Germans executed his father.' Friis grinned. 'Whenever he crossed the border he carried weapons, illegal newspapers and documents. He risked his life every time. One dead informer made no difference to him.'

Jomar mulled this over.

Friis half stood up. 'If there's nothing else…'

'So Berkåk knew he was risking his life crossing the border,' Jomar said.

Friis angled his head.

'But he was killed neither by German soldiers nor the Norwegian Stapo. He must've been killed by a civilian in the forest.'

'It's a mystery.'

'Could he have stumbled across a refugee?'

'Possible, but I doubt a refugee escaping from Norway to Sweden would want to kill anyone, least of all Daniel Berkåk.'

'Norwegian refugees are interned in Kjesäter,' Jomar said. 'You people here in the Press Office sometimes pump them for information, don't you?'

'Pump is *your* word.'

'Could you send me there?'

Friis grinned again. 'Why would we do that?'

'Daniel was killed just by the border. A refugee might've heard or seen something.'

'Why would that interest you?'

Jomar mused for a few long seconds. At length, he took a deep breath and took out the document signed by Terje Wold and Trygve Lie.

Friis read it, raised his head, stared at Jomar and then re-read it.

'That commits you to an oath of silence,' Kraby said drily.

Sigurd Friis slowly absorbed this new information. 'Come here early tomorrow morning,' he said at last. 'At six. Outside the building.'

7

Jomar chose the street called Karlavägen because he liked walking down a tree-covered central aisle between carriageways. It reminded him of strolling down La Rambla and made him dream about other times.

At the Sturegatan crossroads he stopped and considered his

next move. Sooner or later he would have to confront Peder Svinningen. According to Gunvor, he had been one of the last people to speak to Daniel. With that in mind, Jomar ambled down to the Legal Office.

He sat down on a bench on the opposite side of the street to the office, with his back to Humlegården Park, and from there he watched passers-by as he sifted through what he knew about the Legal Office's strong man. Svinningen was the brain behind the initiative to carry out surveillance on what he called 'the opposition', who in fact were Norwegian Communists. The Legal Office carried out wide-reaching intelligence and counter-espionage work, had a controlling influence over job appointments and was preparing for a showdown with Norwegian Nazis the day the war was over. In that context, Svinningen was the brain behind the move to censor all post to Norway. All correspondence had to be sifted through, in his judgement, to separate the chaff from the rest of the Norwegians living in Sweden.

Jomar could imagine him, bent over his desk chewing his lower lip and writing long letters to the exiled government in London about the right line to take, which Svinningen called the 'legal' line, as opposed to the 'desperado' line, which in Svinningen's view was that pursued by militant Communists back home in Norway and the dreamers among the Norwegian refugees who joined British units as commandos and SOE agents. Jomar had heard Svinningen give talks on how the main efforts against such destructive forces should be made in Norway, but how a lot could also be done in neutral Sweden – in Stockholm – by supporting Svinningen's 'new scheme', which involved stepping up discipline generally, plus actively enforcing the 'legal' line in particular. Svinningen was a lawyer with a natural talent for detecting the most elaborate conspiracies in any everyday event, a dedicated and determined sophist, with whom Jomar Kraby was looking forward to crossing swords.

A cat slunk alongside the wall. It ensconced itself in front of a door and coiled its tail neatly around its legs. It was waiting, Jomar deduced, as he was too. A woman opened the door. She was holding a bowl of food, which she placed in front of the cat; it let her close the door before it crept over and started to eat with intense concentration. It nudged every morsel with its nose and then chewed. Its sharp fangs punctured the food, its molars ground it, until the cat suddenly sat quite still, swallowing, enjoying the experience of taste and nourishment before nudging another morsel. Jomar was so fascinated by this process that he almost missed the man, who had managed to cover a considerable distance before Jomar was able to stand up and cross the street.

'Peder Svinningen,' he shouted over to the man in a hurry.

He stopped, turned, and subjected Jomar to a critical gaze.

It was the narrowed, fiery gimlet eyes that caught people's attention. Svinningen's forehead was reminiscent of the crest of a hill, either side of which a bank of snowy-white hair grew over his ears, losing its fight with gravity.

'What is it?' he asked in an oleaginous voice.

'I'd like a few words with you.'

Svinningen's eyebrows rose two further notches.

'I understand you're the head of the Legal Office.'

'A few words about what?'

'I've heard you're so interested in the flow of refugees between Norway and Sweden that you'd like the Legal Office to assume responsibility for them. What is the reasoning behind that?'

Svinningen narrowed his eyes again, obviously provoked. 'I don't see that's any of your business, but is it so strange? The Refugee Office secretariat has been infiltrated by Communists and desperadoes. I believe I've read things you've written. You're one of them, aren't you? You were in Erling Falk's *Mot Dag* leftie group, weren't you? You're a literary radical who believes the world will be a better place if we let Bolsheviks and illiterates into our governing organs. Perhaps you think *that*'s the future now that the Germans are retreating from the east?' Svinningen straightened his back like a schoolmaster on a dais. 'In this war you have to make choices,' he said, wagging his forefinger. 'You have to choose which side you're on. My government is based in London, and I act on their behalf. They don't want Reds running wild and causing trouble in occupied Norway. Every time the fanatics blow up a railway bridge or bomb a factory, the Germans conduct reprisals and murder innocent Norwegians. It's a recipe for chaos in our home country, but we, the government-in-exile in London – that is I, because I represent them – want to have some control.' He repeated the word as if it had a soothing effect on his temperament: 'Control. I want to know which of the Norwegians who come over the border to Sweden are good Norwegians or Nazis or, for that matter, Communists. As an educated person, as someone who purports to be a writer, you must understand the logic in that, surely?' Svinningen tilted his head, as though he were still a schoolmaster and had reprimanded a naughty boy, and was waiting for a subservient nod in return.

Jomar cleared his throat. 'How far are you willing to go to gain control?'

Svinningen studied him. 'What is this?' he said at last. 'Why are you even talking to me? You've spilt soup on your shirt, you stink of alcohol and tobacco, you stand here blocking out the sun and asking me questions that do not concern you.'

Jomar changed his tone now. 'I've been tasked with a mission by the London government. My job is to analyse elements of the Norwegian Legation's organisation. Accordingly, I assume I have your full co-operation, and discretion.'

Svinningen still had the same expression on his face and held the same posture, but now he changed his tone. 'What, sir, are you daring to presume?'

Jomar stuck a hand into his inside coat pocket and took out the letter from the Norwegian government. He unfolded it and waved it like a white kerchief in Svinningen's face. 'Full authorisation. You – and all the staff at your disposal – are duly obliged to answer my questions.'

'Let me see that.' Svinningen read the document, re-read it, looked up at the sky and read the authorisation once again, still speechless.

Jomar watched the man's face pale. Then he plucked the document out of Svinningen's hands and put it back in his inside pocket.

Svinningen changed his tone again. 'If this document is genuine,' he said, 'who do you report to?'

'Torgersen.'

The answer was clearly another body-blow. 'Torgersen?'

Jomar immediately realised that reading this document must have had a much greater effect on Svinningen than he had anticipated. He saw himself as the London government's right-hand man, and now his government had not only issued an order he knew nothing about but implemented it through Torgersen, a man he presumably disliked and looked down on.

Svinningen's eyes were miles away and both his fists clenched.

'The next question is about Daniel Berkåk.' Jomar felt he should strike while the iron was hot.

'Torgersen,' Svinningen repeated, thunderstruck, it appeared, and shook his head. It was clear the man was not listening.

'Daniel Berkåk,' Jomar repeated. 'His father, Sverre Berkåk, was executed by the Germans in Trandum with two others. Why did that happen?'

'They were a group of patriots who were infiltrated by Nazis and later informed on.'

'Have you any details?'

'I don't know any.' Svinningen's mind was still elsewhere. 'It happened in Norway. We're in Sweden.'

'You were aware that Berkåk was going to Norway, were you?'

'So?'

'We both know he suffered a brutal end.'

'Yes, and so?'

'Who else in your office knew that he was going?'

'I have many pre-conceived opinions about you, Kraby. However, I didn't think you were that naïve.'

Now Svinningen had his self-importance and arrogance back. 'You have a document bearing stamps from the highest authority and, before the ink's dry, you're charging forth with blinkers on. Let me share a little secret with you: in war time it's the soldiers who die, not the generals pulling the strings and despatching them. Go home, Kraby. Have another think. Ask yourself who stands to gain what by sending you into battle.'

'No one stands to gain anything in this. The initiative comes from London.'

Svinningen leaned back but refrained from answering. Without saying a word he spun on his heel and went on his way.

Jomar Kraby watched him. He wasn't fooled by the arrogance. Two ministers' signatures on a letter Svinningen knew nothing about must have sent tremors through the ground beneath the feet of this pompous individual. He must have been wondering what this might mean for him, in the future.

Jomar turned and set out in the opposite direction. He smiled as he walked. He had given the old fox something to think about. The question was: how would he strike back? He would find a way to exact his revenge. Svinningen couldn't allow a humiliation of this kind to go unpunished.

I'll deal with that when the time comes, he thought. With the vodka bottle in his pocket, Jomar walked home to prepare for an early start the following day.

8

Kjesäter Manor House appeared in all its grandeur at the end of an avenue of trees. The building had three floors, and there were eleven tall windows in every row. Borgar Stridsberg pulled up in front of the main entrance and all three quickly alighted. First, Sigurd Friis and Ester, a young woman from the Intelligence Office, followed by Jomar, grateful to be able to stretch his legs finally, but still tired after getting up at five in the morning.

By the entrance he stopped to take in the sight of the refugee camp: the huge main building was supplemented with barracks and, beyond these, meadowland. Here Norwegians wandered around idly and compensated for their idleness on a sports ground. A group of refugees in short trousers and white vests were doing marching manoeuvres.

Jomar was introduced to the camp commanders and shook their hands one by one, then Sigurd led the way into an office, where they made themselves comfortable. Ester sat at a desk with a typewriter. Both she and Friis tidied papers into a pile and took turns to sharpen pencils in a desk-mounted machine.

Ester gave Jomar a copy of the list of the latest arrivals.

Jomar thanked her, took the list and found a seat at a desk under the window.

Then she went to the door and summoned the first interviewee.

He shuffled in and sat down – almost two metres tall and wearing breeches and a T-shirt. He said he was from Oslo, twenty-two years old and had escaped to Sweden to avoid having to do forced labour for the Germans. Roadwork. How he was going to pass the time in Sweden he wasn't sure, but he wanted to do something useful. He had heard there were opportunities in forestry.

When he folded his enormous hands, Jomar thought that this job could actually suit the man.

Ester typed up the man's answer. This routine had its own rhythm: questions, clatter of typewriter keys, pling, more clatter and then another round of questions.

Jomar looked out of the window. Behind the sports ground there were more barracks, and the ranks of men who had been marching were now lined up and doing gymnastics.

Behind him Sigurd Friis continued with the questioning: 'Where do you stand politically?'

'Stand?'

'Where do your sympathies lie?'

'I don't actually have that many sympathies.'

'And what do you mean by that?'

Jomar peered up, curious to hear the answer. It was clear the young man was prepared and had planned what to say. It transpired that he wasn't interested in politics.

Friis straightened up and pressed him harder. 'You risked your life crossing the border because you didn't want to work for the Germans. If you're not interested in politics, surely it doesn't matter whether you work for them or not?'

Jomar concentrated on the list of names.

Soon the door closed behind the gaunt man.

Jomar leaned forward, holding the sheet of paper. 'Fourth line from the bottom.'

Friis studied the list. 'What about him?'

'I'd like to hear what he has to say.'

'Now?'

Kraby nodded. 'If he's the Kai I think he is, I knew his father.'

'So?'

'As I said, I knew his father.'

Friis motioned to Ester, who got up and went out. Shortly afterwards, she came back with a young man in his late twenties. Jomar recognised the eyes and the jaw of the man's father, and racked his brain to remember when he had last seen this fellow.

Friis readied a form on the desk in front of him. 'Kai Fredly?'

The man nodded and sat down.

Ester's typewriter rattled away.

Friis waited until the noise abated before asking Kai why he had decided to cross the border.

'I want to do something for Norway,' he answered, and started to talk. He had been arrested by the Germans. He had escaped doing forced labour on a boat but had been arrested and interned in Grini. When he was released, he had only one thought in his head: to get to England. He wanted to train as a soldier and fight for Norway.

Jomar coughed.

Friis glanced across at him.

'Your brother's a Nazi, isn't he?' Jomar said.

Kai Fredly looked back and gulped before answering. 'My brother's dead.'

That was news to Jomar. He suddenly felt sympathy for the young man. 'My condolences. How did he die?'

Fredly took his time, gave the question a lot of thought before answering: 'He went missing and was gone for a while. Then they found his body. I don't know much about it, because I was in Grini when it happened.'

The typewriter rattled away.

'He was a Nazi though, wasn't he?'

All three of them looked at Jomar. The silence persisted.

Kai Fredly squirmed uncomfortably on his chair. Eventually he spoke up:

'My brother was a member of the Nasjonal Samling, if that's what you're asking me, but I don't know much about that either. I was at sea when my brother joined the NS. I was at sea when the Germans invaded our country, and I was in Grini when he died.'

Kraby waited for the typewriter to stop.

'I knew your father a little. We used to have quite a bit to do with each other – politically.'

Fredly looked straight at him.

'I was at his funeral,' Jomar continued. 'You probably don't remember me.'

Kai shook his head.

'Five or six years ago I heard one of his boys was in Spain. Is that right?'

Fredly nodded.

'What did you do there?'

'I fought.'

'Which company?'

'Thälmann battalion.'

'You fought against the fascists?'

Kai Fredly nodded.

'And the Germans?'

He nodded again.

'What about your brother?'

'What about him?'

'As a Nazi, I suppose he was on the German side?'

Fredly was quiet. The typewriter was also still.

Jomar pushed him: 'What do you think about that?'

'I think about it as little as possible.'

'What kind of answer is that?'

'This war is hell,' Kai Fredly said. 'All my folks are dead, and that's bad enough. I don't have the energy to think about what my brother did or why. He's gone. The only thing that has any meaning is to finish this awful war. That's why I want to go to England to do my bit.'

'So defeat for the Germans has some meaning for you?'

'Yes.'

'You're here now because you got out of Grini,' Jomar said. 'Why did the Germans let you go?'

'You'll have to ask them that.'

'Did they interrogate you?'

'What do *you* think? It's a prison camp. Of course I was interrogated.'

'What did they want to know?'

'What I knew about Norwegian Communists.'

'Did they know you'd been in Spain?'

'Strangely enough, yes, they did.'

'What did you tell them – about Norwegian Communists?'

'Very little. After Spain I went to sea for a couple of years. Then I came home. I hadn't had any contact with Norwegian political circles for many years. That's what I told them. I said I had nothing to tell the Germans.'

'Did they believe you?'

'I don't know.'

'Your father worked for the party. You know lots of Communists. As far as I can see, you would've had a lot to tell the Germans.'

Kai Fredly didn't reply. Just glared defiance at Jomar.

'What form did these interrogations take?'

'They asked questions.'

'And when you didn't answer…?'

'What do you mean?'

'Did they hit you to get an answer out of you? Were they violent?'

'No.'

The typewriter fired another salvo, and Kraby waited for it to die away. 'They thought you could give them names of Norwegian Communists, but you couldn't tell them anything. When you kept your mouth shut, they didn't try to force you to answer. Instead, you were released. That's very unusual.'

'It might've been very unusual, but I'm not German. I don't know how they think.' Fredly seemed annoyed. 'When I left the gates of Grini behind me, I just wanted to get away. I didn't object to being released.'

'What actually happened? Why were you arrested?'

'It was because of the recruitment office. I was doing forced labour on a two-thousand tonner called the *Harvesthude*. They wouldn't let me sign off. In the end, I did a runner. When we were moored in Stavanger. A stroke of luck for me. Because she was torpedoed last year at her anchorage in Stadtlandet. Then I worked for a farmer in Jæren. I had to lie low as I was a wanted man, but after the potato harvest there wasn't much work on the smallholding. So I think the farmer blabbed to get rid of me, because one day four soldiers and a Gestapo man showed up. Then I was taken to Grini.'

The typewriter rattled away for quite a while this time.

'When did you get out?'

'Just over three weeks ago.'

'You were released from a German prison camp. You hang around in Norway for two weeks and then you travel to Sweden. Why?'

'I've told you why. I want to do my bit for our country.'

Jomar studied the list of names. In the right-hand column there were brief notes about individual possessions. 'When you came here, you had five thousand kroner on you. That's a lot of money.'

'It's my accumulated wages. I'd been at sea since before the war started.'

'Was it good pay?'

Fredly didn't answer.

'It's at least a year since you left the ship. Haven't you spent any money since then?'

'What is this?' Kai Fredly said, flailing his arms around. 'Don't you two believe what I'm saying?'

'By which route did you come to Sweden?'

'Kongsvinger.'

'Why that route?'

'Because Kongsvinger's closer to Sweden. Why d'you think?'

'Most people cross the border at other points because the Värmland police chief has a bad reputation.'

'I wasn't aware of that.'

Jomar studied the papers again.

'You were arrested by the Swedish border police. To the police chief you said that you fled because your brother had been arrested by the Germans, but that you weren't political.'

'I said that so as not to be sent to prison. I'd heard the Swedes lock anyone up who travels via Sweden to England.'

'How did you get to Kongsvinger?'

'From Youngstorget. I got a lift on a market-stallholder's lorry, under a pile of vegetables. He drove me to a barn outside Kongsvinger. The man who ran the farm showed me the way across the border.'

'What was his name?'

'He didn't say.'

'Did you notice any police activity around the border?'

'No.'

'A murder took place in the border area. A man was shot. The police carried out enquiries. Did you notice any of this?'

Kai Fredly shook his head, but he was warier now, it was visible in his eyes.

Jomar Kraby scrutinised him.

The young man glared back.

Jomar tried to read him, but failed. Nevertheless, he felt he had touched a nerve in this son of one of his old friends. He had triggered a reaction that had made the young man go on the defensive.

Sigurd Friis stood up looking annoyed and beckoned with his head to Kraby. They walked into the corridor together. 'This is going nowhere, and there are lots more people we have to talk to. This guy is no Nazi. He fought in Spain.'

'The Germans let him go, from Grini, even though he didn't tell them anything. I don't buy that.'

'You think he was recruited as an agent?'

'That's one possibility.'

'If he was, why did he come to Sweden? No, Jomar, I think he's telling the truth.'

'He crossed the border at the same time as Daniel Berkåk was killed.'

'Many more did too, but we've taken note that he's a Communist, and we'll add his name to the list of unreliable Norwegians. This is routine. The Communists have their own file in the archives. We send them into the forests where they can do least damage. We have to move on. Talk to more people.'

Jomar was lost in thought.

'Well?'

'He wants to go to England.'

'He believes in fairies.'

'I have a suggestion.'

Friis's brow furrowed with suspicion.

'Let's send him to Stockholm.'

'That's against the rules.'

Kraby said nothing, just raised his eyebrows.

'Why do you want me to break the rules?' Sigurd Friis said, seemingly nettled.

'He's got money. He doesn't want to be a burden to anyone. Being in Stockholm will make it easier for him to try and move – to Scotland or Canada. Then it'll be possible to see whether he means what he says, whether he is the patriot he claims to be.'

Friis shook his head in resignation.

'I'll assume responsibility for following him wherever he goes,' Jomar said.

Friis took a deep breath.

Kraby did the same, then put his hand in his inside pocket and showed a corner of the document signed by the ministers in London.

Friis shook his head again, opened the door and went back into the office.

Jomar followed him in and watched as Friis dismissed Fredly. Then Jomar took out Daniel Berkåk's notebooks. Sigurd Friis and Ester whispered, sending him glances. Jomar let them as he flicked through the notebooks and realised that the only interesting find he had made in this case so far was the newspaper cutting about Daniel Berkåk's father.

Reading the article, Jomar was reminded of Hjørdis, who was still sticking it out in Oslo. A little more than two years ago she had written to him and said she never wanted to see him again. He hadn't been entirely sure she was serious, however, he had crossed the border to Sweden without her. Without visiting her first or saying goodbye. He still imagined he could feel her presence whenever she thought about him. Presumably it was the same for her, but what was she thinking? The memory of her despair still hurt him. What pained him most, however, was that he hadn't defied her warning and met her face to face before he set off.

Jomar looked out at the men on the sports ground. He had a sense it had been a waste of time travelling to the refugee camp, and he would have to focus on other elements of the case if he was going to make any progress. Daniel Berkåk had been shot on the Norwegian side of the border. Jomar couldn't understand that Torgersen didn't realise what seemed so obvious now: the solution to this mystery lay in Norway.

9

The rhythmic clickety-clack of the train was soporific. Kai slept in his seat. Whenever he opened his eyes, he looked out on forests of spruce, stretches of deciduous foliage and white birches. Tranquil water glistened behind the trees. A meadow became a field of potatoes and a darker green. Evening was approaching, and Kai was thinking that what he saw could have been Norway, except that there were no soldiers or police boarding the train and demanding to see their travel permits. This was also something new: sitting on a train without feeling anxiety.

Soon the train was pulling into Stockholm. There were no blackouts on the windows here. The station lighting shone through the glass. No soldiers in sight, and when the train finally stopped in Stockholm Central Station, he threw his kit bag over his shoulder and walked past the crowd of Norwegians congregating on the platform.

Kai was at ease in his own company, and now he wanted to wander around to explore what peace meant. So, he left the station and went wherever the mood took him. He paused by a restaurant window and looked inside at the guests. Muted tones from a band were just audible through the pane. The music became louder, and voices and laughter burst through the door as it opened. Two women spilled out. One almost collided with Kai, but she leapt to the side with a giggle and staggered on, arm in arm with her friend, both scuffing high heels along the pavement. Kai avidly inhaled the perfume they left hanging in the air, thinking this isn't real, was he daydreaming?

When they were gone from view, he saw three passengers he recognised from the train. Refugees shuffling along the pavement. Grey, shapeless figures with sunken cheeks. Norwegians – poor people who stank of sweat, dirt and inadequate nutrition. He was still one of them. Irresolute, he watched them before setting off himself. Together, they found their way to Sturegatan 60 and Jernberg's boarding house.

Here, he queued and filled in the forms he was given by the man behind the counter. When the man told him his bed was number six in the dormitory, Kai asked what a single room would cost.

The man eyed him warily. Peered at the board behind him. Yes, in fact, there was a single room free. Kai nodded and took out the banknotes he had kept at the ready in his pocket. For a week's advance he was given a key. Then he walked up the dark stairs and into a corridor where a mumble of voices from behind closed doors could be heard.

After locking himself in, he threw his kit bag on the bed and walked over to the window. To the left, treetops towered over a small park. Then, out of the corner of his eye, he spotted something. In the street opposite, on the corner beside the park, a stooped man was staring up at his window. He resembled the interrogator from Kjesäter, Jomar Kraby. Their eyes met. The man raised a hand, doffed his hat and inclined his head.

Kai walked away from the window and sat on the bed. Was that even possible? Could that be the interrogator standing there? Was he being followed? He stood up and went to the window again, but the old bag of bones was nowhere to be seen. Had he imagined him? Were his nerves playing a trick? What Kai had enjoyed least during his sojourn in Kjesäter had been the interrogation. Finding out how small the world can be. As though the scrawny man grilling him knew. As though Kraby were playing with him.

This wasn't how Kai had wished to be received in Sweden, with probing questions from dubious authorities, and certainly not from someone who had known his father. Someone who knew about Atle.

Was it chance that Kraby was down in the street? Probably not. Kraby worked for the authorities. Presumably he knew who left Kjesäter and when.

Kai lay down on the bed and stared at the ceiling. How much could this man possibly know? He had talked about a man being killed in the border area and had asked awkward questions, but had then been stopped when the interview had begun to become unpleasant. Or had he been?

Kai realised that he would have to concentrate on other matters. So, he started to count the wooden panels in the ceiling to calm himself down. The interrogator is not here. He is not asking any more questions. Be present, here, now, in the moment. Stay calm. Tomorrow is another day.

10

On his way up the stairs to the third floor of the tenement block that was Grev Turegatan 45, Jomar Kraby could already hear the soft tones of a piano. When the door opened, he stood for a few seconds listening. 'Claude?' he asked.

Torgersen nodded and stepped aside. Without a jacket he seemed smaller than usual. His embonpoint was more obvious and the taut braces either side of his stomach emphasised his age. Torgersen strode ahead, pointed to the table, on which sat a backgammon board, and continued to the kitchen for glasses and a bottle of cognac.

Jomar was still holding his present behind his back.

When the glasses were on the table and the record on the gramophone had stopped rotating, Jomar decided it was the right moment. He held it out.

Torgersen stood holding the bottle. 'What's that?'

'A present.'

The cognac gurgled into a glass. Torgersen stared sceptically at Jomar's still-outstretched hand and the flat package it was holding.

'It's for you. Marius-François Gaillard playing "Claire de Lune".'

Torgersen was dumbstruck.

'Ragnar,' Jomar said. 'Let's listen to it. Put it on.'

Torgersen went to the gramophone and lifted the record on the turntable with the care and precision of a music lover. Slipped it into its sleeve and laid it down before taking the present. He unwrapped it, and through his pince-nez studied the cover before sliding out the black disc and balancing it on his spread fingers. Read the label. Lowered the disc onto the turntable and gingerly raised the pick-up arm. And sat down. Neither of them said a word while the piano notes filled the room.

At such moments Jomar could appreciate Torgersen's passion. This was music that did not search for a theme or a reiteration of it, but merely declared its presence and continued its reasoning, first sequentially, then in intricate harmonies, almost as if it was being playful, seemingly unruly, but nonetheless following a strict logic. Like floating phosphorescence, he reflected, or swallows' acrobatics against a steepling sky.

Jomar sat with his palms pressed together as the magic slowly dissipated and everyday life reasserted itself in the flat.

'Backgammon?' Torgersen asked.

'I spoke to Svinningen.'

Torgersen shook his head in resignation.

'He got a shock when he read the document.'

Torgersen was still silent.

'I don't want to be used in any disagreements you might have with the head of the Legal Office. If you have any.'

'It annoys me that he interferes in my domain. It's nothing personal, but he's a manipulator. That's where it ends for me. Any conflicts exist solely in his own mind. You were sent a letter signed by two government ministers. Fair enough, I nominated you for the job, but, that apart, I'm a middle man. Svinningen will have to go to London to fight his case.'

Jomar took out the cutting from *Håndslag*. Placed it on the table and pushed it over to Torgersen, who read it.

'Sverre Berkåk was Daniel's father,' Jomar said. 'Sverre was first arrested by German soldiers and later the same evening executed by a firing squad. He belonged to a group of Resistance fighters that had been infiltrated and betrayed. The informer responsible was then expedited by the Home Front. It's rumoured that the Stapo wanted to interrogate Daniel Berkåk about this matter.'

Torgersen leaned back in his chair, nursing his glass.

'This tells me one thing,' Kraby continued. 'If the solution isn't to be found in Norway, then there is at least some important information about this case there – in Norway.'

Torgersen twirled his glass of cognac. Pensively, he stared at the contents. 'And you buy me a present?'

'I have to cross the border. Can you arrange that for me?'

Torgersen sipped his cognac, swallowed and put down the glass. 'I seem to remember I asked you to investigate leaks here in Stockholm. I doubt you'll find them if you leave Sweden.'

'Why don't you want me to cross the border?'

'Out of concern for you, Jomar. The people sent to Norway have to be fighting fit with a military background. And not without good reason.'

'You also appreciate that there is information relevant to this case that can only be found in Norway. You said so yourself when we were discussing this. Any leaks here most probably go straight to the German authorities over there, but the likelihood is that it wasn't a German soldier who killed Daniel. This mystery alone is justification enough for me to cross the border.'

'Nothing's impossible, but you risk being arrested. If you're caught entering the country you'll be treated as a courier and a spy. And shot.'

Jomar didn't answer.

'You'll be interrogated and tortured before you're executed.'

Again, he didn't answer.

'Transport across the border doesn't constitute part of the deal we made.'

'I accepted the job and I'll keep my promise. As far as I can judge, Daniel Berkåk doesn't seem to have had any enemies in Stockholm, but in Norway there was a price on his head.'

Torgersen didn't respond to that.

Jomar tapped his middle finger on the press cutting. 'This can't be chance. Daniel was said to have been devastated by the death of his father. Now he's been killed too. Something tells me there's a link. We'll never crack this unless we know more about the past.'

They stared at each other until Torgersen released a long sigh.

'You'll need ID papers, won't you?'

Kraby nodded. 'A new passport. A new name. And a legitimate reason for travelling to Norway.'

Torgersen rose to his feet and walked over to the gramophone. 'I'm too old to carouse with you, Jomar, but how will two men pass the time in any other way? The only other suggestion I have is a game of backgammon. If you win, I won't deny you any request you make.' With infinite care, he raised the stylus and played the record again.

11

When Kai first woke up, it was because of the racket the dustmen were making, emptying bins down in the street. He lay listening to them but fell asleep again. He had all the time in the world. In Kjesäter they had been keen to keep people on their toes. Wakey, wakey, rise and shine, tidy the barracks, make your bed, exercise drills before breakfast. One duty after another. Now he had nothing to do, and no one expected anything from

him. Kai had experience of being a poor role model for others
and slept until late.

Eventually, when he did get up, he went out to get to know
Stockholm. In many ways the city was reminiscent of Paris, with
wide open spaces dominated by massive buildings, but there
were also districts, such as in the Old Town, where timbered
houses straddled cobbled streets and alleyways. There was a liberating sense of a world without war in Stockholm, apart from
the long queues outside butcher shops and cars rear-mounted
with a wood-gas generator.

Kai went into a café and ordered a herring smörgås and a cup
of ersatz coffee, which tasted pretty good. He sat on his chair
and observed the Swedes' carefree lifestyle, bustling in with
shopping bags, hugging each other and bursting into laughter
at the drop of a hat.

Kai was aware that even though the town was large and unfamiliar to him, he was sure to know some people here. There
were thousands of Norwegians in Stockholm, and now he
recalled some of the names from the list Sara Krefting had
slipped into his hand before he left her villa. He suspected that
one of the women at the Refugee Office had attended the same
school as him.

Should he go there? How do you combine making your
presence known with the desire to make yourself scarce? What
if Gunvor *was* the girl he'd known when he was a boy? Would
she remember him? No, he told himself the very next moment.
He couldn't disappear though. Not yet. His name was on the
register. They had it, his papers too. So he had to be patient. To
bide his time. No matter what, he had to orientate himself, get
an overview of the situation. Sooner or later, he would have to
go to the Refugee Office, put on a good front and demand his
five kroner a day in pocket money – however little he needed it.

Still he was unable to get the Kjesäter interrogator out of his
mind. If it had been Jomar Kraby outside his boarding house,
Kai wanted to know why. There had to be a reason. Kraby was

one of the principal figures in the Refugee Office. If Kai was going to find out how he was viewed by the authorities he really would have to go there. The sooner, the better, he thought. So he drank up and left the café with the firm intention of finding the office before he could change his mind.

◈

The building was one of many in the gently sloping street. A man stood outside the door. He was his age, perhaps a couple of years older, an athletically built guy with an authoritative presence. Kai's trained eye noticed that he was armed. The bulge by his armpit was unmistakeable. The Refugee Office had an armed guard posted at the front.

Kai crossed the street, nodded to the guard, told him his name and said he was supposed to report to the office.

They shook hands, and the guard introduced himself, in a Trondheim accent, as Borgar Stridsberg. He looked at his watch and said that it was rare for anyone to be working on a Saturday. 'I think Gunvor's here though.'

Stridsberg instructed Kai to wait there and went inside. The door slammed behind him.

Gunvor, Kai thought, with butterflies in his stomach. It was too late to pull out now. He would have to go through with this. Anyway, what harm could it do if they were acquainted? There were lots of Norwegians in Stockholm. He had to expect to meet people he knew here.

Kai turned. On the opposite side of the street stood a man of his age leaning against the wall, staring in his direction. Could he be a guard too? No, this one had a more nonchalant appearance.

The door opened again. Stridsberg filled the doorway. 'Up the stairs,' he said, with a toss of the head.

Kai went inside and climbed the stairs. Gunvor was waiting on the landing.

'Kai, is it really you?'

She was unchanged, even though her childish features had matured into a woman's attractive face. They had never been close friends, but he remembered her open expression and the kindness in her blue eyes.

'It's been a long time.'

'Ten years? Twelve?' Kai recognised the furrow she got above her nose when she was thinking. 'Was it the summer before I started at upper secondary?'

'Probably,' he said.

They stood gazing at each other, both with smiles playing on their lips.

'And here we are?' Gunvor pushed open the door to an ante-chamber and led the way in.

'A lot of water's flowed under the bridge since we left Hersleb School, Gunvor.'

'That's one way of putting it,' she said, making for her desk. She shuffled a few papers together and put them in a drawer.

The wall behind her desk was covered with index-card cabinets. At the back was a door that presumably led to another office.

Gunvor straightened up and turned to him. Kai searched for something to say, something about the old days. But she was first to speak.

'There's no one here today. And actually I was just off. Could you come back on Monday, do you think? Do you need food vouchers for the weekend?'

Kai shook his head. 'I have some money, but I was asked to report to the office. Then I heard you worked here. I thought, Gunvor knows me, she'll believe me.'

'Believe you?'

'Me and Atle. You remember Atle, my brother, don't you?'

She didn't answer; she went to the coat stand where a jacket was hanging from a hook.

'He was a few years older than us,' Kai hastened to add.

She put on her jacket.

A hint that I have to be brief, Kai thought – almost a rejection, a subtle indication that my presence is a little inconvenient.

He didn't want her rushing off. So he stepped across the room to signal that he wasn't going at once. Took up a position by the window. Told her about the interrogation in Kjesäter. Told her he had been at sea when the Nazis invaded Norway.

'Before that I was in Spain and I hadn't spoken to Atle for several years. Now I've come to Sweden and I find I'm being lumped together with my brother, who was a Nazi. I'd like to know what they suspect me of.'

He looked out as he was speaking. Down on the pavement he spotted the gaunt interrogator. The old man was like him. One-hundred percent Norwegian and one hundred percent unsure about his home country's authority in Sweden.

'I doubt anyone suspects you of anything,' Gunvor said. 'But there are *agents provocateurs* everywhere. Stockholm's a magnet for them. It's not only people who are under fire at home who come here. Fortune hunters drift in too. And spies. Nazis cross the border. The situation affects everyone's security. Part of our job here in the office is to maintain an overview, find out who's coming here and why. The Swedish authorities demand it, and so does our government in London. I'm sure you told them why you're here, didn't you?'

For a few seconds Kai wondered how honest to be. 'I want to go to England,' he said. 'I want to be a soldier. I want to make up for lost time, for my brother too. I simply cannot fathom why this should be so hard to understand.'

'Don't raise your voice, Kai. There are informers everywhere. This is Stockholm. The Germans have lots of people working here. Keeping an eye on our offices – Germans and Swedes and maybe many other nationalities. Don't talk aloud about your plans.'

Some devilry in Kai urged him to ask: 'Do you know a Norwegian called Daniel? Daniel Berkåk?'

Gunvor raised her head and seemed suddenly so taken aback that he thought he had gone too far.

'Why do you ask?'

He looked out again, to hide his face while searching for an answer. The man leaning against the wall had disappeared. 'Just someone I met once. A couple of years ago. I heard he was in Sweden.'

'Daniel Berkåk's dead.'

Kai realised he couldn't look away now. He steeled himself and met her gaze. 'Dead?'

'Shot,' she said. 'Murdered.'

Kai could feel his hands trembling, and he cursed himself for not having kept his mouth shut. 'Dead?' he said again, clearing his throat. 'When did that happen?'

'Not so long ago. At the border.' Gunvor glanced at the door. Tilted her head.

Kai could hear it too. Some people talking. Raising their voices. There was an argument going on, outside, in the street. Kai made for the door to find out what was happening.

Gunvor grabbed his arm.

They exchanged glances – the racket was now on the stairs outside the ante-chamber door. More than one person was running. One man yelled.

They were staring at each other when two shots rang out in quick succession. Kai felt a stinging pain in his ear and dragged Gunvor down with him as he fell.

'Make yourself as small as possible,' he whispered, taking a splinter from his cheek. They locked their eyes on the closed door where one of the shots had torn open the wood.

Another shot rang out, and there was a heavy thump on the floor above.

Then silence.

All he could hear was Gunvor gasping for breath. She was lying flat on her stomach, her eyes wide open.

Kai pressed his palms on the floor; the sight of the splintered wood in the architrave around the door told its own story. It had been millimetres away.

Gunvor's hands found his arm.

Kai whispered: 'You alright?'

'Think so,' she whispered back, raising her head. 'You've got some blood on your cheek.'

He showed her the splinter of wood and thought about the thump they had heard above them. Someone had been shot. Perhaps the guard.

The ceiling creaked. Footsteps could be heard clearly. Someone was walking around up there, and whoever it was had a weapon.

Kai freed his arm from Gunvor's grip, rose to his knees and scanned the room for a means of escape. The door was out of the question. The only way out was the window, but it was several metres down. He would be OK if he jumped, but what about Gunvor? He couldn't leave her here.

Everything was quiet, outside and above them.

Kai stood up, his gaze fixed on the door handle. He grabbed it. And heard Gunvor whisper: 'Kai, no.'

Nevertheless, he pressed it down. Leaned his weight on it and opened the door a fraction without making any noise. Peered through the crack. There didn't seem to be anyone around. He opened the door a little more and could see the stairs to the next floor. There was no one outside. Only an oppressive silence.

Perhaps he was being stupid, but he wanted to know what had happened.

He was about to open the door wider when Gunvor came up behind him and shouted: 'Borgar?'

Kai clenched his teeth. Now whoever was upstairs knew where they were.

'Borgar Stridsberg, are you there?' Gunvor shouted again.

'I'm here.'

The voice came from upstairs. A door slammed and footsteps resounded.

It was the guard, and he had a gun in his hand.

Stridsberg stopped in front of them. Pale and shaken, he returned the gun to his shoulder holster and straightened his jacket. Looking up at the attic, he said in a low voice: 'A man forced his way into the building against my orders. When I chased him, he pulled a gun on me and fired.'

Before he could say another word, Gunvor had dashed up the stairs. Kai and the guard followed close on her heels. In the attic, she knelt down beside a figure on the floor. It was the man who had been leaning against the wall outside. He was lying on his back with a revolver in his hand. His face was white. His mouth was open, and his hair flopped over his forehead. Gunvor felt his wrist for a pulse. She let go of his hand and felt the man's neck. 'He's dead.'

The words made Kai go weak at the knees. It didn't seem to matter what he did, he ended up at the centre of disaster. From his crouching position, he tried to catch Gunvor's eye, then the guard's. And failed. They were both focused on the body on the floor.

'Who is he?' Gunvor said, to no response. 'He must've been drinking. He smells of spirits.'

'If he hadn't been so drunk, he'd still be alive,' Stridsberg said.

Gunvor stood up, clearly distressed. 'What happened?'

'He wanted to come into the building, but I told him the office was closed. Then he replied "You're not telling me what to do" and barged right past me. I recognised him and said so: "You're Vardenær. Leave this building at once." He ran up the stairs and drew a weapon. I ran after him and told him to stop. Then he turned and fired and kept running. He was standing here taking aim when I set off after him.'

'Vardenær?' Gunvor said. 'So you know him?'

Stridsberg shrugged. 'What I do know is that he's caused a lot of trouble.'

'A Nazi?'

Stridsberg nodded.

Kai listened to the conversation, unable to free himself from a sense of doom. He was still struggling to control his breathing.

Stridsberg turned to him. 'And you,' he said. 'What are we going to do with you, now?'

Kai and the guard eyed each other for a few long seconds, but Kai had no answer. Instead, he wrested the revolver from the dead man's hand.

'A Webley,' he said, smelling the muzzle. It had been fired, that much was clear. Kai placed it on the floor.

'We'll have to consult Torgersen.' Gunvor was agitated. 'He's at home. I'll run over and ask him what to do.'

Stridsberg grabbed her arm and held it. His voice hissed as he spoke: 'Where's your brain? Getting Torgersen involved? This office is part of the Norwegian Legation. People can't get shot here. We can't have corpses lying around. It has to be disposed of.'

Gunvor chewed her nails, frightened and unhappy. 'We *have* to talk to Torgersen. He's in charge here and he'll know what the best course of action is.'

Kai cleared his throat.

The other two looked at him.

'Gunvor, you told me that German and Swedish agents keep an eye on this office. Maybe the police saw the incident. Perhaps they heard the shots.'

His words had an effect. For a moment the two were unsure of themselves, their minds clearly racing furiously.

'No one's reacted so far,' Stridsberg said firmly. 'Grab his arms.'

Kai felt drained, and cold, but did as he was told. Took off his coat and dropped it. Together, they managed to turn the dead man over onto his stomach. There was a pool of blood on the floor.

Gunvor went down the stairs as if in a dream and returned with a bucket and a scrubbing brush. She knelt down, scrubbed the floor with the brush and rubbed at the unplaned wood with a cloth. The dim light from the bulb in the ceiling didn't make it easy to see whether the red stain had gone or not. Stridsberg said he knew where they kept a carpet in the cellar. He went to look. Kai held the door open for Gunvor, who staggered down the stairs to a broom closet with a sink, where she could change the water.

There were bloodstains on the stairs too. The sight of them made Kai retreat into the attic, where he stared at the dead man's revolver. Now he was alone. Unseen. He seemed to wake from his stupor, squatted down, took the gun, made it safe, wrapped it in his coat and left it on the floor.

From below he heard Borgar calling.

Kai ran downstairs, two steps at a time. Met Gunvor on the way up. Told her about the stains on the top stairs. Grabbed one end of the carpet with Borgar and carried it up. Back in the attic, it was a struggle to wrap the body. The carpet was stiff and unwieldy, the body heavy and awkward, but finally the carpet was completely rolled up, many kilos heavier and larger than it had been. They each took an end and manoeuvred it down the stairs. Stridsberg at the front, walking backward. Kai leaning back so as not to be pitched forward. They took one step at a time, not speaking, gauging their progress in each other's eyes. The weight was so great that both his hands and his arms ached, but Kai didn't want to be the one who asked for a breather. The landings, where they had to turn, were the worst part.

At last, the guard kicked the door open. Outside, it was a normal summer's day. The fresh air on Kai's face made him feel he was waking from a nightmare. The street life and noises were real, not the horror movie in the attic.

They lowered their load to the pavement and stared at each other for a few seconds.

Stridsberg patted his pocket. 'Hang on a mo,' he said and ran off.

'Where are you going?'

'To get a truck.'

Kai ran back in and hurtled up the stairs.

Gunvor, who was on the landing outside the attic, gave a start when he snuck past her. 'What's the matter?'

'I left something up here.'

Inside the attic he grabbed his coat and put the revolver in a pocket. With the bundle tucked under his arm, he ran back down as fast as he had come up.

The sight of the rolled-up carpet brought him to a halt. Inside it was a dead man, shot – and *he* was carrying the discharged firearm. His gut instinct told him he shouldn't be hanging around; he should get away, go back to the boarding house and make sure he didn't show his face here again. He fought the impulse. This office was the sheet anchor for Norwegians in this country. If he was going to create a life for himself, of whatever kind, he couldn't run foul of regulations or fall out with other Norwegians. Not yet, at any rate. So he forced himself to stay put. And mulled over what Gunvor had said about people keeping an eye on the office. What if someone was in a window taking photographs now? What might that lead to – right now, or in the days to come? He kept his head down, without looking up, even when people stepped out into the street to pass him or a car drove past. When he did finally raise his head, he saw a man in a uniform coming up the hill on the other side of the street.

The policeman crossed over. And stopped in front of him.

'We're doing the place up,' Kai said, uneasily.

'You're Norwegian?'

'Yes.' Kai pointed. 'The secretariat. The Refugee Office.'

'I know,' the constable said. 'The Nazi bastards are not having it so easy now. The Russians are chasing them across the steppes.'

'We're moving a carpet,' Kai said in a strangulated voice. 'My pal will be here soon. With a truck.'

'I was staying with my uncle in Umeå when the Germans invaded Norway. It was bloody unbelievable.'

The door opened and both of them turned. Gunvor stood there holding a bucket. She stopped, paralysed, mute.

The policeman and Gunvor seemed to know each other. He nodded and she lifted the bucket in a kind of feeble greeting.

'I'm doing some cleaning,' she said.

At that moment a small dropside truck pulled into the kerb, and Stridsberg jumped out of the cab. He, too, knew the officer and waved to him.

'Is that you, Borgar?'

'Sure is,' said Borgar Stridsberg as Kai went to the cab, opened the door and put his coat on the seat.

Borgar motioned with his head. Kai closed the door. Borgar grabbed one end of the carpet. Kai hurried over and took the other. The police officer went over to help. When Gunvor did finally react, she rushed forward, tripped and fell headlong. The policeman turned and helped her to her feet.

From the corner of his eye, Kai saw Gunvor straightening up and brushing down her skirt. Borgar and he lifted the carpet while the other two were busy. He had forgotten how heavy it was. Stridsberg rested one end on his shoulder and loaded it onto the back of the truck. He clambered up after it.

Behind them, the policeman was asking Gunvor if she had hurt herself.

She mumbled something or other, and Kai pushed at the carpet. It buckled and Kai felt something on his hands. He looked down. Something red. Blood. Once again, the policeman asked if they needed any help.

'We're fine, thanks,' Kai said, panic-stricken, staring at Gunvor, who was holding her knee. She asked the policeman if he had a lot of work on. He answered as Borgar pulled and Kai shoved as hard as they could.

There. At last, the body was on the truck.

Borgar Stridsberg jumped down and secured the tailboard.

'Have you got a handkerchief?' Kai whispered to Stridsberg, who took one from his pocket without looking at him. Kai stood with his back to the policeman and wiped the blood from his hand.

Borgar said it was time they got going.

'OK,' the officer said, waving his truncheon. He and Gunvor watched them climb into the cab.

Kai whispered that he had blood all over his hand.

Borgar Stridsberg stared back at him, with a poker face. 'You can keep the handkerchief then.'

He smacked the truck into gear and they set off.

12

Silence reigned in the cab. Kai held on to Borgar's handkerchief, staring out at a lazy Saturday in Stockholm. Was the world really so grim? he wondered. Was there a curse hanging over him? He felt as though he was being chewed up and spat out. Was there an invisible force driving him into crisis after crisis? At the same time, he tried to compel himself to think differently. Life was hard, but he was still alive, after all.

It was Stridsberg who broke the silence: 'Why so quiet, Fredly?'

'Who was he?'

Stridsberg didn't answer.

'Has it occurred to you that he might have a family?'

'Everyone has a family. That's how we're born.'

The silence persisted for longer this time.

'What I do know is that he wanted to play the big, powerful man in the war,' Stridsberg said at length.

'Did you know him?'

'No. I only know that he was always up to no good. In Trondheim, among other places.' Stridsberg concentrated on the rear-view mirror. 'A friend of mine and his father had a radio in the cellar, where they listened to London. They received messages, which they passed on to the boys in the woods. Our man in the carpet raised hell in the block where the radio was. He spied on them and told the police. My pal managed to escape to safety. Here, in Sweden. He's in Scotland now, but they killed his father. The Germans wanted to know who he was working with, who he was passing messages to. They beat him to death in the mission hotel in Trondheim.'

'Why did he come to the Legation? What did he want?'

Stridsberg shrugged. 'The man was drunk. Extremely drunk. Said he wanted to report something.'

'What?'

'He said he'd seen someone. Then he asked what we'd pay for information. I said we don't pay for information. To which he replied that he'd talk to someone who had a bit more about him than I did. I stood in his way and said the office was closed, but he pushed me aside and ran up the stairs. When I followed him, he pulled a gun on me. Why would he force his way in? Why would he draw a weapon on me, a Norwegian guarding Norway abroad? Why shoot? Because he was drunk? I don't care what he wanted to report. And now we'll never find out.'

Stridsberg fell quiet. Kai fell quiet. There was nothing to say.

They were out of Stockholm now. Kai recognised the terrain from the previous day's train journey, but soon Stridsberg turned off the main road. The forest was getting denser. Houses were few and far between.

Again Stridsberg broke the silence. 'We forgot to take his gun. Hope Gunvor has the nous to hide it.'

Kai looked out of the side window.

Shortly afterwards Stridsberg drove into a gravelled area and parked.

Kai was glad to escape the oppressive atmosphere in the cab. Spruce trees towered around them. Stridsberg came out with a length of rope coiled around his shoulder. Kai's mind was still in disarray. He had no idea what the man had planned, nor what he was thinking. All he knew was that the man with the rope could shoot and kill him if he was so disposed.

Stridsberg let down the tailboard and jumped up onto the back of the truck. 'Grab your end.'

Kai obeyed and lifted the carpet.

At first they followed a path. The body became heavier and heavier. His hands ached. His arms ached too, but he didn't want to complain.

Then they left the path and zigzagged between the trees. They had to lower the roll of carpet to pass under low-lying branches. A crag loomed ahead of them. Now they had to drop the bundle, grab the top end and drag it over the rock. Kai was utterly exhausted.

'Have you been here before?' he asked. 'Where are we actually going?'

'Be patient and walk.'

Soon the distance between the trees increased and the ground became wetter. Further ahead the terrain widened out into a broad bog. At length they were able to lay the body between a flat rock and a pine tree. Kai shook himself and massaged his forearms as Stridsberg pointed to the eastern ridge and the lower hills on the opposite side and said that this bog land bore all the signs of being an overgrown mere.

Stridsberg unwound the coiled rope and passed one end to Kai. 'Strip off,' he said.

Kai didn't understand what he meant.

'We have to find a spot out there that's deep enough,' Stridsberg said, talking to him as if he were a child. 'It's going to be muddy. We don't have any spare clothing and I don't suppose you'll want to wear the dead man's clothes afterwards, will you. They're soaked in blood. You lead. Tie the rope around your waist for safety.'

'Why should I? It's your plan. You lead.'

'You lead because it's me who gives the orders here,' Stridsberg said. 'And because I'm still not sure how far you can be trusted.'

Kai loosened his belt. Without another word he undressed

and laid his clothes on the rock. The rope prickled against his skin as he tied it around his waist. The bog squelched as he moved into it, step by step. At first, it was springy beneath the soles of his feet, but it gradually began to give way, the further out he waded. Soon he was in it up to his knees, but the bog water rose, and the ground beneath was deeper and slippery. Suddenly there was no solid base and he was searching for firmer footing, which didn't exist – that was how it felt anyway, because he was sinking deeper, up to his waist, and as he began to flounder it was like struggling through cold porridge. The mud pressed against him, around his body, sucking him down, and in Kai's mind the bog was like an animal, he imagined he was being held in jaws that were trying to devour him, surrounded by a putrid stench bubbling to the surface, and he tried to grab hold of something, anything, in the swamp around the hole he was in, as the mud made it harder for him to move, and all the time he was sinking deeper, up to his chest, and even deeper.

'Borgar!' he yelled. 'Pull me out!'

Stridsberg was a long way away. Kai heard a voice calling, but he couldn't make out the words and all he could think was that he had walked into a trap. Stridsberg wanted to get rid of a dead body and now he was disposing of a witness at the same time.

Kai cursed himself and his stupidity as mortal fear numbed his brain. Through the haze he saw Stridsberg busy at work and realised that the man was tying the rope around a tree trunk. Kai focused on the rope. Infinitely slowly, it tightened as he sank deeper. Soon the rope was as taut as a tensioned cable and the slime was up to his chin.

Then, finally, he managed to raise both arms. And grip the rope. His hands were greasy and slipped.

'You pull too,' he yelled.

Stridsberg shouted back something unintelligible.

The jaws of the bog refused to let go. Kai thought about his parents. They had fought tooth and nail for a better world. They'd had two great hopes. One son had been killed. Now, their last hope was going to perish in a marsh in the country where he had sought refuge. What a defeat. Was there a devil sitting somewhere laughing at the pathetic lives all four of them had led?

Kai pulled for all he was worth, seething with fury, with an ire that he directed against himself, against fate and German soldiers; he raged against God, the world and its injustice. He saved his greatest wrath for the arsehole standing on dry land, nice and warm, and responsible for Kai's plight.

Kai roared and yanked at the rope. Then it happened. Gradually the mud began to release its grip. Kai was pulling so hard his arms screamed with pain, and slowly, to the squelching sounds of the morass, the bog allowed him to slither to freedom. The stench was foul, and he imagined he had been submerged in a mass of rotting matter, a profusion of decomposing animal carcasses. At last, both legs were out of the bog's jaws. He dragged himself along the surface before daring to stand upright. When he tried, he still couldn't feel the bottom, so he lay back down and tugged feverishly at the rope. Eventually he found firmer footing and stood up. He waded until his knees were free, then sat down and rolled in the water to rinse the filth from his body. He kept walking, reached a birch tree and staggered on, breathless, wet and cold.

Now Borger Stridsberg was as naked as he was. Kai's teeth were chattering and he said he needed to rest. Stridsberg said they couldn't stop now. Kai stood shivering as Stridsberg dragged the carpet across the bog towards the brown mud-hole. Soon the carpet was half-covered by the muddy water. Then Kai gave Stridsberg a hand. Together, with the rope to hold onto, they coaxed the dead body towards their goal. Two naked men under a naked sky.

Afterwards, still undressed and wet, they sat on a crag, waiting for the bundle to sink below the surface. Two small humans in a vast forest, sharing a gruesome secret. The silence was oppressive.

At length, Stridsberg began to talk – about himself and about his father, who travelled to the Soviet Union to work as a lumberjack when his mother died, and brought one Ivana back to Norway.

Kai realised that Stridsberg was tormented. The certain knowledge that they had killed a man made the silence hard to bear.

'Ivana didn't settle. She never learned the language, and the women in the street thought that her moving in and taking my mother's place in his bed had happened too fast. My father moved to Oslo with her to avoid the gossip, but that didn't go well. Ivana returned to the Soviet Union.'

'Is he still alive?'

'He died three years ago,' Borgar replied. 'There were rumours circulating about a battle, and my father was worried about me and my brother. He hitched a lift in a lorry going north and it drove straight into an ambush in Morskogen Forest. The Germans dragged him and the driver out of the lorry. They pummelled Dad with the butts of their rifles and chased him towards the Norwegian positions, shooting at him. He was hit in the neck and died.'

Kai thought he ought to say something. Perhaps talk about Atle, or his father's death, but he kept quiet. He couldn't bring himself to say anything. They remained silent. Then both gave a start when they heard a sound from the marsh. They stood up. The carpet had tilted and unravelled. The carpet was lost in the bog while the top part of the dead man stood like a sculpture, staring at them.

'Must be the rigor mortis,' Borgar said. 'He'll be gone soon.'

Kai couldn't help but stare, and had the impression the corpse was staring back. Gradually, eerily, the body sank – so slowly that Kai began to think it wasn't going to disappear. They would have to wade out again. They – or rather he – would have to stand on the skull and force the man down.

Even more minutes ticked by. Kai got ready to plough

through the bog again, but now only the head was visible. The process was speeding up, and it seemed to Kai that he could feel the cold water rising, up to his nose. That could have been him, Kai thought, but it wasn't.

Eventually the top of the man's head was covered. All of a sudden everything was as it had been before they arrived. A flat wetland, insects dancing in the air one late-summer afternoon. A human body had been swallowed up by nature, and nothing had happened. Had it not been for the gentle breeze caressing his skin, Kai would have thought it was a dream.

They walked back to the car and drove towards Stockholm in silence. Again it was Borgar Stridsberg who broke the silence as they approached the residential district of Vasastaden. He reached into his inside pocket, found some money and passed it to Kai, who refused to accept it.

Borgar waved it impatiently. 'We're bound by a secret now, Kai. It's something that'll always bind us.'

Kai didn't answer.

'Can I trust you to keep your mouth shut?' Stridsberg was still holding out his money.

Kai nodded.

'Swear you will.'

'I swear. What's happened here this evening will stay between you and me.'

'Don't tell Gunvor either. If she asks, keep mum.'

Kai nodded again.

'What is it with you? Don't you want any money?'

Kai shook his head and unfolded the coat. From a pocket he took the dead man's revolver.

'I'll keep this. This is the only payment I want.'

Borgar pulled in and brought the truck to a halt. He looked through the windscreen, his hands on the wheel. 'We've talked about the Webley before.'

Kai didn't answer.

'You didn't say anything about having it in your pocket.'

Kai didn't answer.

Borgar turned to him. 'How much is your word worth, Kai?'

Still Kai didn't answer.

They sat eyeing each other for some moments. Both with their fists clenched.

'Alright,' Borgar said at last and started up the truck. 'Don't forget that I know you have it.'

'I won't.'

Borgar asked where Kai lived. 'We'll go there first.'

13

Ragnar Torgersen's face had assumed the expression Gunvor never liked to see. So she sat at her desk looking at the type-writer, as if to summon some strength before she raised her head and used the only argument she had.

'I had to leave it to him. What else could I do?'

Torgersen didn't answer. Instead he continued to finger the damaged architrave, shook his head with a grim air, then inhaled, opened the door and went into the corridor. He called Borgar Stridsberg.

Torgersen stood in the doorway, waiting. Gunvor watched. Dreading what was going to happen. Stridsberg's footsteps sounded on the stairs.

They exchanged glances when he entered. The door closed behind Torgersen. Stridsberg turned to him and spoke before Torgersen had a chance to ask anything.

'I had no choice, and you don't want to know what we did with the roll of carpet.'

Torgersen took his pince-nez and began to clean it.

'This won't leak out,' Stridsberg added.

'Roll of carpet?' Torgersen queried. 'We're talking about a man, aren't we?'

'We're talking about an informer – Vardenær. The man forced

his way in, drew a gun on me and fired. What should I have done? Let him pick us off? First me, then Gunvor, and then the other guy. And what do you think he'd have done afterwards? Ransack the office for compromising paperwork and information about Norwegian patriots in Sweden. Paperwork he could run off with, straight to the Germans. That's why I'm bloomin' here, to protect the place and everyone inside.'

You've been practising that little speech, Gunvor thought, not without some admiration.

Torgersen was moved, that was clear. 'But disposing of the body as though he were unwanted carrion?'

'Should we have called the police? Should we have let them accuse us of murder, let them arrest us in the Norwegian Legation? Should we have unleashed a whole damn flood of gossip and political slander in Stockholm's papers? Given carte blanche to all those who wish us ill?'

'Thank you. That'll do. I want you to bring the body back here.'

'That cannot be done.'

'It must be. We need to have an orderly relationship with the Swedish police and authorities.'

'I'm telling you this can NOT be done.'

They sized up to each other. Two fighting cocks, Gunvor thought, and was about to say something, but didn't get that far.

'The other fellow,' Torgersen said, 'Who was he?'

'Kai Fredly. A Norwegian refugee.'

Torgersen threw up his hands in horror.

'He happened to be here at the time. And obviously got involved.'

'The office was closed. What was he doing here?'

'He came to meet me,' Gunvor was quick to say. 'We went to the same school. In Hersleb.'

Torgersen still had his gaze fixed on Stridsberg. 'Is he trustworthy?'

Stridsberg glanced over at Gunvor. And eventually, Torgersen did the same.

'My gut instinct tells me he is,' she said, slightly piqued that she was the one to decide the matter. 'Kai was in Spain, fighting for the Republic. Not that that means much, but it tells me his heart is in the right place. I was in the year above Kai. The summer before I started at upper secondary, he signed on with the merchant navy. He's a seaman.'

'Oh yes?' Torgersen said, pinching the pince-nez onto his nose. 'Don't stop there. Tell me more.'

Gunvor talked about Kai, his parents and his brother. 'I didn't know Atle. He was five or six years older than me. What I do know is that he became a Nazi. He's dead now. The Svartholmen business last winter.'

'Was that his brother?' Torgersen asked.

Gunvor could only nod.

'Atle Fredly,' Torgersen said, nervously stroking his chin. 'So that's his brother. Are you sure that Kai Fredly's a better man? And not an *agent provocateur*?'

Gunvor was unsure what to say.

Torgersen turned to Stridsberg. 'Could the two of them have been in cahoots? Vardenær and this fellow? Could Kai Fredly have come in first to check the lie of the land? To keep Gunvor talking?'

'Out of the question,' Stridsberg said. 'If they'd been working together, Kai Fredly would've made his getaway afterwards. He wouldn't have stayed to help us.'

Silence.

Torgersen cleaned his pince-nez again. 'What do you think, Gunvor?'

She took a deep breath. 'I think Borgar's right. Kai's as solid as oak.'

Torgersen was pensive.

Gunvor and Stridsberg exchanged looks.

'Vardenær,' Torgersen said. 'Will he be missed?'

'I think so,' Stridsberg said. 'He knew people here in Stockholm. They'll certainly miss him.'

'Family?'

'He had family here and in Norway. He was half Swedish. Lived for several years in Trondheim.'

'Could he pop up at any time?'

'He's dead, Torgersen.'

'I know he's dead,' Torgersen responded petulantly. 'Gunvor said you and the other fellow took the body away in a truck. What I want to know is if the body's in a closet or something similar that someone might open. Can the body fall out? We don't want a knock at the door, and there's a diplomat or a policeman standing there asking us what the hell has been going on here.'

'I understand,' Stridsberg said – calm on the surface.

'So, how likely is it that this might happen?'

'It won't.'

'And you want me to believe that?'

'We drove out of town to—'

Torgersen raised both hands. 'I don't want to know.'

Borgar said nothing.

Torgersen was now so angry his hands were trembling. 'You, Gunvor, and you, Stridsberg – you carried out a series of actions without conferring with me or a superior of any kind.' Gunvor eyed Borgar, and he gave her a nod. 'There's only one way we can get out of this situation. You two will have to face the consequences of your actions. In other words, you'll have to take complete responsibility for what you've done. Should your confidence prove to be misplaced, Borgar, should this body fall out of a cupboard, or whatever, you two are responsible, and neither I nor anyone else in the Legation can help you. Is that understood?'

Gunvor nodded. Borgar Stridsberg nodded.

Torgersen opened the door to his office and stood musing before he spoke again. 'Don't let him out of your sight, Borgar. Follow him.'

'Follow whom?'

'Kai Fredly. He's the weak link in all this.'

'I can see that, but what can we do?'

'Employ him,' Gunvor said, as quick as a flash.

The two men turned to her.

'Then we could keep an eye on him.'

'I can't employ everyone we're keeping an eye on.'

Borgar and Gunvor exchanged glances.

Torgersen reflected. 'Besides, we'd have to find him jobs to do.'

'I think he can drive,' Borgar said.

'You think?'

Borgar shrugged. 'I can ask.'

'This is moving too fast,' Torgersen said. 'I'll have to give this more thought.'

This was a sign that the conversation was over.

Gunvor cleared her throat, and Torgersen turned to her. 'Yes?'

'Svinningen was here, before you arrived.'

'Did he see the damage to the door?'

'I don't know. He didn't comment on it, anyway.'

'What did he want?'

'He gave me a lecture on how important it is that the Legal Office takes over responsibility for refugees from Norway and controls the flow. Afterwards he wanted the names of the border guides and a map of the courier routes.'

'Will he ever stop nagging us? When you go to fetch the post from the Legal Office, give Svinningen a map.'

'There is no map of the routes that are used.'

'Find a blank one and draw in a few routes.'

'I don't know any.'

'I know you don't, but I want an end to this. Make some up and give the man the map.'

With that, he slammed the door behind him.

The two of them looked at each other for a few seconds. Stridsberg gave her a double thumbs-ups, turned and left.

Gunvor went to the extensive shelving system and searched for a map of Norway. Then she used a fine felt pen to dot a few lines from Norway to Sweden. One from Halden, another from Ørje via Aremark, and she continued in this vein, drawing lines from Elverum, Østerdalen, Meråker and near the border posts in the north, such as from Mo i Rana and near Junkerdalen.

Afterwards she sat looking at the map, unsure whether Svinningen would buy it. Every day she dreaded going to the Legal Office. And pulling the wool over Svinningen's eyes didn't make this visit any easier, but she had no choice. Despondently, she folded the map, dropped it into a bag and set off.

14

When Gunvor opened the door to the Legal Office's antechamber, she found herself looking straight into the face of Lotte Bendiksen, a woman who had been born with the innate ability to fawn on those above her and trample all over those below her. Bendiksen signalled her status in the office with her appearance: pearl earrings, gold-rimmed spectacles and a neck as high as a ski jump.

Gunvor grabbed the pile of post for her office and placed it on the table. Directive after directive, and an envelope addressed to Ragnar Torgersen. It had been opened. She was so taken aback that she stood holding it in her hand.

Frøken Bendiksen must have been expecting this reaction because now she was peering over the edge of her gold rims.

'This envelope's been opened.'

Bendiksen craned her neck and nodded. 'It has indeed. A perfectly accurate observation, Gunvor.'

'How come?'

Bendiksen was once again concentrating on her typewriter and didn't look up. 'I don't know,' she said, winding a sheet of paper into the carriage, rotating the roller and adjusting her glasses.

Gunvor angled her head. The way frøken Bendiksen was deliberately ignoring her revealed that she knew very well why but was neatly sidestepping the question.

The envelope contained a passport and a number of train tickets. She took out the passport and opened it. Jomar Kraby had been issued with a new name and passport. Why would anyone in the Legal Office be interested in such a letter? Gunvor knew about the leaks and shared her boss's concern. The fact that this letter had been opened on its way to him was alarming, to put it mildly. She knew it wasn't her job to flag up this incident, but she couldn't contain herself. 'This is an official dispatch from the Passport Office to Ragnar Torgersen. It was sealed and someone has opened it. That should not happen.'

'Yet you stick your big nose in,' Bendiksen said. 'Put your proverbial own house in order, Gunvor. By the way, have you anything for us?'

'For Svinningen,' Gunvor said, taking the map from her net bag.

Frøken Bendiksen stood up, hurried over on long, slim legs and knocked on the door at the far end of the room.

Svinningen opened the door and came out. He looked at Gunvor, who was holding the map.

'From Ragnar Torgersen,' she said hastily. 'I said you'd been by the office. This is the map you requested.'

Svinningen came over to the desk, where he spread the map out and followed the black dotted lines with a nicotine-stained forefinger. 'Well, well,' he mumbled. Then he fell quiet, slowly straightened up and looked into Gunvor's eyes. 'There isn't a route via Kongsvinger and Austmarka.'

Gunvor stepped closer and studied the map. Svinningen was right. How could she have forgotten it?

'Daniel Berkåk told me that he crossed the border at Austmarka when he went to Norway. Shouldn't that route be on the map?'

'I know nothing about that,' she stammered. 'This is the map we have.'

Svinningen eyed Gunvor in a way that made her spine run cold.

'I'd assume,' she burbled, 'that both the Press Office and the Military Office have some routes they keep hush-hush.'

Svinningen seemed to accept her answer, because he shook his head in resignation, like a teacher confirming a child's bad behaviour in class once again. He folded the map.

Where she got her courage from, Gunvor had no idea, but she held up the opened envelope.

'Little Miss Pernickety here is apparently displeased with our internal mail service,' said Lotte Bendiksen, intervening before Gunvor had a chance to speak.

'Is she now?'

'A sealed letter to Torgersen has been opened,' Gunvor said.

'So?'

'I think my boss prefers to open his own post.'

'Has Miss Pernickety heard about censorship?'

Gunvor didn't answer.

'In this office we decide which letters are opened and which are not.'

'This is internal mail from the Press Office's Passport Section to Torgersen. If our people are issued with cover names and new papers, this is a security matter. Letters like this should not be opened by anyone but the addressee.'

Svinningen's glare sent a chill through her body, but the ice in his eyes soon melted.

'Miss Pernickety has a new name,' Svinningen said, winking at Lotte Bendiksen. 'Miss Impertinent suits her better. Take your post. If your boss has any objections, I'm sure he can contact me without your help.'

Gunvor swallowed the humiliation and leisurely dropped the directives into her bag.

'Tell Torgersen I want a list of names,' Svinningen said.

Gunvor turned back to him. Both he and Lotte Bendiksen were standing in the doorway, and he had a hand on her hip.

'Names?'

'Of the border guides. Sooner or later the Legal Office will be administering the traffic of refugees. So we need the names of the people who do it. Is that so strange?'

Gunvor said, as was the truth, that she didn't know any names.

Svinningen tilted his head inquisitorially.

'They all operate with aliases,' Gunvor hastened to add. 'I don't know who has which name. You have the map. If you want any more information, you'll have to see my boss, but he'll contact you anyway when he sees this letter.'

With that, she stuffed the opened envelope into her bag and made her exit.

15

Jomar Kraby fought a daily battle with himself. His arsenal consisted of a Parker fountain pen, an inkwell and a black notebook. He used to own a Remington typewriter, but he had been forced to leave it in Oslo. With his pen he still tried to exercise his creativity, though without much success. During the fourteen months of his exile he had written some epistles and finished a play the Swedish authorities had banned. There had been no official grounds given.

He didn't want to spell out his stagnation. If he did, it would become clearer and more frightening. Perhaps that was why he imagined he could hear his pen talk, and that it spoke to him if too much time elapsed between refills of life-giving ink. Now he had – as he lit his third cigar from the box on the windowsill – penned a defensive argument. A dialogue that was interrupted by the doorbell ringing. The sound freed his mind and sowed a kind of idea. It made him think about James M. Cain, who had used a British/Irish tradition as the title of his great, and impressively short, novel. A reference to infidelity and doorbells, which in its own way reflected parts of the novel's theme. So Jomar grabbed his pen and wrote down the idea. In this way the page in his notebook was no longer blank and his pen no longer had a justified reason for mocking him.

Again the bell rang.

Jomar left the pen on his notebook and the cigar in the groove on the edge of the ashtray before going to answer the door.

In the corridor was Ragnar Torgersen, carrying a bulging bag. Jomar stepped aside and held the door open, then hurried back to the sitting room and his cigar.

'Thank God,' he said, puffing on it. 'It's still alight. You're not bothered by this as a cigarette-smoker, but the pleasure of a good cigar isn't only a good cigar. If a cigar goes out, the taste is ruined when you re-light it. The taste will also change after the first flick of ash, just ask Hans Castorp. When he was at the sanatorium, he ordered cigars with the capacity to retain the ash after being lit. Did you know, by the way, that Sherlock Holmes wrote a monograph on cigar ash? He uses that knowledge in his investigations, in *The Hound of the Baskervilles* among others. Now, of course, out of politeness, I would've offered you a Robusto from my small collection, but you don't smoke that kind of thing, do you, so please excuse me. And I'm afraid I have only Swedish brandy.'

Torgersen didn't answer at once. He was looking at the sketch of Hjørdis hanging in a glass frame on the wall. 'Quite a woman,' he said at length.

Jomar nodded in agreement.

'I saw her in the play you wrote,' Torgersen said. 'She played a woman who was a bit gaga.'

'When?'

'Seven or eight years ago, maybe.'

'*The Glowworm.*'

'Exactly.'

'That lady was never gaga.'

'Well, you know her better than me,' Torgersen said, using both hands to lift the heavy bag onto the table, then went back to the hallway to hang up his coat.

Cigar firmly clamped in the corner of his mouth, Jomar went to the cupboard in the kitchenette to fetch two glasses, took the bottle from the floor beside his armchair and poured.

Torgersen was by the table. Bag in one hand, he took the glass with his other.

'*Skål.*'

They drank, and Torgersen winced before taking another sip, then asked if Jomar still wanted to go to Norway.

'Why would I change my mind?'

'London considers a trip of this kind to be beyond the original commission, so, to help you, they would be willing to do you a favour – which of course requires you to respond in kind.'

'Of course.'

Torgersen put down his glass. 'There's a rumour going round that Daniel Berkåk was killed by a former German soldier. A few months ago, a German deserter crossed the border with his Norwegian sweetheart and wanted to stay in Sweden. The chief of police sent the soldier back to Norway while the girl was offered residence. They both did a bunk. Now it transpires the couple have been hiding in the forest on both sides of the border. Local farmers have helped them with food and shelter. The police have been hunting for them for months, unsuccessfully.'

Jomar shook his head. 'Why would a German deserter kill a Norwegian courier and steal a pile of illegal newspapers and documents meant for the Home Front?'

'The rumour's doing the rounds anyway.' From the bag Torgersen took a tin of pineapples.

Jomar's eyebrows arched.

Torgersen placed the tin on the table and lifted out four more tins.

'Tinned food?'

'A mixture,' Torgersen said. 'The big question is: do you have a hacksaw?'

'I'm afraid not.'

'That's what I thought,' Torgersen said, and took a little hacksaw from the bag. 'Pan for boiling water?'

Jomar said he had one.

'Put it on to boil then,' Torgersen said. 'We have to steam off some labels.'

They worked in silence, Torgersen with a fierce expression on his face, Jomar assisting and refraining from asking questions. They held each tin in turn over the steam, and removed the label, which they carefully placed on the table top. Afterwards Torgersen held the tin over the sink and painstakingly sawed it in two. The juice leaked out. The tin was opened in the middle and the fruit put into a bowl that Jomar had taken from the kitchen cupboard.

When all the tins had been sawn in half and the parts rinsed and dried, Torgersen went back to his bag for the banknotes.

Jomar's eyes widened as Torgersen counted out the thousand-krone notes. There were many.

'It takes time to count money,' Torgersen said on reaching sixty-four.

'I've never viewed bankrolling as poetry before,' Jomar said. 'If I were handy with a brush, I'd paint your portrait.'

Torgersen rolled the first hundred thousand into a tight sausage. This roll was precisely the same size as the tin. Jomar pressed the two halves of the tin together around the money. Torgersen fetched more equipment from his bag: a soldering iron and a roll of tin. He plugged the soldering iron into the kitchen socket. With great care the two halves were soldered together. Then Torgersen went over the joint with a small file and smoothed it over. Afterwards the label was glued back on.

They repeated the process five times. Five hundred thousand kroner in five pineapple tins.

Standing over the table afterwards, they regarded their handiwork, and Kraby could no longer hold himself back. 'Where does the money come from?'

'Nortraship. The merchant fleet's earning as much money today as it ever has.'

Torgersen took an envelope from the coat hanging on the hook. He spilled the contents onto the table: a Norwegian passport, a number of train tickets and a wad of stamped papers. Torgersen told Jomar that his new name was Olaf Døvle and he had a majority shareholding in a company called AB Robsahm.

'You charter ships. You're the managing director of the Swedish office. Last year you arbitrated between the German and British authorities over the Kvarstad boats. You've been hired by Nortraship here in Stockholm. These papers entitle you to travel between Norway and Sweden.'

'I know nothing about shipping.'

'You don't need to. As MD of a charter company you just count the money. What you have to do is litter your language with seafaring terms, such as: "tonnage", "charter", "bareboat" or "shiver my timbers". The latter's a joke, but you're an artist, use your creative mind.'

'What about the tins?'

'We can't send you across the border without a genuine purpose. The Germans have arrested thousands of men. Their families need food and clothing … I can see now that the gravity of the situation's sinking in. If you want to drop this trip, now's the time to say.'

Jomar shook his head.

'You're responsible for this money now and the handover. Your official business today is shipping arbitration. That's why you commute between Oslo and Stockholm. Your company, AB Robsahm, has its Oslo office in Skippergata 9.' Torgersen picked up a bunch of keys and laboriously removed one. 'Take the tins there. You go every morning at eleven and stay there for a minimum of four hours. Do that until you're contacted.'

'And if I'm not?'

'You will be.'

'How do I know that the person who contacts me is not a traitor?'

'You'll be given a password.'

Jomar raised his glass. It was empty. He casually refilled their glasses. 'Have you got time for a hand of backgammon?'

Torgersen studied his watch. 'Another day. I have to go back.'

Jomar nodded.

'The money...' Torgersen started.

'Yes?'

'If anything happens, the banknotes are more important than you.'

Jomar mulled over this formulation. He didn't understand it.

'Jomar?'

'Yes.'

'Be careful.'

'Of course.'

They stood looking at each other.

'What is it?' Jomar said at length.

'I'm not sure if it means anything,' Torgersen said, 'but I'm not the only person to know about your trip and your new ID papers.'

'Not the only person...?'

'I don't think it means anything,' Torgersen said again, rolling his shoulders as if he were trying to shake something off. 'What could it signify that others have seen your passport?'

'Others have seen my passport? What do you mean?'

'The letter was opened before it got to me.'

Jomar angled his head, still not in the picture.

'In other words, more people than you and I know that you've been given a new identity. Soon you'll be on your way into the lion's den.'

'Do you think someone wants me arrested?'

'That's what I'm saying: What could it signify if someone has seen your passport? It's only me who's worried about you and the money. Take care of yourself, Jomar.'

'I'll be careful.' Jomar patted him reassuringly on the shoulder. 'And I'll guard the money.'

16

Kai sank slowly into the mud. The cold slime reached up to his chin. He pressed his mouth shut as his body sank deeper. Clamped it so hard that his canines crumbled, but he didn't feel any pain. Only the wet bog oozing upward to his nose and filling his nostrils. Then he held his breath until the pain in his chest was so great that he had to have air. He let out a gasp and opened both eyes. He was drenched in sweat, and recognised the walls and ceiling of his room in Jernberg's boarding house.

It wasn't night. It was late afternoon. Evening was approaching as he lay in bed thinking about the dead man, who perhaps had a sibling, one who would never see his brother's grave. And what about the man's mother and father? But this was war. There were so many surviving family members who had no grave to visit. This was how he tried to balance the accusations from his own conscience, by repeating to himself that it was no worse for the poor dead man than for the soldiers who were blown to smithereens in the trenches in Spain.

At last he got up, found himself some clean clothes and dressed, hunger gnawing at his insides. He wanted to get drunk, forget the brutal reality of the world and transport himself into dreamland with alcohol, with a woman.

For a few seconds he was back in Oslo. Thinking about Sara and the creaking door hinge when she slipped into his room at night. The little click when she locked the door behind her. He would have given his left arm to be back there, feeling her nails claw his back. He would have given an arm to be anywhere other than here, in this musty, grey, boarding-house room.

As he was going out, two Norwegian men were sitting, smoking on the stairs. They didn't make any attempt to move. Kai stepped over them and carried on down. To the street. It was late, but this was a city that was still alive at night.

Suddenly he saw his brother again. Saw Atle the way he would often see him in men with their backs to him. The trigger could be the profile, an arm movement, a certain gait. Then the man would cross the street, and his own particular identity would reassert itself. He would turn out to be a casual bystander. A man who would be lost in the crowd.

The same happened when his father had died. After the funeral Kai saw him everywhere – at tram stops, on the way into and out of shops – but in the end it was always a stranger, someone walking ahead of him, someone he had never seen before.

The street sign on the wall told him he was in Nybrogatan. A man went in through a front door. There was a guard posted outside the entrance. A Swedish policeman. A car was parked by the kerb. A car with a swastika on the door. Kai retreated. A stream of people came out. They were speaking German. This had to be a German office, and as Kai slowly walked down the street, he thought he saw the same person he had seen before. This time he decided to follow him. The man turned down an alleyway with Kai on his tail. They emerged into a larger, broader street. Kai felt that he was back in his dream. Dreaming that he saw a man and dreaming that he was walking through unfamiliar streets, but he had no idea where he was. The man stopped. Kai stopped. The man turned round. Stood still, staring at him. Kai told himself that he couldn't behave like this. He mustn't follow people.

At last the man turned round and walked on.

Kai let him go and discovered that he was standing outside a restaurant. The name was emblazoned on the windows. *Mona Lisa.*

When the door closed behind him, a different universe
opened up. No street sounds could be heard. A man dressed in
black was tickling the ivories at the back of the room. The piano
notes engulfed the place; it was like an enclave, secluded from
the world. People sat in muted conversation around tables
decorated with lit candles. As a waiter with a white apron tied
around his waist guided Kai to a table for two by the wall, none
of the customers showed any interest. The waiter lit the candle
and placed a menu on the table. Kai shook his head. In a
whisper he asked the waiter for a double whisky. The waiter took
the menu with him.

Kai looked around. An aura of affluence hung over the
clientele, gentlemen in dinner jackets and ladies in elegant
dresses. He was wearing his best suit, but it was dowdy in this
company. Despite being in the same room as the others, despite
the piano tones reaching him too, he was a stranger here, a
refugee. An invisible wall separated him from the other
customers, who were completely at their ease chatting with each
other and laughing. One man stretched out a hand to flick ash
from his cigarette into an ashtray, revealing a gold wristwatch.
A woman at the adjacent table was wearing a triple-strand pearl
necklace. This was the wealthy at their leisure. In an hour or
two they would return to beautifully furnished homes, discuss
the waiter's ability to fulfil his role as a humble servant, sneak
under down-filled duvets and round off a successful evening
with pleasures of the flesh.

Kai knew that whatever he did he would never be part of
what this class represented, but he could tolerate it for one
evening. Sitting here was beneficial to his body and soul,
isolated from others in a reality that wasn't his and never could
be.

The waiter returned and placed a tumbler of whisky on the
rocks in front of him. The candle and Kai's hands were reflected
in the glass containing the golden liquid and ice cubes.
Eventually he noticed that the waiter was still standing by the

table. Kai raised his head. In a low voice the man asked if he was going to order from the menu. Kai shook his head. The waiter grimaced and placed a bill on the table. They exchanged glances.

'I may order something else,' Kai said. The man didn't react; he wanted the money at once.

Kai noticed someone behind the cash desk, at the back of the room, watching them. So the head waiter wasn't taking any chances with him, and he wasn't going to give him any credit. Kai felt his hackles rise, but the pleasure of being able to retreat into this silence overcame any urge to complain. So he took out his wallet and placed a banknote on the table. The waiter left and returned swiftly with his change.

Kai raised his glass and knocked back the contents. He sat swirling the ice cubes and wanting more. Then a high-pitched, angry voice pierced the idyll. Kai turned to the commotion. The head waiter had seized a woman's arm and was pushing her towards the door. She was protesting and trying to maintain a modicum of dignity by leaving under her own steam, but the head waiter wasn't giving her that pleasure. He shoved her and she lost her shoe. '*Jävlar!*' she said in Swedish. You brute. She wriggled loose and retreated two steps to grab her shoe. She stumbled, but the head waiter was only interested in ejecting her. He grabbed her again, and the rest of her entreaties were drowned in the rattle of glass as the door slammed shut.

The head waiter returned with an erect back and a contented look on his face.

Kai stood up and walked out. The woman was stooped over the shoe she had lost. When she had finished putting it on, her hands were still trembling, her body shaking with indignation. She lit a cigarette. Her jacket was bespoke, with broad shoulders and a belted waist. Her skirt was knee-length. Both it and the jacket were of elegant tweed. Her left elbow squeezed a slim, black bag to her body. The brim of her hat formed a sharp line that told you where to look, only to be met by two dark eyes.

'What happened?'

She appraised him before answering. 'They don't allow women to sit alone at tables.'

'Couldn't he have just asked you to leave?'

'The head waiter's a *skitstövel*,' she said without any further explanation. A bastard. Then she threw away her cigarette and subjected him to closer scrutiny.

'So why are you alone?' he asked.

'I was waiting for someone.'

'Who?'

'That's none of your business. When you came in the door, I thought you were him.'

'I'd never have kept you waiting.'

'Aha. A real gentleman?'

She wasn't shaking any longer. The light from the streetlamp made the strands of hair by her ear glisten. Her earlobe seemed almost transparent in the glare.

Her eyes were deep and dark enough to drown in, Kai thought. She seemed to have run out of conversation, but no sooner was the thought articulated than she spoke again.

'Are you Norwegian? What are you doing in Mona Lisa? This is a restaurant for the affluent.'

'What do you know about me and my money?'

'So you're rich, are you? Could you lend me enough for a taxi ride?'

Now he didn't know what to say, suddenly afraid that she would be gone.

'Can you lend me some money for a taxi? Yes or no?'

She wasn't particularly tall. Auburn hair framed her face, which lit up like a jewel when she finally flashed a broad, white smile, as though the scene with the head waiter had never happened.

'I have to go,' he said. 'You can join me.'

Her heels scuffed on the tarmac as they walked side by side towards the line of parked taxis in the distance. He guided her to the one at the front. Gallantly, he held the door open for her. She liked that and raised both eyebrows in acknowledgement before placing herself on the seat and lifting her legs together and in. Kai closed the door, rounded the car and got in on the opposite side. He asked where she was going. She leaned forward and gave her address to the driver, who turned the key and started up.

A silence filled the car, the kind that can only arise between a man and a woman sitting side by side in the dark while a black-and-white film runs behind them. Kai looked out at the illuminated shop windows behind the hustle and bustle of soundless shadows as her silence grew more obtrusive. It made him think they were holding a taut cord between them. They were sharing a feeling of rejection. But, beyond this community, there quivered an attraction that had been noticeable since they first exchanged glances outside the restaurant. The taxi made a sharp turn, and she slid across the seat. Their knees touched. His skin burned. With every bend they slid closer. Soon they were sitting pressed against each other, and neither of them showed any sign of wanting to move. When the taxi stopped, Kai paid, and after the car had driven off, he ruminated on the fact that she had waited for him to pay and to open the door so that she could step out.

'Weren't you going home?' she said when he turned to her again.

'I've just met you, haven't I.'

'I'm not like that.'

'You're not like that? How do you mean?' The words that tumbled out his mouth were different from those he had wanted to utter. What he wanted was to be close to her, because she'd had to put up with contempt and disdain, as he had. Not only that, he wanted to erase from his retina the image of a dead body in the forest, and he'd got it into his head that she could expunge such images, not only because they seemed able to talk so freely to each other, but also because she was a warm-hearted person, a woman who smelt good, who had a captivating lilt to her voice and two bottomless eyes he felt he could immerse himself in.

'I just want to get to know you.' The words slipped out of his mouth, and he immediately regretted them, because it felt as if they revealed his loneliness and desperation.

'We can go for a walk. Around the block.'

So they walked, suddenly shy with each other. First she looked up at him, then once again. The third time she hooked her arm under his; his stride shortened, hers lengthened. They fell into a rhythm, one they could share.

It was a quiet evening, and when they rounded the corner the sound of their footsteps echoed against the walls. He broke the unbearable silence and asked:

'Have you got a boyfriend?'

'What kind of question is that?'

'What kind of answer is that?'

She looked down, with a smile on her lips.

He waited.

'No,' she said, and looked up. 'I don't have a boyfriend.'

'Have you got a job?'

'I'm a secretary.'

That was as much as she said about that. 'Have you been here long, in Sweden, I mean.'

'About two weeks.'

'Two weeks?' She laughed.

'I don't know anyone in Sweden. Will you be my friend?'

Now her eyes were sceptical as she glanced up. 'What do you mean by a friend?'

'Someone I can meet and chat with.'

Someone who was different from what he was ensnared in, someone who represented the state of mind they all craved: the insouciance of peace.

'Someone who lives without fear,' he added.

'I suppose you must know a lot of Norwegians? There are

thousands of them in Sweden, and Stockholm. I'm sure you have lots of friends, and you don't know what frightens me and what doesn't.'

That was true; he knew nothing about her and was lost for words. They walked on in silence, a quiet street where the tall houses made them feel small while the echo of their footsteps mocked and uplifted them at the same time.

Soon they were back in front of the entrance where the taxi had dropped them. They stood looking at each other.

'I have to go in now,' she said.

'Why?'

She smiled. 'Because it's late. I have to eat and sleep.'

'Eat? Let's go to a restaurant.'

'It's late. We have to go our separate ways.'

'I'm hungry too.'

Her white teeth flashed again. 'What's your name?'

'Kai. And yours?'

'Iris.'

He repeated the name, tasted it on his tongue and produced another smile. 'Just a little chat,' he added quickly, 'before we part.'

'A chat? About what?'

'About life, dreams, what you like and don't like, about why you were let down this evening. I hate the man who let you down. I want to be your solace, your friend.'

'I'm not the kind of woman who takes home strangers, Kai.'

'But I'm not a stranger. I'm already your best friend. I promise not to touch you. I just want to talk.'

Again she sent him an appraising look.

In the end, she took his hand, turned on her heel and led him. He followed her up the stairs. Her in front. The seamed stockings disappeared up under her tight skirt. Immediately his thoughts made him feel unclean, and he looked down at his shoes to escape his fantasies.

She lived on the second floor. There was no hallway – they

entered straight into what he assumed was the sitting room. She told him to wait and went through a door further inside. A fresh fragrance wafted over from a huge display of flowers on a small table by a sofa. A card had been attached to the foliage, and he imagined they must have been sent by the man who'd stood her up. He had to be wealthy to send such a bouquet.

To the left was an alcove that formed a kitchenette. He could see a gas stove, and behind a small dining table, a door. No plants on the windowsill. Just a line of toy soldiers on the narrow strip of wood. This wasn't any army. One soldier was holding aloft a flag with a dark-purple stripe at the bottom. He had been painted with such detail: creases in his uniform, lines on his face. Kai showed her the figurine when she returned on stockinged feet.

'The Spanish Republic?'

She took it from him and put it back. 'Alcoy,' she said. 'That's five years ago.'

'You worked at the hospital there?'

'I went with the Swedish Clarté League. Why? Did you go to Spain?'

The subdued light from the window softened her facial features.

'Did you go there?' she repeated. 'To Spain?'

'I went to Barcelona from France.'

The tension between them had been replaced by something else, something he couldn't quite put his finger on, but he interpreted it as solidarity, as though he had met kith and kin in a foreign land.

'We went from Paris,' he said. 'Crossed the Pyrenees on pack-horses. We had to climb at night, and I only had espadrilles on my feet. It's the worst mountain hike I've ever been on in my life. Then we arrived in Figueras. And from there we went by truck to Barcelona.'

What he could have said was that he was transporting weapons, and that one of the packhorses fell from a mountain ledge on the way, but he kept that to himself. What he wanted to say was that they had something in common: war experience.

Iris went back to the front door and flicked a switch on the wall. The ceiling lamp came on, and a bright, yellow light filled the little flat. Then she disappeared into the kitchenette and immediately returned holding two chicken drumsticks. They each ate, standing close and chewing, and the sight of her mouth hungrily gnawing at the meat and her tongue licking her lips was enough to make him feel faint.

He had to put his arm around her, he thought, he had to do it. Had to. He had to do it now.

Then the doorbell rang. The shrill sound pierced the atmosphere like a referee's whistle. They gave a start, both of them. And stared at each other.

'Who would visit at such a late hour?' he asked.

Something happened to her at that moment. Her eyes narrowed. 'I'm different nowadays. I'm no longer the foolish girl who wanted to save the world.'

The bell rang again. An impatient, angry insistence.

'You have to go,' she whispered. She really was a different person.

He didn't want to. He made a grab for her, but she stepped back.

'Move it,' she said, suddenly furious. 'Get out of here. Otherwise I'll scream as loud as I can, and you'll be arrested for assault.'

There was no misinterpreting her marching orders. So he made for the door as the bell rang again.

'Not that way, you chump. Down the rear stairs.' And she shoved him into the kitchenette. Pointing to the door at the end.

He opened it and emerged into a staircase. Then he turned back to say something, to arrange to meet again, to revive some of the good feeling they had when they were checking each other out, but Iris was already by the front door. He heard her open it, and when he heard how happy and relieved she was to see whoever it was, the enthusiasm she displayed, the forced, high-pitched laughter, the pain of it stung him.

He closed the door behind him. Walked down the stairs and discovered he was still holding the greasy drumstick.

In the yard he found a dustbin.

There was a car parked outside the door. Behind the wheel sat a chauffeur. The car had a symbol on the side. A swastika.

Kai stood in a gateway on the opposite side of the street. He stared up at the one window that was illuminated in the dark wall. There were two of them staring. Kai and the chauffeur in the German car. Both leaned back and stared until the light went out.

17

The thought of returning to Norway was like studying a quadratic equation: two solutions, two possibilities. Perhaps Jomar ought to go, but he ought to stay where he was too. The mission he had from the exiled government in London was in a way a legitimate reason, but once the thought of travelling to Oslo had been planted in his head, it was his heart that took over. What really galvanised him was the desire to see Hjørdis again.

Accordingly, he chose a rucksack that could hold much more than five tins of fruit, packed his clothes in a suitcase and the provisions in his rucksack. He thought about Hjørdis as he filled it with salami, ham, herring, tins of rissoles and chocolate. As for bottles, he chose her favourites: absinthe and advocaat. The rucksack was so heavy he almost toppled backward as he lifted it and strapped himself in.

Even though it was early in the morning, he self-administered several doses of anaesthetising alcohol to quell the jangling nerves in his abdominal region.

With the rucksack on his back and the suitcase in his right hand, he trudged off to Stockholm Central Station, unease raging through his body like a fever.

Unease turned to shock on entering the concourse. The railway station was swarming with the Wehrmacht. Jomar tried to force a way through them, but had to give up. There were so many uniformed young men that it was almost impossible to make any progress. Instead it was like being caught in a river – he was carried along by the current, his suitcase and rucksack wedged between German warriors. Jomar couldn't help but go with the flow, an endless stream of murderers all catching his train to Oslo. Where did they all come from? Had they all been in the Soviet Union, killing women and children? Had they fought side by side with the Finnish soldiers in Karelia? One moment Jomar was cursing the Swedish authorities for placing the railway at the disposal of Hitler's murderous regime. The next he was so frightened that he almost crapped his pants as he passed carriage after carriage full to the rafters with armed soldiers as he looked for his seat. He was smuggling half a million kroner into Norway accompanied by a horde of young men who would not hesitate to mow him down the second they received the order.

A single carriage was reserved for Norwegians able to show the correct documentation. After the conductor had checked his, he was finally allowed to manoeuvre his luggage in and discovered to his relief that he had the whole compartment to himself. That was always something, but once the train was in motion, not even here could he escape. The soldiers had room in their own carriages at the back of the train, but they yelled and sang and told each crude jokes, and when the train stopped their gales of laughter could be heard right up to where he was sitting. At regular intervals soldiers stomped through the train to find an unoccupied toilet. This was a visit he himself was studiously trying to avoid.

However, the body is merciless. When the pressure in his

bladder became intolerable, he took his courage in both hands, slid the compartment door to one side and staggered out. And, as expected, a couple of green-clad murderers were queueing outside the toilet, full of confidence and irrepressible youth, and owners of excessively loud voices.

Jomar was about to turn back to his compartment, but one of them called out to him. 'Old man, you can go first.'

'*Ich bin kein alter Mann*,' Jomar answered. I'm not an old man.

Both soldiers grinned.

'Swedish?' one said.

'Norwegian.'

'We're going to Norway too.'

The toilet door opened. The soldier coming out was doing up his flies. The two soldiers in the queue held the door open for Jomar, who shook his head. 'I'll wait my turn.'

The soldier nearest to the door went in.

The noise from the rails was deafening in the gangway between the carriages.

'What do you do when you're not on the train?' shouted the soldier waiting.

Jomar took the fountain pen from his top pocket and waved it. 'I write,' he shouted back.

'Ah, a Norwegian Goethe?'

Jomar shrugged.

'I write too,' the soldier shouted. 'I write poems, like Goethe.'

Despite his nervousness, Jomar managed to squeeze out a smile. All poets deserve to be met with an open mind.

The young soldier was a good-looking, dark-haired man with regular features in a face marred by a birthmark on his cheek. His eyes were swimming with drink, and now three more soldiers stomped through the corridor. Also in high spirits. Jomar was surrounded by the enemy while the clickety-clack of the rails and the wind outside made louder voices necessary.

'Goethe wrote about his travels, about visiting other countries, as we're doing now,' the soldier yelled.

'When Goethe travelled to Italy it was to learn,' Jomar shouted back. 'Goethe escaped from hospital and all he had with him was a pen and paper, not weapons. When he arrived in Italy he studied Palladio's architecture. Humble and full of admiration, he praised the houses that Palladio designed. What do you admire and praise in my homeland?'

'The women,' the soldier shouted. 'Norway's tall blondes.'

'Is that all? Weren't there enough women at home in Germany?'

A spark of irritation lit up the soldier's eyes. Then he reflected. 'The stave churches,' he shouted at length. 'Architecture and craftsmanship, *dei gratia*.' The others nodded. Two of them were holding bottles of spirits. One held his out. Jomar accepted. Gin.

'Viking ships,' the soldier shouted over the din. 'They're wonderful. We're Vikings too, but the Norwegian ones were worse than we are. They travelled the world, fighting, pillaging and killing. They raped the women they encountered. We don't need to do that, at least not in Norway.'

'As you're so enthusiastic about Vikings and women, have you heard about Kark the slave and Earl Håkon?' Jomar took a swig, passed the bottle back and continued: 'Håkon loved women so much that even though Olav Tryggvason, the Viking king, was after him, he determined to stay with Tora, his lover. Håkon had a chance to flee but preferred to remain in bed with her. Only when soldiers were outside in the yard did he show any sign of haste; he jumped into his trousers and fled. Håkon and Kark ran into the barn. There they hid in a pig pen. As they lay trembling with fear in the pig muck, Olav Tryggvason promised a reward to anyone who could tell him where Håkon was. When Kark heard what the king said, he stabbed Håkon and decapitated him. He clambered out of the pen and ran to the king with Håkon's head to collect his money. As soon as the king understood what had happened, he cut off the slave's head.'

'What's that supposed to mean?'

Jomar realised he had managed to offend the soldier who wrote poems like Goethe. He didn't understand why. It was true he had embroidered the story a little, but, after all, he was a dramatist.

Goethe grabbed the lapels of Jomar's jacket; he was strong. The green-uniformed soldier, eyes glassy and insensate, nostrils flaring angrily like a bull's, lifted Jomar off the floor. He could hardly breathe.

'Who's the king and who's the earl and who's the slave in your story?' Goethe snorted, spit flying everywhere.

Jomar pointed to his neck. Goethe let go and Jomar gulped in air. He was no longer afraid now, surprised only that it was possible to end up in such a predicament, to find himself threatened with physical violence by a German soldier as he travelled back to his homeland – before he had even left Sweden. This did not bode well for the rest of the journey.

'The moral,' Jomar said, clearing his throat, 'the moral is clear enough: If you occupy a country to conquer the women, one day a slave will cut off your head.'

The soldiers burst into laughter. There were many of them now, at least ten queueing up for the toilet. When the door opened, Jomar pushed ahead of Goethe. Once inside, he felt light-hearted enough to sing. In the soldiers' honour he sang about Lili Marlene and the lantern. He took aim at the rails through the hole, emptied his bladder and sang at the top of his lungs.

When he went out, he was mobbed. The soldiers patted him on the shoulders, shouted *skål* and offered him drinks from their bottles.

◈

Later, when he woke up from a doze and peered through the window, the train was standing still, in the border town of Charlottenberg. Loud singing from the soldiers filled the train, which was still stationary. Outside, the weather was in tune with his fears. Rain was hammering against the window.

Jomar wondered why the train wasn't continuing its journey. Finally, he heard doors slamming. The noise made him uneasy. The train was in the last station before Norway. Something had happened on board, but what?

Then the compartment door slid open with a bang. It gave Jomar such a shock that he thought his heart would stop.

A small, lean Mephistopheles stood in the doorway, silently observing him. Mephistopheles had his coat belt tightened and the brim of his cap pulled down over his eyes. All Jomar could see of his face was a thin moustache.

Behind him stood two uniformed men.

Mephistopheles asked for his papers.

'The ticket?'

'Papers, you idiot.'

Jomar produced his passport and travel permit.

Mephistopheles took both, opened the passport and looked from it to Jomar, glanced at the uniformed men, nodded and pulled the door to.

What had just happened? Jomar felt another layer of unease on top of the nausea he was already feeling. Why did Mephistopheles take his papers? What was he going to do with them?

He sat listening, without moving. Through the walls he heard the dull thud of doors being closed. Then the conductor blew his whistle, and the train jerked into motion. He looked out. Mephistopheles was standing on the platform looking up at him. In his hand he was holding Jomar's passport and papers. Then his carriage was past him and gone.

At that moment Jomar was back in his flat, looking at Torgersen as he told him that he was not the only person to know about his papers.

Stunned, he watched out of the window as the train accelerated and trees flashed past. The train was steaming across the border to Norway, and he couldn't get off. At once his mind pictured what was going to happen. He had crossed the border without papers. The border police were waiting. He would be arrested. They would at first handcuff him, then open the rucksack with the tins. They would find the money, and he would find himself promoted up their hate list. They would see him as a spy for the exiled government. He would be driven blindfold to Trandum and stood against a wall to be shot. He had failed.

What diabolical irony. As the train approached the border, Jomar tried to hold his nerve, to rehearse what he would say to the border police, but he stumbled every time and kept coming back to the same thought: someone must have known he was travelling to Norway under a false name. Whoever it was would have arranged an arrest in Norway. He had walked straight into the trap like an arteriosclerotic mouse.

Could Ragnar Torgersen have imagined that this would happen? No, he told himself. The time wasn't right for speculation; he had to think proactively. In a few minutes he would be dragged off the train and driven to a dark cellar, where he could expect to be kicked, punched, subjected to water torture, leg clamps, and finally blindfolded and led in front of a firing squad.

The train slowed down and signs flashed by. They had crossed the border. He was in Norway. The curtain had fallen. The second act of the great comedy was about to begin.

Jomar stood up. Reached down his rucksack from the luggage rack. Undid the buckles, opened the flap and looked inside. Tins of pineapples, Swedish salami, meatballs, wine, absinthe and a bottle of advocaat.

With his rucksack on his back and the advocaat in his hand, he slid the door back. He staggered on, through the corridor towards the sound of communal singing, opened first one door and then another. The singing was getting louder. Another door had to be pushed open. Then he had to walk through a freight car and pass a line of soldiers' baggage, green canvas rucksacks. He stopped, unhitched his own and jammed it between the others. Then he continued down the train into a carriage packed with German soldiers. Now they were singing at the top of their voices about the girl under the lantern. Jomar could join in with that one. Jomar raised the bottle of advocaat and bawled along '...*mit di-i-i-ir, Lili Marle-e-e-ene...*' as another voice cut through the chorus.

'*Hallo, Schriftsteller.*'

The seat beside Goethe was free. As the train came to a halt, Jomar fell onto the seat. He offered his advocaat round, to laughs and jeers. It didn't matter. He drank and sang along with the soldiers in a rendition of 'Wir fahren gegen Engeland'.

This was his chance. This was acting like a wolf – if not in sheep's clothing, then at least mixing with the flock. There was one thing he was sure of: Norwegian police would never come in here and make German soldiers show their ID. So he stayed where he was. He was offered more to drink and became drunker and drunker. He didn't even notice the train start.

When silence finally fell in the carriage, he was dozing in a stupor. A little later he opened his eyes. At last they had shut up, he thought, and raised his head. Right. Most of the soldiers were asleep. He straightened up and looked out. A white house and a red barn disappeared behind rocks. Behind them glittered Oslo Fjord. The train would soon be arriving and he was sitting on a seat with a German soldier's arm around his neck. Goethe had fallen asleep. Jomar gently removed his arm, stood up and made his way out. Found his rucksack and staggered on to his compartment.

He found his suitcase on the floor. It had been opened. His clothes had been thrown around. The border police had been here. So the nightmare wasn't over yet. The police were bound to have taken a description of the suitcase. Accordingly, Jomar opened his rucksack and squeezed in as many clothes as he could.

When he heard his fellow passengers gathering their luggage and queueing in the corridor, he looked out again. The train was going through Lodalen and approaching Oslo East station. Was this really possible? Could he have made it?

When, shortly afterwards, the train came to a halt, he waited for the stream of German soldiers to hurry past. Even though the platform seemed to be deserted and safe, the border police were probably waiting somewhere and keeping an eye open for the owner of the suitcase. Jomar got up, left the suitcase where it was, swung the rucksack onto his back, took a deep breath and stepped off the train.

He was one of very few civilian passengers. At the end of the platform stood the conductor, accompanied by two uniformed men. The man would recognise him. But now the die had been cast. Jomar was off the train and couldn't turn back. Jomar focused on the ground and kept walking. In the end, however, he had to look up. He and the conductor exchanged glances. The conductor looked past him without a flicker of recognition. Jomar's legs seemed to be walking of their own accord. The two policemen were on the lookout for someone. Jomar doffed his hat and bowed. Neither of them took any notice. They were waiting for the conductor to point out the suspect. Jomar walked past, his back burning, and he imagined that every single person in the station had their eyes on him. He waited for a shout behind him, an order to stop. But he heard nothing. He concentrated on walking without a backward glance. Soon the exit was only ten metres away. Five. Two. Outside.

He was in Oslo. It was getting dark, and he was still a free man. He immediately crossed the square outside and continued up Karl Johann, mentally thanking the conductor from the bottom of his heart.

It was only when he was crossing Dronningens gate that a reaction kicked in. His hands began to tremble, and he tottered towards a wall to support himself. The conductor had saved his life. Jomar tried to take measured breaths. Telling himself that he had made it. He had survived. Now he had a good story to tell his children or grandchildren – should they ever exist and should they ever come knocking on his door one day. But he had to commit to his role, carry on without attracting attention. So he forced himself to continue walking.

As he passed under the Freia clock and observed the flags on the royal palace fluttering in the wind there was still enough daylight to make out the swastikas. The sense that you were a spectator of your own experiences was reinforced when he read the banner at the front of the Norwegian Parliament, which asserted that Germany was winning on all fronts.

We know that is a lie, he thought, and the main reason we know is because they have to say they are.

All the shop windows were blacked out, but he was able to find his way to the Grand Hotel blindfold. A group of German officers were standing and chatting in front of the entrance to the café. Jomar raised his hat in a friendly manner, walked to the front desk and introduced himself as Olaf Døvle. The receptionist, a man in his forties, took out his ledger with feline grace and welcomed him to the hotel. Without glancing up from the book, the man told him his room was ready. With the same feline movements, the man turned, whisked a key from the board and passed it to Jomar with a wry smile and a knowing wink. Jomar refused the pageboy's offer of help and bowed once again to the German officers, who stepped aside so that he could make his way to the lift.

He went up to the second floor. The carpet in the corridor muffled the sound of his footsteps. The room was large, the ceiling was high, and on the floor was the biggest bed Jomar had ever seen. There was a blackout curtain draped over a tall window. Curious to see the view, he switched off the light and nudged the curtain to one side. He discovered that the window was in fact a glass door that opened onto a narrow balcony.

He stood, gazing around him. Not a single streetlamp, not a single shop window was lit. There wasn't a sign of any activity outside. In this country the occupiers obviously had to live with the same fears as its citizens. It was late, and Jomar had never felt as tired as he did now. He let go of the curtain and threw himself onto the bed.

18

It was quite a chilly morning, and a gusting wind tore at Jomar's clothes as he passed Engebret Café with his rucksack on his back, making his way down Revierstredet. The streets were bare. Only the outline of armed German soldiers could be seen by Oslo Fortress square and the entrance to Norges Bank. Skippergata 9 turned out to be an apartment block with a gateway and a crooked front door, whose hinges screamed when he pushed it open.

There was a smell of mould in the stairwell. Or perhaps it was the smell of an empty town house. Eventually, on the third and top floor he found a door with a sign. Robsahm A/S. He rummaged in his pocket for the key. It fitted. He turned it and opened the door.

It was a relief to take his rucksack off. The room was furnished with a desk and chair. Some ring binders were crammed into a shelf on the wall. He removed them one by one. They all turned out to be empty. He opened and closed the desk drawers. They were empty too.

On the desk there was a flowerpot. He touched the white flower protruding from the soil. It was made of silk, but an intricate design. He mused on this: why would anyone plant an artificial flower in real soil?

He became aware of the need to answer a call of nature, went out and down a floor, where he found the door to a toilet. The small room was pleasantly clean and there was a pile of news-papers beside the bowl. A chill wind rose from the chute when he sat down on the toilet seat. He flicked through the newspapers until he found a picture of Quisling. He tore this page out for use as bumf.

Afterwards, relieved in all ways, he walked back to the office and sat down to wait. He had a book in his rucksack. In case he had to explain himself to Nazis, he had chosen some Nazi literature. Minister of Police Jonas Lie's own book, *A Shark Follows the Boat*, written under the pseudonym of Max Mauser, apparently inspired by the journey Lie made when he accompanied Leo Trotsky from Norway to Mexico.

Jomar opened the minister's novel. He put his feet on the desk and read, but struggled to concentrate. He couldn't move beyond the thought that the writer had been alone with Trotsky for weeks and instead of using the time for his intellectual benefit, or composing a portrait of a historical person, he had dreamed up a story about a robbery and murder on a liner. This was the legacy from Trotsky's stay in Norway: a yarn written by a traitor.

Jomar lost interest in the novel. He yawned, put down the book, folded his arms across his chest and fell asleep.

❧

He woke with a start when the door slammed with a bang. A stranger stood in the room.

The person by the door resembled a bird.

For a few seconds Jomar thought he was still dreaming. It was only when the person adjusted her mask that Jomar realised she was real and what he had first mistaken for plumage was hair.

'Ah, a mask,' Jomar said, putting his feet on the floor. 'I suppose I should've hidden my face too.'

The Mask said it wasn't necessary. A woman's voice. Kraby sat up. The Mask's coat was a cape. A skirt hem protruded and beneath it two shapely legs.

'What do strawberries cost on the market?' he asked, looking at her chestnut hair.

'Fifty øre a punnet, but I can get them even cheaper.'

'How much?'

'Forty-two øre.'

'Hello and welcome.'

'I've been informed that you have something for us.'

Jomar dragged the rucksack over and took out the tins. The Mask took a net bag from inside her cape and dropped the five tins inside.

'Don't you want to check them?'

'That won't be necessary.'

The woman behind the mask was young and loose-limbed. Smooth, suntanned skin was visible between her ear and the edge of the bird's beak. Her speech was articulate and revealed West Oslo origins.

Jomar told her he was there on behalf of the exiled London government. On a mission concerning Daniel Berkåk. The courier who was shot in the back on the Norwegian side of the border with Sweden.

'We were warned you were.'

Jomar nodded, impressed. 'What can you tell me about him?'

'Daniel Berkåk came from Odalen. He grew up on a farm by Lake Storsjøen. The youngest of three. Two sisters. He was going to take over the farm, but he was also a skilled mechanic. He was working in a garage in Kløfta when he joined up to fight on the Finnish side in the Winter War. The same day that the Germans invaded us – the ninth of April – he was discharged. When he came home from Finland, he started up an illegal press, but someone grassed on him. He had to flee and managed to get away. As he was both a good patriot and knew the border district well, he was used as a courier.'

'His father was executed by the Germans, I heard.'

'His father was in a unit we had in Skarnes. It was blown apart when a railwayman in Kongsvinger infiltrated it. Atle Fredly, a discharged Eastern Front soldier. Our boys knew nothing about his background or his beliefs. One of them had made a deal with Fredly to supply arms. When they met for the handover, they walked straight into a German patrol and were arrested. Three of them were shot the same night. Sverre Berkåk was one of them. One died as a result of torture. Rumour has it, the last man was deported to Germany.'

Jomar said aloud what he was thinking: 'This must've had a huge impact on Daniel.'

'Of course. And not only because his father was killed. The death affected the whole family. He was worried about his mother and sisters. And the Germans had taken over their farm.'

'I've been told that Atle Fredly is dead now.'

'He is.'

'How did he die?'

'He went missing and was later fished out of the Glomma, near Svartholmen.'

'Drowned?'

'Shot.'

'What happened?'

The Mask didn't answer at once, she just shifted her feet and cleared her throat. 'All Norwegians who help the Germans will be punished when the war is over, but it's a bit different with people like Atle Fredly. He reported our resistance activities to the Germans. This caused a lot of damage. It led to Resistance men being arrested and killed. Anyone who does that has to be stopped. We can't wait until the war is over to settle scores with informers.'

'So he was killed by the Home Front?'

'Norway is at war – his death must be viewed in that context. We're fighting the occupying power. Those who spy on us, infiltrate our units and betray us – have to be stopped. That's the law of war. Nothing happens by chance. Atle Fredly's punishment was decreed and justified by a practising judge.'

'What's actually known about the sequence of events leading to his death?'

'Some say he was going to buy coffee on the black market

and disappeared. After a month he was found floating in the Glomma near Svartholmen, as I told you. The man who performed the execution had attached a couple of car batteries to his body, but they didn't keep him submerged for much more than a couple of weeks. The body floated up and snagged on something in the river. Then it was brought ashore.'

'If Atle Fredly was going to buy coffee on the black market,' Jomar said, 'someone must have made him an offer?'

'I'd assume so.'

'Who was that?'

'I don't know.'

'Can you find out?'

'Fredly got his just deserts. He's a forgotten man. He should stay that way. No decent Norwegian's interested in digging up that particular past.'

'But now Daniel Berkåk's been shot and killed. We don't know who by, but I believe there may be a connection with his father's execution by the Germans. And it may be something to do with Atle Fredly's treachery.'

The Mask didn't answer.

Jomar pondered before asking his next question: 'Why actually was Atle Fredly interested in infiltrating a Resistance unit?'

'Fredly became a member of the Nasjonal Samling as early as 1934 or 1935, and had been in the Hirden paramilitaries just as long. He volunteered to fight on the Eastern Front as soon as the Germans started their offensive. He served for a long time but was discharged after being injured. Back here he continued to work for the Germans. He was recruited as an agent for the Abwehr and reported directly to Fritz Preiss, the chief of their Intelligence Office. He was rewarded for informing on Norwegians fighting for a free Norway.'

Jomar nodded. He understood.

'Atle Fredly was in Sara Krefting's circle,' The Mask said. 'She's still one of Preiss's most trusted agents. We know that Krefting was involved when the Skarnes unit was smashed, so we keep an eye on her. As you're asking about Fredly, I have something that may well interest you. Atle's brother, Kai, was interned for six months. When he was released, he stayed with the Kreftings for more than a week.'

She was right. It did interest him. 'How do you interpret that?' he asked.

'It gives us reason to believe that Kai Fredly has also been recruited as a German agent.'

Kraby nodded. This thought had occurred to him too when he interviewed the man in Kjesäter. 'I can inform you that Kai Fredly is now a refugee in Sweden.'

'I don't think that changes anything about our view of him.'

'Where does she live, Sara Krefting?'

'She and her husband lived in Slemdalsveien. Her husband, Managing Director Krefting, died a short while ago. Apparently, his widow is already engaged to a Swede, a certain herr Dahlgren. We think the unseemly haste is because Sara Krefting wants to go to Sweden. We don't know what her plans are, but my guess is that the couple will travel as soon as they're married.'

'What's known about Daniel Berkåk's last trip?'

'He was expected in Oslo, but never turned up and was found by a forester from Eidskog. Berkåk had been shot. His body lay undiscovered for days. There are no reports of anyone hearing shots. When he was found he had a gun in his belt, but the papers he was carrying were gone.'

'Have you considered who might've shot him?'

The Mask shook her head. 'We're stumped, but this is a serious matter. Berkåk's murder shows that there are still collaborators in the area. So we're pleased you're investigating the case. We'd like to hear about anything you turn up. Anything that can shine a light on the case.'

The Mask looked at her wristwatch. Her hand was slender and her nails red. She made a move to leave. 'Is that everything?'

'There was one last matter.'

The Mask turned in the doorway.

'Have you got anyone in the Stapo?'

'Why?'

'Would it be possible to get some details about the three men who were shot in Trandum?'

'That should be possible.'

'If I could have some info regarding Atle Fredly too, I'd be grateful.'

'I'll pass on your requests. If you want to get in contact, put the flowerpot on the windowsill.'

She left and closed the door behind her.

19

Jomar walked down Madserud allé in the late afternoon. He counted the lampposts instead of looking for house numbers, the tension in his body like a battle between fear and expectation. To calm himself, he thought about his old friend – the now-deceased father of the Fredly brothers. His elder son became a Nazi; the other, Kai, had the same political sympathies as his father. Two brothers and so different. It was almost poetic, not unlike the Jacobsen brothers. Rolf was a distinguished poet and editor of a Nazi newspaper while his brother Anton was in a German prison camp for patriotic activities.

Kai Fredly, with a past in the Communist party, had spent days in the home of Sara Krefting, a dedicated Nazi who knew his brother. Could the masked woman be right that he had been recruited as an agent for the Nazis? Jomar had a lot of questions to ask him when he returned to Stockholm.

If he ever made it back to Stockholm.

Now at his destination, he stopped. He stood on the pavement for a few seconds, taking in the sight of the small flag-stoned area, where flowering pelargoniums in terracotta pots made the entrance resemble a house in Italy. Then he walked up to the blue door, more nervous than ever about who would open. Nervous that the meeting would be stiff and cool, or perhaps as he hoped.

Jomar clenched his fist. Extended the tip of his disfigured middle finger. Took aim. Leaned forward and pressed the button.

No going back now.

When the door swung open, Jomar was holding his hat in his hand. He bowed like a head waiter, from the hip. 'Hjørdis.'

'Jomar?'

He held a finger to his lips. In a pregnant silence they gazed at each other. Jomar was unsure whether his voice would carry as he formulated his first question: 'Are you alone?'

She nodded and whispered back: 'But – how can you possibly be here?'

'Where's Gunnar?'

'At work,' she said, stepping aside and holding the door open. In this house the ceilings were so low that he had to duck to avoid the beams. On the wall hung the painting of a nude Hjørdis when she was young beside the photograph he had taken of her as Ibsen's green-clad troll princess. On the opposite wall hung Gunnar's diplomas, which had never particularly interested Jomar. A new picture had appeared. Of a group of serious gentlemen. One of them was Gunnar. Another was Vidkun Quisling.

Hjørdis stood in the kitchen doorway. When she smiled, two dimples appeared in her cheeks, and the little gap between her front teeth was revealed. She narrowed her eyes and her green irises glittered like emeralds in the sun. Seeing that, he regretted not having spent every single day and night of his miserable life enjoying the sight. Instead he had made the wrong choice. It was his lot in life to make the wrong decisions time and time again, and he wondered if the Maker – if He existed – would ever forgive such a proliferation of stupidity.

Then she turned serious again. 'You're taking a risk coming here. Imagine if Gunnar had opened the door.'

He didn't reply.

'How long have you been in Norway?'

'One night and this morning.'

'You come to visit me, and I have nothing to offer you,' she said, flashing the jewels in her eyes.

Jomar took a bottle of absinthe from the pocket inside his coat. Her smile was wry and knowing. She went to the cabinet and took out glasses, forks and sugar cubes.

Jomar twisted off the cap, poured absinthe into the glasses, balanced the forks on top and placed a sugar cube on each.

Hjørdis filled a jug of water. She lifted it and with the poise of a ballerina poured water over the sugar while they watched the colour of the anise-flavoured spirit change from golden to grey.

'How long are you staying?'

'As long as you allow me to.'

'Gunnar will be back soon.'

'Something tells me you should be alone when he returns.'

The sugar cubes had gone, and she put away the jug. They looked each other in the eye and said, '*Skål.*'

Hjørdis, glass in hand, was pensive, then she took the plunge and asked: 'How's Pandora?'

Jomar bought himself time by putting down his glass. Hjørdis, as always, was direct and never failed to hit the target. But, he reflected, she probably knew no more than that Pandora was in Stockholm, as most actors in Oslo had crossed the border the previous year. 'I assume she's fine.'

'Don't you know?'

He shook his head.

'So you're not together?'

'No, Hjørdis. I live alone.'

'But you meet her?'

'That's a long time ago now,' Jomar said, thinking to himself that 'long' was a relative concept. A second can last an eternity for lovers. 'Come closer,' he said, patting the cushion on the sofa beside him.

She smiled again, the way she had when she opened the door. At first he saw surprise shine in her eyes, before joy took its place in her vulnerable smile. Now he saw her the way he had more than twenty years ago, and it struck him that it hadn't been him who had tormented Hjørdis and aged her, it had been the responsibility she had felt for those who were close to her; and the war, of course. Whatever is repressed inside us has no chance against the relentlessness of time.

20

The quickest way to pass time is inside a cinema. You can forget yourself. Watch others' lives. The auditorium's vast, anonymous obscurity evokes sympathy, laughter and tears. There, in your seat in the darkness, you see there is pain greater than yours. You see that trivialities, such as a look or a carefully chosen word, can cause profound distress or open the gates to an outburst of elation. Stockholm had many screens, probably a hundred.

Kai stopped to peruse the posters mounted in cases on the cinema wall. Gary Cooper and Ingrid Bergman were starring in one film, but more important was the fact that it was about the Spanish Civil War. It had to be a sign from above.

The queue was painfully slow, but when it was his turn at the box-office window the woman still had a pile of tickets. He bought two and went to invite Iris.

As soon as he rounded the corner, it was obvious he was too late. He was still a hundred metres away from the front door when he saw Iris coming out. She hesitated for a few seconds, gauging the sky. The rain was getting heavier.

Kai speeded up as she tightened the belt around her cape. He wanted to shout, but held back when she hurried off without an umbrella.

His legs did their own talking. He followed, feeling there was something wrong about all this, following instead of running over and patting her on the back. But his dark side wanted him to conceal his presence. Because his dark side thought the haste in pursuing this Iris who no longer wanted to save the world could not bode well.

At the intersection with Kungsgatan she dashed across the street and into the door of a stately hotel. He stopped and examined the façade. Carlton Hotel. She was probably meeting someone there.

Then he saw her behaviour in a new light. What he was doing was ridiculous, bordering on stupid. So he ambled aimlessly down the street. Someone shouted, and he looked back. He caught a glimpse of a woman's hardened face in a gateway. He shouldn't be here.

He turned and walked back to the door that had swallowed up Iris. He made a decision, nodded to the page boy and walked past him, into the hotel lobby. Stood at the entrance to the restaurant. There was a high ceiling. Beneath immense chandeliers waiters snaked their way between tables, carrying plates of food or bottles. The restaurant was quite full. There was barely a vacant table. The clientele was a motley assortment: the women were dressed to the nines, and uniformed men outnumbered the civilians.

Kai scanned the tables, but Iris was nowhere to be seen. Had she gone out again? Or was she visiting someone staying in the hotel?

The door to the bar was open. She wasn't there either. The clocks on the wall told him what he already knew: Kai wouldn't have any company in the cinema this evening. He had lost all desire to see the film anyway, so he scrunched up the tickets and threw them in the bin by the entrance.

He walked back the same way he had come and stopped outside the block where she lived. He crossed the street and found the same gateway where he had stood gazing at her window.

The windows were dark. The rain was bucketing down, and he leaned against the wall and waited. What was he waiting for? Kai had no answer to that, except to say that he wanted to see Iris again. What he should do was go back to the boarding house and bed. Nevertheless, he waited.

As the evening dragged on, people did occasionally go through the front door. Each time it gave him a start. Each time he had to lean back against the wall because it wasn't her. At regular intervals a police constable plodded past on his patrol. Whenever Kai heard the heavy footsteps he crouched down behind the dustbin in the gateway and waited for the man to pass and the sound of his boots to die away. Then he stood up, but continued to avoid looking at his watch, as he didn't want to provide himself with arguments for giving up. However, church bells struck every hour. The dull chimes made him realise that slinking around at midnight was utter madness. And yet he stayed.

At last a car pulled up on the opposite side of the street to the gateway. The figure who stepped out from the rear seat was unmistakeable.

As soon as the car drove off he ran across the street.

'Iris!'

She recoiled with fear and backed against the wall.

At that moment he appeared under the streetlight.

When she recognised him, she relaxed and angled her head in surprise. 'Kai? What are you doing here?'

'Waiting for you.'

Her pupils widened. It was what he expected. She would be thinking he was crazy.

'Where have you been?'

She stiffened and glanced up at him with serious eyes. 'That's none of your business.'

She must have read something in his expression, because her tone softened as she continued in a low voice: 'It's late. It's the middle of the night. You can't come here at this hour.'

He didn't answer. Of course she was right. He was an idiot.

'I'm going to bed now,' she continued. 'You have to go home and sleep too.'

With that, she turned to go in.

'Can we meet again?' he said quickly.

She stopped with her back to him. 'How long have you been waiting here, actually?'

'A while.'

Then she turned round. Her expression was resigned, condescending, as though she was dealing with a child, as though he were a dog.

'You're soaking wet.'

'Will you? Meet me? We can go to the cinema. There's a film about the Spanish Civil War.'

'I've seen it.'

He was lost for words.

'It's way past midnight, the rain's pelting down and you're waiting here?' Again she shook her head.

'A drink. We can have a glass of something. Find somewhere quiet and chat. Not today or tomorrow, but a day that suits you.'

Her hand was still holding the door handle.

'Would you like to?'

'Will you go home if I say yes?'

He nodded.

'OK.'

'When?'

'One day.'

'Tomorrow?'

'Not tomorrow. Goodnight, Kai.'

The door closed behind her.

It was as though a spark of hope had released the knot deep in his stomach. From this spark rose an inner jubilation that filled his chest and transported itself to his legs and made them so light he began to run in the rain. One part of him wanted to scream and shout, while another didn't want to let the jubilation out.

When he stopped running, it was to stand with his eyes closed and feel the rain on his face. He didn't care that his shoulders were soaked or that his trousers were sticking to his legs. Because, on the inside, he felt better than he had done for ages.

21

After a simple breakfast in the Grand Café, Jomar walked back to his hotel room with a copy of *Aftenposten* under his arm. The maid was finishing her work and collecting her dustpan and cleaning equipment. He waited patiently for her to take everything with her, then closed the door, pulled the armchair over and braced himself for the Nazi version of the state of the world. He had barely been sitting down for ten minutes when there was a knock at the door.

When he opened it, Hjørdis was leaning against the door frame and looking at him. 'I forgot to ask you something yesterday.'

He held the door open, but she didn't budge.

'I've got a few things for you,' he said. 'From Sweden.'

Hjørdis didn't move. They stood looking at each other in silence. Until he had to swallow.

'What were you going to ask me?'

'Do you remember that I wrote to you two years, four months and two weeks ago to say that I didn't want to see you anymore?'

Jomar nodded. He remembered that very well.

'Then you turn up yesterday anyway, as though the letter had never been written.'

The words that usually flowed with such ease deserted him this time. Instead he gazed at her, thinking that for the chosen few it was as though beauty was not a veneer that fades over time but something that shines from inside, as though its features are only mediating fragments of a larger identity. And he tried to understand how he had ended up in this situation – facing this shining light of a woman and knowing that it had probably been his perfidy that made her settle down with someone else. 'It's war,' was all he could find to say. 'War casts aside everything in its wake.'

'Also normal decency?'

'"Love is blind, and lovers can never see their own foolishness."'

'That's Rebecca's line. It should be spoken by a woman.'

'You do it, Hjørdis.'

Now she was unable to suppress a smile.

'Won't you come in?'

Again her eyes became serious.

'What do you think would've happened if Gunnar had been at home yesterday?'

He shrugged.

She shook her head. 'Why do you think I actually wrote that letter?'

Jomar didn't want to articulate an answer to that question either. So they eyed each other for several long seconds. He tried to read what was going on behind those green irises, but was forced to give up, as always.

A man and a woman walked along the corridor behind her. She came a step closer to him to let them pass, then pushed him aside and entered the room. She had her hands down by her side, in a pose not dissimilar to the one he had seen when she was playing Mor Nille.

He closed the door and leaned against it.

'I didn't want to see you anymore because I couldn't bear you leaving again. When are you leaving this time?'

'As you've come here, it's you who has to leave me.'

Her smile returned. It was as if she had calmed down, then

she came closer and rested her hands on his shoulders. She stood up on her toes and touched his lips with hers.

◈

Later, when Hjørdis went back to her husband, Jomar lay in bed, speculating whether one experience of happiness can be compared with another. Is it possible, he wondered, to preserve an experience over time, wrap it up, keep it unchanged inside and take it out whenever the need arose, use it as balsam for bruised feelings? If it were, unfortunately he didn't possess this ability. Is it possible to manage your own life choices without them having an impact on other people? After all, Hjørdis was married to someone else. And then another question reared its head: what if she had married Jomar? What kind of life would that have been? Would they have succeeded in loving each other as unconditionally as they did whenever they met? Would she have put up with him? Would he have been enough for her? Or would their love have succumbed to the triviality of everyday life? Such questions should be forgotten as quickly as they arise, he reflected a second later. Such thoughts are the devil's work. The ones that lie in wait to seize their chance to whisper malicious speculation into the ear of the happy but unguarded.

He lay idly dozing, but gave a jump when he heard noises by the door. An envelope was pushed underneath. Jomar lay on his side, watching the flitting of shadows across the floor and the movement of the envelope. Soon the footsteps faded and were gone, and he sat up. What would a real agent do in such circumstances? Launch himself at the door, wrest it open and grab the messenger outside? Jomar Kraby was not a real agent. Besides, he wasn't dressed.

He wrestled his way out of bed, went over to the door, took the envelope and opened it. It was full of papers, blue carbon copies of police documents. He was immediately gripped with panic. Then he tried to calm down. This was why he was here after all, to find out such things. So he lay back on the bed and started to read. A small note fell from the pile. It detailed his instructions. After reading the papers, he was to burn them.

He raised his head. Looked around. The waste-paper basket. It was made of metal.

The top sheet in the pile was the directive that had cost three good Norwegians their lives. Sverre Berkåk was the oldest of the three. The other two were men in their early twenties. When he read the Stapo report on the investigation into the murder of Atle Fredly, one conclusion was very clear: he would have to talk to the masked woman again.

◈

A few hours later, he strolled down to the kiosk in Studenterlunden. There, he bought a pack of cards, before continuing to the office in Skippergata. Here, he placed the flowerpot on the windowsill and played patience for a couple of hours, but the masked woman didn't show up. He had to go back to the hotel, mission unaccomplished.

However, when he went back the following day and inserted the key in the lock, someone had already unlocked it. Instinctively, he retracted the key. The hairs stood up on the back of his neck, and he spun round to make his escape down the stairs as he heard the door open.

'Relax.'

It was the masked woman.

Jomar stood frozen on the top step, already out of breath.

She held the door open. 'Come inside.'

Jomar walked past her and had to sit down. 'Sorry,' he said, placing a hand on his chest. 'I'm not used to this.'

'The flower was on the windowsill,' she said.

He nodded, but waited until his breathing was back to normal before explaining what he wanted. 'I have to get closer to the Swedish border,' he said. 'Can you get me a travel permit?'

The masked woman didn't consider this a problem.

'And I'd like to thank you for the police reports.'

'You shouldn't be thanking *me*.'

'There's one thing I was wondering with regard to Atle Fredly. The Stapo regard the matter as an unsolved mystery, not as a liquidation carried out by the Home Front.'

'That's right.'

'Why not?'

'They always try to win the propaganda war with such cases. First, Atle Fredly went missing, and then a search operation was mounted, and that gave them a pretty good hand. When his body was fished out of the river, the missing-person case became a murder investigation.'

'Who did liquidate him?'

'Only the executioner knows that.'

'Are you sure the murder wasn't private score-settling?'

The Mask nodded.

'The Stapo's main suspect was Daniel Berkåk. The police think Berkåk killed Atle Fredly to avenge his father.'

'That's not true,' she said. 'Daniel Berkåk was in Sweden when Atle Fredly was killed.'

'He went back and forth across the border several times. The police claim that Berkåk was in Kongsvinger the day Atle Fredly went to buy black-market coffee and disappeared.'

'Don't believe the Stapo. They're rotten to the core.'

'Why not? The case they're building against Daniel Berkåk seems solid enough.'

'The police will never admit that we have the power to execute informers. Their version of events is that he had personal motives for shooting Atle Fredly. This way they kill two birds with one stone: they disempower us and simultaneously turn Berkåk into a monster. The press writes whatever the police want them to, anyway. The truth is that Fredly was executed because he was a traitor who did a lot of damage. The death sentence was passed by our own court, subject to the jurisdiction of the government in London.'

'Could Berkåk have been ordered to liquidate Fredly?'
'No.'
'Why not?'
'Because then the execution would have become a personal matter, not a case of treason and betrayal.'
Jomar nodded. He understood. 'In Stockholm the suspicion is that Berkåk's murder was planned in Sweden.'
'I don't want to speculate,' The Mask said. 'The more you can find out, the better.'
Jomar had no more questions. The Mask told him the plant would be on the windowsill when his travel permit was ready.

22

Hjørdis accompanied him to the train. They had left it to the last moment so as not to drag out their parting at the station. Nevertheless, they stood in front of the carriage looking at each other for several long minutes before the train's departure. He was searching for something meaningful to say, when the conductor with the green flag went to close the door.

Then she placed a gentle finger on his lips. 'Go now,' she whispered and pushed him. 'I'll be fine.'

He backed towards the door. Hjørdis had grown into her role now. Her face was hewn in stone.

The conductor blew his whistle.

Jomar pulled down the window as the train jerked into motion. The woman in his life was only one of many silhouettes on the platform, but when she raised her hand, it seemed to Jomar that he had never seen her so alone, not even on the stage.

'We should both be leaving,' he said to himself, convinced she was thinking the same.

Soon she had become small and unrecognisable. Jomar sat down and kept his face turned to the window so as not to reveal his emotion to fellow passengers.

◈

In Kongsvinger he got off and waited at the taxi rank. A Ford soon arrived and pulled in. The driver jumped out and stowed Jomar's rucksack in the boot. Jomar got in and asked him to take him to Skotterud.

When he recognised his surroundings, he told the driver to stop. The driver took his fare and asked no questions. Jomar scanned the forest and the countryside. He waited for the taxi to round the bend. Only then did he shrug on his rucksack, turn, set out on the path and stride out alongside a rail fence. Before long he was walking between trees on a narrower path. He passed a farmhouse, where a little girl was sitting on the front doorstep playing with a cat. In the adjacent yard a dog was lying down, tethered to a wall. It stood up, stretched and emitted a few low growls until Jomar had walked past. Then it fell silent and lay down again.

After half an hour a small field came into view. A breath of wind caressed the spikes of barley and a darker-green hue billowed across it. Behind the field appeared the farm called Bråtan, a log-cabin construction, an equally sun-scorched haybarn with a privy leaning against the north wall.

Bråtan was one of those slash-and-burn farms built by a Finnish immigrant. Here, the original settler had first built a house and a barn with logs from the trees he felled. Then he set fire to the rest of the vegetation and sowed rye in the ashes. After a few years, when the yields began to dwindle, the settler had moved on to harvest crops in the same way as he had here, while one of Arnfinn Bråtan's ancestors took over the farm.

Jomar knocked on the door, to no effect. Then he pushed the door. It wasn't locked, but the house was silent. Nonetheless, he poked his head in. Something smelt good. There was a pot simmering on a wood stove. Probably a soup. It couldn't have been long since someone had stoked the fire.

Jomar sat down on the flagstone by the door to wait. Arnfinn

lived alone here and took jobs as a border guide. So he was
naturally wary of any stranger that came by. Jomar knew that
from the first time Arnfinn guided him across the border.
Arnfinn must have seen him when he was walking beside the
field, but obviously hadn't recognised him. Then he had made
himself scarce. The only sign of life was a few chickens strutting
around the yard. From the kitchen the clock cuckooed eight
times. It was eight o'clock.

Jomar stood up and shouted: 'If you don't come out this
minute, I'm going to eat your soup.'

After sitting back down, he heard some sounds emanating
from the haybarn. And Arnfinn appeared. Lean, wearing blue
trousers and a work smock. With his long, jowly face he looked
like a priest in a Renaissance painting.

'Is that you, Jomar? Been a while.'

They went in and sat at the kitchen table. Arnfinn served
potato soup, then brought over a leg of mutton and cut slices
off it. The soup was thick and creamy with green herbs, and it
was good. Jomar asked about the recipe, and Arnfinn explained
that it contained nothing but leeks and potatoes, which he grew
himself. Jomar countered that you couldn't get that taste from
just leeks and potatoes. Then Arnfinn put down his spoon and
said he used stock too, chicken stock and a couple of other in-
gredients, also green. This was the parsley and wild garlic he
harvested and dried in the spring. Jomar said he knew nothing
about herbs, but the soup was a taste of heaven.

The cuckoo burst out of the clock and announced that it was
half past eight. After a second portion of soup, Jomar was full
and pushed his plate away. Outside, evening shadows were
falling across the countryside. They waited for darkness
although neither of them said this was what they were doing.
Jomar told him he was on a job for the Norwegian Legation in
Stockholm. An investigation. The issue was what could have
happened to Daniel Berkåk, the courier. So he asked Arnfinn
for details about when he found the body.

Arnfinn said he had been hunting small game, and it wasn't a good idea to tell either the police chief or the border police that you owned a weapon. Accordingly he had to hide his hunting rifle before contacting the local police. Arnfinn had seen a raven flapping its wings over a cleft in the rocks and thought an elk or a deer had fallen, so he circled round to see. He found the dead man face down. Fortunately the raven hadn't pecked out his eyes. It had mostly fed on his clothes.

Arnfinn stood up and told Jomar to follow him.

They went behind the house. Here, a rusty steel barrel had been stood on its end, and used as an incinerator. Arnfinn walked over and raked through the ashes. He pulled up a pile of papers that hadn't been fully burnt. On the top sheet was the logo of the *Håndslag* bulletin.

'After the police had taken the body I spent a few days searching. The newspapers were in bundles inside a rucksack. I brought them back home and distributed them to people I knew. Those left over I burned.'

'Where was the rucksack?'

'Down another cleft in the rock a few hundred metres away from his body.'

'Apparently he had some more official documents with him as well.'

'That was why I went to search. The rucksack was full of newspapers, but there were no documents.'

'The person who killed Daniel Berkåk must've taken them then?'

'Maybe.'

'What do you think happened?'

'Only the killer knows that, but there's one thing I don't understand. Berkåk must've taken the train to Arvika as usual. He had the train ticket in his pocket. I know he had a bike at the station. He usually cycled from there to Austmarka. Where he crossed the border on foot. And he had another bike waiting for him on the Norwegian side. He used this one to get to Kongsvinger, but he can't have taken that route this time.'

Jomar was all ears. 'He took a different route?'

'Berkåk must've entered the country further south. His body wasn't far from Lake Leir.'

'Why do you think he crossed the border there?'

'I can think of only one explanation: he intentionally avoided the usual route.'

'Why would he do that?'

Arnfinn pondered the question before answering. 'On the usual route he probably had somewhere to stop over. I'd guess a farm, a place he could pop into, and get food and rest, maybe sleep if he was late. If this is somewhere the Home Front uses regularly, I imagine it was important for Berkåk not to reveal the location to others. I reckon he crossed further south because he was with someone.'

Jomar nodded. In fact, Daniel Berkåk may have been travelling with his killer.

'Has his bike been found?'

'Not as far as I know. It's probably where he left it, in Sweden.'

'He might not have used the bike this time?'

'He must've done. It's quite a distance from Arvika to Lake Leir. He wouldn't have considered it on foot.'

'A tragedy, whichever way you look at it.'

Arnfinn nodded. 'It is. His father was shot by the Germans. Him and two others. They were arrested after they let Atle Fredly join the group.'

'Fredly was snuffed out too.'

Arnfinn nodded. 'He disappeared. I can't imagine who would miss such a man, but there was a search for him. Someone had seen him driving off with a woman. Apparently a woman who was supposed to be taking Fredly to someone who sold coffee, but it wasn't coffee the man sold. She was probably a decoy.'

'I read about it in the police papers. Do you know who she might've been?'

Arnfinn shook his head.

'The police think Daniel Berkåk killed Atle Fredly.'

'So I've heard. If they're right, that's fine by me. Fredly was an absolute shit, the worst kind. Now he's dead. Good riddance, I say.'

'If no one knows anything about this woman – and stop me if I'm wrong here, Arnfinn – but it's possible she may've crossed into Sweden.'

'You're wondering if I took her over? I don't know. I've taken women over, but never ones travelling alone.'

'Think back. Does anyone stand out?'

'You're putting me on the spot now, Jomar. Who we take over the border is secret, and we never ask for names.'

'The people who saw her with Fredly, didn't they describe what she looked like?'

'She's said to be around thirty, dark-haired, that's all.'

'Any obvious candidates?'

Arnfinn shrugged. 'For all I know, she may've crossed further south, in Aremark, Ørje, or north in Finnskogen.' Arnfinn grinned. 'There was a woman in Magnor who moved north at that time, but I don't think it was her.'

'Why not?'

'She was a widow with a young child, and I doubt she would've exposed herself to such a risk. Anyway, I heard she went up north somewhere, not out of the country.' Arnfinn looked up. The first stars were shining dimly in the greying sky. 'Let's go, shall we?'

'Ready when you are,' Jomar said, following him.

◈

They had been walking for almost two hours when Arnfinn told him to wait, and sneaked off on his own. The mist was nigh on impenetrable. The ground was wet; his shoes were wet, trouser legs too. Jomar sat down on his rucksack and listened, but heard nothing apart from the dim drone of an engine and water dripping from leaves. Occasionally there was a breath of wind between the tree trunks, and the mist lightened. Then he could make out the outline of trees in the distance. The engine noise stopped, but the silence was broken by voices. They were so far away that he couldn't distinguish the words. However, he knew they were German.

Soon the voices were drowned by engine sounds, which died away once again, and silence returned. He listened, his shoulders tense with the strain.

When he heard footsteps in the heather, he held his breath and leaned his head against a tree trunk. A figure in the forest stopped. The shadow wasn't wearing a helmet – but a peaked cap. He breathed out.

Arnfinn crouched down. 'The coast is clear,' he whispered. 'We'll go our separate ways now. Run across the border and don't look back.'

Jomar struggled to his feet. His back ached, and he could feel the tiredness in his stiff legs and hips.

'Go now, Jomar.' Arnfinn was impatient. 'You haven't got much more than seven to eight minutes.'

Jomar gripped Arnfinn's outstretched hand. Thank you, Arnfinn. What do I owe you?'

'I get my reward in heaven. Stir your stumps, Jomar. Run. Now.'

Jomar turned. Strode quickly to the border road that ran ruler-straight like a firebreak through the forest. He stopped and took a deep breath. The line that separated freedom from the Third Reich seemed insuperably wide.

Not a sound to be heard, not a soldier in sight. And with that he was off. He didn't run; running was an art Jomar had learned as a child but had lost in the intervening years. However, he moved as fast as his legs would allow. Rushing through tall heather and shoots that wrapped themselves around his ankles, trying to hold him back. He stumbled and tottered, but managed to stay upright and hurry on. On his back his rucksack swung from side to side. Jomar gasped for breath and wanted to rest, but forced himself to keep going, plodded his way to the wall of trees that formed a protective screen around freedom.

That was when he saw the shadow. The second before he reached freedom he saw the arm with the torch that sprang into life and dazzled him. Jomar raised both hands.

'*Nicht schießen*,' he shouted.

23

The woman behind the counter was wearing a pink dress buttoned at the front and she was so heavily made up that small flakes of powder fell from her cheek when she stretched her lips into a strained smile. Almost like a badly applied plaster finish, Kai thought, who knew very little about perfume, but remembered the name on the bottle Sara Krefting took from her bag when she dabbed some fragrance behind her ears.

The name was like a password. The woman bowed her head, then reached backward, found the bottle of Shalimar without turning and held it as though it were made of gold. Kai wondered if it was really made of gold, because the price was exorbitant.

What should he do next? Write a letter to Iris and ask her out? Devise an excuse? Something had clicked into place the evening he saw her last. If there was a God, it must be Him behind this, who guided his footsteps towards the restaurant, who turned the head waiter into a thug, a God who made Kai stand up and go outside, a God who stood behind a corner and breathed a sigh of relief when Kai spoke to Iris. How likely are you to meet a woman who is as beautiful as a spring day and who shares elements of your terrible past that you thought you would have to live alone with for the rest of your life?

As one day succeeded the next, it became harder to recreate an image of her. Kai would wake up in the morning and not remember what she looked like. He panicked, thinking she could walk past him in the street, and he wouldn't recognise her. The next moment he thought: if that's the case, if her face, her body and her appearance were of such little significance that he couldn't recreate them in his mind, what was lacking in him? He realised he was being ravaged by something he was unable to control. The word eluded him, but whatever it was that was lacking could only be made complete when she was close. By talking to Iris and getting a response, by being in a room and knowing she was there too.

In the end, he could wait no longer. He was in a hurry, overwhelmed by the thought that she might not exist, that she might be just a figment of his imagination. He ran the last stretch, took the stairs two steps at a time. Arrived at her door gulping for air. He rang the bell. Again and again, but no one opened up. Iris wasn't at home, and Kai had to return to his boarding house with nothing to show for his efforts.

Here, in Stockholm, there was nothing to do except drift around with other Norwegians, who spent their time eternally discussing the war, especially the Eastern Front. Kai couldn't bring himself to take part. While others were speculating about what Stalin would do if the Red Army managed to overcome the German and Finnish troops, his thoughts were with Iris. In fact, he didn't believe the theories that the Soviets wouldn't be satisfied with annexing Finland and would continue westwards and swallow up Sweden while they were at it. Stalin led a dictatorship of the proletariat. Why would the working class want power over anything but the means of production? Kai kept these thoughts to himself. He was just killing sluggardly time until he could go and see Iris again. When discussion turned to the Nygaardsvold government, which hadn't been able to give the mobilisation order until German troops were already in Oslo, he continued to sit quietly smoking. Others could work themselves up about a government that had left the country at the moment of crisis and escaped to London before the fighting started. Kai kept his mouth shut. After all what did they themselves do? Beneath the surface of such discussions lurked sticky questions that Kai definitely didn't want to address: why are you here? Who are you, actually? Why did you come here? Why didn't you stay in Norway? Didn't you want to fight? You could have joined the boys in the forests, couldn't you? Instead you came here. What do you want here? To lead a life of idleness?

◆

The next day it was the same again. Breakfast. Then go to see Iris and dejectedly accept that no one was going to open the door. The same happened on the third day. Fatalism took control of his mind. It was as though he already knew while walking there that she wasn't at home. He imagined there was an invisible cord between them. If they were in contact, the cord was taut, and he could feel in his whole being that she was thinking about him, but when he stared up at the darkened window, he felt nothing. She had her focus on others; he was forgotten. When he went to her flat it was to confirm that she was no longer there for him. Self-contempt took over; he was a fallen dreamer who spent his life searching for a woman in the middle of a war. Nevertheless, he repeated the same routine on the fourth day too. Only on the fifth was there light in the window.

The square of yellow light became a portrait when Iris looked out. He remained in the shadows, feeling the cord binding them together slowly becoming tauter. As soon as he stepped forward under the streetlamp, she saw him. Then he crossed the street and heard her open the door while he was on his way up the stairs.

Iris was waiting in the doorway when he burst out with what had been on his mind:

'Where have you been?'

'You don't want to know.'

The answer was crushing, and she understood that. Her expression changed and she seemed genuinely desperate. 'In Helsinki. I was visiting my fiancé, Heikki.'

He didn't believe her. Engaged? But she didn't have a boyfriend, did she?

She looked away. 'Heikki's a bit older than me. He's from Suojarvi, a town in Karelia. Actually he's a journalist, but now he's serving in the Finnish army. He was on leave. I caught the ferry to Åbo and then the train.'

'That's not what you said last time,' he said, cringing at his own spinelessness.

'Because I'm engaged,' she said, looking him in the eye. 'Heikki and I met in Spain. He was working as a reporter for *Helsingin Sanomat*.'

At the same time as wishing this was all lies, he was telling himself he should have known. This was the same as when he was in Paris, where he learned that beautiful women are never alone. Beautiful women always find a suitor they choose over you. But he didn't want to pull back. Not this time.

'I came here to ask you out.'

'I've just come home.'

It was what he had known all the time: she was a lost cause. Now she was making it clear. So he turned to leave.

'Wait,' she said, closing the door behind her and holding a finger to her lips. She led the way up the stairs and into the loft. Here, between the panel doors of the storerooms there was a ladder leaning against the roof light.

'Don't look,' she said, climbing up first. As she lifted the roof light, she cast a stern glance over her shoulder. He looked down when she hoisted her skirt and clambered out. Only then did he follow her. Up here they could sit on a ledge with their backs against a low wall and their feet resting on tiles while the reflected glow from the street lay like a matt spider's web under the eaves.

'This is my secret hideaway,' she said.

Kai leaned his head back and discovered it was possible to see stars the way you could on evenings in the forest. His hand found hers. When she interlaced her fingers with his, he breathed out.

'What are you thinking about?' she said.

'I'm just stargazing. I like to find constellations.'

'Which ones?'

'The rifle,' he said, letting go of her hand and pointing. 'Those four there, forming a square, that's the rifle butt.'

'That's the plough, and you know that very well.'

'That arch, that's the trigger guard.'

'You're being silly.'

'Your turn. What can you see?'

'It's too early,' she said. 'It isn't dark enough yet.'

'Are there any special ones you look for?'

'Berenice's Hair.'

'I've never heard of that one.'

'It's a constellation made up of dim stars. Besides, I like the story behind it, about a queen who cuts off her hair for the gods to have her husband return safely from the war.'

Now they were no longer alone on the roof. The shadow of a stranger had sat down between them.

'I only see things I know when I stargaze,' he said, in an attempt to coax the atmosphere back. 'I don't want to see what others have seen.'

'And what do you call what you're doing?'

'It's what's on my mind,' he said, feeling the distance grow between them again. 'Your fiancé. He fights for the Germans then?'

'He's fighting for his country.'

Kai looked up at the sky and felt something unsaid looming. 'I came to Sweden to find a way to do the same. I hope I'll manage it.'

'Hope?'

'Well,' he said, to take the conversation away from himself.

'Well what?'

'Do you believe deep down that it doesn't matter if he's fighting alongside the Germans?'

'What are you trying to say now?'

'The Nazis persecute the Jews, gypsies and Communists. They have some notion that if you have blue eyes and you march to their tune, you should rule the world. Do you believe deep down that it doesn't matter that people with that ideology are now fighting side by side with your fiancé?'

'I believe you're rambling now. Have you been drinking?'

'It wasn't your fiancé who rang your doorbell when you threw me out.'

'No, it wasn't.'

'Who was it?'

'Why do you want to know?'

Silence hung in the air. Here they sat, side by side, while she was building a wall around herself, claiming she was going to marry another man. But he wanted to get behind the wall and the contradictions. He wanted to talk openly and easily, as they did the first time, before the stranger rang the bell.

She met his gaze but couldn't hold it.

'When you arrived in the taxi the following day, you came from a hotel.'

She looked up again. Her eyes were harder now.

'You were leaving the house when I got here that day. I couldn't catch up with you. You went into a hotel. I followed, but I couldn't find you in the restaurant.'

'You cannot behave like that.'

'I wanted to ask you out to the cinema.'

'There can never be anything between us.'

The silence between them continued. Kai leaned back, stared at the sky and searched for something conciliatory to say.

'I come from Edsbyen,' she said. 'A small place in Gävleborg county. A long way from here. In the north. My family owns a factory there. They manufacture wooden tools: rakes, broom handles, scythe handles, kitchen equipment, stuff people need.'

She sat searching for words and he wondered whether to take her hand again.

'It's always been a good business,' she continued. 'The house I grew up in is nicer than other houses. My siblings and I were looked after by a nanny and when I was old enough to realise how different my life was, compared with everyone else's, I was ashamed. I just wanted to leave. Everyone knew everyone else, and everyone thought they knew everything about everyone. You rarely met with anything but a set of prejudices. It felt as though the place was asphyxiating me. I moved here, trained as a nurse during the day, and attended study groups in the evening, where it was explained to me how my father and his father before him were able to get rich. I learned that the production of goods was a zero-sum game, as energy is in physical systems, because a finished article is no more than its constituent parts. I learned that the constituent part that punctured this zero-sum game was the worker, because workers have a magical ability to renew their labour power every day. It was the workers' ability to renew their labour power that allowed my father to sell a finished article at a higher price than the value of all the individual raw goods together. It was the worker who added value in the production of goods. I learned that my father and his father before him had stolen the good's surplus value from the workers who rightfully owned it. I sympathised with those who had been robbed. I distanced myself from my own family, had some vague idea of paying penance and was ashamed of my upbringing. My ideal was class solidarity and community in areas where there was poverty. I wanted to be a different person and I was determined to do just that, to be someone else. The nursing profession was the tool I would use to atone for my family's crimes. I took work in areas of Stockholm dominated by poverty before leaving for Spain. I saw myself as a kind of Salvation Army soldier, but I didn't realise that I was, and would remain, a foreigner, that I revealed my origins through my attitudes, actions and language. I had no experience of being kept down or suppressed.' Her voice deserted her, and she looked away. 'That was the lesson I learned. One night I was crossing the plaza where I lived. I'd done several shifts in a row. There was a soldier sitting by the fountain. He asked if I had any cigarettes. I didn't answer, I just walked past him, looking down at the ground as I knew I had to because I was a woman and alone. He came after me. Then I turned and ran back. He ran after me. I ran into the house where I'd been working. The family had sat down to eat. I shouted for help. He came after me and hammered on the door. I told them not to open, but he did, the father in the house. The soldier dragged me out, by the hair, and beat me up, then tore off my clothes and finished the job, the way men do with women. No one lifted a finger to stop him. I'd been in and out of that house for days, providing medicine and care; I'd kept alive two young men with bullet wounds and a woman with TB, but when I needed help there was none forthcoming. They just closed the shutters. Why? They thought I was rich, spoiled, naïve and privileged. I had forced my way into their domain and demanded a place with them while foolishly rejecting a life they dreamed of. I wasn't like them; I was different in every way, in my behaviour, background, reflections, vocabulary. I represented something they hated. They thought I deserved to be sullied. It was my turn. I was so devastated, so humiliated, from then on I began to despise everything to do with the working class. Later, if anyone mentioned the word "solidarity" I laughed in their face. But I have grown. I think I've distanced myself from the hatred, as I've put the physical assault behind me, but the pain, the degradation and the shame are impossible to forget. Do you understand?'

Her words had a numbing effect on him, but he shook off the paralysis and cleared his throat: 'Marx distinguishes between enlightened workers and the lumpenproletariat.'

'What are you trying to say now?'

'Marx writes that a rotten part of the old society's lowest stratum will always let itself be bought to enact reactionary chicanery.'

'Are you trying to excuse what happened to me?'

'No.'

'So what are you trying to say?'

He understood how she felt. It wasn't him who had just quoted Marx; it was the young man he had once been. But he couldn't stop himself countering what she said, because doing this was about holding on to her, being close to her, as much as anything else.

'You were subjected to a disgraceful crime. The fact that no one came to your aid was also a crime, but I still think it's a mistake to lose your faith, because if you reject what you believe in, something else will sneak in and replace what you abandon. If you deny solidarity and humanity to others, the alternative will be worse.'

She studied him, searching for words.

'The Nazis legitimise their fight against human dignity with a perverted belief in evolution,' he continued before she had a chance to say anything. 'In their lexicon there are no words for solidarity. If someone suffers, they only have themselves to blame. The weak and the sick have to either die or accept their status as Untermenschen. When Hitler usurped power in Germany, his message was that what happened was an act of nature – it wasn't because of party propaganda, warmongering or repeated agitation for simple solutions to ordinary people's everyday problems. Do you want to stand with the masses that support him?'

'Are you saying I'm a Nazi?'

'Of course not.'

'I tell you about a rape that that has shaped my life and you belch forth a load of theoretical hogwash.'

He had no answer to that. Of course he felt for her. There was something in her fury he had reacted to, not the crime she was subjected to, but he also thought she understood this.

'I was treated like detritus. They left me lying there like litter. This feeling was so clearly defined and so strong that all I wanted to do was die. Heikki found me and helped me to the field hospital. I hadn't been injured on the battlefield and had no right to demand medical help, but he wouldn't let them turn me away. I was given the help I needed and I was not the only person who saw reality differently that night.'

It was no longer warm on the roof. A chill went through him. Everyone has anguish they hide, he thought. Everyone has experiences that can be used to justify sides of their personality or behaviour. All anguish is unique and personal and cannot be measured and weighed against that of others.

'What about the man who rang the doorbell when you threw me out?'

'He doesn't concern you.'

Before he could respond, she forced a smile and shook her head. 'You think you know all about the man, don't you. You think you know about a man at Carlton Hotel. Now you're ransacking your vocabulary instead of giving expression to the contempt you think I deserve. I've come across looks like yours before. Many. You don't need to pretend. I'm a woman, and I have control over my own life, Kai. I decide who I spend time with, and where and when it will happen. That's it basically, and you'll have to accept it. Now I'm here with you, but don't take our sitting here for granted. We're here because I invited you. I'm not sure I'll do it again though. You have an intensity I don't think you're aware of. Because of it you now know my shame. And talking about it makes me feel besmirched again. I want to escape this feeling, but there is more to life. I know this feeling will go in time and it scares me that you've made me talk about it. I want to keep my distance from men who frighten me.'

When she fell silent, the silence lingered for quite a time, and he racked his brain for something to say, anything that could erase the oppressive awkwardness, but he couldn't find the words.

'Nordahl Grieg wrote in a poem that faith in human dignity

is a bulwark against violence,' she said. 'I hope he's right, but I'm
not sure. What I *am* sure of is that however our relationship
develops, the sun will rise sooner or later, and when it does, we
will wake up. You'll also wake up from what you call your dream,
and when you do, it's best for both of us if you wake alone.'

They gazed lingeringly into each other's eyes, until he casually
leaned forward and kissed her. She let it happen, but didn't
react, she just sat still staring at him. Then he leaned back,
turned his eyes skyward and felt hers burning on his cheek. It
was all too complicated. He had no idea what to say that would
not provoke or offend her. They sat in silence, side by side, their
backs against the wall and their feet resting on the roof tiles,
until he felt her place her hand over his.

'Who are you, Kai?'

'What do you mean?'

'I think about you a lot, but I can't see who you are. You're a
refugee but with enough money to go to Mona Lisa, and now
you quote Marx without blinking. Every time I try to place you
in a picture frame, you wriggle out and show me new sides.'

'Is that so wrong?'

'I need to know who I'm dealing with to feel secure. I need
to feel secure.'

Her eyes were searching and her lips slightly apart. He had
to wrap an arm around her, he thought. He had to do it now.

'Shall we go now?' she said. 'I'm cold.'

He was first to climb down the ladder. When he turned to take
her hand, she stumbled on the lowest rung and tumbled forward.
He caught her in his arms. She weighed nothing. He lifted her
and held her tight. She laughed and was so beautiful it hurt.

Her smile slowly faded. 'What's the matter?'

'Nothing.'

She freed herself and went down the staircase first. Stopping
outside her flat, she turned and said goodbye.

Then he remembered the present in his pocket and handed
it to her. 'Here you are.'

Motionless, she stood looking down at his hand and the package.

'Take it. It's a present.'

She lifted her chin and shook her head.

'Take it. It's for you.'

'When you accept a gift you have to return the favour.'

'What do you mean?'

'I'm not ready to return any favours.'

The answer drew a gasp from him, deeper this time. 'I decided to do this because I appreciate you. You've made my life in Stockholm sweeter. That's what you've given me. This present is me returning the favour.'

Hesitantly, she raised her hand.

'Take it.'

At last she took it.

'I'll be back, Iris.'

She leaned forward and pecked him on the cheek.

Then she closed the door, and he was alone.

Kai turned and went down the stairs. Iris had talked about herself, opened her soul, and he had been unable to do the same. All he had focused on was holding her hand.

When the extent of his spinelessness became clear to him, he wanted to go back upstairs and make amends. He wanted to tell her about himself, lay bare his soul and ask her to do what she wanted with it, but that was too late now. If he went back and knocked on the door, she wouldn't open up. This would only increase the distance between them, instead of reducing it.

It would have to be next time, if she gave him another chance.

24

Jomar Kraby opened his eyes in the blackness of night and heard a jangling noise without at first realising what it was. Gradually reality returned and he remembered he was in a prison cell. He was lying on a bunk, and the jangling was coming from the door. Someone was opening it. When he realised that, he swung his legs down onto the floor and sat rubbing his face.

He was in a prison. Thank God it was Swedish. When the door was finally open, the light came on as well. It was the same grumpy chief of police there, ogling him. With his bony face dominated by a bushy, moustache-less beard and his firm, square jaw, he resembled a figure from another era.

'Good morning,' Jomar yawned.

'It isn't morning.'

There was nothing he could say to that.

'Gustav Møller sends his regards.'

'I don't think I know who he is,' Jomar said, yawning again. 'Is he a friend of yours?'

'He's the Swedish minister of social affairs.'

'Right.'

'You don't know him?'

'I'm fairly sure I know someone who does. If that helps.'

The chief of police didn't answer.

'I asked you to contact the Norwegian Legation,' Jomar said. 'Ragnar Torgersen. Have you contacted him?'

The grumpy chief of police didn't answer. The door slammed shut.

Once again Jomar was alone, and he lay back down on the bunk. Staring into the darkness. Vainly trying to remember the dream that had ended so abruptly.

◈

The next time he woke up, the cell was lighter. From a small window high in the wall a strip of light beamed down onto the lavatory bucket in the corner. So it was a new day and outside the sun was shining. The shutter in the door slid open with a click, and another beam of light bore in and met the first.

Someone looked at him. The beam of light disappeared. Shortly afterwards the lock rattled and the door opened. The man standing in the doorway this time was the uniformed stripling who had arrested him.

'Yes?' Kraby said.

'Come with me,' the policeman said, waiting by the door.

Inside the office, on the floor above, in front of the police chief's desk, stood Torgersen, his coat open and his hat in his right hand. He didn't utter a word, nor did he seem to be in an especially good mood during the time it took for Jomar to be given his things – coat, shoes, hat, cigarettes, wallet and a comb – and his rucksack, which the officer lifted onto the table, opened and asked Jomar to check.

The car was parked outside. Borgar Stridsberg stepped out and took Jomar's rucksack.

'Nice to see you, Jomar. Everything alright?'

Jomar said yes and lit a cigarette.

Borgar stowed the rucksack in the boot. 'What was it like being back in the old country?'

'So-so. Actually, the visit wasn't all about the Norwegian tragedy,' said Jomar, who sensed that Torgersen was becoming impatient.

He took a couple of quick drags, dropped the cigarette and crushed it with the toe of his shoe. Torgersen held the rear door open. They got in.

'I appreciate that there must be an explanation for you returning on foot, but we can deal with that later,' Torgersen said. 'Drive, Borgar.'

With that, Jomar leaned back in the seat and closed his eyes.

25

They stopped at the Stadshotell in Karlstad, where Jomar entertained the other two with the latest jokes he had brought back from his homeland. 'Speaking of food,' he said, pushing his plate to one side. 'And this is absolutely true. I went to Saga, the cinema, with a lady friend. Before the feature film there was a propaganda newsreel. In which one German cargo boat after the other was unloading food onto the quay in Oslo harbour. A man in the row behind us shouted: "Stop. Stop the film. You're showing it the wrong way round."'

Jomar and Strisberg grinned. Torgersen gave a measured smile and asked if they had finished eating. He wanted to have a few minutes with the Norwegian explorer on his own.

They left, and Torgersen led the way to the bridge. He continued to Theatre Park, where the lawn was divided into rectangular flower beds beneath huge deciduous trees.

'The fact that you weren't the only person to know about my new passport was actually significant,' Jomar said. 'The border police had a name to search for. They confiscated my passport in Charlottenberg. When the train crossed the border, I was left with no ID papers. The plan was to arrest me on the Norwegian side. Fortunately, the train was full of German soldiers, and the Norwegian border police didn't see me in that carriage.'

'Swedish railways transporting German troops,' Torgersen snorted. He stared into the air. 'The rumours say there'll soon be an end to this outrage.'

'It was handy for me, but it meant I had to cross the border on foot coming back. Who knew about the passport?'

'I don't know.'

'You said the envelope was open. Who opened it?'

'I don't know.'

'Could it have been someone in the Legal Office?'

That hit home. Torgersen struggled to keep his hands under control. 'It's impossible to know. Why do you think so?'

Torgersen's body language was eloquent, even if his mouth said nothing, and Jomar thought back to the confrontation with Svinningen and to showing him the document the London government had signed. And, importantly, to Svinningen's reaction when he realised he had been kept in the dark with regard to the government's decisions concerning Daniel Berkåk's murder.

Svinningen knew how to strike back, that much was certain, but it was still hard to accept that the man was willing to curtail Jomar's work with an initiative that could have been fatal. Was Svinningen really so callous, or was it just the protected life he lived in Stockholm that had made the man lose any sense of the war's realities?

'I don't think anything,' Jomar said. 'It was a question.'

'We've both been naïve,' Torgersen said, gazing towards the river. 'You because you wanted to go to Norway. Me because I tend to think people are better than they are.'

Jomar chose to hold his tongue.

'What did you actually learn from the trip?'

'It's evident that the murder of Daniel Berkåk is linked to another incident – in Norway. It makes the fact that there's a Norwegian refugee in Sweden interesting.'

'Who?'

'His name's Kai Fredly.'

'I know that name.'

'Kai's the brother of Atle Fredly, an informer who was liquidated last winter.'

'I know a bit about that case too.'

'The Stapo think it was Daniel who killed Atle Fredly.'

'That's nonsense.'

'It's actually what the Stapo think.'

'And I say that's ridiculous,' Torgersen said, pointing to a bench with a view of the hotel across the river, which curved just there; at the edge children of all ages were wading through the water in the sunshine.

Jomar waited until they were both sitting down.

'The Stapo think Berkåk had both the motive and the opportunity to do it. Atle Fredly was the man behind the Germans' execution of Berkåk's father.'

Torgersen heaved a heavy sigh. 'Let's get a couple of things straight here,' he said, with a weary expression. 'It's correct that Atle Fredly was an informer. Many people were arrested and tortured, and many were executed as a result of his treachery. Daniel Berkåk's father was one of the many men he had on his conscience. Fredly had to be stopped. The order came from the highest quarters. The person entrusted with dispatching Fredly was professional. There was no personal angle to this case, not from anyone.'

'Sooner or later, killing someone is always personal.'

'No,' Torgersen growled. 'Atle Fredly's no longer alive because of politics – nothing personal. Blood vengeance is a ritual that went out with the Vikings. And you and I should be glad it did.'

'Before you reject everything I have to say, listen to this: there were two people involved in destroying the Home Front unit in Skarnes. Atle Fredly was working with another Nazi, Sara Krefting. My sources tell me that Kai Fredly stayed with Krefting before crossing the border to Sweden. That's alarming.'

'Why should it be alarming?'

'Atle Fredly knew Sara Krefting because both were members of the Nasjonal Samling and Germanske SS Norway. They both worked for Abwehr intelligence. Sara Krefting comes from the upper classes, a Bergen shipping family, which is the closest you can get to aristocracy in Norway. Kai Fredly's a working-class boy from Oslo who went to sea when he was fourteen. When he was arrested for escaping from forced labour, he'd been working for a farmer in Jæren for four months. Before that he was at sea. Before being at sea he was crawling through International Brigade trenches in Spain. Kai Fredly couldn't possibly have known Sara Krefting or her husband. Yet he moved into their house the day he was released from a German internment camp, and he stayed there for days.'

Now Kraby had Torgersen's undivided attention.

'His brother, Atle, infiltrated the Home Front unit in Skarnes,' Jomar continued. 'It was Sara Krefting who was responsible for organising the arrests of the unit members. So they

combined to commit this crime. Then, one day, Atle Fredly
vanished without a trace. Sara Krefting must've realised he'd
been killed and feared for her own life. After all, she was an
accessory. Later, when Fredly was found dead and the Stapo
singled out Daniel Berkåk as the murderer, she had all her sus-
picions confirmed, and was terrified Berkåk would come after
her and kill her too. So she decided to have him liquidated
before she suffered the same fate as Fredly.'

Torgersen listened without a comment.

'Sara Krefting's on intimate terms with German officers and
Nazi-friendly police officials,' Jomar continued. 'She's on first-
name terms with the Stapo boss. Krefting must've known the
police suspected Berkåk. So it's logical she feared him and
schemed to find a way to get rid of him.'

Both men paused as two women strolled past. The younger
of them was pushing a pram. The older was sprinkling bread-
crumbs from a bag over the water, where the quacking and
flapping wings told their own story about the struggle for
existence.

Jomar waited until both were out of hearing: 'I think Sara
Krefting paid Kai Fredly five thousand kroner to kill Daniel
Berkåk. At about the same time as Berkåk was killed on the
Norwegian side of the border, Kai Fredly was arrested by the police
on the Swedish side. He had five thousand kroner in his pocket.'

At first Torgersen considered what Kraby had told him. Then
he shook his head. 'This is a fantasy,' he whispered. 'If Kai Fredly
shot Daniel Berkåk, he must've had a weapon.'

'Krefting would've given it to him. I think Kai Fredly shot
Berkåk, threw the gun away and kept going, across the border
to Sweden and straight into the arms of the Swedish border
police.'

'If he killed Berkåk, he must've known Berkåk was on his way
to Norway. He must've known when he was coming and which
route he had taken. How could he have known that?'

'The Legation has leaks. I've discovered that to my own cost.'

Torgersen stared at him, still with a frown between his eyebrows.

'The information that's being leaked,' Jomar said, as though talking to a child, 'goes through either the Swedish or the German intelligence service, or both. *Nota bene*: everything the Abwehr in Stockholm finds out about the Norwegian Legation goes across the border to the Abwehr in Norway. Who to? The head of their intelligence service in Oslo: Fritz Preiss, who is Sara Krefting's controller.'

Torgersen was still tight-lipped.

'There's only one way to find out,' Jomar continued. 'We have to establish whether Daniel Berkåk was involved in Atle Fredly's death or not.'

'I know he wasn't.'

Jomar shook his head. 'You don't. You *think* you know.'

'How are you going to find out?'

'I have to know who was assigned to liquidate Atle Fredly.'

'You never will. Whoever knows anything about liquidations in Norway keeps their mouth shut tighter than a clam.'

'I think I will.'

'How?'

'They used a decoy. A woman apparently offered Atle Fredly an opportunity to buy genuine coffee on the black market. The last time Fredly was seen alive was when he and the decoy got into his car and drove off. Presumably going to the place where the executioner was waiting for them. This woman knows who the executioner is.'

'Are you sure she wasn't the executioner?'

'What do you mean?'

'Our Resistance movement consists of men and women, Jomar. Why wouldn't it be the woman who shot Atle Fredly?'

'Regardless of whether she was a decoy or the executioner, she was observed. The Stapo tried to find her without success. Why did they fail? Because she crossed the border. She's a Norwegian refugee in Sweden, and I'll find her.'

Torgersen sighed loudly and stared up at the sky.

'What's the matter?'

'I asked you to investigate leaks in the Norwegian Legation, Jomar. So you listen carefully now: no one wants you to rake up the Atle Fredly case.'

'Rake up? What do you mean?'

'The liquidation of Atle Fredly, the informer, was a military act. There are no grounds for the death sentence in Norway during peace time. It was legitimised exclusively by the fact that Norway is at war. When this war's over, there are many Norwegians who'll be punished. Sara Krefting and other Nazis will be called to account for their actions, but our soldiers, those fighting in the war on our side, they won't be punished. We don't want to punish the man who liquidated him. It's our enemies who want to. It's the Nazi regime we're fighting who will punish that man. Let me be absolutely clear, neither I nor the government nor anyone else of a patriotic disposition wants you to stick your nose into a liquidation carried out by the Home Front. I thought you were clever enough to realise that without any help. I'm starting to regret giving you this job.'

Jomar glanced across the river at the Stadshotell. Borgar Stridsberg was walking with a pile of newspapers tucked under his arm. He stopped by the car and placed them on the roof, leaned against the bonnet and started to flick through them.

Torgersen put a hand in his pocket and pulled out a packet of cigarettes. The genuine article: Philip Morris. When Torgersen offered him one, Jomar wasn't slow to take advantage and helped himself to two. Torgersen lit up and held the lighter out for Jomar.

'What if I employ him?' Torgersen said.

'Whom?'

'Kai Fredly.'

'Have you gone crazy?'

'Not at all. If he works for me, we can monitor what he does.

If your speculation is correct, we have him to hand when the evidence is on the table.'

'You may be able to monitor him. Perhaps. When I was in Oslo I had regular contact with a masked woman from the Home Front. She's sure the Germans have recruited Kai Fredly.'

'If he's a German agent, he'll give himself away sooner or later while working for us.'

'It's a high-risk strategy. The Germans might find themselves gifted an inestimable source in your office.'

'I'll give the matter some thought,' Torgersen said, as though the employment suggestion had come from Jomar.

Jomar wasn't sure he liked that attitude. He sat finishing his cigarette as Torgersen got up and signalled to Stridsberg, who folded the newspaper he was reading and got into the car.

'We'd better get going,' Torgersen said. 'Are you coming?'

26

Driving into Stockholm, Borgar Stridsberg first headed for Torgersen's address. After the head of the Refugee Office had been dropped off, Jomar looked at his watch. The Legal Office was still open, so he asked Stridsberg to drop him off there.

'I just need to see if Svinningen is in. Have you got enough time?'

Stridsberg did and set a course for Sturegatan, where he pulled into the kerb and stopped.

Jomar nodded to the guard, entered the building and went up the stairs. On opening the ante-chamber door, he saw Svinningen's back at the other end of the office. Svinningen was standing, looking over his secretary's shoulder. Frøken Bendiksen was reading aloud from a document:

'"…and as I've come to Sweden and have nowhere to live, I'm asking for a small contribution of two thousand kroner."'

Frøken Bendiksen stopped and laughed. Svinningen guffawed.

Jomar cleared his throat.

Two heads swivelled round.

He tried to read their expressions. It wasn't easy. He therefore raised his hat and smiled at them. 'Yes, indeed it's me. Here I am, alive and kicking. Aren't you happy on my behalf?'

Lotte Bendiksen stood up. Without dignifying him with even a glance, she turned and marched out of the room, straight-backed.

Jomar addressed Svinningen. 'Did I disturb you?'

'What do you want?'

'I see you let your secretary read confidential papers.'

'Everyone in this office is accredited and enjoys my confidence. This also applies to frøken Bendiksen.'

'Which one of you is it who opens mail from the Passport Office?'

Svinningen shut his mouth so tight his jaw muscles went white. 'Enough tomfoolery,' he hissed. 'What do you want?'

Jomar thought on his feet. It was a long time since he had felt such a desire to strike someone. However, an offence of that nature would give Svinningen a good opportunity to stop the investigation, and now more than ever Jomar wanted to get to the bottom of this matter. So he chose once again to smile. 'Atle Fredly.'

Svinningen's eyebrows curled so they resembled the wings of a bird of prey ready to pounce.

'Informer, liquidated.'

The hawk hovered in the air.

'The man's fate was sealed by the wise men you worship in London. I want to know who was given the assignment; as head of the Legal Office I'm sure you will've been informed.'

'Wrong, Kraby. I have no idea what you're talking about. My government does not order killings.'

'Let's consider this matter a rumour. Have you any idea who could've carried out such an action?'

'Let me put it like this,' Svinningen said, oleaginously: 'If it's a rumour that an informer was lying belly up somewhere in Norway that has brought you here today, I'm fairly confident one man knows who's behind the killing.'

'Who?'

'Osvald. He's used for that type of job.'

'In person?'

'I doubt it. Osvald's an agitator and a Communist with a gang of lunatics around him who cause us and the Germans a lot of trouble. He's the bubonic plague in person, but in cases like this he's useful for our Home Front. Osvald delegates the assignment to the person he considers best suited for the job. The pre-condition is absolute silence.'

This gave Jomar food for thought.

Svinningen strode past him to the door, grabbed the handle and was about to leave. 'That was all, I take it?'

'I've read the Stapo documents. Atle Fredly was fished from the Glomma. Do you know who dealt with the corpse and what happened to it afterwards?'

Svinningen shook his head.

'You're the head of the Legal Office. Can you find out?'

Svinningen seemed irritated now. 'Absolutely not. I don't want to know who's been doing this kind of thing, and it would undermine my legitimacy to react in any other way.'

Jomar was about to speak, but Svinningen didn't give him a chance.

'This so-called assignment you were given was ludicrous from the outset if you have to start querying actions that lead our struggle for freedom closer to victory. No one needs to know who eliminated Atle Fredly. The fact that he was stopped has saved many Norwegian men's lives. People who perform such necessary acts have a right to anonymity and protection. No one should be digging up the Fredly case, least of all you or Torgersen. Does he know you're raking up this matter?'

Jomar chose to ignore the question. 'Atle Fredly worked with Sara Krefting. She's either already in Stockholm or on her way

here. As a matter of form, she's married a Swede, one herr
Dahlgren.'

'Has she divorced Krefting?'

'He's dead. Now his widow has remarried and is perhaps
already in Stockholm.'

'So?'

'If she's here, there will be a reason. She has a plan. As you
have agents everywhere, perhaps you could take the trouble to
find out what the reason is,' Jomar said, turning to Svinningen.
'That's all. Now you may open the door.'

Svinningen tore open the door. Jomar raised his hat and
walked through.

27

Kai waved to the girl behind the counter in the lobby and
continued into the street. Here, he stood for a few seconds
scrutinising the weather, then strolled along the pavement, not
knowing what to do. It was a late-summer evening and the air
was warm.

A sudden impulse made him turn round. And there he saw
the interrogator from Kjesäter: Jomar Kraby. The hat and the
open coat were unmistakeable. A skeleton of a man. Stationary
now. The man looked up and pretended to be staring at
something in the sky. Kai decided to ignore him. He walked on
down the street, but had to stop at the intersection, where a
policeman was directing the traffic.

A quick glance over his shoulder confirmed that Kraby was
still there. The policeman waved people and traffic on. Kai
hurried across the street and quickened his pace, to channel his
annoyance and shake off his shadow. It wasn't good to lose your
temper, not with an old man.

A trolley bus pulled in at the stop. Kai jumped on, bought a
ticket and found a free seat by the window. He got off in

Östermalmstorg. From there he ambled down to Berzelii Park and crossed it, still unsure what to do.

As he walked along the harbour, something happened. Several cars drove up and parked in front of the entrance to the large building with the verdigris copper roof, on which pennants from various countries fluttered in the wind – Stockholm's Grand Hotel. This was the catwalk for the bourgeoisie. As each car drove up, a page boy ran out and opened the rear doors for the gentlefolk inside. A Mercedes was at the head of the queue. A door opened and a leg appeared. Soon a woman was standing in the street, waiting for her gentleman escort, who got out on the opposite side. Kai had seen this woman before.

At first he couldn't understand how it was possible, but it had to be her. It couldn't be anyone but Sara. The profile under the blonde curls was hers. A cape draped across her shoulders, she turned to her escort, a man dressed in black with a bow tie. A third person joined them, a young woman. All three disappeared through the door held open by two liveried employees.

Kai walked closer to the windows to check his own appearance. An ordinary man in a jacket and tie looked back at him from the glass, neither a proletarian, nor exactly a *petit bourgeois*. He took a comb from his inside pocket and tidied his fringe. The suit fitted him well, but the crease in his trousers left something to be desired, and his shoes weren't polished. The door beyond led into the citadel of the snobs. This operation would require nerves of steel and a steady course.

Before he could change his mind, he put the comb back in his pocket and set off. When he strode up the stairs to the entrance, the doorman held open the door. Kai had a coin ready to give him before entering.

If Stockholm was an illuminated carnival compared with Oslo, this had to be the main stage, thought Kai, standing under the chandeliers and staring into a large restaurant packed with guests, busy waiters and an orchestra playing smooth jazz.

Kai breathed through his stomach and went in.

The first person he clapped eyes on was Iris, who was sitting with three other women at a table by the wall. All four were dressed for a party. Iris was wearing a red dress, short-sleeved, with a low neckline and a belt around her waist. She had been served a cocktail with a straw protruding from the glass. Her black gloves reached up to her elbows, and at this moment she was reaching for a packet of cigarettes. A man approached her table and held out a lighter. Iris puffed her cigarette into life, made a comment to him and laughed, the cigarette dangling from between her fingers. The two of them obviously knew each other. They knew each other well. This was somewhere she came frequently.

Kai walked on. He caught her eye for a fraction of a second before she looked away. Passed her without slowing his pace. What had been his objective in coming here?

Immediately the orchestra stopped playing and the buzz of voices rebounding from the ceiling filled their ears for a few seconds, until a sharp sound penetrated the hubbub and a hush fell. It was the conductor tapping the music stand with his baton. The orchestra struck up a slow waltz. It was a signal. People turned their heads and twisted round on their chairs. Something was about to happen by the entrance.

In the doorway stood the house's leading lady. Kai had seen her face on the cinema screen many times. Some of the guests rose to their feet when the film star walked past with her entourage. The waltz died as she sat down.

The moment was past. The buzz of voices rose again, and then it was as though Kai was discovering himself anew. The light was stronger, the tables and the orchestra clearer, and Iris merged into the mass of people forming the backdrop. This clarity made him feel more self-confident.

At the table closest to the diva sat Sara Krefting, who had just made an amusing remark. Her gentleman friend and the younger woman burst into laughter. The woman held a hand over her mouth. That table could benefit from another pair of male legs, thought Kai, and headed towards it.

The orchestra struck up another tune. When the saxophone came in, Kai was standing next to Sara's chair. He bowed. She angled her head as though a reunion at the Grand Hotel in Stockholm was something she had actually been expecting. With a wry smile on her lips, she pushed back her chair, stood up and allowed herself to be led onto the dance floor.

'Good to see you, Kai,' she whispered into his ear as he put his arm around her waist.

He loosened his grip around her slim figure and let her move an arm's length away.

'Just as good as knowing you're the man I'd hoped you would be,' she continued when he held her tight again. 'Why didn't you write? I've been worried about you.'

'Sorry,' he whispered, 'but I don't like being ordered around.'

'And that was what I was doing?'

Kai noticed that they were being watched by Iris, who was sitting with the man who had lit her cigarette. Her escort was talking to her, but Iris was staring in Kai's direction.

This inspired him. He pulled Sara closer and asked what she was doing here in Stockholm,

'Maybe I have another job for you. If you're a good boy.' They looked into each other's eyes. 'But I want a report from you immediately afterwards,' she whispered. 'I don't want to read about it in the newspaper.'

The tune was over.

Another job, Kai mused, as they walked back to the table. Good boy, he thought as he pulled out a chair and was introduced to her companions. The woman was called Brita and was a friend of Sara's. She spoke Swedish. The man was Swedish too, but he wasn't just making up the numbers.

Sara fanned her face hectically with her hand. 'I was widowed, Kai. I was in mourning, but now I've remarried and I'm happy.' She leaned forward and kissed her husband on the lips.

Kai visualised the man in the wheelchair, the man who

refused to speak to him. Now he was dead. How quickly can you re-marry after becoming a widow?

Sara turned in her chair. A German officer bowed. Sara took his hand. The officer helped her from her chair and guided her onto the dance floor.

Kai had had enough and rose to his feet. Scanned the room for Iris without success. But he did see Jomar Kraby, sitting alone at a table by the wall. Now he was talking to a man at the neighbouring table. Kraby pointed to Kai. Both looked towards him.

Kraby raised his beer in greeting.

Kai could feel his blood beginning to boil and walked towards the door. As he went past Kraby, he knocked his glass off the table. It smashed as it hit the floor and someone shouted, but Kai took no notice. He just kept walking.

The restaurant door closed behind him. Kai continued through the lobby and out into the street. He turned right, up Stallgatan, to walk off his fury, but he got no further than the first intersection. He heard quick footsteps behind him and a familiar voice.

'Kai.'

He swivelled round.

Iris was gasping for breath. She had been running. That much was obvious.

'Are you going?'

He nodded.

'Don't you feel like staying a bit longer?'

'What have you done with your gentleman friend?'

Something happened to her face then. Kai didn't want to know what, he just turned to go. She grabbed his arm.

'The woman you were dancing with,' she said. 'Is she Norwegian?'

Kai looked down at her hand. Then she let go.

'She's Norwegian, yes.'

'Is her name Sara?'

'Sara Krefting.'

'Do you know her?'

Kai couldn't help but notice her expression. It was midway between impressed and enthusiastic. 'Now she's called Sara Dahlgren. She's married to the guy sitting at her table.'

'The other woman sitting there – what's her name?'

This directness surprised him, and he parried with a counter-question: 'What's the name of your friend?'

'Helmut.'

'You seem to know him well.'

'I know no more about him than I do about you.'

'Such as what?'

'He's a colleague of my fiancé, Heikki.'

'What else?'

'He's a member of the SSS, the Swedish Socialist Party.'

'Nazis. Fine friends you choose.'

'You're my friend too, aren't you? And the woman sitting at the table with Sara Krefting, what's her name?'

'Brita.'

Iris shook her head, smiling. 'No, Kai. Her name's Ulla.'

'Why do you ask if you already know the answer?'

'I want to know if they're being straight with you.'

Kai looked at her with fresh interest. This was a new Iris. Not only had she run after him and stopped him; she wanted something from him. 'Why would they lie about her name?'

'Perhaps it's Ulla lying. She works in a special office. The people who work there gather information.' Iris looked around her and stepped closer before whispering: 'Even if Sweden isn't a participant in the war, all of those who are, are here in Stockholm. What do you think the Germans, the British, the Americans and the Soviets are doing in town? They're keeping an eye on each other, and Sweden's keeping an eye on them. The government wants to know if Sweden's being dragged into the war. Norway's occupied. Denmark's occupied. Finland's fighting against the Soviets. The Baltic States are occupied.

Sweden's surrounded by war, and that means genuine information can be valuable.'

'So you *are* still politically engaged! This is a different tune
from the one you played when we were on the roof.'

She cast down her eyes. 'I still think about that evening.'

'Do you?'

'I'm wearing it, your present. Smell.' She uncovered her neck
so that he could smell it better. 'Imagine you knowing what I
like best.'

They were standing close to each other, and the gentle
evening light softened her face.

'Sara and Ulla are lying to you, Kai, but I'm not.'

'Well,' he said. 'You ask me in and when another man knocks
on the door you give me the heave-ho.'

'I'm honest with you. It's important for me to be honest.'

'When you talk like that, you remind me of my brother.'

'Have you got a brother?'

'He was a Nazi. You would've liked him.'

'Was?'

'He's dead.'

She said nothing. Seemed to search for words to fight back
with. He was beginning to feel heartily sick of her game-playing.
So he turned to go.

'I'm sorry to hear that,' she said quickly, as if to hold him
back.

'When you say something like that, why don't you mean it?'

'Why do you think I don't?'

His breathing. He had to control it.

Iris looked him in the eye. 'Why did he end up with the
Nazis?'

'What do you mean?'

'You were passionate about a cause. Your brother went the
opposite way. Why did that happen?'

'I don't know.'

Iris stepped even closer. 'Are you sure? I went to Spain as a protest against what my family stood for. Who rebelled in your family: you or your brother?'

'You have your story; I have mine. What do you want actually? Why have you come after me?'

'You know Sara Krefting,' she said. 'Perhaps you should find out what her plans are here in Sweden?'

'Why should I do that?'

'You could do it because I've asked you to and then you can tell me.'

'So what you said was all lies. You're still politically active.'

'Not at all.' The hand wearing the black glove stroked his arm, and her voice was almost a whisper. 'Politics is for idealists and people in positions of power. I'm neither. I care about my life in this world. Like you. Because I think you and I are quite similar, Kai – two veterans of Spain with no other baggage than the illusions we no longer believe in.'

He wanted to say 'speak for yourself', but held back. In silence they looked into each other's eyes.

'Will you do this for me?'

'I don't need you, Iris. I've met Ulla now, the woman who works in an office gathering information. If I find anything out, it doesn't have to go through you.'

Now she was hurt, and he realised that was exactly what he'd wanted to do: hurt her.

When he turned to go, he was allowed to do so without restraint. She didn't follow him, and he didn't look back.

28

Atle and his father had been enemies for as long as Kai could remember. Atle got up to mischief, and afterwards there was a thrashing. His father hauled him up the stairs by his ear and gave him a beating in front of an open window. On one occasion Atle took his revenge by yanking his clothes off the

wardrobe rail and pissing on them. Having done that, he
marched into the sitting room and announced what he had
done in a clear and defiant voice. Then there was another
thrashing, harder than ever before, while his mother sat holding
her ears in the kitchen.

The yellow rectangle on the floor told him the sun was ready
for a new day. Kai got up to go to the bathroom, but came to a
halt in the doorway. Someone had pinned a piece of paper to
the corridor wall. It was a missing-person poster with a picture.
The police were searching for a man: Kåre Vardenær.

Kai quickly loosened the drawing pins, took down the poster
and backed into his room. He perched on the edge of the bed
and read. It said that Vardenær was thirty years old. Kai had only
caught a glimpse of him through a window before he was confronted by the man's dead body, but now he wondered whether
he had seen Vardenær before. The print wasn't the best, but there
was something familiar about the hair – the way it flopped over
his forehead. And about the face, which was slightly feminine.

If you knew anything about the disappearance, you were to
contact the police.

Kai stared into the air. So far, life in Stockholm had been like
walking in a hazy dream, aimlessly going through the motions
without a thought in his head. Spying on a Swedish woman.
Being jealous of the men she met. Fantasising that she thought
as he did and dreamed about him. Sitting up late at night and
feeling sorry for himself. Sleeping in. Staring at the wall and
pondering whether there was any meaning to all this. Then this
poster turned up, like a slap in the face.

In the corridor a door banged. The bathroom was free.

◈

After shaving and getting dressed, he folded the Vardenær poster
and stuffed it into his inside pocket. Then it was down the stairs
and into the street, where he came to an abrupt halt.

Jomar Kraby was leaning against a wall, smoking a cigarette. 'Nice to see you again, Kai.'

Kraby dropped the fag end and trod it into the pavement. 'And nice of you to knock over my beer. The head waiter didn't know what to do to make amends. I got good and drunk – at a discount.'

Kai said nothing.

'It struck me you and I should have a little chat today.'

'You and I have nothing to chat about.'

'Apart from what you did before you came to Stockholm.'

'Why would I waste my time on you?'

'You would profit from it.'

'Another day. I need some food.'

'Me too. And the meal's on me.'

They walked side by side past the newspaper kiosk. Kraby stopped outside a café and said he could recommend it. He held the door open for Kai, who was thinking he would give Kraby a morning and no more. Find out what the man was actually after.

The aroma of baking and pastries filled their nostrils as Kraby led the way past the counter full of delicacies, where women in white aprons were serving customers, who left with cakes and freshly baked bread. In the café part, most of the tables were full. People were eating, reading newspapers and chatting. By the window two women were getting up to leave. Kraby stood by the table. A waiter appeared, removed the cups and ran a cloth over the table. Kraby ordered eggs and bacon for them both. And milk and ersatz coffee.

After the waiter had gone, Kraby looked at Kai with a smile on his face. Or, thought Kai, was it a smile? It was more appropriate to say he bared his teeth. Kraby's smile was a wolfish grin. His face was gaunt; his skin appeared to be too small for it. It stuck to his forehead and chin in a way that made his head resemble a skull, which in turn showcased his long, voracious teeth.

'May I ask you something, Kai?'

Kai didn't answer.

'Why do you think Hitler invaded Norway?'

Kai peered up, suspicious. Was this a trick question? 'Presumably he wanted Norway's coastline,' Kai said. 'The Germans are building bunkers there, aren't they, from Halden to Kirkenes.'

'What the Germans said was that they wanted to protect us. They said they would save us from a British invasion. Do you believe that? Do you think the Germans need Norwegian harbours to fight against England? If England was the cause of the occupation, why didn't the Germans withdraw from Norway when they overran Holland and Belgium and France, whose coasts run the length of the English Channel? It costs money to occupy such an extended, rugged landscape like Norway's. Hitler has transported an army of several hundred thousand men up to this barren country. Why has he done that?'

'He needs *Lebensraum* for the Aryan race,' Kai said in a low voice. 'The soldiers do what they can. Most of the ones I saw in Norway had a Norwegian girl on their arm.'

The food was served. Kai was so hungry he had to force himself not to wolf it down. Eggs and bacon was a rare treat. He chewed slowly, eyes closed. Kraby didn't speak while he was eating either.

After Kraby had finished, he pushed his plate aside. 'Around the autumn of 1940, when it became clear that the war was going to be long,' he said, taking a toothpick from the holder on the table, 'the Germans needed some nodding dogs to administer Norway for them, some loyal idiots who spoke Norwegian. They chose Quisling and his entourage for the job. Why did they do that?'

Kai shrugged, suspecting that Kraby wasn't interested in any answers he might come up with.

'They chose Quisling to mobilise a Home Front, Kai.'

Kai had to shake his head at this conclusion. 'The Germans? Do you mean to say it was the occupying power that mobilised the Home Front?'

'The Home Front was and is a pain for the Germans, but it is also useful.'

'How do you make that out?'

Kraby leaned forward. 'The same day the German army marched into Oslo – and it was clear that the king and government had fled – Quisling attempted a coup over the radio. He claimed he was taking power on behalf of his Nazi party, but he didn't get any support, from the Norwegians or the Germans. When it transpired that the invading German army didn't support Quisling's coup d'état, the Norwegian Supreme Court appointed the Administrative Council. It was supposed to be a kind of senate consisting of good Norwegians whose task it was to administer the country under German occupation – because the Norwegian government had made good its escape to London. But the Germans didn't want good Norwegians governing Norway. They wanted loyal sycophants. So the Germans dissolved the Administrative Council and brought Quisling back in from the cold. They allowed him to establish a so-called "sitting" government. My contention is that Germans dissolved the Administrative Council and appointed Quisling and his lackeys as cabinet ministers for one reason only: to make Norwegians form a Home Front.'

Kai's eyes widened.

'It was a masterful move. Josef Terboven knew that the appointment of the traitor Quisling as minister president of Norway would result in organised resistance among Norwegians, and the formula's working. The more the dreadful, scheming Quisling ravages our country, the more the Home Front's attention will be focused on that and away from where the Germans want peace and quiet.'

'And where is that?'

'Norwegian industry,' Kraby said, putting down the

toothpick, taking the cigarette from behind his ear and lighting it. When he took a drag, his cheeks hollowed, and his head resembled a skull even more. 'In fact, the Wehrmacht has only one main interest in Norway, and that's its industry. Norsk Hydro aluminium, Norsk nitrite, the Zinc Company, the copper mines in Sulitjelma, the iron-ore mines in Sydvaranger, the Orkla and Foldal companies. We're talking raw materials here, Kai. We're talking ferro-alloys from Odda, Sauda, Fiskå and Notodden, aluminium from Høyanger, Eydehavn and Vigeland. Dynamite and trotyl from the Norwegian explosives industry. The Engene and Gullaug factories. Molybdenum and vanadium from Knaben and Christiania Spigerverk.' Kraby placed the cigarette on the edge of the ashtray. 'Germany's a military nation. It's products such as these that deliver their strike power.'

Now it was Kai's turn to take a cigarette from the packet he kept in his inside pocket.

Kraby tore off a match and held it close for Kai to light up. 'The Home Front does nothing to blunt the German interest in Norwegian industry.'

'Nothing?'

Kraby nodded. 'The Home Front distributes illegal newspapers to resist Hitler's propaganda machine. In addition, they train Norwegians to handle weapons while we're all expecting a British invasion. The people joining the Home Front are teachers, students, children, workers, doctors, lawyers, trade unionists – but no industrialists. At the same time the Germans don't have a single Nazi in Norwegian industry. They don't want any disruption to exports. To be sure of peace, they maintain their activities around the Home Front. The Germans and Quisling harass people in the streets. The Home Front reacts. And so the game goes on while industry grows exponentially, and exports to Berlin are undisturbed.' Kraby sipped his coffee and took a long drag on his cigarette. 'There's only one group of Norwegians who have seen through this and actively sabotage

Norwegian industry, in order to hit the Germans where it hurts most. That's the Communists, like Osvald and his gang.'

'I see,' Kai said, somewhat irritated. 'But what has that to do with you and me? Why are you talking about this?'

'Because you and I have to agree on one thing,' Kraby said, his teeth bared in another skeletal grin. 'The world is not the way it appears. Nothing is the way it appears. Do you know Max?'

'Max?'

'Max Hodann. He was at the Grand yesterday. Sitting at the table next to mine. Quite a man. He's a German refugee and Communist. Had to flee Germany when Hitler came to power. Lived in Norway for a few years, with Lise Lindbæk, who wrote a book about your brigade. The Thälmann Battalion.' Kraby bared his teeth again and crushed his cigarette in the ashtray. 'You served in the Thälmann Battalion when you were in Spain. Max thought he'd seen you before and was wondering who you were. "He's Kai Fredly," I told him. "He served in the Thälmann Battalion." Max didn't agree. "That's not where I saw the guy," Max said. "There was no Kai Fredly in that battalion." Then Max and I had a few drinks and he remembered where he'd seen you. "Kai Fredly. Yes, now I know. He was one of the men smuggling arms. He sold guns to the units." So you didn't fight in Spain, did you, Kai.'

Kai stared back hard. 'Do you think the Republic would have stood a chance without arms?'

'The Republic collapsed.'

'Unfortunately, yes,' Kai said, and added: 'Injustice can only be fought with weapons. This war is proof of that too.'

They eyed each other in silence.

'So you know Max Hodann and his wife?'

Jomar Kraby nodded.

'She wrote for a Norwegian newspaper when I was in Spain, didn't she?'

Kraby nodded. 'That's correct. *Dagbladet.*'

'How did you get to know her?'

'I don't remember, but I'm a writer. I've worked on several newspapers, and I published books while I was still living in Norway.'

'Do you know any foreign journalists?'

'The odd one or two.'

'Do you know a Finnish journalist, someone called Heikki, who was a reporter on the *Helsingin Saanomat*?'

Kraby nodded. 'Heikki Virtanen was a reporter on the *Helsingin Saanomat* during the Spanish Civil War, but now he's dead.'

Kai stared blankly at Jomar.

'What's the matter?'

'He's dead?'

'Virtanen died in Spain.'

'Are you sure?'

'I am. Why?'

'Nothing.'

Kai's thoughts were with Iris. Why had she lied to him? Or to be more precise: what had she and what hadn't she lied about? Why had she said she went to Finland to see a man who no longer existed? Or perhaps it was not so surprising that she made things up. He'd seen a new side to her the previous evening when she ran after him to pump him for information.

'Did you think Virtanen was alive?'

Kai nodded.

Kraby smiled. 'The world isn't as it first appears. Nor are you, Kai. The sailor who was supposed to have fought in Spain, who fled to Sweden with five thousand kroner in his pocket, who stays in a cheap boarding house, but goes without any hesitation into the Grand Hotel and asks Sara Krefting to dance. It was obvious to everyone that she enjoyed being held in your arms. Have you two had a bit of how's-your-father?'

Kai could feel the fury rising and banged his fist on the table. 'What's that got to do with you?'

The plates and cutlery jumped into the air. Frightened faces looked in their direction.

Jomar Kraby bared his teeth again in the same grin. 'Take it easy. The exchange of body fluids between men and women is entirely normal. Most men would sleep with Sara Krefting if they got the opportunity, but what made her show such tenderness to you, Kai?'

Kai looked around. The other tables were no longer interested in them.

'Krefting's a woman who differs from you in many respects, Kai. She comes from a family that sees itself as God-given aristocracy. She was fifteen years old when the Bolsheviks took power in Russia. When they killed Tsar Nicholas and his family, Sara Krefting realised one thing: that those who wished to remove her privileges, and topple God's order, were Communists. From then on, even though she was so young, she started registering Communists in Norway and keeping a watchful eye on them – together with her extremely reactionary father. During the next twenty years she became the person on the right who knew most about the left. When the Germans occupied the country, she became a spy and an informer for the German authorities. In the last two years she's been working for Fritz Preiss, the man leading the Abwehr in Oslo and responsible for Communist affairs. Preiss is a perfect match for Krefting; he dislikes Communists too. Preiss carried out surveillance on Communists, and arrested and executed them when he lived in Germany. In Norway he does the same, and he has people like Sara Krefting work for him. She has devoted her life to working for the Wehrmacht, in Norway, and also here in Sweden. A few days after her husband died, she married a Swedish businessman. Accordingly, she had a Swedish passport and could travel into this country without soiling her hands by escaping over the border. You and other Norwegians had to run from tree to tree, hoping not to be shot during your escape. When you succeeded in crossing the border, you were first arrested, then interrogated by the chief of police, who speculated whether to send you back to the German internment camp or boot you on to the refugee camp in Kjesäter. Depending on how the mood took him. When you came here, there were ten or twelve of you per billet, farting your way through the night. The next day you had pea soup in the refectory, more interrogations and more medical checks. You reeled off one explanation after the other, were interviewed by Norwegian court officers and journalists who dug up your past, before you were finally allowed to come to Stockholm. Here, you and other Norwegians can claim five kroner a day pocket money, worn shoes and clothes Swedes no longer wear. Sara Krefting, on the other hand, was able to catch a train straight from Oslo to Stockholm, and she lives here like a millionaire. You and Krefting are from two different planets. Yet she chose to lie back and part her lily-white thighs for you. I'm curious by nature, Kai. I ask myself: why would Sara Krefting pamper a sailor, who was, furthermore, a fully paid-up member of the Norwegian Communist party? Was there something in it for her? If the answer is yes, there is a further question: what did Sara Krefting get from you?'

Kai didn't answer.

The elegant woman at the adjacent table stood up and marched out. Jomar Kraby sat watching her, then turned back to Kai. 'Where were we?'

'You were asking about something, and I was keeping my mouth shut.'

'Exactly. Did you know that Sara Krefting knew your brother?'

Kai didn't answer.

'She was the one who supplied the weapons.'

'What kind of weapons?'

Kraby waved to the waiter, who rushed over. Kraby passed him a few banknotes and the waiter handed over the change.

Kraby waited until he had gone before continuing: 'If Sara

Krefting hasn't told you, I will. And if she has told you what I'm about to say, you'll have to put up with hearing it again. Your brother worked as an agent for the Abwehr. First he went to the Eastern Front with a regiment best known as the Fifth SS Panzer-Division Wiking. There, he killed Jews, gypsies and other bipeds the Nazis considered worthy of extermination, then was shot in the shoulder and officially rendered *hors de combat*. So he was sent back to Norway. As soon as he was at home and had recovered sufficiently, he started to cause mayhem for the war effort. As you know, he had a job on the railway. One thing he did was to infiltrate a Resistance group in Skarnes. They planned to move into the forest and go into training while waiting for the British invasion, but they didn't have any arms to train with. Your brother told them he could procure some. Sara Krefting hooked up with him; perhaps she devised the plan herself, who knows? At any rate she requisitioned eight Krag-Jørgensen rifles from her handler, Fritz Preiss. She passed the weapons on to your brother, who was supposed to pass them on to the Home Front in Skarnes. But when the Resistance boys were due to meet your brother and get the rifles, they only met German troops. It was five unarmed men against a unit of twenty soldiers. Shit odds. All five were arrested. Three of them were executed the same evening. By a firing squad in Trandum. One of the five is still in a concentration camp in Germany, and the last man died during torture in Grini. Did you know that?'

Kai shook his head. 'I don't believe it,' he said gruffly. 'My brother was a Nazi, but he wasn't heartless.'

'The eight rifles and the five men who were betrayed are the reason your brother's no longer alive.'

Kai said nothing. They eyed each other, and he didn't want to look away.

'One of Sara Krefting's opponents – I'm talking about a Norwegian who was involved in the Skarnes affair – was shot on the Norwegian side of the border recently. Do you know anything about that?'

Kai shook his head again. He could feel himself sweating now.

'The man who was shot was Daniel Berkåk. Does that name ring a bell?'

Kai shook his head again. His mouth was dry. He didn't want to speak. Or clear his throat or swallow. He didn't want to reveal his feelings.

'Berkåk knew a lot about the death of your brother,' Kraby smiled. 'His father was one of three men the Germans executed. So he was a convenient suspect for the Stapo. Their job was to catch the man who killed your brother.'

Kraby paused.

They were still eyeball to eyeball, and Kai was not going to give way.

'The man the Stapo considered the main suspect for the killing of your brother was found shot by the border,' Jomar Kraby said, still smiling. 'At about the same time as you appeared as a refugee – by the border.'

Now Kai had to clear his throat and swallow. 'What do you mean?'

'What do you think I mean, Kai?'

'I have no idea what happened to my brother, and I have no idea what you're talking about.'

'Did you shoot and kill a man by the border?'

'Is this your assignment? To solve a murder?'

Kraby didn't answer.

'Why?'

Kraby didn't answer.

'Is this Berkåk's death more important than my brother's? You're lying about Atle. You want me to believe he was a bad person. Why? To cast your assignment in a better light? My brother was killed, but you're as happy about his death as the king is. No one mourns the death of my brother; no one wants to avenge the injustice of it. Why not?'

'You have every right to mourn your brother, Kai. There you

have my full sympathy. It's reassuring to hear that blood's thicker than water, and I appreciate that you want to avenge an injustice, but you still haven't answered my question. Did you do that? Did you shoot and kill a man by the border?'

Kai's hands were trembling, and he gripped the edge of the table to hide it. He kept his mouth firmly shut.

The silence hung between them. They bored into each other's eyes. Kai still wouldn't look away.

'Know anything about Anarcharsis, the Greek philosopher?' Kraby asked.

'Should I?'

'You're a sailor, aren't you? Anarchasis considered that there were three types of human being: the living, the dead and the seafarer. The seafarer travels between the known and the unknown. All the time he is balancing on a thin line, always on the edge of the abyss.'

'What do you mean?'

Jomar leaned forward. 'Regardless of whether you shot Daniel Berkåk or not, you should know one thing: Berkåk did *not* kill your brother. Your brother was liquidated by the Home Front because he was an informer, or in other words, a rat. You can tell Sara Krefting that when you see her again.'

Kraby stood up.

'Why would I?' The inside of Kai's mouth felt like sand now.

Jomar looked down at him with the same grin playing on his lips. 'Kai,' he said in his wheezing voice. 'Sara Krefting's the kind of person who thinks she knows everything about your brother's death. Now you know more than she does. Get a taste of what that does to you.'

Jomar Kraby turned and left.

Kai sat watching him through the window in a state of paralysis. Thinking to himself that this man was not to be underestimated. His gimlet-eyed curiosity was both unpleasant and unwanted. First the questioning in Kjesåter. Then searching him out in Stockholm. He had stood outside spying on him,

he had followed him, he had been carrying out his own investigations. How much did Kraby know? What did it mean that
he knew anything? What would he do with whatever he knew?
Which led to the next question: what should he himself do
about Jomar Kraby? Or, to be more precise, when should he do
what he needed to do?

29

When Kai left the café, his legs decided for themselves where
he went. Thoughts were racing through his mind, vying with
his footsteps. Daniel Berkåk was gone forever, and here he was,
walking around a country untouched by war. Should he stick
to his word? Try to reach Scotland and join a Norwegian army?
Would that release the pressure on him? Would that give him
the peace of mind he needed? No. His top priority was to do
something about the meddling leech he had just spoken to.

As he swung round the corner by the Refugee Office, Gunvor
was coming out of the door. Kai stopped and leaned against a
building, waiting. He saw her exchange a few words with the
guard, then continue along the pavement.

Kai backed away a few metres and was motionless as she
passed on the crossing. He gave her a few metres and then
followed.

It wasn't long before she stopped and turned round.

'Hi,' she said, but her smile faded when she saw his expression.

'There's a guy bothering me,' Kai said.

Gunvor raised both eyebrows in surprise.

'Jomar Kraby. Who is he?'

'He's a writer, but here in Sweden he's a refugee like you.'

'Is he working for the Legation?'

'Why do you ask?'

'Because he searches me out and grills me.'

She said nothing.

'I want him to lay off, and you can do something about that.'

'I'll tell you something you might not know. It was Kraby who brought you here. Most refugees have to go to the forests and chop firewood for the Swedes. You were allowed to come here because he put in a good word for you.'

'Why would he do that?'

Gunvor shrugged. 'I think he did it to help you. Apparently, he knew your father.'

'I want him to leave me alone.'

'Tell him.'

'I have done, but he persists.' Kai produced the cutting about the investigation into Kåre Vardenær, unfolded it and showed her. Gunvor peered up without saying anything, but in her eyes there was an anxious expression.

'They're searching for Vardenær. His friends are. And they've gone to the police. Sooner or later the police will start focusing on you, perhaps they already have.'

Her eyes had an anxious expression now.

'Don't forget I know what happened.'

'What do you mean?'

'I want Jomar Kraby off my back.'

'What's he got to do with the case?'

'You and I saw a dead man in the attic, Gunvor. What do you think will happen if I tell the police what I know?'

Gunvor didn't answer at once, but her face was serious, and she weighed her words carefully.

'Kai, think before you open your mouth.'

'I always do. Just get that man to leave me in peace.'

'Remember what the three of us swore to each other. Go home and think about your mother and father, think about your comrades who fell in Spain, think about what happened to your brother. Go home and think, and come back to talk to me tomorrow.'

With that she turned and ran across the street, away from him.

Kai stood still watching the pretty woman, who seemed so carefree. There was something relaxed and clean about her as she strode down the pavement. But when she reached the corner of the street, she turned and stared at him with hunted eyes. He could feel the distance increasing between them. Then she was gone.

He was alone, Kai thought to himself. His mother and father were dead. Atle was dead. It was just him now. Just him in the whole, wide world. This was how he explained to himself that what he had done was right. Obviously, he would have to speak to Gunvor again, but she would have to think things over first. They would talk more the following day.

30

Jomar had wanted to explain the situation and bring his guns to bear on Kai Fredly. That was done now. He had achieved what he set out to do. Now he could reward himself with a glass of nectar and wait for a reaction.

Walking in through the door to the Anglais a little later, he espied his regular table and had barely sat down before a chair scraped on the floor opposite. He looked up and saw Pandora holding the chair. She looked wonderful with her long black hair cascading over her shoulders and her voluptuous figure swathed in a man's clothing, today a dinner jacket. Neither the jacket nor the white shirt was able to do anything other than enhance her figure, a captivating elasticity that would soon be marred by the rasp of her voice. Years of cigarette-smoking and many a glass of strong liquor had given her a huskiness that suited jazz and late nights, but now it was the middle of the day, and there was no grand piano to strike up a tune or create a mood. From her haughty glance and the angle of her hip he realised that she was not best pleased. And he was right. Her voice was particularly gruff as she slid down onto the chair and asked him where he had been.

'I haven't seen you for weeks.'

'Weeks?'

'Days then. I've knocked on your door at least three times.'

'I was in Norway.'

'Norway?'

Jomar raised a hand and motioned to the waiter to bring him a drink.

'With Hjørdis?' Pandora's voice was croakier than ever. She would have been a good mother; she would have been firm, strict. She wouldn't have let her child out of her sight for a second.

Jomar nodded. 'They send their best wishes. Both Hjørdis and Gunnar.'

'Both of them? The three of you were together?'

Jomar didn't answer. Instead, he cast around to see if there was anyone he could invite to their table to derail her. It was too early. There were no obvious candidates sitting at the tables around them.

'Gunnar's an arch Nazi. High-ranking. If he'd seen you, he would've had you arrested.'

'You believe too much of what you hear, Pandora.'

'I believe a lot, but there's one thing I know: Gunnar hates you.'

The waiter brought drinks for them both: beer for Jomar and red wine for her.

'They'll be punished when the war's over,' Pandora said.

'Gunnar will be, but not Hjørdis.'

She burst into laughter. 'Hjørdis will have to stand trial. She's making a film in Norway. Nazi propaganda.'

Jomar sat up. Hjørdis hadn't mentioned this. 'What kind of film?'

'At first, she was going to play Edvard Grieg's wife. Quisling and co wanted a film to celebrate the hundred-year jubilee this year. Nothing came of the Grieg film, but now she's going to play an Aryan in an expensive Viking production, and Gunnar's the director and producer.'

Jomar tried to hide his reaction behind the glass as he drank. Rumours were always circulating around Stockholm. Malicious rumours. And nowhere was this worse than among the artists in the Anglais. But Pandora could be right. Gunnar was a film producer, and he could have pressurised Hjørdis into accepting a role.

'After all, this is Oslo's Theatercafé in exile,' Pandora gloated. 'In a couple of hours the place will be full to the rafters with the crème de la crème of Norwegian actors. Loads of them have come to Sweden to avoid having to perform for the Nazis. Hjørdis stayed on in Oslo and now she's doing forced labour with her eyes wide open.'

Jomar didn't want any part of this conversation. Besides, he considered it too early in the day. There were other things he needed to establish some clarity on, so he couldn't stay here too long.

Pandora reached out an arm and stroked his cheek. 'Don't give it a thought. Don't let it upset you,' she said, getting up and walking to his side of the table. She perched on the chair next to him. She leaned forward and tenderly nuzzled his cheek, then straightened up and smiled. 'You have to forget Hjørdis, Jomar,' Pandora whispered. Her brown eyes softened, and a small hand slipped under his shirt cuff and gripped his arm. 'Hjørdis could've crossed the border like everyone else,' she whispered. 'Instead she's chosen to stay with that imbecile of a man. Can you and I be bothered to worry about that?'

Jomar smiled back at her. Worrying about Hjørdis was something he would never be able to stop doing, however much he wanted to. He raised his glass, expecting her to do the same, and drank up.

'One more?' she asked.

'Another time, Pandora. I have things to do. I'm going to Stocksund.'

'What are you going to do there?'

'Look for a woman,' he said without waiting for a reaction. He got up and walked out.

It was a sudden exit, but she was used to that, and soon others would be there to entertain her.

31

Jomar stepped off the trolley bus in Karlaplan and continued on foot to Banérgatan and the Press Office. Here he realised that rumours had preceded him. People sat up and exchanged glances as he entered and marched to the editor's office.

Sigurd Friis was sitting behind his desk, and he didn't so much as blink when Jomar told him what he wanted. Instead, he swivelled round and organised the matter with a telephone call.

Afterwards Jomar stood outside waiting on the pavement. The man who drove up was Borgar Stridsberg. Jomar got in the back. He asked Stridsberg if he knew the way to Stocksund.

Stridsberg opened the glove compartment and pulled out a map.

Jomar took out the piece of paper on which he had scribbled the address and passed it to him. 'This is a house owned by American Aid. Norwegian women are supposed to be quartered there.'

◈

The road led out of Stockholm. They raced along beneath the green treetops, and Jomar sat in silence. Perhaps, trammelled by his own sentimentality, he had been completely mistaken at the station in Oslo. Perhaps, deep down, Hjørdis had been happy that he was leaving her. If the rumours were true, she couldn't have been having an easy time. Just keeping from him what she had been forced to do must have come at a heavy cost. He felt a kind of sorrow or melancholy as he realised that despite the intimacy and tenderness they had shown each other in Oslo, they had probably both had to lie just to achieve that closeness.

◈

The impressive house stood on a ridge at the top of the road. Laughter and the buzz of voices reached them through the open windows, and on one of the windowsills sat a dusky-haired beauty reading a book, barefoot, wearing dark trousers and a summery yellow top.

Borgar Stridsberg was pensive and looked up. 'Maybe I should go with you, Jomar?'

'You'd only distract us. You'd better stay here.'

Broad steps led up to the building. The woman in the window waved, and Jomar responded by doffing his hat. A terrace revealed itself behind a low gate at the top of the steps. Here, around a table, sat a group of women, their heads bowed over their handiwork. Jomar stopped and watched them, fascinated as he had always been by knitting and the mystery of how individual stitches can, in skilled hands, evolve into functional adult clothing with intricate patterns.

The gate screeched as it opened. The four women looked up and said hello. Doffing his hat again and making his way towards the front of the building, he was reminded of when he went a-courting to a nurses' home in his youth. A brass bell hung outside the entrance. Jomar hardly had time to reach for it before the door was opened by a woman in her thirties, who introduced herself as the director. She had a narrow face under a haystack of pinned-up hair and a wry, knowing smile that Jomar liked and wanted to see more of.

'Jomar Kraby, exiled writer,' he said, without too much affected bashfulness.

'I know,' she said, stepping aside and holding the door open for him. 'I've seen several of your plays.'

The woman put Jomar in a good mood. 'Perhaps you can tell me what you think,' he said as immodestly as he could.

'*The Glowworm*. That's my favourite. I think I've seen it three times.'

A young girl came up the stairs behind them.

'Just fancy,' she said to the girl. 'We have a famous writer visiting us.'

'Fame is like old age,' Jomar replied with lowered eyes. 'It's a two-sided coin, and only the owner has the privilege of knowing both of them.'

'Says a man in the prime of his life,' she said, her eyes holding his, then took his coat and hung it on a hallstand.

It was a long time since a comment had warmed the cockles of his heart like this, and Jomar freely admitted, as they walked side by side, that his writing was not going so well now that he was in exile, but he had been lucky enough to find employment at the Norwegian Press Office. They had been asked by American Aid to write articles about people living here in Sweden for consumption back home – about their everyday lives and most of all their dramatic stories. The job was to hunt out the fates of ordinary people. So he wanted to speak to women who were willing to share their tales. Some he had already spoken to, but now he was looking for a woman from the Kongsvinger area.

They had reached a wide door.

'My office,' the director said, opening the door into a large, airy room with oak flooring and a solid desk placed judiciously between two tall windows.

Jomar stood inside the threshold, envious of both the desk and the atmosphere the light created as it flooded through the windows. In addition, he had to admire the woman's sense of order. On the desk there was a vase of lilies stretching for the light. She took a seat behind the desk and indicated the chair on the other side. Jomar pinched the creases of his trousers and sat down.

The director opened a drawer and took out a ledger, which she leafed through while telling him that they had almost thirty women in residence. There were many dramatic stories. Three of the girls were Jewish and had managed to escape before the deportations the previous autumn. She opened the book and ran a finger down one page, then the next.

'No one from the Kongsvinger area, I'm afraid. What about a genuine Trondheimer? A Nordlander? A sweet young lady from Bergen who, furthermore, likes to write poetry?'

Jomar put on his saddest expression.

'Have you been to Kumla Manor?'

He hadn't.

'They have single women with children there. The last time I visited I met a lovely girl from Magnor, Jenny Enersen, who lives there with her four-year-old daughter.'

'There you go,' Jomar said with a smile. 'But I must write something about this place too. Would you mind showing me round?'

◈

When Jomar took his leave after half an hour, he promised to return if the trip to Kumla proved to be unsuccessful.

After walking down the steps to the gate he found the woman from the windowsill sitting in the passenger seat of the car, being entertained by Borgar Stridsberg.

Jomar cleared his throat.

She opened the door and shot out.

Once they were on their way again, Stridsberg told him that he had been to Kumla Manor on jobs a couple of times. It was on the other side of Stockholm.

Jomar remembered that Arnfinn Bråtan had mentioned that a widow from Magnor had travelled north at more or less the same time that Atle Fredly disappeared. How many young widows can there be in such a small place in Norway? At the same time it struck him that a bit of background information about Jenny Enersen could be handy before they met face to face. So he asked Stridsberg to stop outside the Refugee Office.

Inside, Torgersen was on his own and about to leave for the

day. Jomar enquired whether they had a register detailing all the names of refugees. They did, and Torgersen walked over to the filing system behind Gunvor's desk. He pulled out drawer after drawer. In the end he looked up. 'Sure that's the right name?'

'She's supposed to have a four-year-old daughter.'

Torgersen went through the cabinet again, but slammed the last drawer shut and shook his head. They didn't have a Norwegian woman registered under the name of Jenny Enersen.

Jomar deliberated. Could the Stocksund director have mis-remembered?

'What's the issue with this woman?' Torgersen asked, putting on his coat.

'I'm trying to trace the woman who sold black-market coffee to Atle Fredly.'

Torgersen was watching him pensively.

'What's the matter?'

'Svinningen's written a letter expressing his concern about you.'

'Who to?'

'London. He considers that you're meddling in matters that have nothing to do with you. Actually I don't think he's that in-terested in you, but he's using your interest in the Atle Fredly murder to discredit me.'

Jomar gave this some thought. 'Do you think there's any chance he'll succeed?' he said at length.

'I don't know, but let me put it this way: you will soon have to come up with some results. It's becoming urgent – for both of us. So I hope your focus on Fredly isn't a wild-goose chase. What makes you think this Jenny Enersen is in Sweden when her name isn't even registered?'

'I can feel it in my bones. It's worth investigating anyway.'

Torgersen shook his head and smiled sardonically. 'A woman who sold coffee on the black market. What do you think, Jomar? Was she a decoy or the executioner? Or does she really exist at all?'

32

Back in the rear seat of the car, Jomar turned his mind to Svinningen. When he had taken on this job, his express intention had been not to be drawn into legation intrigues. As if a cork could float up rapids, he thought now. Intrigue ruled in Stockholm. If Svinningen chose to use Jomar as a lever to improve his standing in the legation hierarchy, the best thing he could do was to solve the case. Draw a line under it. And smack it into Svinningen's smarmy mug.

However, he wasn't feeling particularly optimistic on his way to see a woman who probably didn't exist. Instead of finding clear answers he was uncovering new mysteries. What could the significance be of a woman who hasn't registered as a refugee?

Stridsberg drove via Södermalm and then on to Farsta. From there it was only a few minutes to Hanviken and the manor, which stood by the shore of Lake Dreviken.

The main building loomed up at the end of an avenue of immense linden trees. The roof was broken by three dormer windows, the central one sited precisely above the pillar-adorned front entrance.

Jomar, who with his upbringing in heavily forested Hadeland had learned to categorise social rank according to winter-wood consumption, counted four chimneys as he got out of the car. There were two smaller constructions on either side of the main building, once the residences of the housekeeper or the gardener. Presumably it had lost its status as a manor now that the place functioned as a residence for single mothers fleeing Norway.

The door was opened by a matron dressed in a blue-striped pinafore and a white cap. She led the way through the building and out onto a veranda on the opposite side.

Shouts and laughter rang out from children playing as Jomar stopped to take in the sight of this idyllic garden. It, too, gleamed with the splendour of the manor's past. A shingle path wreathed by low box hedges cut an axis through the garden's layout. Halfway, it widened into a circle with a flagpole in the centre. Here three benches had been placed around a table.

Jomar had to smile at the little girl leaning her forehead against the pole and covering her eyes as she counted aloud while her friends dashed away and hid behind the fading rhododendrons.

He stood on the steps, watching the group of women who had gathered on the benches. They didn't notice his presence, preoccupied as they were with their own activities.

Jomar didn't move.

One of them finally raised her head. Her dark hair was held in place with slides and pins. She was in her late thirties, wore a plain blue dress and had an attractive face, which had now assumed a hunted expression.

You, Jomar thought at that moment. *You* have been waiting for the day a man would appear in this doorway looking for someone – someone who didn't belong here.

Jomar raised his hat and bowed when she stood up.

Motionless, they studied each other. Her dress reached down to mid-calf, and she was wearing flat walking shoes. Her forearms were pale white and her hands red from scrubbing and hard graft. Her pinned-up hair revealed her neck and her vulnerability.

The little girl by the flagpole had become aware that something was happening. She went over to her mother. 'Mamma, what is it?'

Jomar descended the steps. He heard the mother tell her daughter to go and play.

'Jenny Enersen?'

The woman nodded. Her face was open, charming, and he imagined that if this woman smiled, the snow around her would melt. But a smile was not forthcoming. Now she seemed anxious rather than curious.

'This is about a consignment of coffee,' Jomar said, trusting that he was holding a trump in his hand, and elaborated:

'Maybe from Brazil or Ethiopia. 'You might know because this coffee was advertised in Kongsvinger at about the time you left town.'

If her expression had been hunted before, now she seemed scared out of her wits. 'Who are you?'

'Jomar Kraby, a bankrupt poet and at present a delegate for the exiled Norwegian government in London.'

'What's the matter, Jenny?' asked the overweight Swedish matron who had joined them.

Jomar assumed she represented the staff at this place.

'Nothing,' Jenny said to the matron and turned her back on her. 'It's nothing.'

The other women didn't pay any attention to them. They were talking in low voices, and one of them giggled at something another said.

Jenny looked Jomar in the eye. 'I have no idea what you're talking about.'

'You come from Magnor, don't you?'

'I do.'

'And you fled to this country with your daughter just over six months ago?'

'Correct.'

'Why?'

'That's none of your business. We have nothing to talk about, Kraby.'

'On the contrary, Jenny.'

'We have nothing to talk about, and you know that very well, especially if you're representing Norwegian authorities.'

Now the other women had finally begun to take an interest in the conversation.

'Jenny, aren't you going to introduce your gentleman friend to us?'

'He's leaving,' she said. 'I'll see him out.'

She set off, and Jomar happily followed her along the shingle, up the steps, through the impressive house and out at the opposite side. Here she stopped, turned on her heel with an elegance he could not help but admire, then stared him defiantly in the eye.

'Your name isn't Jenny,' he said. 'No Jenny from Magnor, with or without a daughter, has been through Kjesäter.'

The determined expression on her face slipped. The fear in her blue eyes was visible. 'What do you want? Why have you come here?'

'You must be registered under another name.'

She said nothing.

'What's your name?'

She still refused to answer.

Jomar chanced his arm again: 'Officially, you travelled to northern Norway. Sooner or later I'll find out what your name is, whether you want me to or not.'

It worked. She had to lean against the pillar.

'OK,' he said quickly. 'Naturally we can call you Jenny. You were the last person to see Atle Fredly alive. Do you know what that means?'

No response even now.

'You may find yourself under suspicion of having murdered him,' Jomar said in a low voice. 'However, I don't think you did. I believe you got in the car to show Fredly the way to the man waiting for you both. You can make things better for yourself by telling me the name of the man who was waiting for you and Fredly. The rat-catcher.'

'I have no idea what you're babbling on about.'

She eyed him defiantly again until Jomar looked away and raised his hat as he left. 'As you wish, Jenny.'

'Wait,' she said suddenly. 'Please don't start any rumours.'

'Rumours?'

'About Jenny Enersen living here. I was promised I'd be allowed to live my life in peace. If you are who you say you are, you'll keep the promise I was made.'

Jomar Kraby nodded. 'I need the name of the man.'

'I'm not allowed to say anything.'

She held his arm as she spoke.

Jomar nodded. He took a business card from his pocket. 'Contact me if you change your mind.'

As he walked to the car, she read the card.

'Kraby,' she called.

He turned.

'No rumours,' she said. 'Promise me there won't be any.'

Jomar didn't answer. As she hadn't given him anything, she didn't deserve anything in return. He got in the car and met Borgar's eyes in the mirror.

'Drive.'

33

As Kai entered the door of the boarding house, making for the stairs up to the first floor, someone whistled. The owner was standing behind the counter in the lobby and beckoned Kai over.

'Yes?'

The man turned to the wall, took an envelope from one of the pigeon-holes and passed it to him. 'A lady,' he said with an enigmatic wink. 'She came here asking after you.'

Kai thought about the meeting with Gunvor earlier in the day. 'Norwegian?'

The man shook his head. 'As Swedish as me.'

Kai tore open the envelope as he went upstairs, but waited until he was sitting on the bed in his room to read the letter.

It was written on thin paper. The name of the boarding house was printed in the top, left-hand corner.

Dear Kai,

I owe you an apology. Obviously, I don't wish to push you into doing things you don't want to do. When we were talking, the conversation turned out all wrong. Actually, there was something else

I wanted to ask you about. If you want the same as me, we can draw a line under what happened and meet again. We can go to Mona Lisa. Let's meet outside the restaurant this evening. I'll be waiting for you at eight.

Best wishes,

Iris

Kai re-read the letter several times. 'Best wishes.' 'Draw a line under what happened.' 'I'll be waiting for you.'

He looked at his watch. It was getting on for eight now. In fifteen minutes Iris would be waiting for him. What did she imagine? That he would drop everything and run like crazy to meet her? The Iris who threw him out when another man knocked at the door? Who lied about a fiancé to keep him at arm's length? Why had she come here? What was suddenly so important that she had to ask him about it? 'I don't wish to push you into…' What did she mean by that? She had certainly been curious about Sara Krefting. But *push*?

He re-read the letter. 'Actually, there was something else I wanted to ask you about.' Iris had come here to talk to him. As he wasn't here, she had asked for a piece of paper to leave him a message.

Was she only after information or was she actually interested in him? Why did she want to meet at Mona Lisa? At the restaurant where the head waiter had given her the bum's rush?

No, Kai decided. Iris can wait. After all, he had knocked on her door in vain for days. Now she could have a taste of her own medicine.

Kai stretched out on the bed. And stared at the ceiling without moving.

When he did finally sit up and look at his watch, it was nine o'clock. For more than an hour he had thought of nothing but her, and if he was sure of one thing it was that Iris had been thinking of nothing but him.

34

For Jomar there was little more comforting than watching animals eat. He felt the need to let recent events sink in, so he considered going to the island of Djurgården, to Skansen Zoo to be precise, to watch the bison ruminating. For convenience, however, on this morning, he chose to do the next-best thing: walk to the harbour to feed the pigeons. This was a contemplative exercise. He strolled unhurriedly, his hands behind his back. Felt the rounded cobblestones under the worn leather of his soles, promenaded alongside the water and admired the massive, baroque constructions from autocratic days.

Jomar didn't understand Norwegians who were irritated by the Swedes' lack of humility with regard to the war. He liked being in Stockholm, in a world where life takes its usual course. Being able to amble along, stop, like now, and watch a woman taking her poodle for a walk. The dog came to an abrupt halt, startled by another dog barking some distance away. The woman stopped too. Both stood sniffing the air to see if the danger had passed before deciding it was safe for them to continue their perambulations. A refugee's first and most invigorating consolation, Jomar thought, was to discover that time can pass peacefully. He found himself a free bench and strewed bits of rusk around for the pigeons as the sun warmed his brow.

He was sitting with his hand in a bag, cooing pigeons around his feet, when two legs stopped in front of him. He raised his head and saw Gunvor standing there, carrying a basket on her arm. It resembled the one his mother used to take on country walks when he was small.

'Can I sit beside you?'

'By all means,' Jomar said, making room for her. 'Are you going for a picnic?'

'I've been invited to go swimming.'

'Invited?'

She smiled with embarrassment.

Jomar realised he wasn't going to be informed who the lucky person was. Instead, Gunvor said she had knocked on his door, but his neighbour told her that sometimes herr Kraby took a bag of rusks to feed pigeons on Sundays. 'So I've come to where most of the pigeons in town are.'

'Good job you did.'

'Why's that?'

'I wanted to ask you a favour.'

'I came to ask *you* something.'

Jomar looked up, his curiosity piqued.

'You first,' she said.

'I'd like to know the name of the man who was hired to take out Atle Fredly. Could you do me that favour?'

'I can't imagine how I could.'

'I'm pretty sure there's one man who could,' Jomar said, scattering the remains of the rusks and scrunching up the bag. 'The man defying the government-in-exile's warning not to take up arms against the Germans. The man leading his own guerrilla army into armed combat back in Norway.'

'Osvald?'

Jomar nodded.

'Why do you think he knows?'

'Because the Home Front go to him when they need someone silenced.'

'That's just your opinion about what happens.'

'Svinningen confirmed it for me. Osvald was given the job, and he delegated it to one of his people. And that's where you come in, Gunvor. Osvald organised the raid on the brothel in Universitetsgata. You were on that one. You know him.'

She fell silent.

Jomar smiled.

'What is it?' Gunvor said.

'What went wrong on that occasion?'

'It's not easy to say.'

Jomar tilted his head.

'We had a table on the first floor of the restaurant,' she said. 'We ate for about an hour. Drank too. Bit too much, in fact. I was as nervous as a cat. The bomb was in a suitcase we'd brought with us. Apparently, it was a new invention, a mixture of dynamite and petrol. That was what Osvald talked about during the meal. Under the cork was a rag soaked in sodium chlorate mixed with sugar. If the bottle was turned upside down, the acid would come into contact with the rag and ignite. When we left, he turned the suitcase upside down, but someone found it before it went off, because the petrol leaked out.'

They sat in silence, watching the pigeons swarming around their legs.

'Now I'm just glad it went wrong,' she said in a low voice.

'Are you going to do me the favour?'

'I don't mean to appear difficult, but I can't see how I can make any enquiries. Whenever he comes to Stockholm, he never drops by our office.'

'Osvald regularly receives post from the Russian Embassy. A letter from Madame Kollontai goes through several staging posts. One's called Orina and the next is Gunvor.'

She said nothing.

'Use your imagination, Gunvor. You know the royal motto: "All for Norway."'

Gunvor still didn't utter a word. They both stared mutely into the distance until he patted her knee and said: 'It'd be nice if you tried, Gunvor. I'd appreciate it.'

Her silence persisted.

'You wanted to ask *me* something,' he said.

'I'd like you to be gentle with the brother,' she said, getting up.

'The brother?'

'Kai. He's fragile. Don't push him too hard.'

Jomar smiled and looked at her. 'Tell me why.'

It was clear she was burning to say something but struggling to find the words.

'Gunvor?'

'We went to the same school.'

'Then you know the boy's anything but fragile.'

Gunvor placed the basket over her arm and took her leave.

Jomar sat admiring her attractive figure. She didn't look back as she crossed the street, and he wondered what she wasn't telling him. She had been to his lodgings, then she had gone looking for him, but she hadn't told him the reason.

35

Gunvor had wanted to ask Jomar to keep away from Kai, but she had changed her mind. It would be wrong to give in to Kai's pressure. She and Borgar had to sort this out between themselves. They had to take Kai aside and stress that they were all in it together when it came to the incident in the attic. They had to knock some sense into him.

When she got onto the bus, it was almost empty. A little later, after Torsvik, she was the only passenger left. As this area was unfamiliar to her, she had sat behind the driver so as not to miss her stop. The driver often addressed a few words to her, but they were lost in the roar of the engine and the wind from the open window. Nevertheless, she nodded and smiled whenever she met his gaze in the mirror. At length, the bus stopped.

'Here you are, love,' he said, indicating with his hand and opening the door.

Gunvor got off. There was a man at the stop waiting for her. He was in his forties, wearing black trousers, a white shirt and no socks on his sandalled feet. He led the way to a quay where an elegant, narrow mahogany boat was moored.

The man helped her on board. Gunvor sat on the stern seat, unsure what to do, especially as the man didn't speak. But the archipelago was showing its best side, the sea-smoothed rocks glittered and the sun was reflected in the water, which was as still as a pond.

The man, with admirable sea-legs, balanced on the gunwale, loosened the mooring rope and shoved off. He started the engine, and it purred into action. The hull trembled as they slowly reversed out, then he turned the bow into the bright sunlight. Gunvor took her dark glasses from the basket and put them on as the slender powerboat picked up speed and rose out of the water.

Further out, the sea was choppy, and the waves began to buffet the boat. The sunglasses weren't much use against the fine shower that sprayed her face, and she regretted not having brought a headscarf to keep her hair in place. The wind ruffled and tore at her curls. So she sat holding on to her hair with one hand while clinging to the gunwale with the other.

Soon the boat slowed down and they approached a wooded island, which had to be Storholmen. Once again the sea was as smooth as a pond. The man cut the engine and stepped onto the foredeck while the boat glided alongside the stone quay. He jumped ashore, tied up and stretched out a hand for Gunvor. She flipped off her shoes and allowed him to help her onto the quay. All went well. He jumped back on board to fetch her basket while she put her shoes on.

Beneath a shelter, there was a kind of rickshaw, a bicycle with a little cart behind, containing a seat with a sunroof above. The man pointed to the vehicle. Gunvor followed his instructions and sat down, then the silent man pedalled up a broad avenue to an immense house. Gunvor felt like nobility somewhere in the Orient, sitting in the shade and watching as the man's white shirt stuck to his back while the pedals creaked as they revolved. She also felt stupid. She could easily have walked this part.

Having arrived at the impressive house, he jumped down from the rickshaw and led the way into the garden. He motioned to her to wait. Gunvor put down the basket and marvelled at the profusion of flowers framing the pond and the fountain. On either side of the water there were pergolas with clematis and honeysuckle clinging to the supports. The house itself was like a palace, with wings and annexes. In front of the central building was a terrace surrounded by a stone wall. Virginia creeper twined around the railings and climbed up between the windows, covering large parts of the tall façade.

Soon the gravel crunched, and Orina strolled over. She was wearing summery apparel – a short-sleeved blouse, a tight skirt down to mid-calf and sandals.

Gunvor was embarrassed and quickly realised that Orina felt the same. To lighten the atmosphere she showed Orina the contents of her basket: the picnic and the bottles of juice and water.

In a surge of enthusiasm, Orina slanted her head and took a step forward. As if on command they moved into an embrace, so clumsily that they almost banged heads. They both burst into laughter and then hugged each other again, this time without any problems.

Orina guided her though the park, which seemed like an extension of the garden, planted with roses and rhododendrons. The path led down to the water. Here they continued over the rocks to a sheltered spot, where Orina spread a rug.

From very early morning Gunvor had dreaded the thought of changing her clothes. She felt small and round compared with Orina, who was long-legged and lithe. Orina didn't seem at all bashful. Without any hesitation she undid the zip at the side and let her skirt fall, unbuttoned her blouse, smiled and winked, then turned and, with her back to Gunvor, kicked off her panties and slipped into her swimsuit. Gunvor tried to do the same, but felt awkward and inelegant and struggled to keep her balance. As she was trying to pull her swimsuit up over her hips she almost fell over and was so embarrassed that her cheeks burned, sensing that Orina was behind her watching. When she eventually turned, Orina stretched out a hand, stroked her shoulder and said she was beautiful. Gunvor felt a warm flush inside and was unable to respond. She gripped Orina's slim hand, thinking she would never let it go as they walked down to the water together. Here she had to put on bathing shoes, and again she felt stupid as Orina climbed barefoot onto the high rock and dived in. Her body was like a brushstroke against the sky until it broke the surface of the sea. Gunvor was impressed and waited for her to reappear. It took time. Orina swam a long way under the water before she reappeared.

Gunvor had never felt secure in the sea and couldn't bear the thought of submerging her head. As she waded out, she found her fears of the sea temperature confirmed. She held in her stomach, concentrated on not uttering any sounds, then closed her eyes, defied the cold and fell forward with a sharp intake of breath. When she could no longer feel the seabed under her feet, she swam a few strokes to control her panic. Orina was nowhere to be seen.

Finally Orina's head bobbed up again. Her hair was stuck to her scalp and drops of water hung from her eyelashes as she gasped for air. Gunvor trod water, but all her movements stopped when she felt Orina's cool lips against her own. Then she sank. And, for the first time, Gunvor experienced happiness while being submerged. Again she could have been gripped by panic, if she had not felt Orina's hands in hers.

Afterwards, lying side by side with Orina on the grass, she closed her eyes and felt the droplets of water on her skin slowly evaporating in the sun. When she felt a light touch on her back, she opened her eyes and met Orina's ice-blue gaze. 'What is it?'

'Where are you going to say you've been today when your boss asks?'

Gunvor considered carefully before replying. 'Here.'

Orina smiled.

'The Legation's investigating a death on the border with Norway,' Gunvor said. 'A Norwegian courier was killed.'

'What's that got to do with you and me?'

Gunvor told her that one of the people working on the case was Jomar Kraby. 'He reckons the murder's connected with the liquidation of an informer in Norway: Atle Fredly. Kraby thinks

Osvald knows who was responsible and asked me to use the postal delivery to find the name.'

'How?'

'Get your boss to ask Osvald to release the name of the liquidator.'

Orina lowered her gaze.

'What's the matter?'

'Was that why you came here?'

'No.'

'No?'

'You were the one who invited me.'

And then it just happened. They kissed again, and Gunvor trembled with emotion as they looked each other in the eye.

'If he wants something,' Orina said. 'He'll have to offer something in return.'

'Such as what?'

'How should I know? This is like shopping. If you buy a loaf of bread, you need money, don't you. Kraby understands that. He'll have to work out for himself how much information from us is worth.'

Gunvor said nothing. The reasoning seemed fair enough to her, but she wanted to be wholly present, here and now, not thinking about Jomar Kraby. And she could see Orina wanted the same.

36

After the pigeons had eaten the last crumbs, Jomar got up from the bench and threw the bag in the litter bin on the nearby lamppost. Then he rummaged through his coat pocket for an object he had been holding on to. Actually, he should have returned Daniel Berkåk's flat key to Gunvor. He fingered it pensively.

Arnfinn Bråtan had found a train ticket in Berkåk's pocket.

It showed that Berkåk had taken the train to Arvika, as he always did. From there, presumably, he had cycled to the border, as he always did – but had then, on this occasion, chosen a different route from his normal one.

Arnfinn thought the explanation for this was that Berkåk had not been alone; he had chosen a different route so as not to give away the usual procedure to whoever he was with. Arnfinn might be right, but Jomar wanted proof. If he was to find any, there was only one logical place to start the search. Accordingly, he strolled off to catch a bus to Hammarby.

◈

He began in Daniel Berkåk's bedroom. Here he examined the wardrobe, the bed, the bedclothes, the mattress and the pillow. He inspected the mattress for new seams and squeezed the pillow and duvet. All without luck. At the top of the wardrobe there was a shelf he hadn't checked properly the last time he had been here. He fetched a chair from the sitting-room and mounted it for a better view. There was a pile of clothes. Jomar grabbed them, went through the pockets and turned the socks inside out. Nothing.

After he was finished in the bedroom, he scoured the sitting room. Turned the armchair upside down and checked between the springs. Scrutinised the back for signs of new stitching. Pored over the desk. Peered behind the curtains. Stepped carefully on every plank in the floor to see if one was loose. Nothing.

In the bathroom he opened the cupboard and went through everything, but all he found was towels and toilet paper. He fetched the chair again. Stood on it and removed the top of the cistern on the wall above the lavatory. Ran his hand through the water, touching the sides and the bottom. Nothing, needless to say.

In the end, there was only the kitchenette left. He opened

the cooking-utensils cupboard, looked inside every pot, lifted the gas rings and peered underneath. Examined the cupboard under the sink, took out the bucket and bottle of detergent. Nothing.

Then he repeated the previous procedure of bouncing on the individual planks in the floor. By the wall one plank gave a few millimetres. He bounced on it again. There was definitely some give.

In the kitchenette drawer he found a knife. He knelt down. With the knife firmly inserted in the crack beside the loose plank, all he had to do was flip it upward. The plank was about half a metre long and covered a hollow.

Inside, there was a folded envelope. With beads of sweat forming on his forehead, he stood up and opened it.

The documents were written in code. These papers were meant for the Norwegian Home Front, but Daniel Berkåk had left without them and chosen a different route from the usual one. So Arnfinn was right: Berkåk had not been alone.

Jomar wondered what to do next. Should he take the documents to Peder Svinningen or Ragnar Torgersen? He opted to wait. If, in time, he was able to finger Daniel's murderer, these documents would be proof. So he put the envelope back. Replaced the plank, got up and left the flat reassured.

◈

Half an hour later, he opened the jangling door of the Anglais and looked straight into the face of Pandora. Wearing a cloth cap and knickerbockers, a workman's shirt and braces, blood-red lipstick and white gloves, she looked very appealing.

'You owe me a beer,' she said.

'Do I?'

'When you ran off last night, you left me to pay the bill.'

'So let me make up for that,' he said, drawing a chair out for her.

37

There was a large, mud-caked magpie's nest in the treetop on the opposite side of the street, at roughly the same height as the window. Even though twigs stuck out in all directions, Kai knew that the inside would be as warm and inviting as any other bird's nest. The architecture and building style were a mystery, and the skills required had to be peculiar to the magpie as a species, he reflected. Every magpie in the world takes coarse twigs and makes the same kind of messy dome with the same internal structure. This was what it was like to have no purpose in a foreign land: you stand gawping through a window musing about a bird's building skills.

Kai turned away, still full of regrets. He should have gone to meet Iris the previous day. He donned his jacket to go out and clear his mind.

Outside, the weather had changed. A fine drizzle was falling from the sky as he opened the door and walked down the stairs to ground level. He flipped up his lapels and ambled along the deserted pavement in Östermalmsgatan. A sudden impulse made him glance over his shoulder. He saw a figure hastily crossing to the opposite pavement. There was something about the man's bearing. A hat drawn down over his eyes. Bent forward in a loping run.

Kai was approaching the park by St John's church. He noted that his legs had found the way there without any help from him. Iris lived a few blocks away. Should he turn round or carry on?

Once again he thought he could hear footsteps behind him, but he was alone as he crossed the street and walked into the park, which was also a cemetery. Between the gravestones it was dark. When he heard footsteps behind him, he walked faster. He was close to the church now and the steps leading up to it. Then he stopped and turned around.

No one.

Kai was out of breath, and again he thought about the man who had crossed the street behind him, but here he was alone with the trees. The trunks were black in the twilight. Rain dripped from the brim of his hat, and he wondered why anyone would be following a poor refugee. Nevertheless, he decided to stand still for one long minute to be sure. It was as he was about to place a foot on the lowest step that someone whistled behind him. Kai went to turn, and the next thing he knew he was lying in the gravel and could feel moisture seeping through the back of his trousers. It was then he noticed the pain in his cheek. His jacket rucked up as he was dragged through the gravel by his legs. The man let go, and Kai got to his feet and fled up the steps, but the man behind him was quick. At the top of the steps Kai was tripped from behind and fell flat on his face. His knees burned like fire, but again he got to his feet. Or almost. He tried to duck a flurry of punches but was forced to his knees. He glanced left and caught a glimpse of a shoe sole. It struck him on the side of the head, and everything went black for a few seconds.

When he reopened his eyes, he was lying on his stomach and could feel a knee in his back.

'I've killed before, Kai,' said a voice that sounded familiar. 'The only reason you're still breathing is that Gunvor asked me to spare your life, but if you so much as whisper a word about what happened while I was with you, you're a stiff. Got that?'

Kai gasped for air and twisted onto his back. He lay, looking up at Borgar Stridsberg, who had grabbed his lapels.

Kai heard rather than felt his head hit the ground.

'Answer me. Yes or no?'

Stridsberg released him. That gave Kai the second he needed. Summoning all the strength he had in his stomach and chest, he thrust the top of his skull forward in a headbutt. And made contact. Stridsberg held his face with both hands, cursed and straightened up. Kai was immediately on his feet. Stridsberg backed away. Kai's arms were firing like pistons. His knuckles smarted from the blows.

Dizzy, Kai stopped and almost fell headlong.

Stridsberg kicked out at Kai, but missed.

Then they heard a whistle in the distance, and from the corner of his eye he caught sight of a policeman running towards them.

'Cops,' he shouted to Stridsberg, limping across the grass and past the bell tower.

Stridsberg came up behind him and ran ahead. 'Follow me,' he shouted.

Kai obeyed, thinking that perhaps this wasn't such a great idea – the smartest move would have been to go separate ways, but he wanted to conclude this confrontation with Borgar Stridsberg once and for all. So he followed him, panting for breath and tasting blood in his mouth.

They ran down a long, steep set of steps. Kai concentrated furiously so as not to stumble. At the bottom Stridsberg turned into the opening of a tunnel. With Kai hard on his heels. They ran inside until Stridsberg stopped in the darkness.

Kai took a handkerchief from his jacket pocket and wiped his face. 'Where are we going?'

'Shh,' Borgar whispered. 'He's coming.'

Then Kai saw the policeman at the entrance to the tunnel. The oval opening was blue against the darkness. The policeman stared into the gloom, then briskly walked towards them.

Kai squeezed back against the wall.

The footsteps were coming closer, and Kai held his breath.

When the policeman passed, Kai could have stuck out a hand and touched him if he had wanted.

The policeman stopped and switched on a torch. A powerful beam of light shone down the tunnel and swept across the walls. What was he doing? Kai was sure the man must have seen him.

The policeman switched off the torch. It was pitch-black again. The man was invisible. But his breathing was audible. Soon footsteps were audible too. And at length the policeman appeared as a silhouette against the blue opening. The silhouette became smaller and smaller until it and the sound of boots on the ground were gone.

'I think he saw us,' Kai said in a whisper.

Stridsberg ignored him. 'You've disappointed me,' he whispered. 'Threatening Gunvor like that. Don't you think she has a past too? You have to show people here more respect. Gunvor was in the big battle.'

'Which big battle?'

'August last year. With the Stapo.'

'Was she involved in that?'

Borgar nodded. 'Osvald broke into the Stapo rooms in the middle of the night. He went up to the fifth floor where the torturers did their work and attached an explosive to a telephone. When the Gestapo boss, Reinhardt, rang the Stapo the next day to requisition some muscle to beat up arrested patriots, the whole place was blown to smithereens. That's why Gunvor had to escape to Sweden.'

'What was her role?'

'She's a legal assistant and worked for the lawyer who managed the house-owner's business. In the office they had access to the keys for the whole building. The night the boys broke in and set the device, Gunvor was on her way across the border. The point, Kai, is that we're all in the same boat. There isn't one Norwegian who's here in Sweden without a good reason. However hard fate has been on you, you're no more entitled to feel sorry for yourself than anyone else.'

Kai sensed that Stridsberg wasn't finished and refrained from answering.

'Torgersen's decided to employ you,' he whispered.

'Perhaps I make my own decisions about where I work…' Kai whispered back.

'You have no choice.'

'Does he know?'

'Does he know what?'

'Does he know what happened?'

'No one but you, Gunvor and I know,' Borgar hissed. 'And that's the way it's going to stay. We'll carry this secret to our graves. Come on.'

Kai followed him. They walked down the tunnel and out the other side. They came out by Humlegården.

Stridsberg showed the way to a parked car, which he unlocked. 'Take the wheel.'

'Me?'

'Can't you drive?'

'Yes, I can.'

'Then get in.'

Kai felt his face smart with pain but got in anyway.

Borgar sat next to him.

'You look terrible,' Kai said.

'Not as bad as you.'

Kai studied his face in the mirror. He was right. He did look worse, but he had a handkerchief in his pocket and wiped his face again. It seemed to help.

'Banérgatan and the Legation,' Stridsberg said.

Stridsberg raised his arms in horror as Kai began to drive.

'What's the matter?' Kai shouted. He saw headlights flashing ahead of him and heard cars hooting their horns.

Borgar grabbed hold of the wheel and wrenched it to the left. 'You're in Sweden, lad. We drive on the left here.'

38

Pandora was breathing quietly and regularly. Her black hair cascaded over the pillow and one of her curls tickled his nose. His thoughts wouldn't leave him in peace, and Jomar had enough experience to realise that tonight it was likely to be several hours before he slept. Sometimes stubborn trains of thoughts made a night owl of him, which he both accepted and liked. So he got up, as soundlessly as he could.

The best work he had written had been at night. Night has a power. Night makes the world your own, and it re-shapes you in the same way that it re-shapes the universe. Objects change form and character, emotions have greater strength, truth is distorted and lies make themselves seem attractive. The loneliness of the night brings death closer.

In the light of a candle, he sat down on the sofa, placed a map of Sweden on the table and spread it out. He found the railway line running west and the stations. Daniel Berkåk had taken the train from Stockholm to Arvika. From there he had cycled to the border. Usually, he would have crossed by Austmarka, but Arnfinn Bråtan had found Berkåk's body near Lake Leir, a good bit further south. He could, therefore, have cycled to Charlottenberg, on the border, but Jomar doubted it. He followed the route on the map with his finger. The few densely populated areas along the border were swarming with police on both sides. Any courier would cross where there were fewer patrols, in the forest. Presumably Berkåk cycled on smaller farm and cart tracks south of Charlottenberg. He must have left his bike somewhere near the border and continued on foot.

Berkåk's job was to smuggle underground newspapers, weapons, money and documents across the border. Bumping into the police or soldiers was a calculated risk every single time, but this particular occasion was quite different. To be sure the documents didn't fall into enemy hands, he had left them in the flat. The plan must have been to overpower his adversary when they were both in Norway. If he had attacked his travel companion in Sweden, the case would have ended up in the hands of the Swedish police. Something took place on the Norwegian side and had a fatal outcome. And it was Berkåk who found himself overpowered, not his adversary.

Why had things gone so wrong? Could it have been because Kai Fredly turned up at the border? Fredly was the only person with a clear motive for killing Berkåk. Could it be chance that Kai Fredly appeared when he did?

If it *wasn't* chance, the reason for his presence in Sweden had to be that he wanted to meet Berkåk and kill him, but how could Kai Fredly have known where Berkåk would cross the border? No one knew the route in advance. In addition, Berkåk had decided on a different route from his usual one. This was an extremely important question: how could Kai Fredly have known where Daniel Berkåk would appear?

Could Kai Fredly really have shot and killed Berkåk? Or could there have been two people involved? Could Berkåk's travel companion have been Kai Fredly's accomplice, a man who forced Berkåk to make for a point where Fredly was waiting for him? Could that be how Berkåk was outmanoeuvred? If it was, it must have been Berkåk's travel companion who decided which route he would take. Was that likely?

Jomar could feel he was getting somewhere, but he lacked information. He closed his eyes and leaned back, but his peace was immediately broken. The telephone rang in the corridor. Patiently he waited for someone to answer it. As it kept ringing, he glanced over at the bed, where Pandora was stirring uneasily. Then he tightened his dressing-gown belt and went into the corridor.

He lifted the receiver from the wall and put it to his ear. Bending at the knee to be able to speak into it.

'I'd like to talk to Jomar Kraby,' a man's voice said.

'Speaking,' Jomar replied.

At that moment a lock clicked further down the corridor. The woman next door had obviously been woken by the telephone ringing and stuck out her head.

'It's for me,' Jomar said, with a reassuring smile.

'It's Jenny,' the man at the other end said. 'The Norwegian. She wants to talk to you.'

'OK,' Kraby said. 'Let me have a word with her.'

'She's not here now.'

'Where is she?'

'Come to the police station in Mariebergsgatan.'

'Am I talking to a police officer?'

'You are indeed.'

'You want me to go to the police station and talk to Jenny Enersen?'

'Yes.'

'When?'

'Now.'

Jomar glanced at his watch. It was getting on for two in the morning. If he was going to go to the police station he would first have to get hold of a taxi. 'Sure this can't wait until the morning?'

'Yes.'

'Who shall I ask for?'

'Nordeng,' the voice said. 'Report to the duty officer.'

After ringing off, Jomar stood with the telephone in his hand. The woman in Kumla Manor must have changed her mind and decided to talk to him, but why had she involved the police? Why had a police officer contacted him and not her?

◈

Nordeng was a thickset man in his forties. He was standing in reception with his jacket open and his hands thrust deep into trouser pockets. He was wearing glasses and lifted a hand to straighten them when Jomar came to a halt inside the door.

From an inside pocket Nordeng took out a business card that had almost disintegrated. Jomar's name and telephone number were barely legible.

'Is this yours?'

Jomar nodded.

'Have you given a card like this to a Norwegian woman by the name of Jenny Enersen?'

Jomar nodded again. 'What's happened?'

The man reached out an arm and opened a door. 'Come with me.'

'Where are we going?'

'The mortuary,' Nordeng said.

39

On the desk there was a photograph of a young man wearing knee breeches and a woollen jumper. He was sitting on a rock in a mountain landscape, peaks steepling up behind him. It could have been somewhere in Romsdal or maybe the Lyngen Alps east of Tromsø. The man's face was young and unweathered, and he had a nice smile. He was holding a rifle in one hand, and Kai caught himself wondering what he was hunting. He lifted the picture and studied the towering mountain tops in the background. Then the door opened behind him.

Kai straightened up, put the photograph back and turned.

The man who introduced himself as Ragnar Torgersen stood in front of the door, weighing him up, then placed a pince-nez on his nose, walked back to the desk and straightened the photograph.

Kai apologised and said he was curious to know what the young man had been hunting.

'Nothing,' Torgersen said. 'He was being hunted. It's my son Hjalmar. He's dead.'

Kai offered his condolences.

Torgersen opened a drawer and took out a document, thumbed through to the last page, took a pen from his breast pocket and removed the top before passing the pen to Kai. 'Sign here,' he said, pointing to a line at the bottom.

Kai leaned forward. 'What kind of document is this?'

'An employment contract and a non-disclosure agreement.'

'Non-disclosure?'

'You have to swear that you will not disclose confidential information about anything you see or hear in this job. If you do, you will be punished.'

Kai slowly skimmed through the pages. It was all fine by him. He signed.

Torgersen took the documents, sat down behind the desk and cast an eye over him. 'There are advantages to working here too. For example, you get a better place to live.'

'I see I should have read what I signed.'

Torgersen half smiled, stood up and went to the door. 'Gunvor?'

Kai heard a chair scrape on the other side. Torgersen passed her the document, then he closed the door and turned back to Kai.

'You look exhausted.'

Kai ran a hand over his face without answering.

'Guards are our face to the world,' Torgersen said, drumming his fingers on the desk as he was thinking. 'Borgar Stridsberg appears to have received the same treatment as you. He's been given alternative duties until he's presentable again. Your face's nothing to shout about either, Fredly.'

Kai said nothing.

Torgersen took a pocket watch from his waistcoat and looked at it. 'Can you drive a car?'

Kai nodded.

'Do you know your way around Stockholm?'

'I should be OK. There are maps if there's any difficulty.'

Torgersen peered at him through the pince-nez, then arched his eyebrows. The pince-nez fell and he caught it in his hand. 'We'll have to give it a go.'

Kai understood and made for the door. Here he turned.

'Yes?' Torgersen said.

'Your son. Would it be impertinent to ask what he died of?'

'Torture,' Torgersen said. 'Hjalmar tried to shoot himself when he was arrested but was only fatally injured. They killed him the following night.'

Kai fumbled for words.

'Ask Gunvor to come in when you leave,' Torgersen said, sitting down behind the desk.

Kai left the room. In the ante-chamber Gunvor was bent over her typewriter. When he closed the door behind him, she raised her head. Her eyes were burning, and he searched for words.

'Yes?' she said.

'I think I should offer you an apology.'

With a taut grimace around her mouth, she nodded and lowered her head over her typewriter again.

'Are you a lawyer?'

Gunvor straightened up again. 'Law student. I never finished my studies.'

He nodded. 'You've always been bright, Gunvor.'

She reacted with a repressed laugh. 'Good at studying. Borgar tell you, did he?'

He nodded.

'There's so much we'll never know about each other,' she said with a weary smile.

'By the way, Torgersen wants you.'

She pushed her chair back and stood up.

Once again Kai searched for something to say but couldn't find the words. So he walked past her and out.

40

The garage turned out to be in the cellar of a huge building by Tantolunden Park. The ramp down was broad, and when he stopped at the entrance, he saw a sea of vehicles. Lines of illuminated bulbs in the ceiling made the car bonnets shine like waves.

He rang the bell hanging from a chain in the ceiling, and soon an elderly man in a grey coat hobbled out. The man took the keys, disappeared and came back driving a black, four-door Volvo. He waved as he shot past, up the ramp to the road and parked by the pavement. The old boy stood with a toothless smile, waiting to hand over the keys.

At first Kai could only gape in wonder: luxurious seats inside and a bonnet that was long enough to have a reserve wheel mounted on either side. He lifted the bonnet and gazed inside. The power of it. Six spark plugs. He closed the lid, got in behind the wheel and started up. The six cylinders purred with consummate restraint. After pressing the accelerator a couple of times, he let out the clutch and drove.

His job was to collect the boss of the Legal Office, Peder Svinningen. As soon as Kai pulled in beside the cinema, the door of number twenty opened and Svinningen came out. At first the man raised both eyebrows at the sight of Kai's black eye, but got in without comment. Kai looked at himself in the mirror anyway before setting off. The facial swelling had gone down and the colouring around his eye was lighter. He had got used to the sight of himself, but he could understand why people reacted when they first saw him.

His passenger behaved in a condescending manner, addressing the window as he issued his orders. Kai gleaned that he wanted to be driven to Police Headquarters. He headed towards Kungsholmen and arrived there without too much trouble. A stocky guy was waiting outside the front entrance, and he got in when Kai pulled up. The two passengers were on first-name terms and Kai discovered that the policeman was called Lennart Nordeng. The man had a broad face, a sensitive mouth and wore glasses beneath a high forehead. The two of them chatted while Kai drove them back to Vasastaden and the restaurant where they were going to eat. The conversation was so interesting that he wished he could have accompanied them inside and heard the rest. Instead, he had to wait in the car. To kill time, he walked to the kiosk on the corner and bought a couple of newspapers.

He was about to get into the car when he heard a familiar voice behind him.

'Kai.'

Sara Krefting was wearing a blue skirt that reached down to her knees and a matching jacket with a belted waist. Her hat was purple and reminded him of an ingeniously folded paper aeroplane.

'I saw Svinningen crawl out of your car,' she said. 'So you've become a chauffeur for the Legation.'

He had nothing to say.

'Congratulations. You're going up in the world.'

'You're not doing too badly either. You're getting on well in Sweden.'

'Not well enough,' she said, inspecting him, her head tilted at an angle. 'Have you hurt yourself?'

'I may have got out of bed the wrong side.'

She came closer and stroked his cheek with a finger. 'I've got a job for you.'

Now he saw her husband. Dahlgren was getting into a low-slung, open-top sports car further down, in the car park.

'Why would I do a job for you?'

'You know you'll be paid well.'

'You can forget that right now.'

The answer made her smile even more. 'What should I forget? That you stayed with me? Perhaps I should forget the gun I gave you or how I told you when to leave for the border and who you should look for? I wager you haven't informed your new employer about these details. Should I, do you think?'

'You cut corners, Sara. You remind me of my brother. When he talked to people, he never listened. He thought he knew what people were going to say the minute they started a sentence. He interrupted and finished the sentence for them. He never realised that he was the one who didn't know what was going on.'

'What is my young boy trying to say now?'

'You and I have finished with each other.'

'Are you trying to say you want to give me back the money?'

As he struggled for a reply, she stood even closer to him. 'What do you think the more inflexible of your colleagues will think about Daniel's death when I tell them about the gun and the money?'

He clenched his fists, and she retreated two paces.

'Just do what I tell you,' she said. 'That would be best for both of us.'

'Forget it, Sara.'

'No, Kai. We collaborated back in Norway, and we'll do the same here. Give it some thought and get in touch when you're ready to do as I say. You're a good boy. Now I have to go so that Svinningen and Lennart Nordeng don't see us talking. That might ruin any work we do together.'

Her husband had started the car. It came to a halt behind them.

'Daniel Berkåk didn't kill my brother.'

'How could you possibly know?'

'I work with people who do. I have my sources.'

Sara became pensive for a few seconds, then turned on her heel without saying a word, opened the low door and climbed in. The engine roared as they drove off.

Kai had had the last word, but he knew her. Sara would be back. Equally arrogant and uninformed. The open-top car crossing the bridge resembled a dinghy on the open sea. Two small heads protruded above it, nonchalant and vulnerable, and for a moment Kai caught himself feeling slightly sorry for them both.

◈

After an hour and a half Svinningen and Nordeng emerged through the front door of the restaurant. The policeman was in a good mood now, while Svinningen was more reserved. Nevertheless, the conversation continued during the journey south, mostly as a Swedish monologue.

When Kai had dropped off Svinningen in front of the Legal Office, he drove Nordeng back to Police Headquarters. The Swede leaned forward, rested his arms on the back of Kai's seat and asked him what his name was and what he had done to his face.

'I walked into a door,' Kai said, and earned a guffaw.

'What do you think of us Swedes, Kai?'

Diplomatically, Kai answered that Swedes were alright. 'Hospitality tells you a lot about a person's good character,' he said, and felt he was being honest when he said that.

'Are you ready to fight for Norway?'

'You bet I am.'

'The Germans will lose the war, Kai. They'll soon be squeezed like a louse between the Red Army in the east and Churchill and Roosevelt's forces in the west.'

'If there's an invasion from the west.'

'There will be. It's just a matter of time. In my view, you and the other Norwegians have to be prepared, Kai. You need general training and instruction on how to use weapons. When Reichskommissar Terboven and his soldiers have to be pushed out of Norway on their arses, it's you and other Norwegians who'll be doing it. Don't you agree?'

Kai didn't exactly disagree.

'I knew you were a good lad, Kai.'

Kai didn't answer.

'I like you, Kai.'

Kai didn't respond to that either. They had arrived.

Nordeng raised a hand and waved before disappearing into the police station.

Kai looked at his watch. After parking the car, his plan was to move house.

41

Dear Hjørdis,

I promised I would write, and I do so with a heavy heart. Not because I regret anything I said or we did during the few days we were together in Oslo – I keep the memory of that carefully sealed and only take it out late at night when my longings for you are at their most intense. I'm writing because something terrible has happened. I feel guilty, and I need to talk, but I have no one I can confide in. You're so far away, and this letter may well be expurgated or destroyed in some way by the censors, but it will have to take its chances. Compared with all the other horrors Norwegians face at home, some may consider this incident such a small matter, but in Sweden where we live in peace, a death hits you hard. A woman I was speaking to a few days ago has died. She was found floating in the sea off Djurgården. She's left behind a daughter of four. This child has no one else, and when I spoke to her mother, the girl was playing with other children in the carefree manner that only a secure future can confer. Her terrible loss has torn my heart asunder. The daughter needs her mother and the safety they had risked their lives crossing the border to achieve, but evil caught up with them. It has transpired that the death was no accident. There was no water in her lungs. The police say she was strangled before she was thrown into the sea, and I feel burdened by guilt. This woman lived some way out of town, in a home for single Norwegian mothers here in Sweden. I had my job to do, and a conversation with her was vital, but I could see that she was frightened. Some of the pain I feel is because I made no attempt to reassure her. The day after our conversation she travelled to Stockholm – perhaps to talk to me, perhaps to meet someone else – but here she was murdered in the cruellest way. A woman with nothing to her name. A single mother who had only her life and her love for her child. I'm tormented by the thought that this happened shortly after I visited her. I don't think I will have any peace until I find out the exact circumstances. I owe the child that.

I regret that this is not a happy letter. It's like many of our conversations in Oslo. You always listened to my complaints without talking about yourself, but I have to articulate this misery. Then we'll have to see whether I decide to send this letter or not. Anyway, you should know that I still think about the days we shared in Oslo with great tenderness and joy. I think about how difficult life is for you, in so many ways. Some of them you can talk about and some you can't. That's how it is for us all. At any moment life can present us with mountains that have to be scaled. You've chosen to be loyal

*to your husband and stay in Norway. And I have every respect for
your decision. I want you to know that is what I genuinely think,
even though I can sit here, as now, missing you more than I have
ever missed anyone. In this wretched solitude I still take great delight
in visiting memories. Right now I'm looking at the snap I took of
you one summer's day on Lake Sogn long before the war. The
sunlight is glistening in your hair and in your eyes. I wish I had
you here so that I could benefit from your wisdom. I'm afraid you
will have to bear with me if I express my longing for you on paper
this time. After all, writing is what I do.*

    A warm, tender embrace from your
    Jomar.

42

After the letter box had swallowed the envelope and the lid had
shut, Jomar mused on the power it had. It was a poetic instal-
lation, and he reflected on all the times he had stood as he was
standing now, thinking this is it, the die is cast. The letter had
gone; it was too late for regrets. There was no going back. The
letter might be received as a kiss or a slap in the face. It was impossible to know. All he could do was wait for a reaction – if
indeed there would be any.

    In the letter he had deliberately avoided mentioning the
rumours that were circulating about Hjørdis making a film for
the Nazis. It was none of his business. If this was what she was
doing, it certainly wouldn't be with a light heart. Life has a
tendency to place individuals in situations not of their own
choosing, but they cannot avoid them without causing so much
pain for others that it also damages them.

    Jomar had, however, made enough intimations of the betrayal
in his letter, in his usual artless way. If Hjørdis read an uncen-
sored version, she would draw her own conclusions, and he
wouldn't be there to alleviate the sorrow or the fury that the

allusions would trigger. He had written many letters, and he had stood in front of a closed letter box on more occasions than he cared to admit, wondering whether what he had done was right or his choice of words had been appropriate.

Now he felt a need to redress the imbalance his emotions had aroused, and so he made a beeline for the remedy he had always sought out when such perceptions required tending – a trip to the library. He wanted to read prose or poetry that would put his own anxiety and despair into perspective, verbal formulations that could put the world in its place, Oscar Wilde quotations or perhaps a few lines from Arthur Rimbaud.

He climbed up the little hump in Humlegården where the chemist Carl Wilhelm Scheele stood on a plinth enjoying the view, then continued down to the avenue leading to the statue of Carl von Linné. As he walked down the shingle, he recognised two figures sitting side by side on a bench on the path. Two women. One was Lotte Bendiksen, the arrogant private secretary from the Legal Office. The other was Sara Krefting.

This was a meeting that piqued Jomar's curiosity. After all, these two women were on different sides in the war. Now they had met up and were sitting together, each with an identical string bag. He therefore walked slowly on, hands behind his back, mumbling to himself a line from Wordsworth's poem about daffodils and thinking that he was the only person on the path. He wandered lonely as a cloud, as it were, certain the two women would notice him.

And, sure enough, they did. That is, Svinningen's private secretary did. She stood up, grabbed one bag and quickly walked towards Linné.

Jomar was keen to see what Sara Krefting would do, but then he realised that she – even if she undoubtedly had his name in one of her files on suspected 'destructive elements' – may not have known what he looked like today, many years after he had been politically active. For that reason, she probably wouldn't recognise him.

And, indeed, she did stay on the bench, a blonde beauty in dark glasses as protection against the sun. When Jomar passed her, he raised his hat and nodded without eliciting any reaction. He could understand that. She was the kind of woman who was used to men's compliments and therefore barely took any notice.

He passed four more benches before sitting down. He sat with his hands thrust into his coat pockets until she got up and strolled past with a bag in her right hand. Jomar gave her a head start, then rose to his feet and followed her.

43

When Jomar alighted from the bus and ambled home, his head was full of conflicting thoughts. At first, spying on Sara Krefting had excited and inspired him. Then he had realised his initiative had very little to do with his investigation. He had the same flaw as a detective as he did as an author: falling prey to the temptation to go off at a tangent, following paths that led nowhere. The challenge now was to find his way back. To re-group and prioritise the key elements. To assemble the pieces so that he could get back on the right track.

As he turned the corner to walk the last few metres home, he saw a familiar figure waiting outside the front gate. Gunvor saw him at the same moment and waved. Jomar's hand moved of its own accord. It raised his hat. Discovering that an attractive young woman had visited him on her own initiative put him in a good mood.

'Been waiting here long?'

She shook her head.

'Come on in,' he said, heading for the entrance.

'I have to be off,' she said, holding an envelope in her hand. 'For you.' She passed him the letter. 'From the Soviet Embassy. They've invited you to a reception.'

Jomar inclined his head, nonplussed. 'And they've asked me?'

Gunvor nodded. 'Both of us.'

'You and me? Sure?'

She nodded again.

He scrutinised her face, but failed to find any evidence of deception there, neither in her eyes nor in her expression.

'And you're delivering this personally?'

She nodded again, but she had something burning to say. That much was obvious.

'Should I go?'

'If you have something to give them in return.'

Again he tilted his head.

'You asked for something,' she said in a lowered voice. 'The way I read that is they will comply if you can give them something.' She glanced at her watch. 'I have to be off. Can I say we'll go?'

'Give me a couple of days,' he said quickly.

Gunvor nodded and spun on her heel.

Jomar stood watching her. Only when she had rounded the corner did he go up the stairs to his flat.

This case had a life of its own. When he thought it was stranded in the wilderness, miles away, back it flew, straight into his open arms. This offered him new options. The question, of course, was whether he would be able to handle the challenge that had presented itself.

44

Kai's movable goods and chattels amounted to the kitbag he had dragged around ever since he had been released from Grini. The move itself was effected with the Legation car, from Jernberg's boarding house via the Old Town to Söder and Urvädersgränd, by Mosebacke square. The stairwell smelled of fried fish.

It was a wonderful feeling to insert the key in the lock, turn it and open up his own private castle. He stood in the doorway savouring the experience and smiled at his new life, then crossed the threshold into the room, where fine dust hovered in the sunbeams entering through the window.

It was a bed-sit. There was a bed with a pile of linen on the mattress, a narrow wardrobe beside it, and a bureau next to the window. In the alcove there was a worktop with an electric hotplate and a Primus stove. A board that could be raised to form a table was fixed to the wall. Perhaps this was where he was meant to cook.

He dropped his kitbag on the floor and opened the cupboard below the stove. Two saucepans, a frying pan and a coffee pot. Luxury. When he opened the window a fraction, a train clattered past, probably on the bridge over Riddar fjord on its way to Stockholm Central. He took his time making the bed before placing his clothes from the kitbag in the wardrobe. He hid the Webley revolver under his pillow. Now there was only the memento of Atle left, the picture he had been given by Sara Krefting that day in Oslo long ago. The picture showed Atle in uniform with comrades at the front. A group of soldiers chatting cheerfully. Probably all of them fighting on the Eastern Front.

Kai held the photograph up to the light, but now his gaze didn't fall on his brother. He studied the soldier sitting on the motorbike. There was something familiar about his face. His mouth was open in a full smile as though he had just said something witty. The others were roaring with laughter. They were all in high spirits.

Why had Atle held on to this photograph? Was it a reminder of good friends or of a special occasion? Had these men just participated in something memorable? Perhaps this was after Atle had been awarded his medal? Whenever Kai looked at Atle his eyes were drawn to the soldier on the motorbike. Had he seen him before? Could that be possible? Almost against his better judgement, he picked up his wallet and opened it. Between the banknotes was a folded piece of paper. He unfolded it: *Missing: Have you seen Kåre?*

Kai looked from the print photograph and back again. The hairs on his arm actually began to stand up. There was a resemblance between Vardenær and the man on the motorbike, but how similar were they really? The print was poor quality. The photograph had been taken from an acute angle.

'No,' he told himself kicking off his shoes, then lay down on the bed and stared at the ceiling. 'The world isn't that small. It can't be the same person.'

The thought wouldn't let go of him. After all, Atle had fought on the Eastern Front with other Norwegians. If it was the same man, what did that tell him?

Kai had no idea. His mind went back to Atle, recognising at the same time that it was important to clarify this. Why? he asked himself. He didn't have a clue. Not yet. Kai understood only one thing: he would know what the significance of this was when he had an answer to whether the man in the photograph was the one they had transported through Stockholm in a carpet. The question was: how would he find out?

'There is an answer,' he said to himself. 'It must be in one of the offices. In a filing cabinet.'

Worth a try. Do a little investigating. Find a cabinet and flick through the files. He should be able to do that. According to the contract, standing guard outside the office was part of the job. Kai knew that Borgar disliked guard duties, but he loved driving. Kai lay back and felt a plan taking shape and details falling into place.

45

A return favour for Madame Kollontai was not something that just presented itself out of the blue. In reality, Jomar only had one option, and even if there was little hope of it succeeding, he had to try. In the end, though, he thought he had devised a reasonable cover for his initiative.

This time there was no one waiting for him at the doors to
Police Headquarters in Mariebergsgatan. It was a busy day –
people were coming out and going in, the queue in front of the
duty officer was long. When it was Jomar's turn, he asked to
speak to Lennart Nordeng. The uniformed officer pointed to
the line of chairs against the wall and asked him to wait there.

A good ten minutes dragged by before Nordeng opened the
door and beckoned him in.

'What can I do for you today, Kraby?'

'The woman in the mortuary.'

'Oh, yes?'

Kraby looked around the large room. 'Is there somewhere
private we could talk?'

Nordeng waved an arm and led the way up the staircase.

'Have you discovered the motive?'

'The murder was sexually motivated. Her dress was torn, and
she wasn't wearing any underwear. On top of that, she still had
money in her handbag, which was floating beside her in the sea.
So robbery is out of the question.'

Nordeng held the office door open. Once inside, he sat down
behind his brown desk.

Jomar brushed down the seat of the other chair in the room
and sat. 'I went to Kumla Manor and spoke to Jenny Enersen
because I'm investigating the murder of a Norwegian courier
on the other side of the Swedish border. Daniel Berkåk. I don't
think Enersen was directly involved, but it's highly probable that
she had information about it.'

Nordeng nodded.

'I think Jenny Enersen was killed by the same person who
killed Daniel Berkåk.'

'I'm a busy man, Kraby. Murders committed in Norway do
not fall under my jurisdiction.'

'Of course they don't, but there's been a small development.'

Nordeng raised his eyebrows.

'I'm sure that Daniel Berkåk was murdered by someone living

in Sweden, and I'm sure he killed Jenny Enersen. The two cases are connected.'

'I doubt that. The murdered woman was found with her clothes torn. She was the victim of a rapist who killed her to hide his crime.'

'I believe the murderer tore her clothes after the murder to put the police on the wrong scent.'

Nordeng's gaze lingered on him for longer this time. 'Last time we met you said you thought the murderer knew that Berkåk was on his way to the Norwegian border by train. You thought the murderer followed him from Arvika.'

Jomar nodded.

'You think the murderer followed Berkåk on a bike. You think Berkåk left his bike on the Swedish side of the border and crossed on foot. You think the murderer did the same and followed him. You think the murderer waited until Berkåk was on the Norwegian side before shooting him. After the murder the man crossed the border back into Sweden without meeting any German or Swedish guards, then cycled to the station to catch a train to Stockholm.'

Jomar nodded. 'With Daniel Berkåk's death, the murderer's mission was complete. I think, afterwards, he cycled to Charlottenberg. The distance from Lake Leir to Charlottenberg is only a few kilometres. I think he caught the train from there to Stockholm. I was considering asking you to speak to the Charlottenberg police and enquire if anyone has seen a stray bike on the station or in the surrounding area. If they have, while it doesn't mean I'm right, it would make my theory more likely.'

Again, Nordeng swung from side to side on his chair.

Jomar crossed his legs and waited.

'Thank you for the tip-off regarding the bike in this murder investigation. However, I have a hunch there's something else behind your visit. Am I right?'

Jomar nodded.

'Then tell me why you're really here.'

'When the Germans invaded Norway and advanced north, there was the terrible Battle of Narvik,' Jomar said. 'Both German and British forces wanted control of the port because it was from there that Swedish steel was being shipped out to the world. Many Norwegians regarded the Battle of Narvik as their country's last hope of forcing the Germans to retreat. Many Norwegians went to Narvik to fight, but it was difficult to get there. Because at that point the Germans controlled all traffic north, so there was only one way open to Narvik, and that went through Sweden. Those who made it to Sweden were able to catch a train to Kiruna and cross the border from there into Norway and Narvik. Many young Norwegians crossed into Sweden and caught the train bound for Kiruna to join the Norwegian troops. But most of these volunteers were arrested by the Swedish police. The few who succeeded in joining up did so by pretending to be civilians on trains that in reality were German troop carriers. Swedish trains to Kiruna were full of German soldiers the Swedes were transporting north to join General Dietl, who led the German army at Narvik.'

Nordeng, irritated, cleared his throat. 'It wasn't the Swedish authorities who sent German soldiers to Narvik.'

'It's the way the Norwegians saw it. They wanted to travel on those trains to join the Norwegian army and fight, but were arrested by Swedish police. It's also how the British saw it. They fought together with Norwegian troops but were forced back because General Dietl had a constant supply of reinforcements thanks to the Swedish railways.'

'The British retreated from Narvik on Churchill's orders, and you know that as well as I do.' Nordeng gesticulated angrily. 'Where are you going with all this?'

'I caught the train to Oslo a while ago. Many of the coaches were reserved for German soldiers.'

'So? I imagine they had tickets.'

'I doubt it. It was troop transport organised by the Swedish authorities. The same is happening on the routes to Finland. We both know that the Germans' 163rd infantry division, Division Engelbrecht, was given safe transit from Norway through Sweden to fight on the Eastern Front.'

Now Nordeng said nothing.

'You and I are both convinced Germany's going to lose the war. There's a rumour doing the rounds among Norwegians living in Sweden that the Swedish authorities have finally decided to insist on their supposed neutrality by refusing to allow Germans on these troop trains. Can you confirm that?'

'Are you out of your mind?'

Jomar merely smiled at the response. 'When will the ban come into effect?'

'Is that why you've come here? To barter information?'

Jomar straightened up and assumed an injured expression 'Me? An exiled Norwegian writer?'

Nordeng blew out his cheeks and shook his head in resignation. '*Supposed* neutrality,' he muttered.

'The rumours are swirling around already.'

Nordeng didn't answer.

'I have something I think will interest you.'

Nordeng didn't respond this time either.

'A Norwegian woman, a Nazi, has just acquired Swedish nationality through marriage. In Norway she's a member of the Nasjonal Samling and the Germanic SS. She and her husband moved to Sweden recently. I know that she is in possession, illegally, of confidential information from the Norwegian Legation.'

'So?'

'I happened to witness the confidential information being passed over. I then followed her to Nybrogatan 27. To the German Legation's Handelsabteilung – the trade department – where we both know Büro Wagner, their intelligence service, is based. This woman procures information from the Norwegian Legation and delivers it to the German intelligence service. In other words, she's a spy operating in Sweden.'

Lennart Nordeng's eyes were like ice. 'A spy in Sweden,' he sighed in despair. 'What's her name?'

'Sara Krefting. She's married to a Swede now and goes under the name of Sara Dahlgren.'

'Why are you telling me this?'

It was Jomar's turn to remain silent.

Nordeng stared at him, then heaved a heavy sigh and shook his head. Eventually he swivelled round in his chair and plucked a ring binder from a wall shelf stacked with them. He placed the binder on the desk, opened it, flicked through the papers and read. Then he closed the binder, put it back and stood up. 'If you would excuse me for a minute,' he said, and left the room.

Jomar waited until the door had closed. Then he stood up and went behind Nordeng's desk and located the same ring binder. He placed it on the desk and thumbed through the papers. Sending glances at the closed door. He sat down on Nordeng's chair and searched through his pockets. He found Daniel Berkåk's notebook and Nordeng's own pen. He began to take notes. Turned over the page and made more. Then he stopped, forced open the metal rings and took out a document he hastily folded and stuffed into his inside pocket.

At that moment he heard sounds in the corridor. Jomar jumped up. The sudden movement sent the ring binder flying. Paper was scattered across the floor. Jomar put the pen and notebook in his coat pocket and went down on all fours. With sweat pouring from his forehead and frequent glances towards the door, he managed to scrabble some of the papers back into the binder.

He could hear voices outside. Nordeng was talking to someone.

There was too much paper. The perforations tore, the documents wouldn't go into the file and then he saw the door handle move downward.

Jomar swept up the last papers, shuffled them together, stuffed them in the binder, pushed it back into its position on the shelf and rushed back to his chair.

The door opened.

A second later Jomar was sitting on the chair, which scraped along the floor as his body weight sent it towards the wall.

Nordeng stood still, observing first Jomar, then the floor. Jomar followed his gaze. Under the desk were two loose pieces of paper. Jomar made himself busy lighting a cigarette.

Nordeng bent down and picked them up. Read them and laid them on the desk before taking a seat.

They sat looking at each other for a long period of awkward silence.

'You were right about one thing,' Nordeng said at last. 'There's a bike at Charlottenberg Station that no one has claimed. The station master had taken the bike in, expecting the owner to come forward. I've asked the police chief to organise a search for Daniel Berkåk's bike in the Lake Leir region. Should we happen to stumble across the bike, Berkåk's murder is still a matter for the Norwegian police. So spit out all you know now. Anything connected with the murder of the woman we found in the sea.'

Jomar took a match box from his pocket and flicked ash into it. He cleared his throat. 'I'm sure that Jenny Enersen knew who killed Berkåk. I think she knew the murderer and also where he was living in Stockholm. I think she left Kumla Manor to meet him in Stockholm and say that I'd been asking about him. She wanted to warn him, but unfortunately she made a terrible misjudgement. She should never have gone to see the man.'

'Why would Berkåk's murderer kill her?'

'Because she knew too much. She knew who he was and where he was living.'

'Berkåk was killed in Norway. It would've been of no interest to us if a woman had turned up here at the police station ranting on about a murder in Norway. The murderer must've known that.'

'She contacted the murderer to tell him I was on his trail. Killing her was a mistake. I think he did it in a moment of panic. He's not worried about the Swedish police, but he fears the exiled Norwegian authorities will discover the truth.'

Nordeng swung from side to side in his chair again, thinking, then said:

'There's a kind of logic to what you say, but I'm still loathe to believe it.'

Jomar didn't answer him. He put the cigarette end in the matchbox and closed it.

Nordeng took the two documents from the desk and held them up. 'While I was away and you so generously re-organised my shelves,' he said with the same dry intonation, 'I also did a bit of digging with regard to the Norwegian woman you mentioned. Sara Krefting AKA Sara Dahlgren.'

'Oh, yes?'

'She was arrested last night on suspicion of spying. Our people had seen her going into Nybrogatan 27.'

'Is she in prison?'

Nordeng shook his head. 'She was immediately released.'

'Why?'

'My reading is that she bought herself off.'

'How did she manage to do that?'

'With a map.'

'A map?'

'The same map I'd guess she sold to the Germans,' Nordeng said, getting up. 'A map of the courier routes between Sweden and Norway. Now I think we're both happy, Kraby. Good afternoon.'

Lennart Nordeng walked over to the door and held it open.

46

As a child, Kai had waited to grow up, as a teenager he had waited to become an adult, as an adult he had waited for a better life, waited to be seen, waited for the sound of the siren, waited for shots, waited for death – and when the bullets didn't hit him, he had waited for the end of the war.

What he was waiting most for now was the light to be switched off on the floor above. Kai glanced at his watch for perhaps the fifth time in the last few minutes. Svinningen's secretary, frøken Bendiksen, had left half an hour before. Only the boss was left there now. Kai had a sense that he was a spectator of his own life. He wondered what could change this. Would he leave this nebulous existence if he did as Lennart Nordeng wanted, if he trained as a soldier in Sweden, did military drills, assault courses, muscle-building, fought with a juddering machine gun in his hands? Once again, he looked up. The window on the first floor was still lit, even if the office was supposed to have closed almost half an hour ago.

Wait, he thought once again. The way he was waiting for an initiative from Iris. Nothing doing there either. To kill time he took a few paces, turned and walked back. The cinema hadn't opened yet, but a sprinkling of passers-by stopped and studied the film posters. Then the door closed with a bang. Kai nodded to Peder Svinningen, who walked past without returning the acknowledgement and continued to the corner, where he crossed Linnégatan with long strides. Svinningen was a man who didn't possess enough generosity in his soul to see other people or even speak to them.

Kai looked up and saw that the light in the window had been switched off. He walked to the corner and waited for Svinningen to turn down the side street and disappear. He looked up again. The light was still off. The usual procedure was that Kai should check the door was locked before he clocked off. Instead, Kai went inside, locked the door behind him and entered forbidden territory. It was one thing to guard the door to the king's private chambers. And quite another for the guard to violate said chambers.

Inside, he listened to the silence – and to his own inner voice, to see if it had any objections to the forbidden acts he was about

to perform. He felt nothing and had to accept that he didn't give
a damn. What would happen if he was caught? Presumably he
would be given the boot. So what? Kai hadn't applied for this job.
He could survive without it. There were some things he needed
to clarify, and they were far more important to him than a job.

At the top of the staircase he cast a quick glance into the ante-
chamber, which was empty and in semi-darkness, but still
carried a slight whiff of the perfume the women who worked
there wore. There were two other doors on the landing. One
was to a room with a sink and a toilet. The other was to a win-
dowless room where all the walls were lined with filing cabinets.
He walked in. Searched for a drawer labelled *V* and flicked
through until he found the file he wanted:

Vardenær, Kåre.

He placed it on the cabinet and started reading. Vardenær had
been born in Meråker to a Swedish mother and Norwegian father.
He grew up in Norwegian Trøndelag and Swedish Storlien. He
was known to be an informer and *agent provocateur*. Member of
the Nasjonal Samling since 1936. Member of their paramilitary
organisation, Hirden, since the same year. Volunteered to fight
for the Nazis in 1940. Joined SS Panzerdivision Wiking.
Discharged in 1942. Reason for discharge unknown.

The photograph that Sara Krefting had given Kai didn't lie.
It was documented. Atle and Kåre Vardenær must have known
each other. Vardenær and his brother had fought side by side
on the Eastern Front.

A click broke the silence. A door downstairs opened. Soon
afterwards light footsteps on the stairs were audible. Kai was no
longer alone.

47

The staircase was broad and every step creaked. On the landing
Jomar knocked on the door. No answer. He knocked again and

waited, but presumably Gunvor wasn't at home. Involuntarily
he glanced at his watch. It could be time for mass. Jomar didn't
know if Gunvor went to mass regularly, but as St Eric's
Cathedral was on the way back, he could drop by.

The cathedral nestled in the landscape like a rather modest
copy of cathedrals in Venice and Rome: a neo-Gothic basilica,
built in redbrick with two spires and a large rose window at the
front facing the street. Jomar opened the door and entered, but
stopped inside and admired the beam of light that cut through
the stained glass and lit up the two altars that welcomed the
cathedral's visitors. The Mother of God to the left and the Son
of Man to the right. The choir was assembled.

Jomar sat down. When he bowed his head, his gaze fell on a
grey cat under the pew – and at the same time two equally grey
kittens – as it lazily stretched its paws, unaffected by whatever
else was going on. Jomar met the cat's yellow eyes and breathed
in the aroma of incense. He liked the smell, liked the red light
in the tabernacle, the Catholics' need to create an illusion of
God's presence in His house. He liked the organ music and the
priest's melodious liturgy.

As the organ faded, he saw Gunvor's back among the group
of worshippers. Then one of the kittens squealed. The mother
had grabbed it by the neck and was carrying it. The other kitten
floundered around blindly. The mother disappeared but was
soon back for number two. After the cat had disappeared again,
Gunvor came walking towards the exit, but stopped, eyebrows
raised, when she saw Jomar, who stood up and whispered he
could walk her home.

Side by side, they walked in silence until they reached the
entrance of the block where she lived.

'Do you feel now that that you've been washed clean of your
sins?'

'Are you making fun of me?'

Jomar shook his head. 'I'm just curious. I admire anyone who
has enough sense to believe in God.'

'I think forgiveness is a basic need for everyone.'

Jomar considered her response for a few seconds. 'I have a more agnostic view of the world myself,' he answered. 'But my egocentric nature tells me that to avoid meeting the Devil I will probably try to secure an audience with St Peter the day I feel death breathing down my neck.'

'You can't plan for death.'

Jomar didn't disagree. 'When did you become a believer?'

'I've always been one.'

'Catholic? Always?'

'After three friends died. We were going to fight, and no one would beat us. The possibility hadn't occurred to us. Not one of them had a chance to say goodbye to anyone. I came here because this church is receptive to mysteries. The parish priest doesn't protest when I tell him about conversations I have with my dead comrades.'

Jomar nodded. 'Perhaps, mentally, I should become a Catholic. If I do, it'll be more because of the aesthetics around the rites than any need for absolution. I think it's more important to be able to forgive yourself than to leave something so important to any perception we may have of God. Love, on the other hand, is a basic need. No one needs forgiveness for being human.'

The look she sent him showed that she was moved, but she said nothing.

'I'd like you to thank Orina and say I accept the invitation,' he said, taking an envelope from his inside pocket and passing it to her.

She took it. 'What's this?'

'A quid pro quo that Madame Kollontai may be able to accept.'

She opened her bag and dropped the envelope inside. 'Do you know the way?'

'You'll be going ahead, will you?'

She nodded.

'You haven't sinned, Gunvor. Remember that.'

The evening sun was shining on her face as Jomar left.

48

The light tread on the staircase made Kai quickly close Vardenær's file and slot it back into the cabinet drawer. Then he shut it and tiptoed to the door.

He groped for the light switch, turned it off, then stood motionless, waiting for the intruder to walk by. The footsteps stopped. Kai bent his knees and clenched his fists. The footsteps carried on. Stopped again. Then he heard a door open. Kai used the opportunity to press down the doorhandle as quietly as he could. He waited for a few seconds, opened the door a centimetre and peered out.

The ante-chamber door was ajar, and a light was on. Kai slipped out from the archive room and was about to close the door behind him. To do so he would have to change hands on the handle. And to do that, he would have to turn. A floorboard creaked as he did so. The noise made him freeze, but nothing happened. There was a vague scent of perfume on the stairs now too. Quietly he pulled the door to and tiptoed over to the next door, which was adorned with a heart. He repeated the process with the door handle. This one wasn't as easy. A hinge groaned. Again, he froze and listened, but no sounds came from inside the ante-chamber. Then he slipped into the toilet.

With the door slightly ajar, he stood breathing through his mouth. At last he heard footsteps again. The person who came out of the ante-chamber was a woman. Frøken Bendiksen. Then she went into the archive room.

Kai stared at his hands. He liked this, being here, in forbidden territory, unseen. He felt powerful because the woman didn't know he was watching her. What was more, he felt an urge to use his power. So he clenched his teeth to control himself, to stop himself from bursting out of his hiding place and going after her. What would he do anyway? This was what it was like when you have been waiting for too long. Emotions had built up inside him and were on the point of exploding. This was not good. Kai realised he would have to get away before he did something he would regret.

So he slipped out of the toilet, ready to dash down the stairs, but he couldn't do it, he couldn't leave. The sense of power was so strong it prevented him. Instead of going downstairs, he stopped and looked through the half-open door. Frøken Bendiksen was bent over an open cabinet drawer. She took out a file and dropped it in her net bag, then closed the drawer. As it slammed shut, Kai nipped back into the toilet.

It was one thing to violate the king's chamber. And quite another to remove treasures from it. The feeling of power grew as, through the crack in the door, he watched frøken Bendiksen go down the stairs holding the net bag in her hand. Once she had closed the front door after her, Kai shot down the stairs.

The tall woman rushed off as the evening sun cast a long shadow ahead of her.

Kai followed her. They went to Stureplan square in the centre of Stockholm. Here, frøken Bendiksen entered a door below an illuminated rainbow. Kai knew the Regnbågen restaurant was a meeting point for Germans, the way that the Anglais was for Norwegians.

There was nothing to lose, so he went in. There were very few customers. Frøken Bendiksen had found a table at the back. She sat down on a long bench with her back to the wall. Kai chose a smaller table for two by the entrance, where the wall was decorated with mirrors that made the restaurant seem bigger than it actually was.

Kai ordered a glass tankard of beer and was halfway down it when the door opened again. He had seen this woman before. It was Sara Krefting's friend from the Grand Hotel.

The woman walked straight over to frøken Bendiksen's table

and stood next to it. Lotte Bendiksen stood up, and they shook hands warmly.

They sat down, and the waiter came over with menus. On his way back, Kai waved to him and paid.

He left the restaurant, his body tense and his blood pulsating in a way he hadn't known since he was in Spain. Now he didn't want to lose that feeling. So he walked over to the nearby tram stop, where people were waiting under the concrete roof.

Kai had to wait for almost three quarters of an hour before they appeared. First Lotte Bendiksen came through the door and disappeared up Sturegatan.

Kai let her go on her way.

A minute later the door opened again. Out came Sara Krefting's young friend. She looked as if she was going to catch the tram, because she was walking towards him. She strolled in under the concrete roof and joined the queue. He stood next to her.

Her blonde hair was straight and lifeless. Her snub nose seemed to lift her sulky top lip and reveal her front teeth. She had tried to camouflage the tiny pimples on her forehead with make-up.

The woman said nothing but left her place in the queue and walked off. Kai followed her. They went down Kungsgatan: the woman in front; Kai fifteen metres behind.

They passed one crossing, then another, but he didn't have the patience for this, and deciding enough was enough, he increased his stride and caught her up.

She stopped. Her eyes glistened with fear. 'What do you want?'

Kai decided to play it straight. 'I want to know what frøken Bendiksen's feeding you.'

'You're imagining things,' she said, trying to walk on.

He snatched her bag.

She stood with her hands hanging down by her sides, helpless. 'Give it me back.'

'You haven't screamed or called for the police.'

'Give it to me.'

'In a minute,' he said, opening it. Inside was a case file. He removed it and passed her the bag.

'Give me those papers back. Otherwise, I'll have you arrested.'

Her words fell on deaf ears. He opened the file. A photo was attached to the top document with a paper clip. A photo of Sara Krefting. There were several documents. Closely typed. Probably most of it containing the mischief Sara had got up to in her life. The same way the Legal Office had notes on Kåre Vardenær. The same way they had notes on his own brother. Perhaps on him, too.

'Who are they for?'

'Who do you think? You know her, don't you.'

'For Sara? I doubt that. Sara would've collected them herself.'

'She can't. The police are keeping her under surveillance. Are you going to give me the papers?'

'You know where she lives.'

She nodded.

'We can walk there together,' he said, tucking the file under his arm.

'It's quite a way.'

'Then let's get a taxi. Come on.'

'I'll show you where she lives, but I won't go in with you. For me it doesn't matter who delivers the papers.'

'Of course,' Kai said, raising a hand and flagging down a taxi.

Gallantly, he waited until she had sat down before getting in beside her. When the driver started up, she told him to go to Karlaplan.

Neither of them spoke for the duration of the journey. When the taxi stopped, Kai paid the driver and followed her. This had to be the quietest and wealthiest part of Stockholm, he thought. The large, round pond with fountains, wreathed by trees and languid lawns resembled the hub of a huge wheel, where avenues radiated outwards, like broad spokes, to a distant horizon.

'Over behind the trees there, in Tysta gatan,' she said, pointing.

Kai continued alone.

The road was adorned with broad poplar trees between rows of multi-coloured apartment blocks. It was obvious that Sara lived well. The open-top car was parked outside a door with a single name under the bell. One name on a door leading into a whole apartment house. Kai stuffed the file under his belt and buttoned up his jacket before ringing the bell. He stood thinking about the time, almost two months before, when the door opened in Slemdalsveien and Sara drew him into the light. Today the door was opened by a servant and the room behind him was dark. Kai asked the man to tell the lady of the house that Kai Fredly had come with the documents. The door closed, and after a few seconds it was opened again, this time by the right person.

'Kai?' Sara came out onto the steps and closed the door behind her.

At once her perfume wafted over him. Her hair was pinned up the way she liked. She was wearing a white cocktail dress that left both shoulders bare and was so tight he thought she would have problems moving. He was wrong there. When she walked down the steps, it was with an agility he couldn't help but admire.

'Is this a convenient time?'

'We were just about to eat.'

'Perhaps you were expecting someone else?'

Sara didn't answer.

'She gave me the papers as I was coming here anyway.' Kai opened his jacket and held out the file. 'You can have it on one condition. Tell me how you could know when and where Daniel Berkåk would appear in Kongsvinger.'

'Why do you want to know?'

Kai turned to leave.

'Wait,' she said.

Kai stopped.

'There was a man in the Legation.'

'Name?'

'Peder Svinningen.'

'You and Svinningen? Conspiring to bump off a courier? You're lying.'

Sara shook her head.

'If you're so cosy with Svinningen you could've asked him to give you the file, couldn't you?'

'That's what I did, Kai. And now you're his errand boy. My guess is that's the file you have there.'

'What are you conspiring with Svinningen for?'

'Peace.'

'Which peace?'

'The war's in a decisive phase,' she said in a low voice, almost a whisper. 'Whoever finally wins, whether it's the Germans or the British, all patriotic Norwegians agree on one thing: victory must not go to the Reds. Communists undermine society's law and order. I know a lot about the Reds. My files go back a long way. I started collecting information about the Reds long before anyone else in Norway realised how important it was to do so. When the Bolsheviks murdered the Tsar and his family, I already had the names of important sympathisers in Norway.'

'When you were a child.'

'I was fifteen and my father's secretary. When he died, I took over his archives and continued the work.'

'Archives? Don't tell me you brought the archives with you when you came here?'

'I destroyed the lists before I left, but I have everything here,' she said, tapping her temple. 'Someone who knows what I can do and what I stand for is Peder Svinningen. I'm as valuable to him as I am to the German authorities.'

Now Kai had to take a step back and take another look at

her. This mythical female elf whose soul had to be as black as her dress was white.

'Why do you do this?' Kai gesticulated towards the magnificent house. 'You live better than most, eat better than most, party more often and more decadently than anyone. How much richer do you actually want to be?'

'Money? You think this is about money? You disappoint me, Kai. I thought you'd seen through the Reds' banal mentality. For me this is all about the future. I want to live in a Norway that is safe and predictable – regardless of whether it's ultimately Hitler or Churchill who's in power. Svinningen and his people are planning how Norway will be if the British win. They're planning to arrest and punish all the Norwegians who, over the war, have displayed German sentiments, but I'm not going to rot in jail. My aim is to be able to walk around whatever future Norway we see without fear of arrest. I believe in a German victory, but if Hitler has to capitulate and Svinningen comes to power after the war's over, I want to be able to travel home without losing any of my privileges. Svinningen needs me and so he does what I tell him.'

He stared at her, stunned.

'And?' she said, not so much impatient as angry.

'What are you actually doing here?'

'What do you mean?'

'Why did you come here, to Sweden?'

'I'm a wife. I have a husband.'

'Good cover story, I'll give you that, but I've heard you're really here on a mission for a German in Oslo, someone called Fritz Preiss.'

Uncertainty filled her eyes for two brief seconds before she blinked it away. 'What a terrible thing to say. Who could be so evil?'

She was so credible that he was unable to stifle a smile.

'You imagine someone has whispered this in my ear, do you? You're forgetting that you and I, and others, can feel safe in this city, that everything has a price and that everyone you meet, whether they're German, British or Swedish, is looking for the highest bidder. In addition, and you know more about this than I do, if there are lots of buyers, your profit will be greater if what you're selling can be divided up.'

'What do you mean by that?'

Kai didn't answer immediately. Instead he passed her the dossier. She took it and started leafing through. She flicked back to her photograph and grimaced with displeasure. 'They could've used a better photo.'

'Maybe Svinningen told you where and when Berkåk would turn up at the border,' Kai said. 'But there was one thing he didn't say.'

Now he had her full attention.

'Berkåk didn't appear where he was supposed to, according to Svinningen and you. When he failed to show up, I crossed the border, thinking I would find him in Stockholm, but when I arrived, almost the first thing I heard was that Berkåk was already dead. He'd been shot by an unknown killer on the Norwegian side of the border.'

It seemed the dossier was of no interest to her now – neither did she have anything further to say. So he raised a hand and turned to leave.

'Kai!'

He stopped.

'Who was it? Who killed him?'

Kai turned to her, shrugged and splayed his palms. 'As you know Svinningen so well, you can ask him. Perhaps he'll sell you the answer. By the way, I wouldn't trust him if I were you. He's not being straight with you.'

'Not being straight? What do you mean?'

'I told you last time we met – in the time I've been in this country I've learned one thing: it wasn't Daniel Berkåk who killed my brother. The person who tried to make you believe that must've known the truth.'

With that, he raised his hand again, turned and left her without looking back.

49

A gentle shower was falling, leaving droplets of water on the car bonnet as Kai pulled into the pavement. He rolled down the window to check the house numbers. There it was. Further down, there was a big clock over the entrance to a watchmaker's. The hands showed he was a couple of minutes early. So he killed the engine and prepared for a wait.

The sky above the roofs was dark, and it wasn't because dusk was falling. It was almost completely black in the east, and now the rain was coming down harder. Just as he rolled up the window, the rear door opened. Kai turned in his seat, silent. The man who stepped in wearing a dinner jacket and a bow tie was Jomar Kraby.

'No need to look so alarmed,' Kraby said. 'It's me.'

'Can't you pay for your own taxi?'

'I'm representing our homeland at a reception in the Soviet Embassy. Hence the DJ and hence the Legation transport. If you don't want to drive me, you'd better say so now, and we can get someone else.'

Kai shook his head and started the engine. 'I was told there would be two of you.'

'Gunvor, whom you know,' Kraby said, passing him a piece of paper. 'She's gone ahead. We're going to Lidingö.'

Kai took the piece of paper, read the address and drove off without saying another word. The silence in the car was emphasised by the rhythmic beating of the windscreen wipers.

On the rear seat Kraby lit up and passed the packet forward. Kai took it, slowed down and tapped out a cigarette. Kraby leaned forward with a lighter in his hand.

Kai puffed, thinking he ought to say something. 'You're an energetic man, Kraby. Are you still focused on Daniel Berkåk?'

'No. I'm mostly focusing on Jenny Enersen now.'

'Jenny Enersen?'

'Haven't you read about her murder?'

'The woman they found in the sea?'

Kraby nodded. 'She was Norwegian, from Magnor. Crossed the border with a four-year-old daughter.'

'Poor thing.'

Kraby didn't respond.

Kai searched for his eyes in the mirror. 'Why are you following up that story?'

'I spoke to her just before it happened. She knew who killed your brother.'

'What?'

'Keep your eyes on the road, Kai. I'd prefer to arrive in one piece.'

Kai concentrated on driving. Thinking that the passenger on the rear seat was good at one thing: startling folk.

A policeman in black raingear and white gloves was directing traffic at the crossroads.

Kai stopped. 'What do you mean?' he asked, looking at the mirror.

'When your brother was killed, they used a decoy. A woman who knew someone who sold coffee on the black market. Your brother and this woman got into his car and drove off. That was the last time he was seen alive.'

Kai was still staring into the mirror. Jomar Kraby's face was inscrutable. He was looking through the side window.

'So that woman came here, to Sweden? And now she's dead?'

Kraby didn't answer. The policeman waved his hand. Kai drove.

'What did she tell you?'

'Nothing. She denied everything. The following day she went to Stockholm, was strangled and thrown into the sea.'

The hum of the engine and the regular back and forth of the windscreen wipers were all that could be heard.

Kai's eyes found Kraby's face in the mirror, suffused with a red glow whenever he took a deep drag on his cigarette.

'What do you think?' Kai asked. 'What happened to her?'

Kraby opened the ashtray in the door. Dropped the cigarette end inside and closed it. 'I've told you what I know. What do you think?'

Kai had nothing to say. Nor did he want to believe anything either. Kai was able to forget the man on the rear seat. To sit and concentrate. To drive, following the signposts. To forget the war, forget the unpleasantness, keep his mind blank.

'When we first spoke in Kjesäter…' Kraby started to say.

Kai found his eyes in the mirror.

'…I asked you what the Germans wanted to know about when they interrogated you in Grini. You said they wanted to know about Norwegian Communists. You said you didn't tell them anything because you didn't know anything. So they let you go. I said I thought that strange. I still think it is. I think you gave them something. Otherwise, they would never have let you go.'

'What do you think I gave them?'

'Loyalty.'

Kai regretted having taken this job. He should have told Kraby to find another driver. He wasn't under any obligation to talk to people he drove around.

'Your loyalty makes sense,' Kraby said. 'You promised to work for them. That explains why they released you from Grini. It explains how you know Sara Krefting. It may also explain why you came to Sweden. You see, I don't buy your story of wanting to go to England.'

Kai looked in the mirror again. Kraby looked back. Kai broke the vow he had made to himself and asked: 'Why not?'

'Because you've made absolutely no effort to get there. My question is actually *which* Kai crossed the border to Sweden. Is it the Kai who went to Barcelona or is it the Kai who vowed his allegiance to the Germans?'

Kai pulled into the kerb and stopped. Applied the handbrake and turned to look the man in the eye.

'It may be difficult for you to comprehend, but neither of them crossed the border. It was me who did. You see, I've become sick and tired of marching to someone else's tune. When I was in Spain, I learned one thing: War destroys. A Communist manifesto can't stop a bullet, nor can racial theories. I was in Grini when I was told my brother was dead. In one fell swoop, my whole family was gone, and I had plenty of time to reflect on being alone in the world. I was alone, but I wasn't free. And I wouldn't be free if I was set free. Making a deal with a German officer in Grini, stroking Sara Krefting's hair were two steps on a longer trajectory for me. Crossing the border was the third step on the way to becoming free. I came to Sweden to be free.'

'So you come here, and you're confronted by unpleasant questions about the murder of the man the police consider killed your brother.'

Kai turned back and started up the engine again.

Now he was allowed to drive on the road in peace, as it had become more tortuous and narrow. The last stretch was a gravel track and cars were queuing as they approached the sea. Guests in dinner wear swarmed around beneath umbrellas and clambered aboard boats. There were lots of them ferrying people to the island beyond.

When they arrived, Kai glanced at the mirror. 'When would you like to be picked up?'

Kraby was leaving the car. 'Would you mind waiting?'

'How long?'

Kraby turned back and looked across. 'I won't be long. A couple of hours, maximum,' he said and closed the door.

Kai looked around for somewhere to park. Thinking he might just as well wait here as anywhere else.

50

Gunvor felt ill at ease because she didn't fit in here at all. It was a place for the élite, the kind of people who didn't look at each other when they spoke – who directed all their comments at the ceiling.

When she turned, she was startled to find herself looking into the face of Jomar Kraby.

'I knew it, Gunvor. I knew you would be the most attractive woman here. It's a scandal to leave you on your own. Have you been here before? This pile must be the closest you can get to Villa Aldobrandini this far north?'

Before Gunvor had a chance to say a word, he had answered his own question: presumably she had been here before; she must have been, as she knew Orina Vasilikova. 'But do you know the history of this house?'

Gunvor managed to collect herself enough to shake her head this time.

A waiter snaked his way through the guests. Kraby tapped the man on the shoulder and took a glass from his tray. The waiter held out the tray for Gunvor, who said no, thank you, as Kraby was telling her that the man who had originally had the palace built had been a filthy-rich banker who traded with the Russian tsarist government before the revolution.

'The banker bought the whole of Storholmen Island from Edvard Söderlund, the so-called *punch-kungen*, the punch-king. Söderlund was called this because he had a royal warrant to supply punch at a time when it was a popular drink.' Kraby sipped from his glass and angled his head. 'Punch. It's good too. What an eye for detail Alexandra has. The only problem is that the Soviet Embassy doesn't spend any money on property maintenance. Have you been to the loo?'

Gunvor shook her head.

'It's like sitting on a throne. The seat is made of marble and the arms of porcelain. All the taps on the bath are made of gold.

I suppose the purpose must be to make having a dump a class issue. For as long as the lav lasts. It leaks, and the stained-glass windows in there are smashed. Repairing the ostentatious trappings of the bourgeoisie is not the Soviets' first priority.' Kraby looked around again.

'Who was the banker?' Gunvor asked, afraid that Kraby would find a more interesting partner for conversation and leave her on her own.

'His name was Kassmann, a capitalist who traded with Russia. By the way, he suffered a terrible tragedy, almost like in Scott Fitzgerald's book. The one about the upstart living on Long Island.' Jomar Kraby clicked his fingers as he ransacked his memory for the title of the novel. *The Great Gatsby*. A big novel. Gripping. Anyway, Kassmann had a young man working for him to operate the boats. His job was to ferry the boss to Stockholm City and back in a speed boat. One day, after delivering Kassmann to the quay in town, the young man brought the boat back here, to Storholmen. He invited the gardener, a shopkeeper and his little daughter on a boat trip. They set off from the quay down here but had only got a few hundred metres into the fjord when the engine burst into flames. The fire spread, and they had to jump into the sea, all of them. It was a disaster.'

Gunvor felt her back freeze. 'Did they all die?'

Kraby shook his head. 'The shopkeeper and the children were rescued, but when they searched for the bodies, they only found the boatman's. The gardener's was never recovered. From what I've heard, the gardener's ghost is abroad here, in the garden and on the first floor.'

Gunvor didn't want to let this affect her, but she could feel goosepimples on her arm.

'This was a terrible blow for Kassmann,' Kraby said. 'When Madame Kollontai took over the place as the Soviet Legation's summer house, she was in reality returning a piece of Russia to the Soviet Union.'

Kraby tilted his head at the sound of drums. Gunvor adopted the same pose. Something was about to happen by the velvet door at the end of the hall. A small band was approaching. The guests moved apart, and in marched a woman beating a drum. She was wearing riding breeches, tall black boots and a tight officer's jacket, and had the drum attached around her waist. She lifted her knees high, and Gunvor was unable to stifle a smile because, despite hiding her hair under an officer's cap and painting a Hitler moustache under her nose, Orina was easy to recognise. Behind her came a clown playing a trumpet. He was wearing the chequered costume of a harlequin. On his feet he wore huge shoes that forced him to lift his knees high too. Around his waist was a rope, which he used to pull a wooden horse on wheels. After the horse came the singer, marching, dressed in tails with a top hat and white gloves. In a sonorous, velvety voice, the revue star Karl Gerhard started to sing his forbidden song to the roar of the admiring audience:

'It's the infamous horse from Troy
Of modern fifth-column fable
Major Quisling is a papegoy
Who parrots as best he's able.'

The Swedes cheered. The British, the Soviets and the Americans perhaps didn't understand what they were so happy about, but slapped each other on the back, excited that there had been such a joyous break from the usual formalities.

Jomar Kraby swung round and grabbed Gunvor by the waist. Many followed their example. They fell into an almost tango-like rhythm. Kraby was, as always, a country clod on the dance floor, but Gunvor managed to manoeuvre them towards the drummer. She managed to touch her in the crush of bodies and received a knowing wink in return.

51

After several glasses of vodka punch and a couple of tins of beluga caviar on dry biscuits, Jomar realised that Madame Kollontai had no intention of attending the reception, so it was up to him to arrange a confrontation. He had met her before, when she was stationed in Oslo and he was younger and more enthusiastic about the revolution. According to rumour, she was still in contact with a few Norwegians, such as Martin Tranmæl, from that time. As for himself, he was intrigued to know whether she would still recognise him.

The broad staircase up to the first floor was made of marble, like so much in this house, but it was worn. There were cigarette ends on the steps. Several of the edges were damaged, and the top steps shone as if they were soaking wet. Well, it was pouring down when they arrived, Jomar thought, unaware that it would rain indoors too.

As he climbed the stairs, the explanation became apparent. Here there were tubs and buckets placed strategically across the floor to catch the rainwater trickling down through the roof.

He looked up. The chandeliers were moving, as though the wind was blowing under the vaulted ceiling. There were cracks in the plaster, and rain was seeping in. Several of the buckets on the floor were full to overflowing. And the water had formed rivulets flowing down towards the stairs and beyond. The light in the ceiling made the pools on the floor reflect like a mirror. This did not bode well. It was just a question of time, he thought; before too long the house would return to nature.

Behind the clutter of buckets and containers, at the opposite end of the hall, a light shone through a half-open door. He walked towards it, but stopped before getting there, unsure of the etiquette.

'Over here, Kraby. Come in,' said a voice he hadn't heard for ages.

So she did remember him. Beyond that, the joys of their

reunion were of the cooler variety. Alexandra was sitting behind a large desk, as attractive as always. Jomar was sure he looked older than she did, even though she had to be around seventy now – he concluded after some swift mental arithmetic. Her curly hair wasn't grey, but nor did it seem to be dyed.

The desk had a thick catalogue placed under one leg to make it level, and on top there was a dazzling white wound where some wood had splintered off. Also on top were piles of books, papers, several pens and two inkwells behind a great big ashtray overflowing with cigarette ends. He could see she was in the middle of writing and immediately felt he was disturbing her.

'You don't look after the house,' he said, for lack of anything to say.

'What kind of comment is that? Are you after a quote for a new novel?'

'I am loathe to come across as a haggler, Alexandra, but I sent you a letter, and in all modesty I'm only asking for a name.'

'I don't concern myself with that sort of thing anymore. Spying is for idealists and patriots. I'm no longer either.'

'Says the woman who helped to plan the October Revolution.'

'Says the woman who hopes to have a natural death, Kraby, but the chances of that happening are small. Of those who sat around the table in those days only Lenin has had that honour. As far as your query's concerned, it's generated some enthusiasm from the recipient.' She inclined her head. 'Something tells me you knew it would.'

Jomar havered. 'I assume he's asked for something in return.'

She nodded, with a suggestion of a smile playing on her lips.

As she lit a cigarette, and the match illuminated her ravaged face. He saw that her hair was a wig. It was slightly askew. In addition, it became clear that water was dripping down from the roof behind her too.

An officer, he thought, an officer stationed in a decaying mausoleum. There were quite a few subjects he would have liked to discuss with her, such as Kirov's murder, which had triggered Stalin's cleansing of the party, and Nikolayev's role in the matter or Bukharin's tragic fate – but he was standing there like a butler outside a lady's bathroom. He could see she had no intention of inviting him all the way in.

'I'm very pleased you invited me, Alexandra. I still remember with great joy the days of political passion in Oslo.'

'There isn't much joy left in the world, I'm afraid.'

'The Red Army's making headway in the east. That's a joy for many.'

'Death isn't headway. I have a dark view of these times, and I see even darker days ahead.'

Her hand groped for the ashtray. She pulled it closer and flicked ash from her cigarette. 'I'm weary, Kraby, weary of company, weary of war and death and political strife. Long before the world's menfolk began to fight each other in this war, I and all the women in the world fought a different battle. This hellish war has put my own struggle back years. I'm much less committed to this world war than rumours would have it.' With the cigarette bobbing up and down in the corner of her mouth, she at first splayed both hands, then pointed to herself. 'The greater the challenges we face in life and work, the greater we yearn for understanding and human warmth, but they never materialise. The warmth or the caring. It's not dissimilar to the disappointment we experience with romantic love. But you won't be leaving here empty-handed. You can console yourself with that thought. Now I'd like to be alone.'

Jomar realised that his audience was over and backed towards the door.

'Leave the door open,' she shouted.

On the way down the stairs he stumbled into a cooking pot full of rainwater. He stepped right in, soaking his leg up to his calf. He tried to shake the pot off, but his shoe was stuck. Wearing the pot like a galosh, he limped down, but lost his balance and fell headlong. He stretched out both hands to break his fall, but they too skidded in the water. It was no surprise that he had tripped, he thought to himself, as he felt the moisture saturating his shirt front. It was probably an hour since his last drink.

With difficulty he struggled to his knees and met the ice-cold eyes of Orina Vasilikova on her way up the staircase with a bottle of vodka in one hand. Jomar finally managed to kick the pot off his shoe and made room for her to pass. They both stood, watching the pot roll down the steps, then Orina hurried after it, caught it and placed it under another leak from the ceiling. Jomar bowed to her and continued down the staircase, both legs dripping with water, his shirt and jacket drenched.

When, shortly afterwards, he took his coat down from one of the hooks, he felt a stiff piece of paper in the inside pocket. It was an envelope. I'll be damned, he thought, she has kept her word, and felt his mood soar. At the same time, he observed that he wasn't the only person to find the time ripe to leave the party. In front of him were two British officers, accompanying women.

52

His temple was freezing cold. Running a hand over his face, Kai felt a drop of saliva on his chin. This was what happened when you fell asleep against a car window. It had to be late because now and then motor launches filled with homeward-bound guests were mooring at the quay. Gentlemen in hats and overcoats and ladies in capes and high heels were dashing through the rain from the quay to a shelter. They stood there waiting for the car that would take them back to the capital. Kai didn't see either Kraby or Gunvor among the gentry. Another boat moored. Strong men helped the passengers ashore. Kai's eyes widened when he recognised the woman tripping along beside one of the gentlemen.

He opened the door and stepped out of the car. The group of four the woman was part of looked in his direction as the car door slammed.

Kai doffed his hat and stared straight at her.

She stopped, stood still and stared at him.

Kai turned his back on her and retreated into the car. Wrapped his coat around himself. Closed his eyes. Thinking back to the night she and he were sitting on the same seat in a taxi. He was startled when Kraby opened the rear door.

'Thanks for waiting in this shit weather,' Kraby said, getting in and closing the door.

He immediately put his hand into his inside pocket and took out an envelope, which he opened. He used a lighter to read the notelet inside, then replaced everything and leaned back with closed eyes and a rapturous smile on his face. Kai watched him.

Kraby opened his eyes. 'Let's go, shall we?'

'What about Gunvor?'

'She isn't coming.'

Kai started up and switched on the lights.

A solitary figure now stood beneath the shelter at the quayside. It was a woman. She suddenly came running towards the car. Soon she was banging on the window beside Kraby, who told Kai to wait and rolled down the window.

The shoulders of her light-coloured summer cape were dark from the rain as she asked in sing-song Swedish if she could have a lift to Norrmalm.

Kraby seemed confused. 'Why are you alone? What happened to your group?'

'There was no room in the other car. Have you got a seat for me?'

Kai opened his door. Walked round the car and opened the passenger door at the front. 'You can sit here.'

He and Iris exchanged glances for a few long seconds before she slipped inside.

53

When Kai pulled in to the kerb, Jomar Kraby opened the door, said goodbye and got out. Iris and Kai sat watching the lanky figure walk up the steps and go inside. After the door closed behind him, Kai put the car in gear. It wasn't a long trip. On the journey from Lidingö the silence had been odd. Now the atmosphere was even stranger. Kai stopped in front of the entrance without turning the engine off.

Iris made no attempt to open the door.

He turned in his seat. 'Here we are then.'

'Have you got time for a drink?'

'In your flat?'

She nodded.

Kai didn't answer straight away. Her eyes wavered as his gaze met them.

'He's dead,' Kai said. 'Heikki Virtanen.'

She nodded again.

'Why did you tell me he was alive?'

She chose to remain silent. But as he was about to repeat the question, she answered:

'Have you never had a sense that someone who's dead can't be because you still need them?'

Kai thought about his brother. Atle's death represented pain mixed with shame and more, something dark concealed behind a door he had little desire to open. The fear of discovering what was hiding there was too great for that, but could he understand what she meant? Kai realised that he was finished with grieving over Atle. It was different with his father. He still missed him a lot. Kai could still lean on him, and perhaps that was what he was still doing, but to answer her question would be to engage in trivialities when all he wanted to do was hold her tight.

'You were gone for several days.'

'Don't ask where I was. I can't tell you anyway.'

He recalled the moment they were in the little flat and there was a ring at the door. He remembered the transformation that took place. It was quite a different woman sitting beside him now. The light from the streetlamp left half her face in shadow. When they had walked around the block she had said she didn't take strangers home. So he was no longer a stranger – but what was he?

'Have you got time? Now?'

'I think I'll give it a miss.'

Something died in her eyes.

The air in the car quivered with tension, and he could feel himself having to swallow. 'You went to my boarding house and asked after me.'

She didn't answer.

'You wrote that there was something you wanted to ask me.'

Still she was silent, then she grabbed the door handle, opened the door and scrambled out.

This stunned him, but when she stopped at the front entrance and sent him a final glance over her shoulder, he realised she mustn't disappear this time. So he switched off the engine.

She waited for him to get out of the car.

She walked up the stairs in front of him, like the first time, long ago. She searched through her bag for the key. They exchanged looks before she opened up. Once inside, he walked to the window and studied the toy soldiers standing in line as before, and heard her close the door behind them and go to the bathroom.

On her return, she was wearing an ankle-length kaftan, and holding a bottle of wine in one hand and a corkscrew in the other. Kai thought about the lies she had served him up, but he was a liar himself. Besides, he had no wish to ask any more questions, to let untruths or laments about difficult life choices sully his time with her. He walked up to Iris, took the bottle and the corkscrew from her, placed both on the table and kissed her soft lips.

Not a word was spoken between them, not when she led him

to the bed in the other room, not when they undressed each other and not in the intervals their bodies needed as night slowly merged into day. Where nature ruled, there was no room for any other thoughts. Explanations, probing questions about lies, about things unspoken, fabrications and gossip, and the unpleasantness this produced – Kai wanted all of this swept to one side, to be consigned to the life that is lived in daylight. And he saw with the utmost clarity that this was what she wanted too.

54

Jomar unlocked the door to his flat, went straight to his desk and took out Daniel Berkåk's notebook. Then he switched on the light, sat down and compared the notes in the little book with the contents of the envelope he was given on Storholmen. It wasn't necessary, but he did it anyway, as if to confirm to himself that he had selected the right jigsaw piece and it fitted. Afterwards he lit his last Cuban Robusto, treating himself to this and a glass of brandy, while reflecting on what the wisest course of action would now be.

Before the cigar was finished, one glass had led to another, and by the time the cigar was out he hadn't noticed that he had fallen asleep in the chair. In some inexplicable way he woke up in his own bed a few hours later. By then it was daytime – the sun had burst through the cloud and was shining through the window.

He got up, driven by a literary impulse. The work on this investigation had developed in a way that had much in common with writing. The information he had been given in the envelope the previous evening was liberating. It felt as if he had reached a decisive moment in his own creativity, and he was reminded of Thomas Mann's Gustav von Aschenbach, who had been in exactly the same position. Aschenbach had stood up from his desk and gone out because he found himself facing a crucial decision in his writing. He had wandered around the town, observed the cathedrals and met the red-haired man. The walk had finally given Aschenbach the inspiration to travel to Venice, an inspiration which, among so much else, would lead to his death.

Jomar Kraby was in Stockholm, the Venice of the North.

The thought sent a shiver through his body. He knew this feeling all too well. At times writing could be as light and compelling as running before the wind in a boat, but sooner or later the moment of decision arrives, when you have to take a firm hold of the text, eschew temptations in order to be true to the inner structure of the narrative. It is the most difficult thing to do, and he felt that drive now, stronger than ever before. What was he going to do with the person Alexandra had delivered to him on a platter? Spy on him? Contact him? Report him to the police?

Jomar did what Aschenbach did. He went out. He wandered through the streets and contemplated the city's grand architecture, imitated Aschenbach in this way too, but he avoided the cathedrals. Jomar had more appreciation for hostelries, but he didn't enter any of them either. Merely glanced at the windows as he walked by. Even though he was a man who espoused the tavern idyll, he could not bear to waste a fresh, unspoilt morning by confronting the evidence of the previous night's alcohol-fuelled shenanigans. And he had no interest in going into a bar made chilly by a gale blowing through doors and windows propped open in an attempt to remove the stench of tobacco and spilt beer. A morning for him should retain its fresh, unlived atmosphere. Jomar liked to arrive in a pub only when other customers were already ensconced and the atmosphere was focused on the moment, not on the previous day.

He strolled across Norrbroen Bridge, to the square in front of the Royal Palace. He stood by the fence, facing the sea. On the opposite side of the water the Grand Hotel stood cheek by jowl with the German Legation. It struck Jomar that King

Gustav probably drank his morning coffee enjoying the sight of the fluttering swastika flag in the secure knowledge that he was still the king in his own country. Perhaps he thought about Princess Märtha, who, together with Norway's heirs to the throne, was denied entry to Sweden when the Nazis were hunting them three years ago in April. The panorama here was the essence of living in exile. Being able to walk alongside German officers, knowing they didn't have the power to touch you. This was what lent the war a touch of unreality in Stockholm. It was so unreal that staff in Norwegian offices could argue about spelling mistakes or take personal offence at being bypassed in the administrative hierarchy, while every day their compatriots at home were fighting for their lives.

Jomar tore himself out of these reveries and walked to the end of Västerlånggatan and crossed over the Slussen locks. The buildings on the island of Södermalm towered over the water like the walls of a big castle. He climbed, taking the steep steps up from Katarinavägen. At the top, he rambled aimlessly through the streets.

When Jomar finally came to a halt outside the apartment block in Skånegatan, he stood for a few seconds, weighing up the pros and cons, then realised it had to be the force of the phenomenon Sigmund Freud had termed the *Unterbewusstsein*, the unconscious mind, that had brought him here. For that reason, he didn't need to check either Alexandra's note or Daniel Berkåk's notebook.

He went through the entrance, continued up the stairs and studied the signs on doors until he found the name he was looking for. A double door. A cast-iron knocker was mounted between its panels. Jomar took it and banged firmly twice. He held his hands behind his back and waited. No one opened. He knocked again. No reaction.

Then the neighbour's door opened. An elderly woman peered out at him. She had grey hair, which fell over her ears, and a thick lower lip under a prominent bluish nose that lent her face a likeable, proletarian aspect. Jomar nodded to her before going downstairs and outside. He carried on walking down the street until he found an ironmonger's, where he bought a solid crowbar. Afterwards, with the crowbar up the sleeve of his coat, he walked back and up the stairs, tiptoeing this time. For safety's sake, he knocked first. No one at home. Then he placed the crowbar under the moulding where the two halves of the double-door met and applied his body weight. The two halves were prised apart and he was able to push the crowbar in further. When he applied his weight again, the door strike slipped out and the door was open.

Once inside, he examined the door. The frame itself was chipped, from the pressure of the crowbar, but the lock was still fulfilling its function. The flat consisted of a kitchen, bathroom, two small bedrooms and a simply furnished sitting room with a wood-burning stove. One bedroom was bare. From this Jomar deduced that the man lived alone. There were a few books on the shelves. Biographies. Literature about military leaders. Nelson and Napoleon. *The Great War*. Analyses of battles during the First World War in English, Swedish and German. He pulled out a book and sat in an armchair under the window to read. Sounds came from the stairs. Footsteps. Voices. Jomar jumped up from the chair. Stared at the front door.

A key was inserted in the lock.

Jomar grabbed the crowbar.

By the time he had reached the bathroom, there were already people in the hall.

Inside, there was a bathtub. Jomar stepped into it and pulled the shower curtains to. He remembered the book he had left open on the chair in the sitting room. Too late to do anything about that now.

Through a crack in the curtain he could see through the half-open door. A man wearing an officer's uniform came into his line of vision. He spoke German. Behind him was the woman from next door. They moved out of his sightline.

Jomar heard them opening and closing doors and cupboards.

The neighbour came into view again. She was holding the book in her hand. The officer said in broken Swedish that there was no one here. She must have been imagining the whole thing. The neighbour disagreed. She put the book back on the shelf. And now she turned, came towards the bathroom and pushed the door fully open.

Once inside, she parted the curtains. Jomar raised his hat and essayed a sort of smile. Her face was as cheery and expressive as a brick. Her thick lower lip resembled a beak as she thrust out a hand and rubbed her thumb across her first two fingers.

Jomar understood the gesture, took his wallet from his inside pocket and proffered a banknote.

It disappeared into her fist. She gestured for more.

Jomar took another banknote, which disappeared in the same way.

Now the officer was on his way over.

She turned and blocked the doorway. 'No one here,' she said in German and left the bathroom, closing the door behind her as she did so.

Their voices through the closed door were muffled. It was impossible to distinguish any words. At last he heard the front door close. He waited in the bathtub for a few long minutes, then stepped out and returned to the sitting room. He took a deep breath. There was nothing in this room that gave any indication of the man who lived here. If indeed someone did live here.

At length he went to the front door and listened. It was quiet outside. When he opened the door he found himself looking straight into the neighbour's face.

'What are you doing in there?'

Jomar went out and locked the door behind him, put his hand in his inside pocket and pulled out the letter from the government-in-exile in London.

She read it, nodded gravely and passed it back to him.

'You keep an eye on your neighbours, do you?'

She didn't answer.

'The man who went into the flat with you, does he live here?'

'The man who lives here travels a lot. I think he's in Germany at the moment.'

'Who was the man with you?'

'He's from the German Embassy.'

'So the man who lives here is attached to the embassy?'

She nodded.

'The name on the door, Asbjørn Fallet, is Norwegian.'

'Then presumably he's Norwegian,' the woman said, handing out the banknotes to him. 'Asbjørn Fallet's probably not the only Norwegian working for the Germans.'

'Keep the money,' Jomar said. 'You've earned it.' He sniffed. There was a wonderful aroma. 'Meatballs?'

She shook her head. 'Beef stew,' she said, stuffing the notes in her apron pocket. 'Hungry?'

'If you're offering,' Kraby said.

'I eat alone far too often. Join me,' she said, shuffling ahead of him to her own flat.

55

What a great pleasure a hearty meal is. First, beef stew with carrots and onions, and then Swedish blueberry soup for dessert. All in all, a luxury Jomar's body hadn't enjoyed since pre-war Christmas nights.

Almost torpid with contentment, he treated himself to a taxi home and then a nap on his bed. He was lying, eyes half open, trying to remember the last time he'd had a lunch without alcohol, when the telephone in the corridor began to ring. Jomar swung his legs down onto the floor and went to answer it.

It was a call from a phone booth. There was a clink as the coin dropped. The voice in the receiver belonged to the woman who had made the delicious meal. Jomar took the opportunity to praise her culinary skills before asking how he could help.

She informed him that her neighbour hadn't gone to Germany, as she had told him. Because he was at home now. Jomar thanked her and rang off.

Jomar went back to his flat. He stood at the window, looking out as he considered various plans of action. And concluded that actually there was only one thing he could do. So he put on his shoes, coat, hat and scarf again. Went downstairs and made the same journey, this time by bus.

From the bus stop it was a hundred metres on foot. On arriving, he went through the front entrance without a sideways glance. Carried on walking up the stairs and hammered the knocker on the door. When the door opened, Jomar raised his hat and extended his broadest smile. The man in the doorway was an athletically built fellow with a knitted waistcoat over a shirt and felt slippers on his feet.

'Was wünschen Sie? Kann ich Ihnen helfen?'

Jomar didn't believe for a second that the rote-learned German was anything but a blind. He pointed to the name plate. 'Sie sind Asbjørn Fallet?'

The man in the doorway didn't react.

Jomar motioned towards the name plate and when he spoke again, it was in Norwegian. 'If you aren't Asbjørn Fallet, where is he?'

The man slammed the door.

Jomar stared at the wooden panel. He waited, but nothing happened. He banged the knocker again. Nothing.

Then he turned, went downstairs and out. He carried on down the street, wondering if he had been stupid. Stopped, thought for a moment, then walked back, into the block and up the stairs. This time he knocked on the neighbour's door.

She opened up and stepped aside.

A vague whiff of beef stew was still noticeable. He hung up his hat and coat and followed her into the sitting room. She was playing patience.

'Let's have a game of cards,' he said.

'Didn't he want to talk to you?' she asked, pooling the cards and shuffling them.

'No.'

'He's rarely in during the evening. He'll be going out soon.'

'That's kind of what I'm hoping.'

'Rummy?'

'Why not,' Jomar said, sitting down at the table.

❖

They had been playing for about half an hour, in which time Jomar had lost most of the games, when she raised her head and listened.

Jomar heard it too. The corridor door closing. Her neighbour was on the move. Jomar stood up without saying a word. Grabbed his hat and coat and left.

Outside, it was growing dark, but there was no mistaking the man. He was heading for the taxi rank, where four cars were waiting in a line. When the first started up, Jomar made for the second. The driver was professional and discreet. He asked no questions when Jomar told him to follow the car in front, but from a distance.

It wasn't to be a long journey. The car in front went via Slussen, through the Old Town and across the next bridge until it pulled over by the Carlton Hotel. A page boy opened the door for Asbjørn Fallet, who walked into the hotel.

Jomar paid his driver and got out, but he hesitated before going in. Through the windows he could see that the man had stopped in the lobby and was now in conversation with the receptionist. Eventually he headed towards the restaurant door.

Only then did Jomar enter the lobby.

The man joined a group in the dining room. Three elegantly dressed women and two men in German uniforms. All five of them greeted him with raised glasses.

Jomar found a seat at the bar where he had a good view of

the restaurant and the table for six. When the waiter came past, he asked for a beer.

The six men and women were served food and wine. They were a merry crew. Jomar managed to down two more beers and visit the toilet once before the man called Asbjørn Fallet signed the bill. Afterwards the whole group left the restaurant and entered the lobby, making for the lift. One of the women tripped. She let out a squeal; Fallet grabbed her and broke her fall. 'I think I must be a bit tiddly,' she said, hooking her arm through his.

Jomar was fairly sure he had heard her voice before.

After the high-spirited crowd had entered the lift, Jomar went to the toilet again. Afterwards he headed straight for the reception desk. The man standing behind it had red hair and a thick red beard.

Jomar said he thought he had recognised Asbjørn Fallet. 'Is he staying at this hotel?'

'We don't have a guest by that name.'

'The man who caught the lady before she fell, wasn't that Fallet?'

'That was herr Lazarus. Johan Lazarus. If you would excuse me,' he said, going through a door behind the desk.

Jomar went outside to find himself a taxi. True to form, there were none to be seen.

◈

At last, one pulled into the kerb to drop off passengers, a woman and a man. Jomar waited until they were both out of the car before getting in. He told the driver to go to Mosebacke Torg. On the hill up towards the market square the taxi passed a parked car Jomar had seen before. It belonged to the Norwegian Legation. After paying the driver, Jomar strolled back to the parked car and looked up and down the street. The flat he was searching for had to be in the vicinity.

There were two entrances to apartment blocks in this part of town. The first one he went through led to a staircase going up through the floors. Jomar walked up, reading the signs on the doors, but didn't see the name he was after. So he went down again and into the next entrance. This was the right one. Kai Fredly had stuck a bit of cardboard bearing his name onto one of the post boxes below.

Jomar went up to the second floor and knocked.

He heard footsteps inside. The lock was turned, and there was Fredly, wearing trousers, a vest and red braces. From inside the flat he heard a voice on the radio.

Jomar lifted his hat. 'Sorry to disturb you so late.'

Kai just stared at him.

Jomar held his ground, thinking.

'Yes?'

'Aren't you going to invite me in?'

'I'd prefer not to.'

Jomar nodded. Actually, there was nothing you could say to a point-blank rejection. 'Do you know the Carlton Hotel here in Stockholm?'

Kai shook his head. 'In fact, I don't.'

'I think you should get yourself over there.'

'For what purpose?'

'There's a man staying tonight by the name of Johan Lazarus.'

'And who's he?'

'I don't know him.'

'So why should I go there?'

'I think it would be of interest to you.'

'You're talking in riddles, Kraby.'

'Lazarus is not the man's real name,' Jomar said. 'He lives in Stockholm, but tonight he's celebrating with some others at a hotel, and calling himself Lazarus. The only other Lazarus I've ever heard of was a friend of Jesus Christ who rose from the dead. I think it's no coincidence that this man has chosen such an unusual name.' Jomar raised his hat. 'Give it some thought, Kai. Goodnight,' he said and left.

As he was walking downstairs, he asked himself why he hadn't told Kai about the woman who had tripped in the hotel reception area. Granted, he didn't know her name, but he could have described her. It wouldn't have been difficult. He wondered whether it was the writer in him or the romantic who had chosen to keep stumm.

On the way down he tried to hear if Fredly had closed the door. He didn't hear anything. Presumably he hadn't moved. He could understand that.

He had given Kai Fredly something to chew on.

56

The sound of Kraby's footsteps faded. At last, he heard the front door slam. Kai went back to the bed-sit, where he watched himself switch off the radio. He sank onto the edge of the bed and sat as if paralysed. When eventually he did raise his head, drops were falling against the window. Raindrops. Probably a storm. How fitting.

After a while he got up and found a clean shirt in the wardrobe. Looked at himself in the mirror while buttoning it up and tying his tie. He was ready, but paused by the door. Went to the sink and threw water over his face. Afterwards he lingered, staring at the bed. And took a decision. He went over and lifted the pillow. Grabbed the Webley. Checked the barrel. Four of the six chambers were loaded. He prepared the revolver, made sure the hammer was down, and stuffed it in his coat pocket.

Then he went out to the Legation car and got in. His hand on the ignition key was trembling. He gripped the wheel tight. And sat breathing heavily before he drove off.

◈

When he drew into the kerb a hundred metres from the main entrance to the hotel, at first he remained in the car. A glance at his watch told him it was close to midnight. Kai took a deep breath and got out, buttoned up his coat against the rain, pulled his hat down over his forehead, walked to the entrance and went inside.

The lobby was quiet. A receptionist dressed in black, pale skin, dark bags under his eyes, red hair and an equally red beard, stood behind the desk.

Kai walked over. The red-haired man lifted his chin and angled his head.

'You have a Johan Lazarus staying in the hotel. Could you tell him that Kai Fredly is here?'

Hesitating, the man looked at the clock.

'I'm expected,' Kai said.

The receptionist rang the bell mounted on the desk. A page boy appeared. He was given a note and ran up the stairs.

Kai found himself a chair by the window. Before long a waiter came over from the bar. His hair was combed back and as smooth and shiny as the lapels on his jacket. The waiter enquired if he wanted anything. Kai shook his head. After a while the page boy returned. The young boy sat on a chair behind the desk, eating a chocolate while staring at Kai, who looked away.

Ten long minutes passed and nothing happened. The page boy was sitting on the same chair.

Another five passed, and Kai started preparing to leave, but when he stood up, the lift motor began to hum.

The cables in the shaft were moving. The lift was on its way down. Through the frosted glass the shadow of a man was visible. Soon it was at ground level and a man pulled the grille aside, pushed the door open and stepped out.

It felt like a kick in the stomach. Not only because it was Atle standing there, but also because of the smile and the scowling eyes that Kai knew all too well.

Kai ignored his brother's outstretched hand, but went straight up to him and sniffed. No evidence of sunshine, only the stench of after-shave, tobacco and spirits. Atle was a big boy now.

Kai took two paces back. His mouth was dry. 'I thought I'd never see you again.'

Atle smiled tentatively. 'Thank you, and the same to you, Kai.' He took a step forward and stopped. 'How did you find me?'

'I hadn't even begun to look. Up until now I'd thought you were dead.'

Atle inclined his head. 'Why are you here then?'

'What's the problem?'

'The name. Lazarus. It's one I seldom use. No one ever asks after herr Lazarus.'

'So who should I have asked to speak to?'

'You first, Kai. Who gave you the name?'

Kai was seeing his brother in a new light. Atle, who had been dead, had sprung up out of nowhere and at their reunion, after five long years, what he wanted to do was barter information. To conceal his disdain, Kai turned away. Tossed his head towards the bar. 'Shall we have a glass of something and chat?'

Without waiting for an answer, he led the way to the bar, which was deserted. No one was sitting at the long counter. Only a few booths beside the windows were occupied – couples sitting either side of a table, leaning forward, whispering. Kai went to a free booth. The same waiter appeared.

Atle asked for a Martini for himself and a double whisky for Kai. 'Only one ice cube in the whisky,' he added with a wink at Kai, who sat observing his brother. The messy hair. The collarless shirt.

'What name do you use when you're not called Lazarus?'

'I can't tell you.'

'Why not?'

Atle composed himself before leaning across the table and looking him in the eye. 'Because I'm working for the Norwegian Home Front.'

Kai was speechless.

'I can't say too much about this,' Atle said, sitting up straight.

'I laid flowers on your grave. Who's in it?'

'I don't know.'

'I've heard a story about a body being dragged from the Glomma.'

'The river story was a fabrication. I had to get away. So they had to make something up.'

'They? Make something up? Are you trying to pull the wool over my eyes?'

'Kai, lower your voice.' Atle seemed worried now. 'I'm telling you this, but you have to keep it to yourself for your own security – and for mine. I'm here in Stockholm on a mission for the Home Front. I have a different name, and every day I live in fear of being exposed and killed. Stockholm's full of Norwegians who hate Nazis, and none of them know what I'm telling you now. That's why I've gone underground. It was the Home Front who made up the story about the river to get me away, so that I wouldn't be exposed. The man in our parents' grave – I don't know who he was. He threw himself in the river. He took his own life.'

'I heard the body was sunk in the river, but it floated up a few weeks later.'

'That isn't right, Kai. This man threw himself into the river of his own free will. Attempts were made to save him, but he was dead when they fished him out. No one knew who he was, but as he was my age, and dead, he became a way of protecting me from the Germans. So they used his body. They said it was me, put his body in a coffin and told the undertaker that the man in the coffin was me. I crossed over into Sweden the same night.'

'You enlisted to fight on the Eastern Front.'

Atle leaned his head to one side, enquiringly. The gesture bordered on surprise. It must have been because of the sudden change of topic.

'Perhaps it was a natural thing for you to do,' said Kai. 'After all, you were in the Hirden long before the Germans occupied Norway. But I've done a lot of thinking about why you of all people would end up fighting alongside the Germans.'

He paused as the waiter brought their drinks.

'I think I know why,' Kai continued when the waiter was out of hearing.

Atle interrupted him. 'The Soviet campaign made me see the world differently, Kai. My eyes were opened to the reality. I understood what the Germanic idea actually was about: killing and the extermination of the innocent. I saw such terrible cruelty in the Soviet Union that I can't even bring myself to talk about it. They forced me to do the most dreadful things.' Atle closed his eyes and composed himself before going on. 'I was ... we were in the SS. We weren't confined by the usual laws. Our orders were to nullify the enemy without mercy. The worst jobs were carried out by Einsatzgruppen, the death squads, but we were forced to be part of the savagery too. No appeal was possible. But I wanted out from the first day. Imagine: I had joined up to fight for a free Norway. Instead, I was forced to kill civilians. I'd had enough when they forced women and children into a church and set fire to it. I was outside and heard the screams when the counter-attack came. I was in the midst of the firing and all I wanted was to die. I was hit in the shoulder. That's how I escaped from that living hell.' Atle took a sip of his Martini. 'My shoulder still bothers me,' he said, putting down his drink.

Kai gazed out of the window. The night was pitch-black. The light from the streetlamps didn't reach inside the hotel. In the reflection he saw the contours of himself, and in himself he saw his brother, the Eastern Front campaigner who was convincingly claiming that he had been converted.

Kai cleared his throat. 'As I said, I think I know why.'

'Why what?'

'Why you ended up there, on the Eastern Front. It was your

rebellion. This was how you could liberate yourself from our father, by rebelling against what he stood for. Grinding into the dirt what he thought was right. What did he say when you joined the Nasjonal Samling?'

'What did he say?' Atle's smile was cold. 'He didn't say a word, Kai. He used his fists. Perhaps you didn't notice. You were Mamma's little prince. That night I hit back, that was the last time. The last time he ever hit me.'

'Are you happy?'

'What about?'

'About your rebellion.'

Atle shook his head, condescendingly. 'You've always been a workhorse, Kai, better with your hands than your head. Stick to your hammer and last.'

'I've seen your medal.'

'Where?'

'At Sara Krefting's place. She let me stay there when I got out of Grini.'

Atle nodded and took a deep breath. 'I was honoured because I spilt blood for the Third Reich. I'm not proud of that medal, but I was lucky and was sent home to recover. As soon I was out of hospital, I contacted good Norwegians. However, I was valuable for the Germans. They wanted to exploit my contacts. The deal with the Home Front was that I'd stay in the Nasjonal Samling but work as a spy for the Home Front. That went fine for a few months. Then my cover was blown, and I had to get out.'

'Why are you repudiating what you stood for?'

Atle frowned. 'What do you mean?'

'You volunteered to fight for Germany. You were willing to die for what you believed in. That deserves respect, but now you're distancing yourself from it.' Kai leaned further forward. 'I did terrible things in Spain, which I'm not particularly proud of, but I did them for a good cause. The decisions I took, I took. The dead are dead, and tears have been shed. I can't change my past and I can't deny who I am or what I've done. You say risking your life on the front was wrong, a terrible mistake. Where are you in all this? What do you stand for, actually?'

Atle glared back, without responding.

'The Oslo police think you were killed.'

Atle didn't respond to that either.

'The man the police think killed you is dead.'

'Who's that?'

'His name's Daniel Berkåk.'

'Don't know anything about him.'

'Are you sure?'

'Daniel? I don't know any Daniel.'

'Berkåk was thought to have been out for revenge. The police in Norway think he killed you because you'd worked with the Germans and you'd had people arrested, people who were then executed.'

Atle hissed as he leaned forward: 'That's a wild accusation. Lies.'

Kai met his brother's eyes and recognised something, a defiance he remembered from their childhood. The sight of it made him shake his head.

Atle leaned even further forward. 'Surely you don't believe people who make up lies about your brother?'

'I know Daniel Berkåk didn't kill you, because you're here. Instead it's Berkåk who's dead.' Now it was Kai's turn to whisper. 'Berkåk was murdered. Why do you think he was killed, Atle?'

'I have no idea, Kai. I don't know who you're talking about.'

'What if someone wanted to snuff out Berkåk to avenge your death?'

'That's madness. Absolute madness,' Atle said, clearing his throat, ready to say more.

But Kai interjected: 'You're a German officer. I've got photos of you in a German uniform with stripes on your arm and a medal on your chest.'

'I care about you, Kai. I always have done.' Atle straightened up, the expression on his face seeming genuinely desperate as he searched for the right words.

'Why are you staying in this hotel?' asked Kai.

'What do you mean?'

'I imagine you have somewhere to live. You don't stay month after month in somewhere as extravagant as this.'

Atle smiled. 'A party. There are a group of us celebrating tonight.'

'Celebrating what?'

'I can't tell you.'

'Any women?'

'There are.'

'And everyone's waiting for you?'

Atle shrugged.

'I can join you. Shall we go up to your friends?'

Atle was silent.

'Are you ashamed of your brother? Don't you want me to meet your friends?'

'No one must know that Atle's still alive, Kai. That's the long and short of it. If the situation were different, if there were peace in the world, I would happily take you up to the room.'

Kai picked up his glass and knocked back the whisky. He gestured to the waiter, who nodded and poured him another tumbler behind the bar.

'Sara Krefting's sure Daniel Berkåk killed you,' Kai said. 'That was why she wanted Berkåk dead and was keen to do something about it. She asked me to kill him to avenge your death.'

Kai was curious to see how his brother would receive that piece of information, but there was no visible reaction.

The waiter came to the table, placed the whisky in front of Kai and took the empty tumbler away.

Atle watched him go, waited until he was out of hearing. 'So you know already. Sara Krefting's a dangerous woman. She's more of a Nazi than Hitler. She thinks she knows what makes the world go round, but she knows nothing, and that's why she's dangerous. You and I are the same blood, Kai. There are enough power-hungry politicians causing trouble everywhere without you and me doing the same. We've fought our battles, but the war we're in now is equally awful, whether the man holding the bayonet is German, British or Norwegian. We're here in Sweden, a neutral country. We're sitting on a dry rock in the middle of the rapids. When the war is over, we can be brothers again. Until then only the fact that I love you and know you're fine makes my life anything but a source of sadness.'

Kai had to smile.

'What are you smiling at?'

'The way you talk. Stockholm's full of Norwegians, but most of them prefer not to pay any attention to German officers. Apart from a few. I think Daniel Berkåk saw you. He would've known who you were when he saw you. He blamed you for his father's death. Perhaps he spoke to you in the street. Perhaps he made a nuisance of himself. Perhaps he accused you. Perhaps you decided to do something about it, perhaps you wanted to shut him up for ever. Perhaps you made sure he couldn't tell anyone else you were still alive.'

Atle stared at him, silent and motionless. The silence persisted and became oppressive this time.

In the end, it was Kai who heaved a heavy sigh and said: 'What are you actually doing here?'

'What do you mean?'

'Are you still a German officer? How do you kill time in Stockholm?'

As no answer was forthcoming, Kai turned to the window and looked out instead.

He heard Atle stand up, wait. At length he felt Atle place his hands on his shoulders. 'Kai, look at me.'

Kai turned and met his brother's gaze.

'I can't tell you everything. If I did, I'd jeopardise your safety. I've already told you too much, but my secret has to stay between us, Kai. You're my brother. Understand one thing though: no one must know I'm alive. No one. No Norwegian, and no one else. Can you promise me that?'

'I'm not the only person who knows you're alive.'

'Who else does?'

Kai knew this version of Atle. The boy who reacted, who wanted to know.

'Who else knows something?' repeated Atle.

'Someone called Kraby, Jomar Kraby.'

Atle nodded slowly.

'Looks like you've heard that name before.'

Atle didn't answer. 'How does he know I'm alive?'

'He's a sort of gumshoe. Goes around asking questions, digging, and he's doing it for the exiled government in London. He's the person who told me to come here this evening and ask after a herr Lazarus.'

'Does he work alone or with others?' Atle's eyes were dark now.

'He's a lone wolf.'

'Thanks, Kai.' Atle raised an arm. 'This is on me,' he said, waving to the waiter. When he came, Atle took out a billfold, handed over a note and gestured that he could keep the change.

'You've made me curious,' he said, pushing the billfold back in his pocket. 'I think I want to meet this Kraby. We can meet him together.'

'Why would we do that?'

'Can you do me a favour and arrange it?'

Kai's brain was churning. Why did Atle want to meet Kraby, and why did he want Kai with him? He was about to ask, when his brother leaned over again:

'Do you know how to get hold of him?'

Kai nodded.

'By phone?'

'Shouldn't be a problem.'

'Give him a ring, Kai.'

'When should I do it?'

'Now.'

'Why?'

Atle smiled. 'You know why, Kai. You're my brother. The fact that you know I'm alive is enough. If you and I are to succeed in sharing a secret, it has to be only us. Don't you agree?'

Kai let the words sink in. He observed that Atle's smile was a grimace, and that there was an unnatural bulge under Atle's armpit. Atle carried a weapon.

'Ring him now? What about your party?'

'They can wait. Do as I say, Kai,' he said, curling his lip into the same grimace, straightening his back and pointing to the telephone box at the end of the room. 'Go on now, Kai. Ring Kraby. Now.'

57

The atmosphere around Jomar felt biblical. A seed had been sown. And the Bible was definitely right about one thing, he thought: there is a time for everything. Now was the right time to wait – and hasten across the cobblestones in Järntorget heading for the Old Town and Den Gyldene Freden pub, where in the evening Norwegian writers often mingled.

Jomar was not happy walking on cobblestones. The unevenness could cause you to trip or to teeter, which might have made him appear intoxicated although he wasn't. Now the thought was in his mind, he tripped and lurched forward. He regained his footing and saw a man in a top hat under a streetlamp ahead of him. It wasn't a man. It was Pandora, wearing a top and tails. He hurried over and hooked his arm through hers.

It was a wonderful evening. Almost like being back home. The poets were all there, and they were enjoying mocking each other and singing their own praises. No one has greater love, no one takes themselves more seriously than a tipsy writer – and no one hates colleagues with more intensity, and no one enjoys insulting each other more.

One round of grandiloquence succeeded another.

It was his turn. When he stood up and opened his mouth, it was with pathos.

'Too many words, Kraby.'

He started again: 'Perhaps you think Beethoven plays too many notes, do you? You should've been a priest. Your monologues are harder to take than a religious service.'

The others laughed, Jomar loudest. There is nothing like being baited by your own kind.

It was the wee hours before he slowly made his way home with Pandora on his arm.

◈

She was leaning against the corridor wall, trying to stand upright, while Jomar, bent at the knee and hip, key in hand, was struggling to find the keyhole, when the neighbour rattled her security chain.

Jomar straightened up and caught Pandora before she fell to the floor.

'I'm bushed,' she mumbled.

The neighbour appeared. She said the telephone had rung several times. A Norwegian had been asking after Kraby.

'Any message?'

'No.'

'Thank you, my dear, thank you anyway,' Jomar said, finally succeeding in unlocking the door.

Pandora staggered over to the bed and collapsed on it, while her top hat rolled across the floor. She lay motionless on her stomach, her face bored down into the pillow.

Jomar poured himself a last glass, thinking about how he hadn't given the murderer a single thought after he had met Pandora in the Old Town. While he was pouring the gin, the telephone rang in the corridor.

He looked at his watch. It was past two in the morning. The

telephone rang again. He walked into the corridor, holding the glass, and, bending his knees, put the receiver to his ear.

'Kraby, this is Kai – Kai Fredly.'

'How can I help you?'

'There's someone who wants to meet you.'

'Now?'

'I've rung several times.'

'So this is urgent?'

'Yes.'

'Who wants to meet me?'

Jomar drank his gin while the young man at the other end deliberated. Jomar, for whom lies had been a source of income for several decades, was intrigued as to what Kai would come up with.

'Someone who knows something,' Fredly said at length, and Jomar could feel he was somewhat disappointed with him – at his inability to lie with panache.

'Knows something about what?'

'About the woman in the sea. The one who was murdered.'

Jomar expelled a heavy sigh. 'You met Lazarus, did you?'

'Let's talk about that when we meet.'

'I suppose the man we're meeting has a name?'

The silence lasted longer this time. Jomar glanced at the receiver before putting it back to his ear. 'What's his name?'

'I don't know.' Kai's voice was barely audible.

'When and where can I meet him?'

'I'll come over now, in the car.'

Jomar stood in the corridor and finished his drink. Then he went back into his hallway and put on his coat. Before leaving, he tiptoed into the bathroom for a pee.

When he got to the bottom of the stairs, the black car was already waiting by the kerb.

Jomar got into the rear seat without a word.

Kai Fredly didn't waste words when he turned to speak. 'This is a short drive.'

Jomar didn't answer. He sat in silence and observed the route they were taking. He knew the road, and he recognised the man waiting on the pavement.

58

As soon as the car stopped, the man opened the door and got in beside Jomar.

'Thought it was you,' the man said. 'Drive around for a bit, Kai.'

The car set off again.

'The Germans take care of their own,' Jomar said. 'What sort of jobs have you got here, at the Legation?'

'I translate mostly. There's enough to do. Stockholm's a busy city.'

'Your neighbour tells me you travel a lot. To Germany, among other places.'

Atle Fredly didn't answer.

'Berlin?'

Fredly still didn't answer.

'I've been there a couple of times myself,' Jomar said. 'Twice in fact. The first time it was a dream. The last time it was hell. It was Nazi Berlin. As a Hitler supporter, you have no idea what you're missing.'

Fredly didn't answer this time either.

'Why do you want to talk to me?'

'I don't actually,' Atle Fredly said at length. 'It's you who wants to talk to me. Have you forgotten that you came to my flat?'

'I can understand why you want this meeting, but I don't understand why you're involving your brother.'

'I'd like to know what you want, Kraby.'

'Involving your brother makes no logical sense.'

'What do you want from me?'

Then Jomar understood the logic in the man's thinking. It made him also see how stupid he had been to agree to this meeting. He sighed heavily, then looked Atle Fredly in the eye: 'I want to accuse you of murder.'

'Who am I supposed to have killed?'

'Asbjørn Fallet. You killed the man who was going to liquidate you.'

'You said it yourself, Kraby. It was him or me.'

'You were left with a corpse and the woman who'd lured you there for the murderer. You could've killed her there and then, but if you'd done that, you'd have blown the disappearing trick you were planning. You dropped Fallet's body in the river and fled, so that everyone would believe it was you who were dead. You took the dead man's name, and with Jenny Enersen and her child crossed the border to Sweden. The two of them were the cover you needed to get across. You told the woman that if she kept her mouth shut, she'd live. You contacted the German Legation under your real name. They could use you. You're working for them now, and you live well, but you're also vulnerable. Stockholm's full of Norwegians. There's a risk you'll be recognised. Daniel Berkåk bumped into you and recognised you. He knew who you were.'

When Jomar fell silent, the noise of the engine was all that could be heard. They were outside the city. It was night. The yellow cone of light met only darkened trees. Jomar glanced at the back of Kai Fredly's neck. He was concentrating on driving.

'Do you think it helps to kill everyone who recognises you?'

Atle Fredly didn't answer.

'When the Germans eventually capitulate, lots of Nazis will try to hide, the way you're doing now, but it won't help them. They'll all be punished. You, too, Fredly.'

'If someone intends to kill you, you don't have much choice. It's kill or be killed.'

Jomar nodded. He could understand that. 'You knew Daniel Berkåk was going to Norway. How did you find out?'

'He was spying on me, but he was never aware that I was spying on him too. It was him or me.'

'That can't be true.'

'Yes, it can, Kraby. Daniel Berkåk wanted me six feet under. That's the only thing that was clear from the first time I saw him in Stockholm. He was out to get me. He told me so when I was cycling after him. He waved. Stopped and waited for me. He was an arrogant piece of shit. He grinned and laughed, and asked if I wanted him to guide me across the border. So I said yes. We cycled together. His plan was to gun me down as soon as we were on the Norwegian side.'

'What happened?'

'He didn't realise my best chance was to act before we reached the border.'

'You shot and killed Berkåk while you were still in Sweden?'

'I had the opportunity, but he was the one who made it possible. He had a boat lying ready, and he simply fell into it. It was a long, risky rowing trip, but I had to get his body to the Norwegian side. Then the matter of his death would disappear in the same way that he did. It worked.'

'And the woman calling herself Jenny Enersen, what was her real name?'

'Eva.'

'You already knew her?'

'She claimed she had some coffee for sale, but was terrified about the whole operation. She told me what was going to happen as soon as we were alone in the car.'

Jomar fell silent, staring out at the trunks of spruce trees caught in the headlights.

'Asbjørn Fallet never knew what happened,' Atle Fredly said.

'After I visited her, she went to Stockholm to warn you,' Jomar said. 'She told you I'd been there at the manor, asking questions. Why did you have to kill her?'

'She didn't come to warn me. She wanted silence money.'

'I don't believe you.'

'What you believe or don't believe is neither here nor there.'

'You had the power to kill her,' Jomar said. 'And as with so many people with power, you made yourself a slave to it. When you were on the Eastern Front, you killed without mercy, and there were no consequences. When you returned to Norway, you killed Norwegian Resistance men and there were no consequences. You killed Daniel Berkåk and there were no consequences. You're an idle, decadent, megalomaniac traitor. When Eva, or Jenny, as she was called afterwards, came to Stockholm and told you that a Norwegian man had visited her, searching for you, the logical conclusion would have been to neutralise the man. Instead, you killed her. As it was in your power to do that, in your stunted brain it was a rational act.'

Atle Fredly didn't answer.

They drove in silence. For a long time. Jomar closed his eyes. In this way he could fantasise that this was a normal car journey, but it was not.

Finally, the car stopped.

Jomar opened his eyes and discovered that Atle Fredly was holding a revolver. 'If you wouldn't mind, Kraby. Get out of the car.'

Jomar obeyed. It was a dark night. The only source of light was a pale moon, which occasionally showed its face from behind scudding clouds. The gravel was wet after the rain, and a chill wind caught the tails of his coat.

Jomar turned to Atle Fredly, who had now extended his arm and was pointing the gun at him. He reflected on the irony that the last thing he would ever write was a play he himself was not satisfied with and which had already been censored. Then he thought about Hjørdis, whom he would never see again, and Pandora, who would wake up in the morning alone.

Jomar glanced over at Kai and had to concede with resignation that there was no help to be found there. Not so surprising really, he thought. Blood is, after all, thicker than water.

'After you've killed me, who's next?'

'No one.'

'What about your brother?'

'What about him?'

'He knows you're alive. He works for the Norwegian Legation. He'll be the witness who convicts you sooner or later.'

Atle Fredly said nothing. Jomar was silent. All that could be heard was the wind in the trees.

'You're so easy to see through,' Jomar said. 'And I don't think I'm alone.'

Atle glanced over at Kai.

'There's only one logical explanation for the situation you've placed all three of us in,' Jomar said. 'You're planning to kill us both.'

Atle ran his tongue over his lips.

'Your megalomaniac brain has calculated and planned it all. There'll be two bodies in a ditch here and tomorrow morning the car will be parked by the pavement somewhere in Stockholm.'

Atle Fredly said nothing.

'Good plan,' Jomar said. 'Who are you going to kill first? Me or your brother?'

Kai stirred.

Atle glanced at him again. 'Don't worry, Kai. The old boy's trying to divide and rule.' He turned back to Jomar.

'Divide and rule? I'm just appealing to the last of any sense of honour you might have. There can only be one reason for involving your brother in this, but this won't end with our deaths. You see, you made a big mistake when you dropped Asbjørn Fallet's body in the river.'

'What kind of mistake?'

'You forgot the propaganda war. When the Home Front liquidates an informer, they leave the body where it fell as a deterrent – a warning to others. When Atle Fredly just disappeared without trace, everyone involved knew that something was not as it should be. Especially because Asbjørn Fallet had also gone missing. As you know, he was supposed to return and write a report. The person who's missed Fallet the most is the man who sent him on the mission to kill you. Sooner or later he'll find out that someone calling himself Asbjørn Fallet is resident in Stockholm. There are many people after you. It's just a question of time.'

'Farewell, Kraby.'

Jomar stared down the muzzle of the gun, knowing he had lost.

Involuntarily, he shut both eyes.

59

A shot rang out. Jomar felt nothing. He opened his eyes.

In front of him on the ground lay Atle Fredly. The figure resembled a bundle of dirty laundry. Above the bundle stood Kai, holding a revolver in one hand.

'Where did you get the weapon from?'

'Shut up, Kraby. I've just shot someone. I'm not a man you should argue with now.'

Jomar had to crouch down. He was dizzy and gasping for air. 'Your brother's blood is calling us from the soil,' he whispered. 'Now I'll have to suffer the burdens of old age and you'll have to live with a cross on your back for the rest of your life.'

'It was him or me, Kraby. Him or me.'

Jomar stood up. 'When did you realise?'

'Don't ask me,' Kai said, his eyes on his brother. 'Atle's a dead man who doesn't exist. He even has a gravestone in Oslo.'

'What are you going to do now?'

'That's none of your business. I want you to go, Kraby. Back to Stockholm.'

Kai motioned with the revolver.

Jomar turned. There, between the mountain ridges, he could see the glow of the city. It was going to be a long walk.

'Go.'

'What are you going to do?'

'Mourn my dead brother. Get weaving.'

Jomar buttoned up his coat and started walking.

If I just keep going, sooner or later there will be opportunities, he thought. At daylight a bus will pass me, or maybe I'll stumble across a train station.

60

Jomar stopped as soon as he was hidden by the trees. He turned to the car and thought about the great Russian novelist who was led before the firing squad and reprieved only seconds before the officer was due to give the order to fire. It is said that this moment did something to the writer, that God, in addition to sparing his life, also gave him perspectives and a reflective profundity that refined his writing. Jomar wondered if surviving this night would do something for his own atrophied writing ability.

He leaned against a tree trunk, staring at the contours of the man kneeling and praying with folded hands for the soul of his brother.

Kai Fredly remained like this for a long time. Jomar was very interested to know what the man would do. Fredly stood up and opened the boot. From it, he took what looked like a coiled rope. Kai tied the rope around his own waist. Then he knelt down and grabbed the body. Lifted it. Stood swaying, with the dead body over his shoulders in a fireman's lift, then turned and staggered through the trees.

It seemed as though the man had a plan and knew where he was going, but what was the rope for? He must have brought it with him intentionally, Jomar thought. Kai Fredly must have planned this. He had driven the car here without any directions. He must know the place from previous experience.

After the trees had swallowed up the swaying figure of Kai Fredly, Jomar waited for a few long minutes before making up his mind. Then he walked to the car and got in the back. It was chilly outside. The man carrying his brother didn't have a spade. It would be a long night. Even though Jomar thought he would never be able to sleep again, he closed both eyes and realised he needed to clear his mind of everything that had happened. So he thought about writing. This is actually two stories, he thought. Two stories, two sets of fabrications. The question was really only where to begin. The right place had to be where the fabrications stopped, he thought. One story had to start with Kai Fredly; the other with himself. But now wasn't the time to write. Soon a new day would dawn. What he should do was prepare himself, spend the last hours of the night in the best way he could. Accordingly, he removed his coat, rolled it up and used it as a pillow against the window. With his head resting on the pillow, he closed his eyes, hoping for a few hours' sleep while waiting for the driver to return.